Swoon

USA Today and International Bestselling Author
Lauren Rowe

BOOKS BY LAUREN ROWE

Standalone Novels

Smitten

Swoon

The Reed Rivers Trilogy (to be read in order)

Bad Liar

Beautiful Liar

Beloved Liar

The Hate Love Duet

Falling Out Of Hate With You

Falling Into Love With You

The Morgan Brothers (a series of related standalones):

Hero

Captain

Ball Peen Hammer

Mister Bodyguard

ROCKSTAR

The Club Trilogy (to be read in order)

The Club: Obsession

The Club: Reclamation

The Club: Redemption

The Club: Culmination (A Full-Length Epilogue Book)

The Josh and Kat Trilogy (to be read in order)

Infatuation

Revelation

Consummation

The Misadventures Series (a series of unrelated standalones):

Misadventures on the Night Shift

Misadventures of a College Girl

Misadventures on the Rebound

Standalone Psychological Thriller/Dark Comedy

Countdown to Killing Kurtis

Short Stories

The Secret Note

ONE

COLIN

As my Uber pulls away from the airport, my driver's eyes in his rearview mirror linger on my face, like he's wondering, "Where have I seen this guy before?" I realize not every Uber driver in every city knows my band, and that if they did, they wouldn't necessarily know our drummer's face. But this is Seattle. Our hometown. The city that's bursting with pride to have spawned 22 Goats. So, I don't think it's crazy to think this driver might be a fan of my band and he's trying to place my face. Or hell, for all I know, he's seen my face on that stupid guest appearance I did on *Sing Your Heart Out*.

"Are you returning home or just visiting?" the guy asks, steering his car onto the main highway.

"Both. I live in LA now but grew up here."

"What brings you home?"

"My childhood best friend is getting married tomorrow. I'm one of his groomsmen."

"Nice."

"Oh, I should probably text him to say I'm on my way to the rehearsal. I'm later than I said I'd be."

I pull out my phone and tap out a quick text to Logan. And since I've got my phone out, anyway, swipe into Instagram to check out whatever reactions people have made to a photo I posted earlier—a photo of me at this afternoon's table read, in which I'm surrounded by the main cast and famed director I'll be working with in less than two weeks.

I didn't post about my first movie role before today because I'd convinced myself the opportunity would fall through for me, either due to a scheduling conflict with my band or because our legendary director, Gary Flynn, would realize he'd made a huge mistake in casting a newbie like me.

But I'll be damned, Gary complimented me today in front of everyone—which, apparently, is fairly unusual, according to the film's big star, Seth Rockford. So, I bit the bullet and posted the jaw-dropping photo. And now, I must admit I'm having fun scrolling through all the congratulatory comments underneath the shot.

Kiera.

I stop scrolling at the sight of my ex-girlfriend's name. She's sending me well wishes, along with everyone else. It's a seemingly innocuous act, but I find it weird. Kiera and I haven't interacted at all, even on social media, since she dumped me four months ago. So why is she bothering to congratulate me now?

I know Kiera and I said we'd always be friends when she dumped me, after taking a job as a backup dancer on a popstar's extended world tour and saying she was planning to "fuck her way around the globe." But since that devastating conversation, I've realized I have no sincere desire to keep in touch with her. I guess I assumed, based on our mutual lack of interaction, Kiera felt the same way.

Against my better judgment, I swipe over to Kiera's Instagram to see what city she's presently "fucking her way through," and quickly surmise Kiera is in London. Which means my ex is no longer getting railed by American dudes, she's moved on to getting shagged by British blokes.

Stop it, Colin.

Why am I even looking at my ex's photos, when I don't even want her anymore? If Kiera dropped out of the tour and begged me to take her back, I'd say no. And I'd mean it.

Admittedly, I was heartbroken for about a month after she dumped me, but after my initial feelings of rejection and humiliation wore off, I realized Kiera had done me a huge favor by ending our longtime on-again-off-again relationship. I realized I hadn't been mourning the loss of Kiera, per se, but the loss of the last-ever girlfriend who'd known me *before* my band hit it big. Before fame and money and the world's projections of me became part of the equation. Before trust became so hard to come by. I think that was the toughest pill for me to swallow: realizing I'd have to return to the dating pool as "Colin from 22 Goats."

"You're the drummer from 22 Goats!" the driver shouts, as if reading my mind. When I look up, he's displaying a photo of Dax, Fish, and me on his phone, his face aglow. "That's you, right?"

"That's me," I acknowledge.

After lowering his phone, the driver bangs his palm against his steering wheel and hoots with glee. "I knew you looked familiar! I just couldn't place you!"

"That happens a lot, thanks to me looking like every other tattooed, brown-haired white guy in a band."

The driver scoffs. "I don't think they pay every tattooed, brown-haired white guy to model in their underwear, sir."

I chuckle. "Oh, you saw that."

"My wife drooled over that shot. You were on *Sing Your Heart Out* this season, right?"

"Briefly."

"My wife has a huge crush on you. So do I—but on your music."

"Thanks."

"Hey, would you mind recording a happy birthday message to my wife? Her birthday is next week. I know she'd flip out to hear you say her name."

"You bet."

"Her name is Maya."

The guy hands me his phone, set to record, and I quickly record a birthday greeting, after which he thanks me profusely.

"So, I gotta ask," the driver says, taking his phone back. "Do you three Goats get along as well as it seems in your music videos?"

I shake my head. "Don't tell anyone, but we despise each other." I chuckle along with him. "Nah, the boring truth is that we get along, exactly as it seems. Do we argue, sometimes? Yes, because we're brothers at this point. But it's never anything major."

"Are the other two Goats coming to the wedding? Is the groom a musician, too?"

"No, the groom's a lawyer. And, yes, the other Goats are coming, but not to the rehearsal tonight. I'm the only grooms-man. I'm the one who lived next door to my buddy, Logan, growing up, so we were always the closest."

"Your buddy won the lottery, growing up next door to

you. Can you imagine being some random future lawyer, and it turns out your next-door neighbor best friend grows up to become the drummer in 22 Goats? Insanity."

I laugh. "I'm the one who won the lottery. If it weren't for my friend, I wouldn't be in 22 Goats today."

"*What?*"

"In eighth grade, he overheard two kids we didn't know in the grade below us, talking about needing to find a drummer for the band they were starting. Logan hooked me up, and the rest is history."

"Holy shit. Your whole life might have been different if he hadn't overheard that conversation!"

"I think about that all the time."

"When was that?"

I tell the guy the year and he freaks out that I'm so young.

"You were only in eighth grade back then? Jesus Christ, I'm old. How old are you?"

"Closing in on twenty-seven."

"Shit! I thought you guys were around my age. I'm thirty-seven!"

I laugh. "Well, if it makes you feel any better, after the rollercoaster ride of the past few years, I often *feel* thirty-seven."

The driver snickers. "You've had some fun, huh?"

"I've had some fun," I confirm.

"I bet women throw themselves at you all the time."

"On tour? Yeah, pretty much. Especially now that I'm the last bachelor standing in my band. But not the right kind of woman."

"Is there a wrong kind?"

"Groupies. Clout-chasers. Honestly, I'd much rather have an amazing girlfriend, than sleep with a succession of groupies. Unfortunately, I've discovered that finding true love is a lot easier said than done."

"*What*? Dude, you're the drummer of 22 Goats!"

"That's the problem. I live in LA. Everyone I meet there is an aspiring model, actress, singer, or influencer who thinks hooking up with the drummer from 22 Goats will somehow boost her career."

"So what? If a woman wants to use you for your connections or money or whatever, let her try. Doesn't mean you have to let her succeed."

I press my lips together and look out the car window at passing traffic. Dudes who've never been in my shoes always think that way. But they couldn't be more wrong about the realities of my situation. The toll it takes on a person to constantly feel like a mark. To never know if you can completely trust someone. Or worse, to trust someone and find out you were wrong to do it. "Let me ask you this," I say, returning to the driver's eyes in the rearview mirror. "If getting used by clout-chasers was such an awesome thing, then why would *both* my bandmates have settled down, the nano-second they found the real deal with someone?"

"Both your bandmates are married?"

"One is and the other might as well be."

"And they're your age?"

"A year younger."

The driver whistles, like I've shocked him.

"That makes me the last man standing," I continue. "And not only in my band, but in my entire friend group. Everyone I'm closest to in the world is all wifed up, or might as well be."

"So what? If all your friends jumped off a cliff, would you jump, too?"

"Absolutely. I'd be so distraught, I wouldn't want to live another day."

He rolls his eyes playfully.

"To be clear, I'd never settle down with the wrong woman, for the hell of it. But, yeah, if I met the right person, someone I trust, someone who loves me the way I love her, and we have awesome physical chemistry too, then why wouldn't I want to jump in, head-first? Dating sucks, man. It's exhausting."

The driver ponders that for a moment. "You know what you should do, Colin? Date another celebrity—someone who's as rich and famous as you are. That way you'd know she was into you for the right reasons."

I smirk to myself. "I've tried that strategy, as a matter of fact. Recently. And it didn't work out."

"No?"

I shake my head. "As it turned out, the woman I'd set my sights on was already in love with someone else."

"*Pfft.* What sane woman would want another guy over *you?*"

I chuckle. "You're an *amazing* hype-man, dude. What's your name?"

"Tim."

"You rock, Tim."

He laughs. "I'm just speaking the truth. If a woman doesn't want *you*, then what hope is there for the rest of us?"

"Ever heard of Fugitive Summer?"

Tim nods. "They've got that song right now. 'Hate Sex High.'"

I'm not surprised he knows the song. That raunchy, addicting tune about a woman riding a "hate sex high" to three orgasms is so wildly popular right now, this driver could turn on his car radio and find it playing on a random station in five seconds flat.

"The woman who turned me down is with the guy who sings that song," I reveal. "He wrote it about her. 'La la la la *Laila*.'"

The driver gasps. "Wait. He's singing Laila there? Ha! I thought he was singing 'la la la' the whole time!" He gasps again. "It was Laila Fitzgerald who turned you down?"

I'm not surprised he's connected the dots so quickly, given his earlier comment about watching *Sing Your Heart Out*. Thanks to that show, Laila Fitzgerald has become a household name—and as a result, her romance with Savage from Fugitive Summer, a guy with endless swagger and a huge social media following, is big pop-culture news these days.

"Hmm," the driver says. "I can't say I blame Laila for choosing that guy over of you. No offense, but have you seen him? He looks like a god."

"I don't blame her, either."

"Plus, he wrote a song about her. Who could compete with that?"

"Not a drummer, that's for sure. Wait a minute. You're saying I don't look like a god?"

"Oh. I . . ."

I laugh. "Just fucking with you, Tim. I'm well aware I can't compete with Savage. Nobody could."

"The good news is, with that guy off the market, the world is your oyster."

"Yeah, but I'm not a *god*," I tease.

"You're a demi-god, though."

We both laugh.

"You really are the best hype-man, ever, Timothy. May I call you that?"

"Please do." His eyes crinkle in the rearview mirror with his smile. "Chin up, Colin. Your dream girl is out there, waiting for you to find her. She might even be at the wedding tomorrow. A bridesmaid, maybe? Bridesmaids are notoriously horny at weddings."

"They are?"

"Of course! They're all dressed up, drinking champagne. They've just watched their bestie exchanging romantic vows of forever. Weddings are the best aphrodisiacs in the world!"

"Well, that might be the case, generally speaking. But this wedding is gonna be more like a family reunion for me than an episode of *Love Island*. I grew up next door to the groom, remember? Both our families will be there."

"But did you grow up with the bridesmaids?"

"No, I haven't even met the bride yet."

"Well, there you go. Bring on the bridesmaids! *Boom.*"

I scowl at him playfully. "Why are you so determined to get me laid at this wedding?"

"Because those who can are obligated to do for those who can't."

Again, I laugh. This guy is a gem.

Tim talks for a while about his good feeling about me finding love, any day now, until, finally, we're pulling into my destination: the parking lot of the church where my buddy, Logan, will marry his dream girl tomorrow evening.

"I hope I made it in time to catch at least the end of the rehearsal," I murmur.

"Parking lot's packed," the driver observes. "That's a good sign."

He pulls the car in front of the church, as I'm giving him a monster tip on my phone. When the car stops, I bolt from my seat and stride to the trunk for my garment bag. But before

I've completed my task, Tim appears and sheepishly asks for a selfie.

"I know you're running late . . ." he says. "But I'd love a photo to show my wife."

"You got it, Hype-man. Of course."

Our selfie snapped, and thanks and handshakes administered, I wish the driver well, grab my bag, and sprint toward the church, excited to spend the weekend with people who know me simply as Colin Beretta—or perhaps, "Logan's longtime friend, Colin"—rather than "Colin from 22 Goats."

TWO

AMY

The wedding officiant—my family's longtime pastor —smiles at my big brother, Logan, and his beautiful bride-to-be, Kennedy, both of whom are standing before him in casual clothes and paper crowns supplied by the bride's niece. "And that's when you'll turn around and lead the recessional down the center aisle," the pastor explains. "Hand in hand, as husband and wife."

Everyone in the church cheers, even though we know the man is only saying those exciting words for pretend tonight.

"Can we practice the recessional?" the wedding coordinator pipes in, her business-like tone in sharp contrast to the pastor's festive one. She begins rattling off detailed instructions to the wedding party—the groomsmen and bridesmaids, including me, all of whom are currently standing in opposing lines. "Amy," she says, shifting her dark gaze to me, "I'll play the part of your assigned groomsman now, so you'll have someone to practice walking with."

Well, that hardly seems necessary, I think. *Walking is walking, right?* But I've no sooner had the thought than a door at the far end of the church swings opens and the groomsman we've been waiting for, Colin Beretta, appears and begins bounding down the center aisle in all his muscled, tattooed, charismatic glory.

Swoon.

That's my body's instantaneous reaction to seeing my life-long crush again, in person, for the first time in nine years. The exact same one I always used to have as a kid.

As I recall, I first swooned over Colin when I was five years old—although due to my tender age, I didn't know how to label the mysterious sensations overtaking my body. It was my first day of kindergarten and my mom had tasked Logan, four years my senior, with walking me to school that day, since my brother would already be making the trek with our next-door neighbor, Colin.

I don't remember the walk to school. All I remember is Logan ditching my whimpering ass in the hallway once we got there. Knowing Logan, I'm sure he left me right outside my classroom doorway, but it felt like Siberia to me. Which is why I started to whimper and freak out.

And that's when Colin swooped in to save the day. As Logan ran away, presumably headed to the playground for some fourth-grade "me time" before the first bell, Colin grabbed my hand and led me into my classroom, straight to my new teacher. "Take extra good care of her," I remember Colin saying to the pretty lady with bright lipstick. "Amy's really *sensitive.*"

I didn't know what that word meant. *Sensitive.* All I knew was it sounded like a beautiful thing, the way Colin said it about me. So much so, hearing him call me that caused a riot of sensations inside me. Butterflies. Warmth oozing like molasses into my core. Shortness of breath. Dizziness. All the things I now understand were the ingredients of my very first Colin-Beretta-inspired swoon.

After that, feeling like my insides were melting over Colin Beretta became a regular thing. Sometimes, it happened after he'd done something sweet for me, like on that first day of kindergarten. Other times, it happened when Colin simply smiled at me from across a room. And still other times, it happened when Colin had no idea I was watching him. For instance, during those last few years, when he'd practice playing his new drum kit in his bedroom at night, shirtless and sweaty, and I'd spy on him from my darkened bedroom window.

Over the years, I came to accept my crush on Colin was and always would be a one-way street. For one thing, our four-year age gap felt insurmountable. For another, he always treated me like a kid sister. But mostly, I knew I'd never get to fulfill my fantasy of kissing Colin Beretta because, instinctively, I knew the flat-chested, frizzy-haired tweener I saw in the mirror would never be able to compete with the stunning, curvy girls I saw Colin regularly sneaking through his parents' side gate, under cover of darkness.

And so, after my parents divorced and Mom and I moved away from Cedar Street, after Logan had gone off to college, and my chances of seeing Colin again in person became slim to none, I started thinking of Colin as my "celebrity crush." The sort of guy I hoped to have as a boyfriend one day—the blueprint of my dream man—but not someone I'd ever meet.

But then one day, about a year ago, I got a text from Colin, out of the blue, telling me he'd arranged a job for me, at Logan's request. He said I could be a production assistant on a world tour, if I wanted. Not with Colin's band, sadly, but with Red Card Riot. One of the most popular bands in the universe. So, of course, I said yes and thank you.

Colin replied that he was happy to do it and that he hoped I'd have a blast on the tour. He told me whom to contact at River Records. Wished me well. And that was that. My long-awaited reunion with Colin Beretta was over. *Womp womp.*

I was grateful for the job Colin had arranged for me, of course. Thrilled. But I can't deny I also felt a bit disappointed he hadn't been more interested in catching up with me. Not that I had anything particularly interesting to tell him.

But then, I had the exciting thought: "Maybe Colin will come to one of RCR's shows and we'll catch up in person!" I'd seen the gorgeous dancer all over Colin's Instagram by then, thanks to my regular stalking of him, so I knew nothing would come of any such in-person reunion. But, still, a girl can dream, right?

But no. One quick Google search shot down any idea that I might see Colin again during Red Card Riot's tour. Apparently, there'd been some kind of kerfuffle a few years ago between Dax Morgan, the lead singer of Colin's band, and Caleb "C-Bomb" Baumgarten, the legendary drummer of Red Card Riot, and the two bands had steered clear of each other, ever since. And so, I accepted the truth that I'd never see Colin again, in person. Not in this lifetime, anyway.

But then, seven months into my job on the world tour, my future sister-in-law, Kennedy, called to tell me some shocking news: Colin had not only RSVP'd *yes* to her upcoming wedding with my brother, he'd not only agreed to serve as one of Logan's groomsmen, but he'd *also* RSVP'd for only *one*e!

In a frenzy of excitement, Kennedy and I both went straight to Colin's Instagram during the call to see if we could discern the reason for Colin's surprisingly stag RSVP. And that's when we discovered yet another shocking thing: Colin had deleted every photo of that gorgeous dancer from his Instagram page!

Obviously, Kennedy and I realized Colin being suddenly single didn't guarantee he'd feel attracted to *me* during the wedding weekend. But, still, I can't deny we were both excited about our discovery, because it meant I stood a snow-ball's chance in hell with him! Not great odds, but better than nothing.

When I hung up with Kennedy, I was buzzing. I told myself to knock it off and not think about Colin again. I told myself celebrity crushes are fine and fun, but delusions are not. I nonetheless couldn't stop my fantasies from coming, against my will. Every time I tried to sleep on the next lumpy mattress during the tour, I imagined Colin seeing me at the wedding and not recognizing me. I imagined him looking me up and down and saying, "You can't possibly be Amy!" and then proceeding to pay special attention to me throughout the entire wedding weekend, until, ultimately, we were naked in Colin's hotel room after the wedding reception, and Colin was making all my sexiest fantasies about him come true.

I knew my fantasies were exactly that. I told myself not to expect anything to actually happen. I vowed to myself I'd remain calm and collected when I saw Colin again. I swore to myself I wouldn't blush or stare—or, God forbid, swoon. Which makes me a liar now, I suppose, given the way my body is reacting as I watch Colin's gorgeous frame bounding down the center aisle of the church.

"Colin!" Logan bellows, as I breathe through the butter-flies ravaging my belly. My brother leaves his post to meet and then hug his old friend, before proudly introducing Colin to Kennedy. Her brown skin glowing with excitement,

Kennedy hugs Colin in greeting—and suddenly, everyone around me, other than the wedding coordinator, seems on the cusp of leaving their assigned positions to head over to Colin, as well.

"Hold on, everyone!" the wedding coordinator pleads. "We only have the church 'til six. Can we finish the rehearsal real quick, and have everyone say hello to Colin when we're done?" Without waiting for anyone's reply, she moves to Colin, grabs his tattooed forearm, and guides him to the end of the groomsmen line—to a spot mirroring mine with the bridesmaids. "When it's your turn to escort your assigned bridesmaid," she explains to Colin, "offer her your arm like *this* and escort her with a big smile on your face for the cameras."

At the words "assigned bridesmaid," Colin looks at me, smiles politely, and returns his attention to the wedding coordinator.

Oh my god. Yes! Colin clearly has no idea who I am! And I couldn't be more thrilled about it.

It makes sense. When Colin last saw me, I was barely fourteen and looked twelve. I was flat as a pancake, with braces on my teeth, zits on my face, and my hair looked like an auburn poodle taking a nap on my head. Plus, I was a hot mess back then, emotionally. My best friend had recently moved to another state. My parents were getting divorced, Logan had gone off to college, and Mom had decided to downsize and get a smaller place across town. The day I said goodbye to Colin, I knew I was going to be attending a new school, where I'd have to make all new friends, and, on top of it all, I also knew, instinctively, I'd never see my lifelong crush ever again.

I like to think I've had quite the "glow-up" since that last goodbye with Colin. Partly, because I was a late bloomer. But even more so, because of my first roommate in college, Lily. On day one, I took one look at my new roommate's sparkling, easy charm and beauty and eked out, "Help me, Lily." And that's exactly what that superstar did, in every conceivable way.

Besides giving me a much-appreciated physical makeover, Lily more importantly laughed at all my jokes, in a way my family never did. She took me along to parties with her amazing friends, who *also* laughed at my silly jokes and coaxed me out of my shell. I doubt I'll ever possess Lily's level of confidence in this lifetime. The woman is a force of nature. But thanks to Lily and her outgoing friends, by the end of my first year of college, I felt like a whole new person. A much more sparkling version of myself than the hot mess Colin had hugged goodbye on Cedar Street.

"Okay, Logan and Kennedy," the pastor says, now that everyone has moved back into position. "After I've introduced you as husband and wife, you'll lead the recessional down the center aisle. Let's practice that now."

As instructed, Logan and Kennedy turn and cheerfully take off down the aisle, followed by pairs of their attendants, until suddenly, Colin is standing mere inches from me, shooting me a breathtaking grin and offering me his muscled arm.

"Hello," Colin says, his dark eyes twinkling. "I'm Colin."

Swoon. "Hi." *Swoon.* "I'm Amy." *Swoon.* "O'Brien. I lived next door to you for the first fourteen years of my life?" I link my arm in Colin's, giggling at his shocked reaction. If I could have custom-ordered Colin's facial expression in this moment, I couldn't have improved on this one.

Colin looks me up and down during our short walk, and

when we reach the end of the aisle and come to a stop behind the already mingling crowd, he exhales, runs his hand through his dark, tousled hair, and blurts, *"How the hell are you Amy O'Brien?"*

A few nearby people swivel their heads toward him, at which point Colin realizes he's loudly blurted the word "hell" in a church—which, not surprisingly, makes both of us burst into laughter.

A gorgeous smile on his face, Colin leans into me and whispers, "Seriously, though. How the *hell* are you Amy O'Brien?"

I'm absolutely giddy. But, somehow, I manage to keep myself from totally spazzing out. "Time stops for no one," I say, returning his grin. "I'm all grown up, Colin. I'm twenty-three."

"Twenty-three!" He looks me up and down again, and this time, I can't help thinking his gaze lingered on my cleavage for a long beat. Or was that wishful thinking? That's certainly what I was *hoping* would happen when I slipped on this lowcut dress and my new push-up bra earlier, even though I knew my mother would have a shit fit and say my neckline is "inappropriate" for church, which is exactly what she did when she saw me. But can I rationally expect *my* tits to impress Colin—a rockstar who must sign his name in Sharpie across at least a dozen pairs of them per week?

"Are you back from the tour for good now?" he asks.

"Yeah, it's been over for a few weeks." I take a deep inhale to keep my voice from quavering, and then clear my throat. "Since then, I've been staying with my mom. Decompressing from the grind, helping Kennedy with wedding stuff, figuring out my next move."

"I feel ya on the 'decompressing from the grind' thing.

Touring takes its toll."

"Ach, it's brutal. Fun, but brutal. Brutal fun." *Stop talking, Amy.* I take another deep breath, and then another, before calmly saying, "Thank you again for getting me the job. It was amazing."

"You've already thanked me. What was your assignment?"

"C-Bomb. I was his personal production assistant during the whole tour."

Colin hoots with laughter. "No way! You were Caleb's assistant, the whole time?"

"Yep. I was his personal assistant, lackey, gofer, waitress, bartender, suitcase-packer . . ." *Therapist.* That last word springs into my mind, but I'd never say it out loud. The surprisingly earnest conversations I wound up having with Red Card Riot's famed drummer toward the end of the tour, when he realized he could trust me completely, are locked in my vault forever. And not because of my NDA. But because I came to genuinely care about that enigmatic, tempestuous man.

Colin chuckles. "I bet you've got some fantastic stories. Caleb is anything but boring."

"I sure do," I agree. "Not only about Caleb, but about the crazy shenanigans of my fellow crew members, too. Too bad I can't tell my very best stories because of my NDA."

Colin smirks. "Come on, Ames. You have to know you saying 'NDA' only makes me want to hear your stories, even more."

Ames. That's what Colin used to call me as a kid. Is it a good or bad thing he's slipped right back into calling me that, like no time has passed?

"I assure you, nothing all that scandalous happened. At

least, not in relation to Caleb. He was honestly pretty chill during the tour—and really sweet to me. At least, once he realized he couldn't make me quit by sending me on a thousand wild goose chases."

Colin looks surprised. "Caleb did what now?"

I laugh. "I don't blame him. I was such a shit show, at first. I would have wanted to get rid of me, too. But what Caleb didn't realize was that the weirder his demands got, the more determined I became. Until one day, out of the blue, Caleb goes, 'Holy shit, dude. You're actually damned good at this shit!'" I giggle. "Is it embarrassing to admit that was one of the best days of my life?"

Colin looks thoroughly confused. "I'm shocked Caleb gave you such a long time to prove yourself. The C-Bomb I know wouldn't bother sending a shitty assistant on a single wild goose chase—he'd tell her to hit the road or get her reassigned."

I shrug. "For the entire first month, that's what I thought was going to happen to me. But it never did."

"What did you do that was so terrible at first?" he asks.

"Oh my God, Colin. I was so star-struck around Caleb and the rest of the band and any celebrity who happened to come backstage after seeing the show, I couldn't speak or control my limbs half the time. I walked into walls and tripped over my feet and dropped things with astonishing regularity. I got simple food orders bizarrely wrong. Oh, and I spilled hot coffee onto Caleb's lap the very first day of the tour!"

Colin has been guffawing throughout my entire description, and the sound of his belly laughs sends tingles skating across my skin. But before our conversation continues, the wedding coordinator yells above the din, "It's time to head to the restaurant now! If you need the address, I've got it here!"

"Did you drive here?" Colin asks. And when I nod, he asks, "Would you mind giving me a ride to the restaurant? You can tell me your best tour stories during the drive. I promise I won't tell anyone you technically breached your NDA by telling me." He winks. "You can trust me, Ames. I promise."

Swoon.

"Okay, I'll take a gigantic leap of faith and trust you," I tease, sounding remarkably calm and collected, compared to how I'm feeling. "Just don't expect my stories to 'wow' you. Anyone else would think my stories are bomb. But to a guy who's toured the world as part of—" I gasp and clutch Colin's tattooed forearm. "*Luke.* He's coming over here. Please—"

"Amyyyyy!" Luke booms, and a second later, my brother's friend is wrapping me in a bear hug that squashes my boobs against his chest. "So great to see you again, pretty lady!"

"Hi, Luke." I disengage from him and motion to Colin, hoping my eyes are sending the latter a telepathic *S O S.* "Luke, this is Colin Beretta, our next-door neighbor growing up. Colin, this is Luke . . ."

"Hammond."

"That's right. Sorry. Luke Hammond, my brother's roommate during law school."

Luke shakes Colin's hand vigorously. "Great to see you again! We met a few years ago, backstage at your show in Seattle. Logan brought me backstage with him."

"Oh, yeah," Colin says, though I can't imagine he actually remembers Luke. "Great to see you again."

"That was a great show."

Blah, blah, blah, Luke says, and Colin nods politely.

"Too bad you couldn't make the bachelor party," Luke

says.

"Yeah, I was bummed to miss it. I had a work thing."

"Well, you missed a great party!"

"I'm sure I did."

Luke babbles about the "amazing" bachelor party for a bit, which seems stupid to me, considering the mind-blowing parties Colin must attend. Until, finally, Colin's eyes meet mine and I know, without a doubt, he's reading my mind.

"So, hey, brother," Colin says, "we'll see you at the restaurant. Amy and I have a lot of catching up to do."

"Oh, are you giving Colin a ride to the restaurant?" Luke asks, looking at me. "If there's room in your car, I could use—"

"Actually, sorry," Colin interrupts. "I want Amy's undivided attention during the drive. We haven't seen each other in years, and I'm dying to hear some of her stories from the RCR tour she worked. With me being signed to the same label, Amy's allowed to tell me anything, despite her NDA, but she can't talk about that stuff when anyone else is around."

I feel dizzy. Like my insides are melting. *The man's a genius.*

"Oh, yeah, sure," Luke says. "No worries. I'll grab a ride from Logan." He winks at me. "Save me a seat at the restaurant. We'll catch up then."

"Aw, shit. I'm such a dick," Colin says, his tone jovial. "I'm calling dibs on Ames at the restaurant, too. Just 'cause it's been so many years since I've seen her, and she's always been like a little sister to me, you know?"

Womp, womp. And the beginning of Colin's comment was so promising, too!

Luke says he understands and he'll find me later. At which

point, Colin slides his arm around my shoulders and escorts me toward the exit of the church.

"Did you see the look on Luke's face as we walked away?" Colin says, once we're out of earshot. "Hilarious."

"Hilarious," I agree. But I'm not feeling all that amused, to be honest. In fact, I'm feeling downright disappointed, thanks to that comment Colin made about me being his little sister, despite my low-cut dress and fancy new push-up bra. Despite the amazing chemistry I *thought* we were *both* miraculously feeling.

Damn! I'm terrible at reading body language! I would have sworn Colin felt at least a glimmer of physical attraction to me! But I guess this situation is the same as the very beginning of the tour, when I thought several crew guys were *super* interested in me, and it quickly turned out every last one of them viewed me as nothing but a little sister too. A funny, amusing friend, a sort of tour mascot, but not someone they'd ever consider banging. Not even when I *thought* I'd made it pretty dang clear I was open to having some casual fun, for the first time in my life.

I smile at Colin as he continues escorting me through the crowd, toward a closet where he apparently stowed his suitcase. "Thanks for helping me out with Luke. He always comes straight for me."

"Not my first time at this particular rodeo, *sis*," Colin says. "I used to do the same thing for Caitlyn and Chiara, once I got big enough to pass as their boyfriend."

Seriously? That's three rapid-fire references to Colin thinking of me as his little sister in the space of as many minutes! *Okay, Colin, I get the message, loud and clear.*

Several people stop Colin on our way to grab his bag, so it takes us a while to get to our destination. But, eventually, we're able to collect Colin's suitcase and make our way outside and into the parking lot, just in time to see Luke getting into my brother's car, along with Logan's future wife, Kennedy, who's sitting in his passenger seat.

Colin and I wave at the trio as Logan's car passes, and the minute they're gone, Colin says, "Does Logan have any idea he's got a monster in his backseat?"

I chuckle. "I wouldn't call Luke a *monster*. More like an annoying, clueless blowhard. At Thanksgiving last year, he sat next to me and talked my ear off about *cryptocurrency* the entire meal."

"A fate worse than death."

"It was. But to answer your question, no, I don't think Logan has noticed Luke flirting with me. If so, he hasn't said a word about it to me." I gesture to my car a few feet away. "That's me. You want to put your bag in the trunk?"

"Thanks." We stow Colin's garment bag and head to our respective sides of the car, at which point Colin says, "Even if Luke's not a monster, he's most definitely a flaming asshole."

"Nah. He doesn't mean any harm. He's just terrible at reading social cues."

Colin opens the door on his side of the car. "No. Only a flaming asshole would even *think* of hitting on his best friend's little sister—let alone, follow through on the impulse." With that, Colin slides into my car, leaving me staring at the space his handsome face filled a moment ago, my spirit thudding into my toes.

"Wompity womp womp," I whisper to myself, before exhaling and slipping into my car. So much for my silly fantasies, huh? Colin couldn't have made himself any clearer: I'm a little sister to him. With exactly zero hope of ever becoming more.

THREE

COLIN

I burst out laughing, yet again. The same thing I've done ten times in as many minutes during this car ride to the restaurant. I don't know why I'm surprised Amy O'Brien as an adult is hilarious, considering how much she always made me laugh as a kid. In fact, sitting here with Amy in her small car now, listening to her talk while studying her various funny facial expressions, I feel like no time has passed since our years together on Cedar Street. Except, of course, for those perfect tits she's now sporting.

I'm a monster for noticing those mouthwatering beauties. Surely, I'm going to hell for all the little peeks I've stolen of them during this short drive. But, come on, how could I *not* peek at them? If they were attached to anyone else but Logan's little sister, I'd already have hit on Amy, *hard*, with the intention of getting those perfect beauties out of that push-up bra and straight into my hungry mouth, as soon as possible. In fact, the minute I laid eyes on Amy in the church, before I knew who she was, I thought, "Here's hoping that Uber driver was right about bridesmaids being hella horny."

Fuck.

I cringe at my inner dialog, even as I'm sneaking yet another inappropriate peek at Amy's cleavage.

"And, lo and behold," Amy is saying, making me realize I've been tuning her out while admiring her tits. "When I walked into that greenroom, the big boss himself, Reed Rivers, was on a couch with her—in the middle of giving her *enthusiastic* oral sex!"

"Wait, go back a bit," I say, realizing I missed the first part of Amy's story because I was staring at her tits. "I got distracted by the . . . pretty view of the skyline."

Amy looks out her driver's side window. "Oh, yeah, it *is* pretty." She returns her attention to the road. "No worries. I was saying Caleb wasn't subtle about his attraction to that music reporter. But when she disappeared somewhere backstage right before RCR was supposed to go on, Caleb ordered me to go find her and make sure she was coming to an after-party as his personal guest." Amy snorts and rolls her eyes. "Mind you, this was only day *two* of the tour—the day after I'd spilled hot coffee onto Caleb's lap—so, I was bound and determined to find the reporter and deliver his message. But when I found the reporter, she was in a green room getting eaten out by Reed Rivers!"

"Holy shit!" I shout.

Amy playfully wags her finger at me. "Now, don't you dare forget I'm bound by an iron-clad NDA! I wouldn't put it past Reed to have me murdered if he found out I told you this story."

"I won't say a word. But I promise Reed wouldn't care if he found out you told me. I'm sure he'd laugh, seeing as how he's engaged to that reporter now."

Amy's green eyes bug out. "What?"

"Yep. At this point, I bet Reed would love for the whole world to know he was eating his fiancée's pussy backstage at an RCR concert, while C-Bomb was doing his mighty best to get her into his bed."

Amy guffaws.

"How'd Caleb take it when you told him Reed had swooped in on the reporter?" I ask.

"Oh, he was pissed as hell. But, thankfully, not at me. Caleb was surprisingly nice about it when I told him. Although . . . when I told Caleb the news, I had a huge welt on my forehead from smacking into a wall after walking in on Reed, and thanks to that welt, Caleb started calling me 'Unicorn' that day and kept doing it for the whole rest of the tour." She unleashes a husky, throaty laugh that sends butterflies whooshing into my belly and arousal zinging across my skin. *Damn.* If Amy were anyone else, that sexy laugh would be a huge turn-on for me, every bit as much as those incredible tits.

Whoa.

Hold on.

It's suddenly dawning on me Amy might very well have just told me, in code, she had a tour fling with Caleb! Because I certainly don't remember Caleb being particularly "nice" to a single staffer during our tour together. And he certainly never gave anyone a cute little nickname, even in jest.

On the other hand, I don't remember Caleb banging any staffers during our tour together. So, I don't think that's his M.O. But I certainly wouldn't put it past him, either. Especially if the right woman had caught his eye . . . like, maybe, a sweet cutie pie he knew he'd be glued to the hip with for the next nine months?

Adrenaline floods my veins. An acute sense of protectiveness. Or is this *jealousy*? I have no right to have an opinion about what Amy might have done during the tour, and with whom. But, still, I can't deny the thought of Caleb's huge hands on her . . .

Oh, God.

I feel sick.

"From what I saw," Amy is saying when I tune back in, "fame isn't everything it's cut out to be. I wouldn't want to trade places with anyone in the band, but especially not Dean or C-Bomb. They can't go anywhere without being recognized."

"It's the same with Dax. I'm lucky. People recognize me, but not nearly as much as Dax or Dean or C-Bomb. And when they do, they're usually pretty chill." I look out my side of the car. "The whole concept of 'celebrity' is a total mind-fuck. *I* know I'm still the same guy who lived on Cedar Street. The guy who used to get teased as a kid. But to the outside world, I'm somehow 'special' and 'set apart,' the coolest of the cool kids, through no particular worthiness on my part."

Amy glances from the road to look at me. "You were teased as a kid?"

"Mercilessly. You remember those older kids who lived on the corner? They were relentless."

Amy is floored. "I must have been too young to notice. What'd they tease you about?"

"For being chubby, mostly. Also, for having the wrong shoes and clothes. This was years before my mom married my stepdad, so money was extra tight in my house back then."

She furrows her brow. "You were never chubby."

I chuckle. "So, you're conceding I had the wrong shoes and clothes?"

She giggles. "I never noticed what you were wearing. But

I certainly remember going to the community pool with you and Logan, and your body was perfect."

"You didn't notice I always kept my T-shirt on while swimming?"

She's clearly blown away. "No."

I nod. "I never took off my shirt in public back then. I was super insecure about my body. That's why I started playing drums, initially. Because I'd heard it's a good workout."

"And here I thought you did it to impress girls."

"Well, that, too."

"Seems like your plan worked like gangbusters, on both fronts."

I chuckle. "Yeah, it's all turned out okay. Once I started getting into drumming, one thing led to another. I started hitting the gym to improve my stamina while playing, and that further transformed my body and attracted even more attention from girls."

"And here you are—an underwear model." She gasps. "Oh my gosh! This puts that underwear ad in a whole new light!" She turns her gaze to me, her green eyes blazing and her mouth wide. "You must have felt such a huge sense of accomplishment when they asked you to model underwear!"

She's exactly right. Was I happy to collect the fat paycheck for that modeling gig? Hell yeah. I bought myself a ridiculous sports car with that cash. But more importantly, the young, insecure teen inside me felt like Rocky Balboa at the top of those famous steps.

"I did," I admit. "When they offered me the gig, it felt like a giant 'fuck you' to everyone who'd ever made fun of me."

"I hope every one of those bullies feels like an asshole now."

I can't help smiling from ear-to-ear. "One of them

contacted my manager a while back, asking him to ask me for tickets to a sold-out show. He was like, 'I grew up with Colin! Tell him the old neighborhood is proud of him!'"

"What'd you do?"

"Told my agent to tell the guy to fuck off."

Amy cackles. "Atta boy!"

We laugh and reminisce some more. Until, finally, we arrive at the restaurant's crowded parking lot. For a while, Amy drives her car in loops, looking for an available spot. But when it's clear we're not going to find one, I suggest we park on the street and hoof it back to the restaurant. And off we go, driving down the street.

"So, what's next for you?" I ask. "Are you gonna join another tour?"

"Not any time soon. I couldn't join the next tour on the schedule, like a bunch of my friends did, because of Logan's wedding. And now that I've had a few weeks to decompress, I've realized I needed a break from the grind. I'm thinking I'll look for a job in LA, doing what I did for Caleb."

"So, what, you'd be, like, a celebrity personal assistant?"

"Yeah. A couple of my friends from the tour said I could crash at their place in LA, while I look for a job like that. Oh! There's a spot."

Amy parks the car, and we begin walking toward the restaurant in the cool night air.

"So, is law school off the table, then?" I ask. It's a natural question. When Logan called me about ten months ago, asking if I could pull some strings and get his little sister an entry-level job with my label, he mentioned Amy was taking a gap year after college to "have some fun and find herself" before following in the footsteps of her father, mother, and brother by heading to law school.

"No law school for me," Amy confirms. "That was always my parents' dream for me. Not my own dream."

"Good for you."

She shrugs. "I'm only twenty-three. I've got time to figure out what I want to do."

"Absolutely."

"For now, I'd be thrilled to get a job in LA that pays the bills and allows me to have some fun along the way."

"Have you asked Caleb to hire you? That seems like a logical place to start a job search."

"I did. Unfortunately, he said he'd rather shove bamboo shoots under his fingernails than have me 'bugging him all the time to be a better person' while he's 'trying to relax like a sloth' at home." She giggles. "Luckily, he also said he'd 'never forgive me' if I worked for anyone else, when he goes back on tour. So, at least I know I'll get to work for him again, one day."

Holy shit. Now I know, for sure, Amy must have fucked Caleb! Because the C-Bomb I know would *never* tell any PA he wanted her to work for him again on the next tour, in advance, even someone as adorable as Amy, if he hadn't fucked said PA six ways from Sunday while traveling the world with her. But since I can't ask Amy about that without coming off like a douchebag, I take a deep breath and force myself to reply, "Sounds like Caleb enjoyed having you work for him."

"By the end, he did. He was really sweet to me, in the end."

Fuck.

Again, I take a deep breath to control my racing thoughts, as we walk silently down the sidewalk together. Finally, I say,

"Well, I'm sure you'll be able to land a PA job pretty easily with Caleb as a reference."

"I'm not sure about that," Amy says. "A couple friends from the tour said it's almost impossible to break into the celebrity PA circuit. Apparently, celebrities like to hire people who've been referred by celebrities they know and trust, and, unfortunately, Caleb doesn't have many celebrity friends, other than his bandmates."

I chuckle. "Yeah, Caleb hates the whole celebrity thing." I purse my lips, contemplating. "You know what you should do? Make it look on social media like rubbing elbows with celebrities is nothing to you—business as usual. LA is nothing but a gigantic game of The Emperor's New Clothes."

"That's exactly what my friend said! She loaded up her Instagram with all her best photos with celebrities from the various tours she's worked, and when she went to an interview with a fancy employment agency in Beverly Hills, they took one look at her Instagram and offered her a nanny position with a huge movie star, on the spot!" She names the movie star and laughingly adds, "And my friend didn't even have any experience with kids!"

"See? I know how LA works. Okay, dude, here's what we're gonna do. At the wedding, we'll take a shit-ton of photos of you partying with Dax, Fish, and me, and then you'll post those shots, along with whatever ones you have with C-Bomb. And *voila.* When you get to LA, you'll interview with that agency and get yourself a kickass job."

Amy squeals with excitement and thanks me effusively.

"Oh! Wait! I just realized something else I can do to help you. *Duh.*" I palm my forehead. "You can work for *me*!"

"What?" Amy shrieks.

"Only for a week," I quickly clarify. "I'm gonna be

shooting a small role in a movie for a week in LA, beginning a week from Monday, and my contract says I can have a personal assistant on-set on their dime. Someone *they* supply to me *or* someone of my own choosing. So, duh, why don't I tell them I choose you?"

Amy hurls herself at me like a missile, shrieking hysterically. And the minute Amy is in my arms, I feel a tidal wave of affection for her—a rush of the same sort of adoration I always felt for her when we were kids. Except this time, of course, my affection is accompanied by something new— unmistakable arousal triggered by the crush of Amy's perfect, bountiful tits against my chest.

I pull back sharply, taken aback by my body's undeniable reaction to her ample curves. "Hopefully, you'll land a permanent job while working for me," I manage to say. "But if not, you'll have a fun adventure and get to load up your Instagram with tons more photos to impress that employment agency."

Amy palms her cheeks looking flushed and glorious. Again, she thanks me profusely. And to my shock, as she does, I feel the urge to lean in and kiss her.

I pivot slightly and place my clasped hands in front of me, in case the tingles zapping my dick turn into a hard-on. "No need to thank me," I say, sounding remarkably calm. "I'm not the one who's going to pay your salary, remember? Which, by the way, will almost certainly be total shit."

"I'd do the job for free!" Amy sings out, before doing a little shimmy that makes my tingling dick begin to thicken. Shit.

"Why don't you stay at my place that week?" I say, even though I probably shouldn't. "I've got a guest room. Why not?" *You know why not,* my brain answers. *Shut the fuck up,* my hard-on replies.

Amy thanks me again, just as a car horn blares in passing.

"Oh, that was Logan!" Amy says, as Logan's car turns into the nearby restaurant parking lot. We pick up our pace and arrive in the parking lot as Logan is parking his car in a spot.

"Logan's always had the best parking karma," Amy murmurs.

"It's bigger than that. Logan's got an uncanny knack for being at the right place at the right time."

"So true."

A moment later, Logan and his two passengers—his fiancée, Kennedy, and that annoying groomsman, Luke—are approaching Amy and me on foot.

"What the fuck, Colin?" Logan shouts, holding up his phone, as he walks—and as he gets closer, I make out the cast photo I posted earlier today on his screen. "When were you planning to tell me you've been cast in a fucking Seth Rockford flick?" Without waiting for my reply, Logan pulls me into an enthusiastic hug and congratulates me.

"Don't be insulted I didn't tell you," I mutter. "I didn't tell anyone."

It's a lie. I told Dax and Fish, pretty early on. Partly, because I tell them everything. But also in the context of our band talking about our then-upcoming tour schedule. Fish had revealed he wanted to take some time off from touring to produce his new girlfriend's upcoming album, so Dax dropped the bomb he also wanted to take his foot off the gas for a bit to spend more time with his wife and young son. And so, in the context of that conversation, I told my fellow Goats about the movie role I'd been offered and was dying to accept.

Before that conversation, however, I'd already told my personal mentor, Ryan Morgan—Dax's older brother—about the movie role. But only because I've always relied on Ryan, more than anyone else, to help me figure out my life's biggest decisions.

After Logan releases me, the other people in the group congratulate me on the movie. Until, eventually, our group begins walking toward the restaurant again.

"Speaking of the movie . . ." I grin at Amy. "You want to tell everyone the exciting news?"

"Is it for sure, though?" she asks, her green eyes hopeful.

"One hundred percent. Tell the world, dude."

Amy squeals and excitedly tells the group about her short-term job with me on the movie set, which prompts Kennedy to hug her and Logan to mouth to me, "Thank you."

Apparently, Logan thinks I offered to help out his little sister, yet again, as a favor to him. But while that was true last time, Logan had nothing to do with my offer to Amy this time. As a matter of fact, I felt inspired to help Amy, on a whim, simply because I was enjoying her company so damned much and thought it might ease my anxiety during a stressful week to have a friendly face along for the ride.

We reach the front door of the restaurant and I open it for everyone to pass, which they do, with Amy hanging back to go last.

"Did you see the look on Luke's face when I said I'll be working for you?" Amy whispers excitedly in the doorway. "He looked like a toddler denied a cookie!"

With a happy little evil laugh, Amy enters the restaurant and I follow. But I can't agree with her assessment. Nope. Luke didn't look like a toddler denied a cookie a minute ago. On the contrary, he looked to me like a man who just figured out the woman he'd set his sights on is way, *way* out of his league.

FOUR

AMY

"No, sadly, none of my scenes will be shot in Hawaii," Colin says, responding to a question from one of the groomsmen sitting across from us at the table. "My character dies at the one-third mark of the movie, before his unit takes off for combat. So, all my scenes will be shot on a studio lot in Burbank, before the rest of the production heads off to Kuai for three months."

Everyone within earshot of Colin peppers him with another round of questions about the movie, which he graciously answers. That's great by me, since it gives me more time to covertly ogle Colin's lips as he talks. To study his handsome profile, his sexy, tattooed forearms, and tousled, gorgeous hair. All without coming off like the lowkey creeper I am.

I'm sitting to Colin's right at our long table, while Logan and Kennedy sit to his left, and several members of the wedding party sit across from us. When we first sat down fifteen minutes ago, Logan told everyone the exciting news about Colin's upcoming movie. And that's all anyone's wanted to talk about since.

"How'd you get the part?" one of the groomsmen asks.

"I got lucky," Colin replies. "Thanks to a modeling campaign I did recently—"

"The one for Calvin Klein?" a bridesmaid interjects.

"Yeah. Thanks to that ad campaign going viral, I got invited to a big Hollywood party, where I met the director of the movie, Gary Flynn. One thing led to another, and my manager got word Gary wanted me to come down and audition for him and his casting director. I went down there, crapping my pants, read a few scenes for them, and two days later, I got word the role was mine."

Everyone at the table explodes with excitement and another round of questions. But this time, Colin says, "Enough about me. Let's talk about the wedding. Has anyone started a pool on who's gonna get the drunkest tomorrow night?"

If he wanted to change the topic quickly, he's a genius. Instantly, enthusiastic conversation about tomorrow night's festivities ensues, and then continues until the waitress appears to take everyone's food orders.

When it's our turn to order, Colin and I give the waitress our information, at which point Colin shocks me by leaning into my shoulder, bumping me playfully, and asking, "Do you not drink alcohol, or are you simply not drinking tonight?" He points at my water glass.

"Oh, I drink, but not when I'm driving. I'll drink like a fish tomorrow night. In fact, don't tell anyone, but I'd advise you to put all your money on *me* in that pool."

Colin laughs at my silly joke, the same way he's laughed at all my jokes tonight. And I can't deny, each and every time

I hear Colin's adorable, heartfelt laughter, especially in reaction to something *I've* said, butterflies—no, *fireflies*—whoosh into my belly. *Wings and lights,* as the famous 22 Goats song says.

"Something tells me Drunk Amy is going to be highly entertaining tomorrow night," Colin says.

"That's a given. With each drink ingested, Drunk Amy's internal filter loses fifty-percent functionality. Give me three drinks, and it's ninety-nine percent likely I'll say or do something highly regrettable. Might even do both."

Colin's dark eyes flicker. "Sounds fun." He leans forward and places his tattooed forearm onto the table, a mischievous smirk on his handsome face. "Did Drunk Amy ever say or do something 'highly regrettable' during the RCR tour?"

I roll my eyes. "Yes, unfortunately."

"Oooh. Tell me more."

"Nothing too scandalous—don't set your expectations too high. But I most definitely committed the crime of 'oversharing while intoxicated' during the tour."

Colin pulls a face like he's not impressed. "Pfft. That's barely a misdemeanor."

"Not the way I did it, honey."

He laughs and arches an eyebrow. "Tell me more."

I blush. "It's embarrassing."

"The best stories always are, my dear."

I pause, and ultimately decide I'm enjoying having Colin's playful, undivided attention too much *not* to tell him the full story. I take a deep breath, gearing up. And then, "It was, like, day three of the tour and I was playing a drunken game of 'Never Have I Ever' with a small group of crew guys. And I guess I didn't realize people aren't usually completely honest during that game, because I stupidly didn't hold back." I snort. "I wound up answering 'never' so many times, one of the crew guys flat-out asked me if I was a virgin." When Colin's eyebrows ride up, I quickly add, "I'm not. I had a boyfriend for almost a year in college. But, obviously, based on my answers to all those raunchy questions, it seems my boyfriend and I weren't anything close to 'adventurous.' In fact, it became obvious during the game my paltry sex life had been embarrassingly unadventurous. Not to mention . . . ahem . . . embarrassingly *ineffectual*."

Colin grimaces.

"Yeah. My ex and I lost our virginity to each other, so I kept thinking it'd get better once we both got more experience. Unfortunately, that never panned out."

Colin grimaces. "Yeesh, Ames. Did you realize you were waving a red flag at a horny herd of bulls during that game?"

"Shockingly, I did!" I giggle. "And I was glad to do it. I actually wanted to make it abundantly clear I was highly interested in turning some of my 'nevers' into 'I sure have's!' during the tour. But after that, nobody even flirted with me, ever again, like they'd been doing the first few days. In fact, after that, they mostly ignored me." I roll my eyes and sigh. "That's how I knew I'd thoroughly embarrassed myself during that game and scared everybody off. Either that, or I'd only imagined they were flirting with me in the first place. Most likely, I just wasn't attractive enough for such experienced guys to—"

"No, that's not it. No, Amy. I can tell you with one hundred percent certainty that wasn't it."

My heart is racing. I know Colin is only reassuring me to be nice, but hearing him impliedly call me attractive feels pretty damned incredible. "You want to hear the most embarrassing thing of all?" I ask, my confidence bolstered.

"Abso-fucking-lutely."

"Caleb overheard the whole game! He heard every embarrassing word I'd said!"

"You mean he was playing the game with you guys?"

I shake my head. "No. We were playing in this lounge area in our hotel, not realizing Caleb had been lying on a couch in the corner when we came in. I only found out he was lying there, eavesdropping, when I got up to throw away a pizza box after the game!"

Colin hoots with laughter. "Nice of Caleb not to announce himself."

"Right?" I palm my forehead at the memory. "You should have seen the smirk on that motherfucker's face when our eyes met. I knew, right then, he'd heard every word I'd said and found *all* of it highly amusing."

Colin furrows his brow, which isn't the reaction I was expecting.

"What?"

"What'd Caleb say?"

"Nothing! That was the weirdest part. He smirked at me, and then got up and grabbed my hand. He was like, 'Time for bed, Drunk Amy.' He dragged me to my room and tucked me into bed. Said he'd stay with me until I fell asleep. And I guess that's what he did because in the morning, I woke up and there was water and ibuprofen on the nightstand, and Caleb was gone."

Colin narrows his eyes, looking like he's trying to solve a Rubik's Cube.

"What is it?" I say, confused by Colin's body language.

Colin smiles. "Are you leaving something important out of your tale, Ames? Hmm?"

"No. What do you mean?"

Colin's smile turns lopsided and wicked. "You can tell me the truth, Ames."

"About what?"

"You had a little tour fling with C-Bomb, didn't you?"

I gasp. "What? *No*."

He's not buying it. "Come on, dude. C-Bomb is a lot of things, but 'patient' isn't one of them. 'Nice' isn't one of them. He's not the kind of guy to hold a drunk girl's hair. Especially not a drunk *PA's* hair. And *especially* not a drunk PA who's as sweet and inexperienced and starry-eyed—and, yes, attractive—as you."

My heart is exploding in my chest. Colin thinks I'm attractive enough to have had a tour fling with the legendary drummer of Red Card Riot—a man known to enthusiastically, ahem, appreciate women? Well, color me complimented!

"You really think I had sex with C-Bomb?"

"I sure do."

"Thank you! Wow!" I take a minute to gather myself. "That's so sweet of you to say!"

"Well, did you?"

I sigh. "Unfortunately, no. I swear it on the soul of my dead dog Fluffy. Remember him? In fact, Caleb didn't so much as flirt with me throughout the entire tour. And nobody else did, either, unfortunately. Not after that game. The whole crew treated me like the tour mascot, from that day forward. I was everyone's kid sister. Frankly, it was totally demoralizing." I furrow my brow, suddenly realizing something horrendous. "Wait a second. Are you telling me Caleb has a weakness for sweet, inexperienced, starry-eyed women?"

"Definitely."

"And yet he still didn't make a move on me, even though I

obviously fit that description and was around him, more than anyone else, for nine freaking months?"

Colin grimaces, apparently seeing my point.

I cover my face with my hands, feeling mortified. "What's wrong with me, Colin? Why *didn't* he make a move on me? Why didn't anyone?"

I touch her arm gently. "Amy, no. Don't feel bad. Hey. Look at me, sweetheart."

I slowly remove my hands.

"Obviously, Caleb really liked and respected you. That's a *good* thing."

I lean into Colin and whisper-shout, so the people sitting around us at the table won't overhear me. "So now you're saying a man can't like and respect a woman *and* want to bang her? Because if that's your point, it's disturbing."

"Of course, that's not what I meant. I'm just saying it's clear Caleb genuinely liked you and probably . . . I don't know, felt like he didn't want to mess up your friendship. He was your employer, after all. Your direct superior. That made you technically off-limits to him, right?"

I'm not impressed with his logic. "Thanks for trying to cheer me up. I appreciate that. But I think Nate was right. He was this douchey crew guy. And he—"

"Sound guy?"

"Yeah."

"I know Nate. I hate that guy."

"So do I! He's such a douche. Nate was the only guy who kept hitting on me, even after that drunken game, until I finally told him to stop. I said, 'Look, I'm never gonna get with you, dude. So, leave me alone.' And you know what that asshole said to me in reply? He goes, 'If you're holding out for C-Bomb or one of the other band members, don't bother.

Those guys can pull anyone they want, three at a time. They're never gonna stoop to banging a lowly PA who's a six, on a good day."

Colin practically spits out the vodka drink he just sipped. "That motherfucker said *what* to you?" Breathing fire, he pulls out his phone and begins swiping. "That asshole follows me on Instagram. I'll spam-like a bunch of his photos, so he looks at my profile. And when he does . . . Come here, Ames." Colin holds up his phone, framing our faces. "Snuggle up to me, like we just got finished fucking in the bathroom. Let that asshole think I just went 'Instagram official' with my hot new girlfriend." I nuzzle close, freaking out he called me hot. And when I get a whiff of Colin's delicious cologne, and he kisses the side of my head in reply, I feel butterflies, even though I know Colin's only pretending to be my boyfriend for the photo.

Snap.

The photo taken and approved by me, Colin posts it like a man possessed, and then, as promised, immediately spam-likes a slew of Nate's photos. But midway through his online campaign, Colin pauses and looks at me. "Nate doesn't know you're like a sister to me, does he?"

Fucking hell. I was feeling like something new had maybe started bubbling between us during this meal! He called me attractive! Said I'm hot! Was all the mutual attraction I thought we were both feeling all in my head, again?

"Uh, no. I didn't mention my connection to you during the tour to anyone but Caleb."

Colin freezes. "You told Caleb about me?"

My heart begins pounding. "Just that we grew up together and you'd gotten me the job." I pause, not understanding Colin's stiff body language. "Did I mess up somehow?"

"No. Of course not. How'd Caleb react when you told him about me?"

"He was super sweet. He said he wasn't surprised you got me the job because you're a good, loyal friend. He even said he missed hanging out with you."

Colin's eyes saucer. "Caleb said that, or he *implied* it?"

"He said it."

"He said he missed hanging out with me?"

I nod. "He did." My heart skips a beat at the excitement in Colin's expression. Obviously, this bit of news means the world to him. "I know Caleb and Dax had some sort of falling out," I venture tentatively. "But Caleb had nothing but complimentary things to say about you."

"Yeah, Fish and I had nothing to do with what happened. Neither did the rest of the RCR guys. Even Dax didn't have any hard feelings, really. It was all Caleb. Dax tried to reach out to him, lots of times. But Caleb Baumgarten is one stubborn motherfucker."

I run my fingertip over a fork in front of me, my heart thrumming. "Do you think maybe you could reach out to Caleb now, since so much time has passed, or would that make waves for you with Dax?"

Colin purses his lips. Takes a sip of his vodka drink. He fiddles with his napkin for a long beat. "Yeah, I think I could do that." He flashes me a crooked smile. "Thanks for telling me what Caleb said."

My heart feels like it's pounding against my sternum. Fireflies are ravaging my belly. *Swoon, swoon, swoon.* "You're welcome."

The air between us feels charged, like Colin's a magnet and I'm steel. I'm not imagining this crazy pull between us, am I? Colin's gaze drifts to my lips, briefly, and then to my boobs, and then to his drink on the table, where it remains. Was Colin thinking about kissing me just now? Or am I falling prey to wishful thinking again?

"Hey, Colin!" Logan says, pulling Colin's attention from his drink on the table. "Do you remember that time when we were about ten and . . .?"

And that's it. The electricity coursing between Colin and me, real or imagined, is gone. Colin is engaged in conversation with my brother now, and I'm looking at the back of Colin's head. Shit.

Exhaling, I pull out my phone and sneak a peek at the photo Colin posted of us, and my heart physically palpitates at the sight of it. Oh, how I wish the canoodling couple in this photo were real.

"Yeah, so this guy named Nate . . ." I catch Colin saying, even though his head is turned. "Such a dick . . . sound guy . . . So, I posted a photo of Amy and me on Instagram, looking like we're a couple."

What's that now?

When I'm able to tune into Colin's voice above the chatter and clatter at the busy table, I hear him explaining that photo of us to Logan. He's telling my brother the shot was meant to "bait" Nate into feeling like an "asshole" for "negging" me during the tour. And Logan is laughing and thoroughly enjoying Colin's story.

"I'm gonna post a bunch of shots with Amy and the Goats tomorrow night at the wedding, too," Colin explains, before launching into describing our strategy for impressing that employment agency in LA. "So, don't be surprised if my Instagram looks like The Colin and Amy Show this weekend."

"That's so awesome!" Logan says, laughing. "Thanks for

doing all that for her. You're the best."

I frown, feeling thoroughly annoyed. I'm grateful for everything Colin is doing for me, of course. I can't wait to head to LA and work for him, however briefly, and stay at his place while doing it. But does Colin have to go to such great lengths to make sure Logan doesn't think, even for a second, Colin and I could *possibly* be interested in each other?

After a bit, Colin returns to me and catches me scrolling through his Instagram account. "Has Nate liked our photo yet?"

"I didn't look."

"Well, let's see." He picks up my phone, taps on my screen, and scrolls for a long beat.

"*Oh.*" Suddenly, there's a shift in his body language—a subtle jolt of his torso that makes me think we've struck gold and caught a fish called Nate on our line.

"Nate liked our photo?" I ask.

"Huh? Oh. No." He puts my phone down on the table and smiles. "So, Amy. I just got yet another brilliant idea to help you. I'm going to a friend's birthday party in Malibu next weekend—the Saturday before shooting starts for me. Tons of famous faces will be there, so why don't you come with me as my 'date' and try to land yourself a job there?"

I gasp loudly. "Are you sure?"

"Why not? I think it'd be a blast to bring you. And who knows? You might get lucky and walk away with a job."

I throw my arms around Colin's neck and thank him effusively for his generosity, yet again, and Colin laughs into my hair.

"This isn't me being generous, Ames. I'm already going to the party. All I'm doing is bringing you along."

When we disengage from our hug, I take a sip of water,

trying to calm down, but my arm is shaking disastrously. So much so, I'd literally be spilling everywhere if my glass had more water in it. "Whose birthday is it?" I ask, my voice quavering.

"Laila Fitzgerald. Her boyfriend is throwing the party at their place in Malibu."

I slam my glass down and shriek, much too loudly for the indoor setting, and my mother throws me a harsh glare from the far end of the table. Ignoring my mother's daggers, I lean into Colin and whisper-shout, "I love Laila Fitzgerald! She's so gorgeous and talented!"

"Yeah, she's a sweetheart. Lots of people from River Records and *Sing Your Heart Out* will be at the party, so I think the opportunities for you to network will be through the roof."

I babble incoherently about my excitement, and then ask Colin a thousand questions. Until all of a sudden, I realize people have been getting up from the table and grabbing their purses and coats.

"Looks like the party's shutting down," I say.

"Yeah, we've got a big day tomorrow."

"Where are you staying?"

"At my mom's place tonight," Colin says. "I'll probably crash in Dax's suite at the hotel tomorrow after the wedding reception."

"Hey, I'm staying at the hotel tomorrow night, too!"

"Awesome. I'm sure we'll party in Dax's suite after the reception. Come party with us."

"I will!" I clutch my heart, feeling like it's in danger of physically exploding and splattering all over Colin and the restaurant walls. I jerk to standing, too excited to sit a second longer, and shout, "I'll drive you to your mom's house!"

Colin chuckles at my exuberance. "Are you sure? I'm fine taking an Uber."

"Don't be silly. Your suitcase is still in my car, remember? And I'd love to say hi to your mom, if she's still awake."

"Cool. Thanks." Colin stands and grabs his coat. "I'm sure my mom will be thrilled to see you again."

We say our goodbyes to everyone remaining in the restaurant, including blecchy Luke, who seems shocked and mildly offended when he finds out I'm driving Colin to his mom's house. *Snicker.* And then, off Colin and I go, out the door of the restaurant and into the crisp Seattle night, to head to our childhood stomping grounds. Only this time, as adults.

FIVE

COLIN

"And then," Amy gushes, "Colin invited me to tag along to a birthday party for Laila Fitzgerald!"

We're sitting across from my mom and stepdad in their living room, and Amy is currently regaling them with all her exciting news. And as Amy talks, it's clear my mother is every bit as enamored with her as she always used to be when Amy lived next door.

"Is Laila Fitzgerald the sassy blonde on *Sing Your Heart Out*?" my mom asks. And when Amy confirms that's the one, the two women chat enthusiastically about Laila for a few minutes, before Amy shifts the topic of conversation to me. Specifically, how "generous and thoughtful" I am for arranging such incredible opportunities for her.

"I think that has more to do with you, Amy," my mother replies, "than Colin's general character."

"Excuse me?" I ask.

"Oh, come on. You've always had a huge soft spot for Amy, ever since she was a baby."

What the fuck? Shocked, I glower at my mother, telepathically commanding her to shut the fuck up now, please. But Mom quickly returns her attention to Amy and totally ignores my death stare.

Mom says to Amy, "When your parents brought you home from the hospital after having you, they came over here to fetch Logan, because he'd stayed overnight with us. And the second Colin saw you, all wrapped up like a little burrito, he asked to hold you. And you know what Colin said when he looked down into your sweet, scrunched-up little face in his lap?"

"*Mom.*" I've never heard this story before, but I can tell from my mother's facial expression, it's going to embarrass the hell out of me.

Mom bats her eyelashes at Amy. "Colin looked down at you and said, '*I love you, baby.*'"

"Mom!" I shout. But it's too late. My diabolical mother is a runaway train.

"And then, after your family left, Colin begged me to give him a baby of his own—one just like you!"

"Mom, stop."

"And I told him, 'No, sweetie, you were an 'oops' baby. I'm all done." Mom guffaws while I shoot her profile daggers. "And you know what Colin did then?" Mom hoots with laughter. "He burst into big old soggy tears!"

While Amy joins my mother in laughing, I mutter, "Probably because you'd just told me I was an accident."

"And from that day forward," Mom says brightly, "from that first time Colin saw you and fell in love with your sweet little face—"

"*Mom!*"

"He always looked out for you. Remember that time you had that lemonade stand to raise money, Amy?"

Amy nods. "For the animal shelter."

"When are Chiara and Caitlyn arriving tomorrow?" I interject, trying to change the subject. But it's no use.

Mom says, "I bet you didn't know all that money Colin gave you for the animal shelter was *all* the birthday and Christmas money he'd been saving to buy himself a video game he'd been dying to play."

Amy looks at me, her eyes like saucers.

Blushing, I murmur lamely, "I like animals."

"I swear, though, Colin only ever did that kind of thing for you," Mom says. "Otherwise, I guarantee we wouldn't have been able to pry that money out of Colin's cold, dead fist."

"Mom!" I say, as my stepfather chuckles next to her. My stepdad wasn't around during my childhood. He came along after Amy had already moved away. But clearly, he's thoroughly enjoying my mother's diabolical machinations. He's a smart man, my stepfather. Surely, he knows what his wife is trying to do—because I sure as hell do.

"And do you remember the time you 'ran away' from home, when you were just a tiny little thing?" Mom asks.

"Enough, Mom," I interject. "Please."

Mom bats her eyelashes at me, feigning innocence. "Sweetheart, Amy and I are just reminiscing." She returns to Amy, her eyebrows lifted in faux concern. "Am I making you uncomfortable, sweetheart?"

"Not at all. I'm loving this walk down memory lane." As Mom flashes me a snarky look that says, See?, Amy laughs and says, "I'm pretty sure I ran away that time because nobody at home would play dolls with me."

"Oh, how you adored those dolls!" Mom says.

"I was obsessed," Amy agrees. "I think that time I ran

away to Genovia. That's the fictitious kingdom in *The Princess Diaries*. But I thought it was real."

Mom and Amy giggle together, while I have a nonverbal exchange with my stepfather that goes something like this:

Please, make her stop. For the love of fuck.

I couldn't make your mother stop, even if I wanted to. And I don't want to, just to be clear.

When Mom's giggling subsides, she continues her story. "I was washing dishes in the kitchen and saw you outside my window, marching down the sidewalk with a doll in one hand and a tiny rolling suitcase in the other. And even from a distance, I could tell you were *pissed as hell*."

Amy squeals with laughter.

"Your little shoulders were set. Your little chin was up. Oh man, little Amy had had enough of whatever mistreatment she'd endured."

Amy guffaws and slaps her thigh, obviously loving the story.

"I was a bit worried about you, when I realized nobody was following you. You were a tiny little thing. Way too young to be marching off, on your own. So, I stopped what I was doing, figuring I'd run after you." Mom winks at me. "But there was no need. Colin had been mowing the front lawn, and when he saw you, he stopped what he was doing and chased after you, without even being asked."

Amy looks at me like I walk on water, and I feel my cheeks turn hot.

"And what did I see a little while later, but Colin escorting you home. He had your suitcase in one hand and your tiny hand in the other, while you clutched your beloved dolly. And I thought, 'What is it about that little girl that's turned my moody boy into a big ol' pile of mush?'"

"Whoa, look at the time," I say, looking at my watch. "We've got a big day tomorrow. We should get some sleep."

"Yeah, you're probably right," Amy agrees reluctantly. She rises from her chair, smiling broadly at my mother. "It was so wonderful to see you again." The women hug warmly and say they can't wait to see each other tomorrow at the wedding. My stepfather shakes Amy's hand and tells her she's lovely. And, finally, I offer to walk Amy to her car.

"Sorry about that," I murmur, as we walk outside into the crisp night.

"I loved every second of it," Amy says. "I've always loved your mom. She's so warm and real. She makes me feel like I can be completely myself around her."

"She loves you, too." *Obviously,* I think. *For fuck's sake, the woman was brazenly matchmaking in there!*

As we stop at Amy's car, she shivers, which prompts me to reach out, reflexively, and rub her arms. And the second I touch Amy's bare skin, I feel a zap of electricity flash through my nerve endings. Jolted, I drop my arms and blurt, "Well, drive safe."

"You, too," Amy says, her cheeks red. "I mean, see you tomorrow."

"Yep. See you tomorrow. Drive safe."

"*You, too.*" She palms her forehead and snorts, before opening her car door and slipping inside—and a moment later, Amy's taillights are gone.

Back inside my house, I search for my evil mother and find her in the kitchen, unloading the dishwasher.

"What the hell is wrong with you?" I demand, coming to a stop on the other side of the opened dishwasher.

"Hmm. Let's see. Well, my therapist says I have deep-seated abandonment issues."

Mom smirks, but she's not fooling me. This woman is a master chess player who's always three moves ahead, while pretending to be clueless half the time.

"Don't BS me, woman," I say. "You were trying to push Amy and me together tonight—as a couple."

Mom leans her hip against the kitchen counter and crosses her arms over her chest. "And what if I was? You two would make an adorable couple."

"She's Logan's little sister! Every story you told should have made it abundantly clear to you she might as well be *my* little sister, too!"

Mom drops the 'innocent act' on a dime, instantly revealing the diabolical creature behind her mask. "When you were kids, yes. Which was age appropriate. But you're not kids anymore, and I could plainly see you have incredible chemistry with her."

"Butt out, Mom."

"Colin, she's had a crush on you since she could walk! Literally. And we all know you're the absolute worst at figuring out and then expressing your feelings! So, I thought I'd pitch in and help you both out."

I feel like my mother just punched me in the gut. That's exactly what Kiera always used to say to me when we fought —that I wasn't communicative enough about my feelings, even though I always felt like I was showing Kiera how I felt, pretty damned clearly, with my actions.

"I saw the way you were looking at her!" Mom says. "Don't you dare pretend you haven't noticed how pretty Amy's become."

"She's very pretty, yes. But, like I said, she's like a sister to me."

Mom's face turns downright wicked. "My darling son, if

you looked at Chiara and Caitlyn's boobs the way you kept staring at Amy's tonight, I'd beat the living crap out of you."

My breathing halts. Did I seriously ogle Amy O'Brien's tits in front of my mother and stepdad tonight? Holy shit. I really am a monster!

Mom adds, "So don't blame me if I seized the opportunity to manifest the Beretta-O'Brien grandbabies I've always dreamed of!"

I'm speechless. Staring at my mother in disbelief. Finally, I say, "You're insane. I've always suspected as much. But now I know it, for sure."

Mom laughs and shakes her head, clearly not getting it, so I decide to make things abundantly clear. Otherwise, God knows what mischief she'll get into at the wedding tomorrow night.

"Listen to me, Mom. I can't make a move on Amy, ever. Yes, she's sweet and beautiful and funny—and I admit I've always had a soft spot for her. But there's no middle ground here. No chance for us to 'date' like normal people. Like you said, she's always had a crush on me, and I'd never want to hurt her. If things didn't work out between us, she'd be decimated and my friendship with Logan would never be same." I sigh. "Amy doesn't even have a crush on the real me, Mom. You heard her. She's crushing on some weird fantasy version of me, who, for some reason, can't stop doing nice things for her—a guy I couldn't deliver to her, in the long-term, even if I wanted to. If you've been dreaming of Beretta-O'Brien grandbabies, then I'm sorry to inform you: you'd better find a new fucking dream."

Mom's eyes become lasers. "You're saying you felt no physical chemistry with Amy tonight?"

My pulse is thumping in my ears. "That's right."

Mom narrows her eyes even more. "Well, great. I suppose that'll come in handy when Amy stays at your house for almost two weeks—at your generous invitation."

"Did you not hear she's going to *work* for me? Of course, I offered her my guest room, when we're going to be driving to the same place every day."

"You're seriously trying to convince me you've offered to help Amy find a job, and offered her a place to stay, for no other reason than because she's like a little sister to you?"

"Mm-hmm. That's right."

Mom cocks her head. "Is that also why you asked Amy to be your *date* to Laila's star-studded birthday party, as well—because she's like a sister to you?"

Mom's dark eyes are boring holes into my face like she's got X-ray vision. So I know, from past experience, I've got to give this bloodhound something, *anything*, to throw her off the scent.

"As a matter of fact," I say, "I asked Amy to be my plus-one at Laila's party, *partly* to help her, but mostly to help *myself*." I tell my mother about the "canoodling" photo I snapped of Amy and me in the restaurant, and how I noticed, shortly after posting it, that Laila Fitzgerald had liked it. "I recently made a fool of myself with Laila," I admit. "I pursued her, romantically, and it didn't pan out—and, unfortunately, Laila's boyfriend knows all about it. So, when I saw Laila had liked that photo of Amy and me, I figured bringing Amy to Laila's birthday party as my date might help smooth over an otherwise awkward and uncomfortable situation for me." I smile like a shark. "So you see, Mother, I'm not bending over backwards to help Amy, nearly as much as you're assuming. And I'm likewise not nearly the saint Amy thinks I am. In reality, I'm much closer to a douchebag who's killing two birds with one stone—helping Amy, yes, since I like her and it's an easy thing for me to do, while also helping myself avoid a potentially tense situation with Laila and her boyfriend. So, I'd appreciate it if you'd stop trying to get yourself Beretta-O'Brien grandbabies and stay the fuck out of my shit."

Mom doesn't flinch at my harsh language and tone. Rather, she purses her lips, calmly, and stares me down the same way she's done my whole life, whenever I've gotten out of line with her. And I must admit, she's scaring me now, every bit as much as she did when I was a kid.

"All right, darling," Mom says. "I'll stay the fuck out of your 'shit,' assuming everything you said is true. I'm not entirely convinced of that, but I'll play along for now, *if* you promise me something."

I sigh. "What?"

"Stop leading that poor girl on."

"Excuse me?"

Mom's dark eyes blaze. "Colin Michael, you were staring at Amy's chest throughout our entire conversation. Laughing at every mildly amusing thing she said. You were absolutely entranced by that woman, and everyone in the room could plainly see it, including Amy. So, if you're sincerely *only* interested in that poor girl as a little sister, then pull your shit together and tell your dick to take a back seat and stop giving her mixed signals. Because the way you were looking at her tonight would make any 'little sister' think her benevolent 'big brother' was thinking awfully hard about incest!" As my jaw drops, Mom leans forward and points her finger at me. "Don't you dare lead that girl on, Colin Michael, or I swear, I'll not only stay the fuck *in* your 'shit,' I'll also beat all your fucking 'shit' clean out of you!"

SIX

COLIN

I turn off the shower and dry off, throw on a pair of pajama bottoms, and drag my exhausted, semi-drunk ass into my childhood bed. I think maybe my mother is secretly an assassin. *Jesus.*

I close my eyes, but as wiped out as I am, sleep won't come.

I look at the time on my phone. *12:07.* That's not too late to call Caleb, is it? When my band opened for his years ago, C-Bomb was always a night owl, the same as me. In fact, we were always the last two guys to go to bed, no matter how long and exciting the day had been.

I grab my phone, scroll my contacts, and push the button to place the unthinkable call. Before my conversation with Amy tonight, I never would have reached out like this. But now, I'm bursting with excitement as I wait for Caleb, or his voicemail, to pick up.

After three rings, Caleb's distinctive, deep voice answers my call, in person—not in an outgoing voicemail message.

"Well, if it isn't Colin Beretta."

"Hey, Caleb. You got a few minutes for me?"

"For you, Colin, I've got all the time in the world. How are you?"

"I'm good. What are you up to?"

"Sitting on my balcony, smoking a blunt, looking out at the moonlit ocean while questioning all my life's choices."

I chuckle. "Sounds fun, if not a little depressing."

"You're welcome to join me. One man staring at the ocean, smoking a blunt, is a possible sign of depression. But two men doing it, together? Now, that's a party."

We both laugh. I forgot how weird Caleb Baumgarten can be. How charming, in his own, unique way.

"I'd come right over, if I weren't in Seattle this weekend. I'm currently lying in my childhood bed. I'm not smoking a blunt, unfortunately. But I'm definitely questioning at least half my life's choices."

A deep rumble of a chuckle escapes him. "You get any pussy in that childhood bed?"

I can't help matching his laughter. Before placing this call, if I'd been asked to predict what Caleb Baumgarten would say when finding out I was lying in my childhood bed, that's exactly what I would have said: *You ever get any pussy in that childhood bed?*

"I did, as a matter of fact," I admit. "Some of it *contraband* pussy, while my mom was fast asleep downstairs."

"Ooh, contraband pussy. Atta boy, Colinoscopy. Get it."

And that's it. With his use of that silly nickname, the one everyone called me during our tour together, Caleb has let me know he's got no hard feelings toward me, despite his years-long rift with my band's frontman.

"But you didn't call to talk about the contraband pussy you got in your teenage bed," he says. "You called to ask if I fucked Amy O'Brien during my tour. The answer to that question, my brother, is no."

I'm shocked into silence for a moment, for a few reasons, not the least of which is Caleb's use of the world *brother*. But finally, I manage to ask, "How'd you know I was calling you about Amy?"

"The magic of Instagram."

"Ah. Yeah, I'm in Seattle for Amy's big brother's wedding tomorrow. He was my next-door neighbor growing up. We were glued at the hip for the first eighteen years of our lives."

"Which means Amy is like a little sister to you?"

"Yeah."

"That's what she told me—that you've always been like a big brother to her. That's why I didn't fuck her, by the way, among other reasons. You're welcome."

"What were the other reasons?"

He sighs. "Amy O'Brien." He snickers. "At first, I think I steered clear of her because she was such a shit show. The worst PA I'd ever had. I literally thought Reed Rivers had ordered a proverbial 'hit' on me by assigning her to me—or maybe he was doing a favor for someone who hated me?" He chuckles. "Either way, I figured I'd better get some more information before I fired her ass or fucked her." I hear the sound of Caleb exhaling in a way that makes me visualize a plume of smoke swirling into the night air on his end of the line. "But then, Amy told me what I needed to know. She told me about *you*. That you'd gotten her the job. That she grew up next-door to you. And, Colin, the way she talked about you . . . I know she *said* you were always like a 'big brother' to her, but the way she talked about you strongly suggested there was something more there. Were you her first love? Did she give her V-card to you? I didn't know. But, either way, unlike someone we both know, I actually *respect* the unwritten rules among brothers. So, I decided she was off-limits to me, right then and there. I'm no hypocrite."

I rub my forehead. "Caleb, Dax didn't get with Violet to mess with you. If that were the case, he's brought new meaning to the phrase 'commit to the bit,' wouldn't you say? They're married with a kid, man."

"A cute one, from what I've seen in photos." He pauses. "You know why I'm pissed, Colin. My issue is with Dax knowing he was like a little brother to me, knowing I loved him like family, and then stabbing me in the back, rather than telling me to my face."

"It wouldn't have changed anything if he'd told you in advance. You're kidding yourself."

"I guess we'll never know." He exhales again, presumably blowing smoke into the night air on his balcony again. "But you didn't call to talk about Dax, any more than the pussy you got in your childhood bed. You called to talk to me about Amy. Your 'honorary little sister.' So, let's talk about that."

Fuck. I wish so badly I could fix the bad blood between Caleb and Dax, the same way as a kid I used to wish I could fix everything between my parents. But clearly, there's nothing I can do about Dax and Caleb, any more than I could save my parents' marriage at age eight.

I sigh with resignation. "What'd you overhear when Drunk Amy played 'Never Have I Ever' with some crew guys? I want complete details."

Caleb laughs. "I overheard Drunk Amy saying the word 'never' a whole lot."

"Be more specific."

"Well, I found out she hadn't, in fact, lost her V-card to you. That she'd only been with one guy—her college boyfriend—and he couldn't find her clit to save his life." He belly laughs. "Poor little thing."

"Amy told me she became everyone's little sister after that," I say. "But that makes no sense, given what she revealed during that game. I would have bet the farm those crew guys were salivating over her like hungry wolves after that game."

"Oh, they were. They would have been all over her, if I hadn't stepped in."

"Ahhh, okay. Everything makes sense now. You laid down the law, did you?"

"Of course, I did. Jesus Christ! Amy wouldn't have gotten a moment's peace during that tour, if I hadn't. You think I was gonna leave my drunk little unicorn to the wolves for nine whole months, knowing she was like a little sister to you? Fuck no. I'm nothing if not loyal to my brothers, even if they'll never know it."

My heart skips a beat. "So . . . what? You brought the drunk little unicorn to her room and then went back out and laid down the law with the hungry wolves?"

"Yep. This was early on, when Amy was still useless to me as a PA. But that didn't matter, because I knew she meant a lot to you. From that moment on, Amy became my little sister. And nobody fucks with C-Bomb's little sister."

"Oh, man. Referring to yourself in third person, eh? This sounds serious."

He laughs.

"Look, man, I know you thought you were helping Amy out," I say, "but you have no idea what a hit that poor girl's confidence took when nobody hit on her for the rest of the tour. Amy spent the next nine months thinking she's not fuck-able enough to get hit on."

Caleb's snorts. "Quite the opposite. Who wouldn't want to

get with a sweet, goofy little born-again virgin who makes the silliest facial expressions you've ever seen in your life?"

"Oh my God! Amy's facial expressions!"

"Hilarious."

"Right?"

We both laugh.

"Poor Amy," I mutter. "Hey, would you mind me telling her what you did to her after the game? I'm sure she'll be relieved to know. Not to mention pissed as hell."

"Go ahead. As long as you explain I did it *for* her, not *to* her. I did that girl a solid."

"She won't see it that way."

"Meh, like I give a fuck. I know she was excited to let loose during the tour and scratch some of those 'nevers' off her list—that was clear as day during that stupid game—but I guarantee you Amy's idea of 'swinging from chandeliers' is riding on top while someone actually knows to touch her sweet spot." He laughs at his own joke. "That college boyfriend of hers? I bet he was gay and didn't admit it to himself. Or maybe he was even running around on her, on the down low. Either way, Amy was that guy's beard, whether she knew it or not. There's no other explanation for a guy being that disinterested in eating a woman's pussy and fucking her right."

In a flash, I see myself doing exactly what Caleb just described: eating Amy's pussy right, until she's screaming my name. Swirling her clit with my fingertip as she rides my cock. What the hell is wrong with me?

"I was *this* close," Caleb is saying, when I tune back into our conversation.

"To what?" I ask, my heart lurching into my throat.

"To firing Amy that first week."

"Oh."

"But then, after she told me about you, I decided to keep her around and keep her busy, so she'd stay out of my shit. But, I'll be damned, that crazy little unicorn kept delivering whatever stupid thing I'd asked of her. Until one day, I realized I'd started liking the kid, despite myself. And not only that, she'd gotten damned good at her job. By the end, she was the best PA I'd ever had. My little unicorn."

"Amy said you called her 'unicorn' because of a welt on her forehead the first week."

Caleb chuckles. "True. But I kept calling her that, long after the welt had disappeared, because she'd gotten so damned good at her job."

My heart squeezes with pride for Amy. "She's looking for a permanent PA job in LA. Hire the girl."

"She already asked me, but I can't. When I'm home, I'm a hermit. Having Amy around would drive me batshit crazy. She'd try to organize everything. Keep me on schedule. Make me do something with my life. Be a better man. Fuck that shit. If I want to sit on a balcony and smoke a blunt and stare at the ocean, that's what I'll do."

"I don't want her working for a douchebag, man."

"Then you hire her."

"I can't. I don't need an assistant, any more than you do. But also . . ." I sigh. "It's complicated."

"Well, if she wants to work in LA, then odds are high she's gonna wind up working for a douchebag."

"Not if I can help it. I'm gonna introduce her around and make sure she winds up with someone who doesn't think dick-sucking is part of a PA's job description."

Caleb snickers. "Do you always work this hard at finding jobs for *all* your honorary little sisters?"

"I've only got the one." I glance at the time on my phone. "Shit. I should go. I'm in my buddy's wedding tomorrow. It's gonna be a long day."

"Get your beauty sleep, Colinoscopy. It was great talking to you."

"You, too, C-Bomb."

"Hit me up whenever you're back in LA. We'll hang out."

My heart leaps. "I will. Goodnight, brother."

"Goodnight, brother."

I end the call and stare at the ceiling for a long moment, feeling an ocean of relief and excitement coursing through me about our conversation. The comradery between us felt the same as it always did. It was like no time had passed.

Amy.

Those same sexual images from before flicker across my mind, against my will.

Fuck.

I roll onto my side, my mind racing, and finally decide to try that technique Ryan told me about to clear my racing thoughts when insomnia strikes. What'd Ryan tell me, again? Oh yeah. *Think of unrelated objects, one after another, and soon, your mind will be clear and you'll drift off to sleep.*

I roll onto my back, take a deep breath, and let my mind wander.

Horse. Barn.

Shit. Those things are related.

Horse. Daisy. Cloud.

Yeah, good. This is working. I'm already feeling more relaxed.

Suitcase. Vodka. Lemonade.

Shit. Vodka and lemonade are kind of related.

Genovia. Curly hair. Green eyes.

Perfect. Fucking. Tits.

In a flash, I see myself devouring Amy's perfect tits. Her head is thrown back and she's screaming my name.

Jesus.

Stop.

I roll onto my other side and realize I'm hard as a rock and my balls ache. With a deep sigh, I grab my phone, swipe into my favorite porn purveyor, and head to my saved videos. I click on the one at the top of my list—a clip that always gets me off fast. As the video gets started, I shove my hand into my boxers and grab my dick, ready to get going . . . and suddenly freeze.

Oh, fuck.

The woman getting banged from behind in the video looks like Amy. Auburn hair. Peaches and cream skin. Full lips. Freckles on her nose. *Perfect tits.*

Obviously, I couldn't have known my porn star of choice resembled the adult version of Amy O'Brien. But now that I do, I'm disgusted with myself. I mean, the resemblance is uncanny!

I swipe into Instagram to look at the photo I posted of Amy and me tonight—and, yep, there's no denying Amy looks like my favorite porn star, though Amy is much prettier.

Whoa. Kiera liked the photo of Amy and me! Why the hell would she do that?

For some reason, that pisses me off. I didn't post that photo for Kiera to see it. I didn't intend to bait her. I posted it for Nate. To make him feel like a tool for negging Amy. And, yes, if I'm being honest, also for Laila, too. I thought maybe she'd see it, which it turned out she did, and show it to her hotheaded boyfriend and say, "See? I told you Colin's not interested in me anymore!" Which, in turn, would hopefully keep Savage from shooting me daggers—or maybe even shooting me—throughout Laila's birthday party.

With a loud exhale, I do something I should have done months ago: I block Kiera on Instagram and delete her number from my contacts list. Those tasks completed, I toss my phone onto the nightstand, close my eyes, and will sleep to come. But all I can see when I close my eyes is Amy riding my cock.

How much vodka did I drink tonight?

She's off-limits, Colin! For so many reasons.

Again, I roll onto my other side and try thinking about random, unrelated objects. But again, it's no use. Finally, I grab a pillow and cover my face, figuring I'll fall asleep like this or suffocate myself to death. At this particular moment, either outcome would be perfectly fine with me.

SEVEN

AMY

I'm trembling as I walk down the center aisle of the church, while concentrating mightily on the wedding coordinator's instructions from last night:

Maintain the proper distance with the bridesmaid in front of me!

Hold my flowers below my bustline!

And, most importantly, smile for the cameras!

It's a lot to remember with all those eyeballs staring at me. Not to mention, when I'm trying not to face-plant, thanks to my high heels, or stumble over the hem of my bridesmaid gown.

As I reach the midway point of my journey, my eyes find Logan at the altar, and the look of elation on his face nearly makes me forget my nerves. *Aw.* I've never seen my brother looking quite this happy. How sweet.

From Logan, my gaze drifts down the line of groomsmen and rests on Colin's handsome face. When our eyes meet, Colin and I share a huge, beaming smile that sends warmth into my belly and makes me completely forget my nerves—at least, for now. *Damn*, that man looks fine as *bleep*—I'm self-censoring because I'm in church—in that dark suit!

I take my place at the end of the bridesmaids, sighing with relief that I made it without tripping, and smile at Kennedy's adorable niece who's sashaying up the aisle amid a swirl of flower petals.

In short order, the overhead music changes and the audience rises. And there she is. Kennedy soon-to-be-O'Brien. Dressed in white.

I glance at Logan and discover he's welled up with tears as he watches his bride approaching him. *Aw.* Not surprisingly, the sight of my usually stalwart brother losing control of his emotions provokes the same reaction in me. As I wipe my eyes, I look at Colin, curious to see *his* reaction to this glorious, tear-jerking moment . . . and the man is cool as a cucumber. Smiling, yes, but basically unfazed. Instantly, I realize: This is how Colin would react to *me* walking down the aisle toward my future husband, whoever he might be. And for some reason, that's a startling epiphany.

Why do I keep swooning over a man who doesn't, and never will, swoon back? If I want to have any hope of finding my person and being in Kennedy's shoes one day, then I need to quit reacting like I always do when it comes to Colin, starting now. Once and for all.

Yes.

What a relief to know my brain has finally gotten the message, loud and clear.

Nodding to myself at my new resolution, I watch Kennedy taking her place next to Logan and swoon at the look they exchange. See? My first swoon since my new vow to myself isn't over Colin! I've one hundred percent turned over a new leaf!

The pastor launches into the ceremony, talking about the power of love and the holy bond of marriage. And I swoon a couple times, *not* over Colin, at the beautiful sentiments he discusses. But after a while, my mind begins to wander. To contemplate the mistakes I've made and the embarrassments I've suffered, while looking for the kind of love Logan and Kennedy have found with each other.

I think my biggest mistake in the past has been my repeated propensity to subconsciously compare every guy to Colin. It's not fair for me to do that, because nobody else grew up next door to me. Nobody else had *years* to get to know me, without sexual expectations or my awkwardness or boobs getting in the way.

Colin never had to make awkward small talk with me online, before meeting me at a coffee house and discovering I'm actually a dork who makes weird facial expressions when I tell a story. Colin never had to meet me in person and discover I'd unintentionally catfished him with a photo taken in really good lighting. Colin never had to chat me up at a frat party, only to find out I'm the kind of girl who wants to have sex with someone only when I genuinely care about them. At least, that's how I felt back then.

I thought being on the road with a group of horny guys for nine months would turn me into a sex machine. Or even better, I'd wind up with an amazing boyfriend at the end of the tour. But after nine months, the only new sexual experiences I got were from a vibrator I'd picked up on sale in Paris. Thankfully, the vibrator did for me what Perry never could, so I'm grateful for that. Although as a boyfriend, the thing was a truly horrible conversationalist.

"Let us pray," the officiant says, and I suddenly realize I've been thinking about vibrators in church. *Yeesh.*

I bow my head with everyone else. And a little while later, listen with tears in my eyes to the beautiful exchange of vows. Finally, the pastor says, "Ladies and gentlemen, I'm thrilled to present to you: Mr. and Mrs. Logan and Kennedy O'Brien!" Of course, I clap and cheer along with everyone else in the church. And as I do, I'm feeling more determined than ever not to let my insides turn to mush over Colin, ever again. Starting now, he's my friend and nothing more! I'm finally free of my crush on him, forever! Determined to open my heart and find true love!

As I bounce in place with excitement, each bridesmaid ahead of me in line links up with her assigned groomsman, until, suddenly, Colin Beretta is standing before me, his dark eyes soulful and his smile breathtaking.

Swoon.

He extends his arm and says, "You look gorgeous, Amy."

Swoon.

"Thank you. So do you."

I link my arm in Colin's—*swoon*—and catch a whiff of his cologne—*swoon*—and practically dance down the aisle with him, buoyed by the cheers and applause all around us. And as I walk with Colin, my arm in his, his cologne in my nostrils, his sex appeal wafting off him like a physical thing, and his smile constantly directed at *me,* I can't, for the life of me, remember a damned thing I promised myself only a few minutes ago.

EIGHT

AMY

Best. Party. *Ever.*

That fancy up-do I wore during the ceremony? Yeah, it's down now. I pulled out the bobby pins holding it together and shook out my auburn waves hours ago, while shaking my booty on the dance floor with Colin and his incredible friends—Dax, Fish, and their beautiful partners, Violet and Alessandra—all of whom have welcomed me with open arms into their group.

At dinner, I snuck away from my stodgy, assigned table to dine with Colin and his four friends, at their invitation, at which point, conversation flowed as easily as the booze we were throwing back.

During the meal, the Goats asked me questions about the RCR tour and laughed at all my stories. In return, they told funny anecdotes of their own, like my experience somehow equated to theirs. Tour talk led to Fish and Alessandra talking about Alessandra's upcoming debut album that was co-written and produced by Fish. And after that, I had an interesting conversation with Alessandra about flowers, prompted by my bridesmaid's bouquet sitting on the table. Who knew there's a whole "language of flowers" from Victorian times? So interesting.

After a bit, I had an amazing conversation with Violet and Dax about their toddler, Jackson, who's staying the night at Dax's parents' tonight. At my urging, the proud parents showed me a million photos of their adorable boy, while telling me stories about him that made me guffaw.

When the boys went off to the bar to grab the table another round of drinks, Violet told me about the cancer charity she started in honor of her young brother who died. Plus, she told me about her passion for designing wedding dresses and showed me some of her sketches on her phone. Currently, Violet only makes actual wedding dresses for her closest family and friends, if requested, but, one day, Violet said she dreams of having her own wedding dress label.

Violet hadn't met Kennedy before today, but I asked her what kind of dress she might have designed for my new sister-in-law, if requested. And Violet's response was absolutely lovely. "Oh, I couldn't have improved on Kennedy's selection," Violet said. "She looks absolutely perfect tonight."

When the men returned from the bar with drinks and shots for all, we started talking about Colin's upcoming movie. Interestingly, however, the conversation about the topic with Colin's best friends bore little resemblance to the same basic conversation during the rehearsal dinner last night. Tonight, among Colin's best friends in the world, he was exponentially more open and vulnerable—real and disarmed in a way he wasn't last night with people he didn't know well.

Plus, it helped that Colin's best friends asked him much more meaningful and intimate questions about the movie and his preparation for his role. They didn't care about whether the lead actor, Seth Rockford, is a douchebag in real life or how much money Colin is making on his small role. No, they wanted to hear about how hard Colin has been working with his acting coach this past month. They wanted to hear about whatever nerves he's been feeling in anticipation. And I must admit, watching Colin's much more vulnerable interactions with his friends made him even sexier to me. And not because of all the booze I was drinking while listening. Because Colin Beretta is a gorgeous freaking man, especially when he lets his guard down.

As promised, Colin also took several photos of me with 22 Goats during dinner, which I then posted to Instagram. And when we checked an hour later and noticed Nate the Asshole had liked my photos—since, unfortunately, Nate still follows me on Instagram—Colin and I high-fived like we were Bonnie and Clyde who'd pulled off a daring bank heist.

When dinner was cleared and the live band had started cranking out dance tunes, our group headed to the dance floor and let loose. And that's what we've been doing, ever since. Presently, I'm on the dance floor with Violet and Alessandra, while the men stand in line at the bar again. But when the present song concludes, I tap Violet's shoulder and gesture, letting her know I'm headed to the restroom, and then bound away to my destination as Violet and Alessandra return to our table to await the next round of drinks.

In the bathroom, I head to a stall and do my thing, wash my hands, and then bop into an adjacent powder room to check my makeup—and that's where I find Kennedy and two bridesmaids, chatting and laughing while touching up their makeup.

"Sister!" Kennedy coos, before wrapping me in a hug. "Isn't this *fun*?"

"So fun! It's the best wedding *ever.*"

I chat with all three women for a bit about the amazing band, but when the other two bridesmaids leave, Kennedy leans in and gets down to business.

"Looks like things are going well with Colin," she says suggestively, her dark eyes glinting.

"Yeah, we're having so much fun. Unfortunately, it's not what it looks like, though." I explain the situation to my new sister-in-law: my job search, Colin's idea for me to load up my Instagram to impress that employment agency, Nate the Asshole, and Colin's kind willingness to keep *blecchy* Luke from flirting with me again.

When I finish talking, Kennedy looks skeptical. "I can't imagine Colin's been spending *this* much time with you, and looking so happy doing it, solely to help you get a job and keep Luke from asking you to dance. I know Colin's an actor these days, but Robert De Niro couldn't fake the kind of chemistry I'm seeing between you two."

My heart is stampeding. But before I've replied to that bit of awesomeness, Logan's amplified voice from the adjacent ballroom wafts into the small powder room.

"Someone, find Mrs. O'Brien!" my brother bellows. "I've got a big surprise for her!"

"Ooooh! Sounds like we'd better find Mrs. O'Brien!" Kennedy jokes, before giggling and grabbing my hand.

When my sister-in-law and I enter the ballroom, we find my big brother onstage, standing in front of all three members of 22 Goats and a couple musicians from the wedding band, with everyone behind Logan poised and ready to play their musical instrument. Not surprisingly, given the obvious performance cued up, every guest at the party is now crowded onto the dance floor, tittering with excitement about whatever is about to unfold.

"Mrs. O'Brien!" Logan calls out when he spots his beautiful bride. "Get over here, baby!"

The crowd parts like the Red Sea for Kennedy as she makes her way to the foot of the stage, while I head to a spot a few feet away next to Violet and Alessandra on the dance floor.

"Hey, baby," Logan says, smiling down at his bride before him. "You remember what I told you the night your all-time favorite 22 Goats song came on the radio during our very first date?" Logan's smile broadens. "You. Give. Me . . . 'Fireflies.'"

Everyone, including me, goes apeshit, because we all know what that means: we're about to enjoy a private performance of 22 Goats' smash hit, "Fireflies"—a melodic song that's been imprinted onto the world's gray matter at this point. Plus, side note, that's an awfully romantic story.

Without further ado, Dax counts off into his mic, and a second later, the lilting, electric guitar-infused introduction to the song begins, at which point Logan hops off the stage, pulls his squealing bride into his arms, and begins swaying romantically with her to the music. Go, big brother, go!

Earlier, Logan and Kennedy danced their official "first dance" to a tune performed by the wedding band. But as sweet as that moment was, it can't hold a candle to this one. How many newly married couples have been serenaded on their wedding day by 22 Goats? I'm willing to guess Logan and Kennedy are the only one.

When his cue in the iconic song arrives, Dax leans into his

mic and begins singing the first verse, and as he does, he looks down at his gorgeous wife, Violet, with such palpable adoration, such intensity and sexual heat and love, while she looks up at him like he's the answer to her prayers, I can't help swooning. As my heart races and pounds, and vicarious fireflies ravage my belly, I shift my focus to Colin behind the drumkit. And that's when my drunken mind instantly imagines he's making those drumbeats for *me*. Serenading me, in musical Morse Code, the same way Dax is singing the lyrics he wrote for Violet.

The first chorus ends and Dax shouts, "Take it away, Fish Tacoooo!" And Matthew Fishberger next to him leans into his microphone, without missing a beat on his bass guitar, and begins serenading *his* love, Alessandra, with the second verse.

I remember seeing Fish singing lead vocals on this song in a recent viral video, recorded during a charity concert in a huge arena, but getting to see him doing it here, in a small, intimate setting, for a hundred people in a hotel ballroom rather than for thousands at Madison Square Garden, is making me swoon, yet again. *Hard.*

Shit.

I've got to get this swooning reflex under control. This is ridiculous.

But it's no use. I'm feeling physically dizzy in response to the romance I'm observing all around me. Logan and Kennedy. Dax and Violet. Fish and Alessandra.

A deep-seated yearning overtakes me. And then, anxiety that I'm not lovable or attractive enough to get to have what they all do someday. Will I *ever* find true love in this lifetime? Will someone *ever* swoon for me the way I swoon for them?

Why'd the sweet boy who grew up next door to me have to grow up to become an actual rockstar—so freaking successful and unattainable, I'd have to be delusional to think he might ever want me, the way I want him?

The crowd around me applauds uproariously as "Fireflies" ends. But I'm too wracked by my racing thoughts to move or react. Why didn't a single crew member even *flirt* with me, during the tour? Why didn't I feel sparks with Perry when we made love? Why can't I jump into meaningless hookups, like all my friends do? *What's wrong with me?*

"Ally, you wanna perform 'Smitten' for a live audience, for the first time?" Fish says, grinning down at his girlfriend on the dance floor.

Apparently, Alessandra has signaled she's game, because as the other musicians, including Colin and Dax, begin exiting the stage, Fish reaches down and pulls her onto the stage next to him. As the crowd applauds excitedly, Fish grabs two acoustic guitars—one for him and one for his love—before returning to his microphone.

"Ally and I wrote this duet called 'Smitten' for her upcoming debut album. It's releasing in a couple weeks." He smiles at the happy couple. "Congrats, Logan and Kennedy. This one's for you."

Colin appears at my shoulder as Fish begins strumming onstage. But before anyone has started singing, Colin leans into me and says, "This is gonna be a huge hit for Ally. Mark my words."

Fish stops strumming. "Oh, hey. Will you guys do me a favor? Record this on your phones and post it everywhere? Let's get some buzz going for my girl's debut!"

Everyone in the audience who happens to have their phone handy immediately takes them out, happy to oblige Fish's sweet request, while Ally thanks the crowd.

As Fish did before her, Ally leans into her microphone and

addresses the happy couple at the foot of the stage. "After witnessing your love today, there's no doubt this song is about you, every bit as much as it's about Fish and me. Congrats!"

As the crowd applauds, Fish resumes his strumming. And a moment later, Ally leans into her mic, beams a gorgeous smile at her boyfriend, and starts singing the song, before soon being joined by Fish:

Oooh I . . .
I love you ever so much, much
I'm living for your every touch, touch
And your every kiss . . . is . . . bliss

Oooh I . . . I love your big blue eyes, love
I'm living for your every smile, love
And your every kiss, kiss, kiss

Every day with you I'm smitten
Every day I have a crush
Feelin' infatuated.
Every day I'm so in love!

It's loooove!
I'm so in love with youuuu!
Just like the sky is bluuuuue!
You're my first. My last. My best. My only.
Looooooove!
Don't want no one but youuuuuu!

Because this love is true!
Can't get enough of you
You're my first, my last, I'll be smitten, always

As Fish and Alessandra reach the end of their first chorus, tears flood my eyes. I wipe my cheek, angry with myself. But I can't keep more tears from falling, no matter how hard I try. I want what Fish and Alessandra are singing about! *And I want it with Colin.* But if I can't have that—and I know I can't—then I want it with *someone.* And in this moment, I don't have a whole lot of hope that will ever be in the cards for me, if the tour was any indication of my ability to attract members of the opposite sex.

As a torrent of tears springs from my eyes, I press the back of my hand against my forehead—because alcohol always turns me into the main character in a period-piece melodrama—and then bolt through the crowded dance floor toward a pair of French doors at the back of the ballroom.

[Go to: http://www.laurenrowebooks.com/smitten37 to listen to Fish and Alessandra perform an acoustic version of their song, "Smitten."]

NINE
COLIN

As Fish and Ally reach their harmonized bridge, I turn to look at Amy next to me, eager to see whatever adorable facial expression has overtaken her now, but to my surprise, Amy's no longer there. Confused, I look around the ballroom, surprised Amy would take off in the middle of Fish and Ally's cute song without at least poking my arm first—and, by chance, I catch a flash of Amy's purple gown as she blasts through a set of French doors on the far side of the large room.

Without thinking about it, I chase after her, worried something's wrong. But when I make it through the double doors and into the cool night air on the expansive patio, there's nobody out here—which makes perfect sense, since every guest at the wedding is presently inside, enjoying Fish and Ally's performance. I turn a corner. No Amy. Retrace my steps and turn the opposite corner, and there she is, slumped over a railing, sobbing her eyes out. *What the hell?*

I bound over to Amy and touch her shoulder. "Amy? What happened?"

She looks up, tears streaming down her cheeks, and my heart squeezes at the sight of her, the same way it did when I chased her down, all those years ago, when she'd decided to run away to "Genovia."

I feel overcome by the impulse to hug her, to try to take her pain away, the same way I did back then. I want to take her into my arms and tell her whatever happened, I'll make it right. But I stop myself this time. We're not kids anymore—and every touch between us nowadays, especially those initiated by me, seems to cause a current of electricity to course between us. Electricity that could easily send the wrong message to Amy. Plus, I think there's a high chance, if I take her into my arms now, I won't be able to stop myself from doing the thing I've been dying to do all night long. Last night, too. Namely, press my lips against hers and then drag her upstairs and scratch a whole lot of "nevers" off her list.

"Amy," I repeat. "Tell me what happened."

Finally, she straightens up and wipes her cheeks. "Nothing happened. Not like you mean. I'm drunk and felt emotional watching Fish and Alessandra singing about being smitten, after watching Dax sing to Violet about her giving him "fireflies," after watching Logan cry at the sight of Kennedy at the ceremony." Another tear falls down her cheek, replacing the one she just wiped away. "It's hard watching all these happy couples, knowing the odds are low I'll ever get to find true love for myself."

"What are you talking about? Amy, you're twenty-three! You've got plenty of time!"

Amy's green eyes blaze. "But nobody even *looked* at me in high school! And then, I was too shy and lacking in confidence to put myself out there in college—so, I settled for the first boy who was nice to me. After that, when I was finally ready to let loose and let my freak flag fly during the tour, nobody even flirted with me for nine whole months!" She throws up her hands. "So, don't tell me I have plenty of time. At this rate, I'll be ninety-three before anyone even asks me on a date!" She wipes her tears again. "What's wrong with me? Tell me the truth. Am I a six on a good day, like Nate said?"

My heart is breaking at the look of pure heartbreak on Amy's beautiful face. "No! I swear on everything I care about in this world you're a stone-cold perfect ten!"

Amy doesn't look convinced. "Then why do guys like Nate and Luke hit on me, but nobody else? It's never anyone I'm interested in. Will I ever feel smitten with someone, who feels the same way about *me*? Will I ever feel fireflies with someone, who feels them for *me*? That's what I want! That's what I deserve."

"Of course, you do."

"I want someone who loves me so much, he feels compelled to write a love song about me, like Dax did about Violet! Maybe not an actual song, if he's not a musician, but I want someone who *would* sing me a love song, if he could!"

"And you'll get that. Of course, you will. You're gorgeous, funny, sweet. Don't listen to that Nate fucker. He—"

"I never had a single orgasm with Perry, my boyfriend in college!" she shouts, out of nowhere. "Not *once*!"

I look around the darkened patio, and when I see, to my relief, we're still alone in this secluded corner, I steer Amy even farther back.

"Shh. Keep it down, Drunk Amy," I caution. "You don't want anyone to overhear you saying that."

Drunk Amy scoffs. "Everyone's inside, watching Fish and

Ally declare their undying love for each other. Nobody will hear me."

"Better safe than sorry, sweetheart." I square my body to hers and take a giant step forward. I'm intending to shelter Amy from anyone who might unexpectedly turn that corner behind my back, but the minute I position myself, my dick begins thickening. Apparently, my penis thinks I'm getting ready to lean in and kiss this girl, the way I've been dying to do all night, and it's voting *yes, yes, yes,* with extreme enthusiasm.

I take a deep breath and tell my tingling dick to calm the fuck down. But it's no use. A boner is thickening in my pants, whether I like it or not. Shit. I should take a step back to send my hardening dick a stern message. I should remind my dick Amy is off-limits for some *very* good reasons.

But I don't.

Indeed, I do the opposite of what my brain is telling me to do and inch even closer to Amy, like she's a magnet, and my dick is made of steel. When I advance on her, yet again, Amy exhales, tilts her flushed, tear-streaked face up toward mine, and nonverbally invites me to kiss her. Or hell, maybe that's wishful thinking.

Somehow, I resist leaning down and doing the deed. But I'm not a saint, as my next words emphatically prove. "Is your college boyfriend the only guy you've ever slept with?" I whisper, even though I know the answer from Caleb—and also that it's very, very wrong of me to steer our conversation in this direction.

Amy nods. "I've made out with other guys. But Perry is the only one I've had sex with."

I take a deep breath. Tell myself not to say anything

further. And then do it, anyway. "You never had an orgasm, while making out with those other guys?"

Amy shakes her head. "Not even close."

"Have you given yourself orgasms?"

This time, she nods. "But not as easily as my friends do it, from what they've said. I really do think there's something wrong with me, Colin. When Perry went down on me, I felt nothing. Actually, that's not true. I was grossed out. I told him to please stop."

Jesus Christ. Does she know she's waving a slab of raw, bloody meat in front of a hungry lion right now? Once again, I command my legs to step back. To put an end to the encouragement my body is surely sending to hers. But my legs don't listen. In fact, they once again do the opposite: they take another step forward.

"He never got better at it?" I whisper, my heart thudding noisily in my ears. "There are videos out there, you know. Tutorials. He could have gotten better with practice."

Amy shakes her head. "If he ever got better at it, then it was with someone else, after me. While we were together, he never did it again to me, which was fine with me. It was totally gross. Like rubbing deli meat down there."

"What the fuck?" I shout, half laughing and half shouting in horror. Quickly, I look around again, worried I've been too loud. "Okay, Amy, listen to me, sweetheart. Your boyfriend wasn't even close to normal, okay? Any normal guy would have taken your reaction as a call to action. A challenge—a wakeup call. It's not normal he didn't want to get better at it for you."

She shakes her head. "Maybe it was me? Maybe he did it right and I don't have all the right nerve endings down there."

I snort. "That's impossible. You said you've made your-self come, right?"

"But with a vibrator. Not with my fingers. And, obviously, I can't reach down there with my own tongue, so . . ."

I laugh again. She's so fucking cute. "Okay, that's fine. I'm assuming you have a clit, right?"

Her eyes saucer.

"You do, right?"

"Yes. Of course."

"And you have a vagina?"

"Colin."

"Answer the question."

"Yes."

"Has any doctor ever told you there's some physiological abnormality inside you?"

She rolls her eyes. "*No.*"

"Okay, then, trust me, with the right guy, you'd go off like fireworks on the Fourth of July."

Amy's chest heaves with excitement. Her green eyes turn to blazing emeralds. Longing—desperation, I'd even say—flickers across her face. She licks her lips and tilts her head back, once again nonverbally begging me to kiss her. And that's it. I can't resist acting on this thumping attraction I've been feeling for over twenty-four hours, any more than I could halt a runaway locomotive by placing myself in its path.

My dick rock-hard, I pull Amy into my arms and press my lips into hers. And the second our mouths meet, Amy swipes her tongue at my lower lip, letting me know she wants more. I don't hesitate. My body on fire, I slide my tongue into Amy's mouth, and she snakes her arms around my neck in reply. I pull her to me, as my tongue swirls with hers, and she presses her body into my hard-on, which, in turn, makes me moan and grind my dick into her sweet spot.

Desire.

Lust.

Fireworks.

As our kiss deepens, that's what I'm feeling and more. I feel swept away on a tidal wave of lust and need.

Oh, shit, are those *fireflies*?

Holy shit!

No.

Not a chance.

I ignore the rippling sensation overtaking my heart and core and concentrate instead on the rockets of desire seizing control of my dick. I focus on the way Amy's perfect tits feel, smashed against my chest. The voraciousness of her tongue and lips as they move in concert with mine. I lose myself to the thumping greed I feel to get those perfect tits out of that dress and into my mouth, before laying her down and devouring her sweet pussy. I'm going to become the first man, ever, to make her groan in ecstasy as her body ripples with the best orgasm of her life. And I can't fucking wait.

A soft but desperate moan escapes Amy's mouth, and I ferociously grip her ass with both palms and press her into me, letting her feel the full length and girth of my arousal. In response, Amy convulses against me like I've shoved my tongue inside her cunt, and that's what makes me lose complete control and do something I know I shouldn't.

"I can make you come, baby," I whisper hoarsely into her ear. "Any way I want to do it, easy as pie. Over and over again—with my fingers, tongue, and cock—you'd be my puppet, and I'd be pulling your strings."

Amy whimpers and babbles an incoherent string of words,

before desperately gripping my forearm and whisper-shouting, "I've got a room upstairs! Take me there and give me an orgasm, so I know I'm not defective. Give me one, so I know the problem isn't me."

I'm out of my head with the need to taste and fuck—to make Amy scream my name. I'm not thinking about consequences. Not thinking about tomorrow. I'm thinking with nothing but my throbbing, aching dick—the part of me that wants to fuck this woman, every which way, consequences be damned.

My breathing ragged, I touch Amy's cheek, making her shudder. "I'm gonna give you a whole lot more than *one*," I whisper. "I'm gonna eat your pussy like it's my last goddamned meal—and show you how good it feels, when a guy does it right. That'll be O number one. After that, I'm gonna do The Sure Thing on you, and make you come at least two more times that way, until you're speaking in tongues and begging me to fuck you. And then, when I finally fuck you, when I give you what you're begging me for, you'll come again. Only this time, with my cock inside you, which is gonna feel so fucking good for both of us, we'll both see God —a whole lot clearer than we ever saw him in that church today, I promise you that."

Amy's legs give way underneath her, so I grip her arm to keep her from melting to the ground.

"This is all I've always wanted!" she shouts. "Let's go!"

Panting, I grab her hand and pull her with me, a man on a mission. But when we turn the corner of the patio, catastrophe strikes.

"Amy!"

It's her mother.

Oh, fuck.

She's sitting with *my* mother on a wicker loveseat on the patio, with both women holding champagne flutes. In a heartbeat, I drop Amy's hand and take a lurching step away from her like she's on fire and I'm covered in gasoline.

"Hello, Colin," my mother says smoothly, as Amy's mother strides to her frozen-in-place daughter.

"Are you all right, honey?" Amy's mom says, as my mother shoots me a death-glare behind her. "Honey, you look flushed," Amy's mom says, putting a palm to her frozen daughter's forehead. "You feel hot. Are you feeling sick?"

"We've been dancing," Amy gasps out. "That's why we came out here. To cool off after dancing."

"Thank you for taking such good care of her, Colin," Mrs. O'Brien says. She grabs Amy's hand. "Come sit down. Both of you. Bianca and I were just reminiscing about the good old days on Cedar Street." She pulls Amy to sit next to her, while I remain in place with my hands clasped in front of my throbbing dick.

"Come sit, Colin," my mother says calmly. But she's only pretending not to be lethal. I know full well she's a spider, inviting a fly into her web. She beckons, her dark eyes blazing. "Join us, sweetheart. We're having such a lovely conversation about the good ol' days."

Amy's mother says, "Bianca was just telling me you gave Amy *all* your birthday and Christmas money when Amy had that lemonade stand!" She chuckles. "I had no idea you did such a sweet and selfless thing for her! That's so Colin."

"Yep, that's Colin for you," the assassin who birthed me says. "Sweet and selfless. It's what I always say." Mom smiles at me like she just wrote my name at the top of her kill list. "Or maybe he was only like that around Amy, come to think of it. He's always had such a soft spot for her, right from the start."

Amy's mother nods. "Some things will never change, huh? Thank you for watching out for her tonight, Colin. Clearly, Amy's had *way* too much to drink." She shakes her head at Amy. "How many drinks have you had tonight? I bet you've lost count." When Amy says nothing, her mother lets out a little *tsk*, hands Amy a glass of water, and insists Amy down the whole thing. "After you finish that, I'll take you upstairs to bed. You don't look well."

"I'm fine. I'm not leaving the party till it's over."

"It'll be over, any minute. The band should have played 'Sweet Caroline' as the last song, five minutes ago. Those surprise performances must have delayed them."

As if on cue, the instantly recognizable intro to Neil Diamond's classic tune begins inside the ballroom, followed by the wedding singer's amplified voice shouting, "This is our last song, folks! Get onto the dance floor and boogie, one last time!"

Amy's mother gestures, as if to say, *Ta da*! Before shoving that same water glass at Amy. "Now, drink up and I'll take you upstairs."

My eyes meet my mother's, and when she arches an eyebrow, everything she said last night slams into me.

I want Beretta-O'Brien grandbabies!

Amy's always had a crush on you!

Don't you dare lead that poor girl on!

Fuck.

I'm a monster. A horny-ass fucking monster.

"I'm gonna find Dax," I shout, way too loudly, before turning on my heel and sprinting away, without looking at Amy or anyone else.

When I enter the ballroom, I find Dax onstage, playing guitar on the famous song, while his wife dances happily with Fish and Alessandra and several members of the wedding party. But the second the song ends and Dax exits the stage, chatting happily with one of the musicians from the wedding band, I barrel straight toward him.

"Gimme the key to the room, Daxy," I command, holding out my palm. I look toward the double doors, my breathing shallow. But, still, no Amy. Thank God.

"I'll come upstairs with you, if you give me a minute," Dax says casually, clearly not sensing my urgency.

"Where's Amy?" Violet asks, striding toward me from the dance floor with Alessandra and Fish in tow. "She said she'd party with us in the suite after the reception."

"She's with her mom outside," I reply. "She wasn't feeling well. Too much to drink."

"Oh no. When did that happen? She seemed perfectly fine a few minutes ago."

"It came over her, all of a sudden." I bat Dax's shoulder. "Key. Now. *Please.*"

"What's your deal?" Dax says, handing me the key. He tells me the room number, at which point I sprint out of the ballroom, without answering him. Without explaining my "problem." And without looking back.

TEN

AMY

Oh my God, that kiss with Colin!

It was better than any fantasy.

"Are you sure this is your room?" my mom asks, after she's swiped my keycard and nothing happened.

And that stuff Colin whispered into my ear right after our kiss was hot as fuck!

Good lord, the stuff Colin said made me so horny, so hot and bothered and ready to go, I felt like I was on the cusp of coming, right then and there, from his kiss and sexy talk alone! In fact, I felt closer to coming in that moment, with Colin, than I ever did having tepid sex with Perry for a whole year.

"Yes, I'm sure," I reply. "Room 709."

Mom tries the keycard again but gets the same result. "Amy, think hard. Don't make me go downstairs to get a new key, if you're too drunk to remember the right room number."

I open my mouth to protest, but a nagging memory at the back of my head stops me. Despite what I just insisted, I'm suddenly not positive this is the right room. "Oh!" I say, pulling my phone out of my little purse. "I took a photo of my room number earlier, in case I got too drunk to remember!" I snort. "That's a little trick my friend on the crew taught me during the tour."

"Lovely. I'm so happy to know you needed such a valuable life hack during the tour."

Giggling at Mom's grumpiness, I swipe into my photos and grimace when I find what I'm looking for.

"Oh." I snort again. "My room is 708."

"Oh, Amy."

We turn around and Mom swipes the keycard on the correct door this time, the one immediately behind us, and I sashay into the room behind her, laughing at her obvious annoyance. Mom's been severely annoyed with me all day long, not only tonight, ever since I dropped the bomb at breakfast that I've one hundred percent decided *not* to go to law school, but instead plan to move to LA to find a job as a celebrity PA.

When I got home from the tour three weeks ago, I informed both my parents, separately, I was seriously second-guessing law school. But back then, I didn't *definitively* say I wouldn't attend. In fact, I remained quiet when they separately insisted on me going and said I'd thank them later.

But when I talked to Colin yesterday about this topic—when I looked into his dark brown eyes and realized Colin had always followed *his* dreams—and was *still* doing it, as a matter of fact, with his amazing movie role—something inside me clicked. A new kind of bravery was born inside me in that moment—one that inspired me to want to follow my dreams, whatever they might be, whether my parents like it or not.

When I told my mother the news at breakfast, and then

told my father at lunch after that, neither of them took it well. My mother accused me of wanting to be a mother and wife, and nothing more than that. Which in her eyes, is a fate worse than death. And my father said he couldn't believe I'd throw away the "expensive education" he'd bought me to become a "glorified celebrity ass-wiper."

I tried explaining it to them. I told them I want to work hard and be useful, before one day settling down to have a family—which I admitted, yes, I do hope to have in the future. I told them how inspiring it was to discover Colin has all the money and success in the world with his band, but is still chasing acting and modeling dreams, simply because he still wants to grow and learn and challenge himself.

"Colin has that luxury, thanks to the money he's making with his band," my mom retorted during breakfast. And during lunch after that, my father said basically the same thing.

"But the tour showed me I don't need a lot of money to be happy," I responded to them both. "I don't need a lot of material possessions. So, why would I pick a career that notoriously chews up souls and spits them out and gives nobody time to spend their big, fat paychecks or enjoy plenty of quality time with the people they love?"

Oops.

It was that last comment about quality time with loved ones that triggered my mother the most. Instantly, I realized my mom has felt judged, all these years, about *her* choices. Her decision to pursue a high-powered career while raising two kids. Of course, judging my mom's life choices was never my intention. My childhood was the only one I knew, so it never seemed weird to me that I barely saw either of my parents. And I've always been proud of my mother for being such an ass-kicker in her career.

But now that I'm older, I realize I want to do things differently than my own parents did. I don't want to follow in their footsteps, if I'm being honest with myself. Because that life wouldn't suit my personality. But that doesn't mean I'm angry with my mom for her choices. Or that I love her any less. Which is what she clearly thought during breakfast today.

"Mom, I'm not judging you," I said to her, when it became clear her outrage at breakfast had more to do with her own insecurities than me going to law school. "I'm glad you've kicked ass in life and followed your dreams, Mom. But *your* dreams aren't *mine*. I'm not the same as you and Dad and Logan and Grandpa. I don't like arguing. I don't care all that much about money. I want to make less but feel inspired every day."

Mom rolled her eyes at that. "How very Gen Z of you, Amy Laverne. But if that's truly your goal, then I don't see how being a personal assistant for a celebrity in LaLa Land could get you there."

I tried explaining it to her, again. I told her how amazing it felt being part of a found family on tour—being on a big crew that worked hard together to make magic happen—to make it possible for the band to do their job, thereby giving so much joy to so many, every night. I told Mom how working closely with Caleb, one-on-one, was especially gratifying because *me* doing *my* job to the best of my abilities allowed *Caleb* to do *his* job, which meant, indirectly, I was part of bringing joy to a whole lot of people across the world.

Mom never got it. When I was finished explaining everything to her, she stared at me, dumbfounded, for a long moment, before saying, "If you didn't have my eyes, I'd swear you were switched at birth." Surely, that's the same thing she's thinking now, as I follow her into my hotel room.

As the door closes behind us, Mom tells me to turn around, so she can unzip me, and then begins barking orders at me. Two minutes later, I'm out of my gown and in soft pajamas, my teeth are brushed and my face scrubbed, and Mom is tucking me into bed.

"Take these," Mom says, handing me two Ibuprofen. And when I've downed the pills with water, she kisses my forehead and whispers, "Now get some sleep. I'll come get you for brunch at ten."

"I'm gonna sleep in," I say. "I'll order room service."

"Suit yourself." Her features soften. "You looked beautiful tonight, Amy. Radiant."

My heart melts. Mom isn't big on compliments. "Thank you. So did you." I twist my mouth. "I'm sorry I'm not what you would have ordered from the Daughter Store."

"Oh, honey." Mom touches her palm to my face. "You're a wonderful daughter. I just want you to be able to take care of yourself in life. You can't depend on a man to do that for you."

"I don't want someone to take care of me," I say. "I know I can do that for myself. I'm just not ambitious the same way you are, Mom. I'd be happy with a different kind of life. But that doesn't mean I don't love you. I do."

Mom caresses my cheek. "I love you, too. Very much." She kisses my forehead again and clicks off the lamp. "Now, get some sleep, party girl. You tied one on tonight, didn't you?"

"Night, Mom."

"Night, sweetheart."

When the door closes behind my mother, I sit up like a

jack-in-a-box that just got cranked and grab my phone, eager to see whatever text Colin has surely sent me.

But he hasn't sent me anything.

Shoot.

I return my phone to the nightstand, telling myself not to worry about it. That Colin will text me any minute now. Perhaps, after taking a shower in Dax's suite? And in the meantime, I'll do some research about that thing Colin said on the patio.

The Sure Thing.

That's the enigmatic phrase Colin whispered into my ear, along with the other stuff he said about eating my pussy and pulling my strings. Lord have mercy on my soul, that was so hot, even though I didn't understand half of what he meant!

I know the phrase "the sure thing" generally means something is guaranteed. But it sure sounded like Colin used the phrase as a proper noun. Does "the sure thing" mean something different in the context of sex and pussy-eating and orgasms and I'm just too stupid to know it?

I search the phrase on my phone, my heart thrumming with excitement . . . but the first batch of results sheds no light on the situation. Apparently, there's an eighties movie of that name. A rom-com, by the looks of it, starring that guy from *Hot Tub Time Machine.* Was Colin referencing a scene from this rom-com? If so, I don't have time to watch it before Colin texts me and asks me for my room number.

Speaking of which . . .

I check my texts. But still, there's nothing from Colin.

Damn.

It's okay. Don't panic. He probably showered in Dax's room and got to talking to his friends and has lost track of time. No worries. He'll text soon. And in the meantime, back to my research.

I grab a large bottle of vodka from the minibar and take a seat on the edge of the bed with it. After taking a couple long swigs, I revise my prior search on my phone, tacking the words "sex" and "orgasm" onto "The Sure Thing" this time. And whaddayaknow? A YouTube video with over ten million views entitled "The Sure Thing" immediately pops up! *Bingo.*

The video was posted by someone named "Ball Peen Hammer," as part of a series called "Ball Peen Hammer's Guide to a Handsome and Happy Life." It seems to be some kind of tutorial. Indeed, the description under the video reads, "I guarantee this fingering technique will give your woman Honey Bunches of O's, lads!"

Giggling at the silly description, I press play and watch in awe as a blue-haired hottie with sparkling blue eyes, a megawatt smile, and two prominent dimples explains his fingering technique in explicit detail, while using combinations of words and slang I've never heard in my life . . . although, come to think of it, Colin himself whispered several of those same words into my ear downstairs. Colin said he'd have me coming so hard, I'd be "speaking in tongues" and "seeing God," both of which Ball Peen Hammer says in this video. To me, that strongly suggests Colin has seen this video . . . which excites me to no end.

"If you've done everything, exactly as I've told you," Ball Peen Hammer says. "Your woman will be so wet and turned on, she'll *beg* you to fuck her. And when you do, it's fifty-fifty she'll have one last O for ya, this time, while your cock's inside her." The blue-haired hottie grins, making his outrageous dimples pop. "And that, my handsome and happy lads, is the holy grail of O's—making a woman come while you're inside her. When that happens, yee-boy! That'll shove you, *hard,* into the best orgasm of your life. I guarantee you: coming with her is gonna be the closest to God you'll ever *come.*" He snickers. "Pun intended. You're welcome."

The video ends and I immediately rewatch it, before checking my phone for a text from Colin that's not there. Shoot. I take a long swig from my bottle and then watch the video a *third* time—this time, while drunkenly trying to do The Sure Thing on myself. But it's impossible. I can't reach the spot deep inside me Ball Peen Hammer has described. And I certainly can't dirty-talk myself—which, apparently, is a crucially important component to this technique. Dammit!

I check my phone again, and when there's *still* nothing from Colin, I decide to bite the bullet and take matters into my own hands.

Me: Hellooooo? I'm still awake and waiting for you to do everything you said downstairs! Are you there?

After pressing send on my text, I stare at my screen for a long moment, hoping to see, at least, three wiggling dots. But when nothing happens, I decide to pass the time by googling this Ball Peen Hammer dude. He looks vaguely familiar to me, but I can't place him.

My search quickly yields results. As it turns out, Ball Peen Hammer is an actor named Keane Morgan . . . as in, the older brother of none other than Dax Morgan of 22 Goats! Which means . . . Holy shit! Colin has definitely watched this video about The Sure Thing and maybe even learned about the technique directly from Keane! Either way, I'm now certain Colin not only knows *how* to do this amazing technique, but he also knows how to do it *well*. And that's got me buzzing like a horny bumble bee!

I take another long swig of vodka and decide I can't wait a second longer for this boy to hit me up. Time to light a fire under that man's hot ass.

Me: Hey, Colin! It's time to get your hot ass to my room to do everything you promised after our kiss. Eat my pussy and do The Sure Thing to me, baby! Fuck my brains out until we see God! Our amazing kiss fulfilled my biggest childhood fantasy about you. Now it's time for you to fulfill my far more ADULT fantasies about you. Room 709. I'm waaaaaaaiting.

A few minutes after pressing send on my text, I hear a bit of a ruckus outside my door in the hallway. Was that someone yelling? My heart in my mouth, I wait for a knock on my door. And when it doesn't come, I stride to my door and fling it open . . . and then furrow my brow in confusion at the emptiness confronting me. There's nobody in the hallway. Nothing but closed doors and a bottle of booze on the carpet in the middle of the hallway. Was that bottle there when Mom and I arrived at my room?

Deflated, I stagger back to the bed and flop onto my stomach on the bed, determined to stay awake for Colin, whenever he finally gets here . . . But soon, I can't keep my eyes open a second longer, so I decide to rest them for a bit, just until Colin knocks on my door . . . And the next thing I know . . . the world blurs . . . and then fades to black.

ELEVEN

COLIN

As Amy rides my cock, a faint rumbling noise slices through my consciousness. Is that a train rolling past Amy and me—a small one, like the kind toddlers ride at malls? And why do I give a flying fuck what's making that noise, when Amy is riding my cock and on the cusp of coming? I return to massaging Amy's clit as she rides me, enjoying the way her perfect tits bounce and jiggle with her gyrations. But a female voice jerks me out of it again.

"Thank you, yes," the woman says.

It's Violet. What's she doing here, while Amy is riding my cock?

Violet continues, "Put everything on the table, please. Thank you."

Suddenly, my mother is standing next to Violet, watching me fuck Amy.

"Well, aren't you going to fuck her on the table?" my mother asks. "You're not going to make me a Beretta-O'Brien grandbaby like *that*."

My eyes wrench open in horror, as a male voice asks, "Will that be all, ma'am?"

Violet replies, "Yes, thank you so much."

There's that same rumbling sound again. And when I turn my head to look, there's a room service cart rumbling past me, pushed by a male hotel employee in uniform.

"Enjoy your breakfast, ma'am," he says.

I rub my eyes and sigh. I'm lying on a couch in Dax and Violet's plush suite. Other than Violet and me and a shit-ton of breakfast food, the large room is empty. Presently, Violet's pouring herself a cup of coffee from a gleaming carafe, her back facing me.

Fuck.

As my brain shakes off sleep, it's beginning to show me jagged swatches of my drunken misdeeds from last night. Oh, shit. *I kissed Amy.* And then whispered something . . . naughty . . . into her ear.

Oh, God.

I remember bursting into this suite last night and immediately guzzling from a bottle of tequila like it was Gatorade, as I tried to erase the bad things I'd done downstairs. But that's all I can remember . . . What happened after that?

"Good morning," Violet says. She's seated at the table now, sipping her coffee and staring at me.

"Good morning," I say carefully. Even though she's smiling at me, she looks like she's plotting my murder.

"How are you feeling?" Violet asks. "You had a lot to drink last night."

"I feel like shit. You?"

"I feel fine. I stopped drinking after the reception and switched to water."

"Good for you. I'm glad one of us was smart."

"You chug-a-lugged when we got to the room. You seemed a bit stressed."

"Mm-hmm." I squint at her. "Please tell me I don't have a Sharpie mustache and beard right now."

"You don't. But only because Fish forgot to pack a Sharpie."

"Small mercies." I rub my forehead as pain rips through my cranium. "Ugh. I feel like I'm dying."

"Coffee?" she says sweetly, motioning to the carafe.

"Thanks. And a huge glass of water."

"Sure thing." She brings me the beverages and takes an armchair next to me. "Is Amy coming to brunch?"

I take a sip of coffee. "I don't know."

"You don't know?"

Ah, there it is. Somehow, I've pissed her off in relation to my treatment of Amy. "I haven't talked to Amy since last night, I don't think—since leaving the wedding reception and coming up here."

"You don't think?"

"Things are a bit hazy, Violet. Gimme a break."

"You didn't think to check on her last night, after coming up here, to see if she was feeling better and wanted to join us?" Her blue eyes narrow. "You'd invited her during dinner to come to our room to party with us, remember?"

"Violet, please. My head hurts."

"I don't know Amy's phone number or room number. After you passed out like a worthless sack of shit without checking on Amy, I had to call down to the front desk to get connected to her room. But she didn't answer."

"Well, there you go. No harm, no foul. She must have crashed the minute she got to her room."

"The thing is, Amy wasn't *my* date last night. She was *yours*. You should have been the one to check on her."

"Amy wasn't my date."

"Maybe she didn't start out that way, but she was your date by the end."

"Butt out, Vi. Amy and I were doing a *thing*."

"What thing?"

"I'm not in the mood to explain it to you."

Violet's nostrils flare. "I don't understand why you didn't call her to see if she was feeling up to joining our party. I asked you to do that and you shrugged me off. How do you know poor Amy wasn't sitting in her room, waiting for you to call and give her our room number?"

I close my eyes and sigh. "You said yourself you called and she didn't answer. Drop it."

"But she could have been in the bathroom. I'm just saying it's weird you dropped her like a hot potato, after having so much fun with her. What happened?"

She stares at me with hard, blue eyes. And I know she's not going to drop it.

"I fucked up, okay?" I bellow, to the detriment of my own cranium's comfort. "I kissed her on the patio, while Fish and Ally were singing their duet, and it was a huge fucking mistake!"

Violet looks confused. "Why is that a fuck-up? Amy is adorable and obviously thinks you walk on water. God knows why. And everyone could see how much fun you had with her."

"She's Logan's sister. Off-limits. I don't want to talk about it anymore."

When I close my eyes, Violet sighs and says, "I'll get you some Tylenol and wake everyone for breakfast. I got us a late checkout, but we need to get moving, so Dax and I can pick up Jackson." When I open my eyes, she's walking toward one of the two bedrooms in the suite. But before she arrives at her destination, she tosses over her shoulder, "Call Amy now and tell her breakfast is here. We invited her to brunch last night, and I don't care how badly you think you screwed up by kissing her, I'm not going to let you ghost that poor girl this morning."

"I would never ghost Amy. She's gonna be working with me on the movie set, remember?"

Violet comes to a stop outside one of the bedroom doors and turns around. She looks deflated. "You didn't feel a spark with her when you kissed her?"

No, I felt a forest fire, I think. *I felt fireflies.* But what I say is, "I don't want to talk about it."

Violet crosses her arms. "Listen to me, Colin. It's imperative you do something extremely un-Colin-like and tell that sweet girl exactly what you're feeling, even if it's going to hurt her feelings. Better to hurt her now and tell her, honestly, you're just not feeling it, rather than stringing her along and giving her hope. The worst thing in the world is having feelings for someone and getting just enough positive feedback to make you keep holding onto hope, when in fact, there's none to be had."

I press my lips together but say nothing.

"Promise you'll be completely honest with her," Violet says. "Let her down easy this morning, if you're not feeling it. It's obvious she likes you. Don't toy with her emotions, if you don't feel the same way."

"Why do you think I came straight here last night and didn't call her?" I shout. "Precisely because I didn't want to lead her on after that kiss!"

"Yeah, but running away after a kiss doesn't solve anything, if you didn't also tell her you didn't feel a spark." She stares me down. "You ran away right after the kiss without saying a word to her, didn't you? Without telling her the kiss didn't do it for you?"

"Uh, no. I definitely said something to her after the kiss. Unfortunately, it was a whole bunch of shit I should never have said."

Violet's eyebrows ride up to her dark bangs. "What does that mean?"

I press my lips together.

"*Colin Beretta.*"

I sigh. "I blew it, Violet. I said a bunch of dirty stuff I wanted to do to her, including The Sure Thing."

Violet gasps.

"And then we ran into our mothers, and I realized my mistake and sprinted away like a bat out of hell."

"And came up here, without talking to her again? Colin! You're telling me *that's* the last thing Amy heard from you last night—you whispering a whole bunch of dirty-talk into her ear after kissing her?"

I nod sheepishly.

"Colin Beretta! You're a goddamned prick!"

"I know. I told you I fucked up!"

"But you didn't tell me how badly you fucked up. That's deplorable. You asshole!"

"I know, Vi. But, hey, on the bright side, Amy and I were both really drunk when we kissed. Maybe she was so drunk, she won't even remember anything that happened on that patio last night. The kiss. What I said after it. The fact that I ran away like a douchebag. Maybe she'll wake up and not remember any of it."

I look at Violet hopefully, but she shakes her head with disdain.

"I wouldn't count on that."

I rub my face. "A boy can dream."

"I think you mean a douchebag can dream."

"Tomato. Tomahto."

Violet exhales an ocean of annoyance with me. "What's the roadblock here? I don't get it. Is it just that she's Logan sister?"

"That's not a minor thing, Vi."

"Yes, it is. Who cares if Logan's her brother? Amy's an adult who's not related to you by blood, and your mutual chemistry last night was through the roof. I'm sure Logan would be *thrilled* for his brother-from-another-mother and his sister to—"

"No. Logan might be thrilled for me to ride off into the sunset with his sister, but anything short of that, if things didn't work out and I wound up hurting Amy—which, let's face it, is the most likely scenario—then my friendship with Logan would never be the same again. It might even be destroyed."

"That seems a tad bit dramatic."

"It's not." I run my hand through my hair. "But you're right that's not the only thing. The bigger thing is how much history there is between Amy and me. The stakes feel way too high, right out of the gate, for me to jump into something with her. I could never casually 'date' her and see where things lead, at any semblance of a normal pace. You said yourself Amy thinks I walk on water, and that's a huge problem. It's way, *way* too much pressure."

Violet rolls her eyes. "Okay, then, be brave enough to

show Amy you *don't* walk on water and take it from there. Problem solved, dummy."

I scoff. "My mother told me last night she's always dreamed of having Beretta-O'Brien grandbabies."

Violet gasps in horror—and, finally, I feel the slightest bit validated by her—like Violet is *finally* understanding my perspective.

"And on top of that little nugget," I add, feeling emboldened, "Amy has never had casual sex. She's not going to jump into a fling with me and see where it leads and not get heartbroken if I don't meet her extremely high expectations in the end. It'd be all or nothing with her, out of the gate, and I'd know that going in, and that's too much pressure and expectation for me to take on. At least, not while sober. No fucking thanks."

Violet doesn't look quite as pissed at me as she did earlier. In fact, she looks mildly sympathetic. "Either way," she says, "you need to talk to Amy now. We invited her to brunch, and she seemed excited about it. Plus, like you said, she's going to be working with you and staying at your place. You can't simply pretend that kiss didn't happen."

"Maybe she doesn't remember it."

"Colin, give it up. I don't care how shitfaced Amy might have been last night, she'll remember kissing you. For fuck's sake, I'm sure she's been fantasizing about kissing you since she was a little girl."

I flap my lips together. "Fine. I'll go talk to her."

"Good. I'll get that Tylenol for you, while you call Amy and tell her you need to talk to her."

I reach for my phone. "Roger."

"Rabbit."

As Violet walks away, I swipe into my texts, figuring I'll

text Amy first and confirm she's awake before calling. But when I swipe into my prior text chain with Amy, I see *two* unanswered messages from her that stop my heart.

Oh my God.

I remember now!

I saw both these texts last night, right after her second one landed on my screen!

In a flurry of memories, I remember myself grabbing the bottle of tequila I'd been chugging and sprinting out of this suite like my pants were on fire, headed straight to Amy's room. *Or so I thought.* When I got to my destination, some old lady, not Amy, answered the door and started yelling at me for waking her up. And that's when I bolted away with my tail between my legs, not bothering to grab the tequila bottle I'd dropped in the hallway in my shock.

But that's the last thing I remember.

The next thing I knew, I was waking up on this couch.

Holy shit. Was I so shitfaced last night I couldn't read Amy's room number correctly? Did I get off the elevator on the wrong floor? I don't know what happened to keep me from successfully reaching Amy's room last night. All I know is, whatever it was, it was divine intervention. I can't imagine how guilty I'd be feeling right now if I'd woken up in Amy's bed, after drunkenly fucking her all night long.

Exhaling, I drag my hung-over ass into the bathroom, mumbling to myself about what a douchebag I am. And when I come out freshly showered fifteen minutes later, everyone's sitting at the table, amiably chatting while eating breakfast. Violet gives me the Tylenol she promised me earlier, which I gratefully accept, along with a huge glass of water and another cup of coffee.

"Get everyone up to speed while I'm talking to Amy,

would you?" I say to Violet. "I don't want to talk about it when I get back, especially if I've got Amy in tow."

"I already told them everything," Violet says with a wink.

"Of course, you did." I put down my coffee cup. "Everyone be chill if I come back here with Amy, okay? Act like you did with her at dinner last night."

"We're not the ones who kissed her and told her about The Sure Thing and woke up to regret it," Dax says. "We'll be perfectly comfortable around Amy. She's a sweetheart."

"I'm sad you're not planning to date her," Alessandra says. "She's so nice."

"I already like her better than you," Fish adds, smiling at me.

I roll my eyes. "This isn't the sort of thing that gets put to a group vote, dudes."

"Maybe it should be," Violet retorts. "If you'd put Kiera to a group vote, I guarantee we could have saved you a whole lot of time, my friend."

Mock-snarling at Violet, I grab a piece of bacon off her plate, since I know she abhors anyone but her son, Jackson, touching her food. And much to my delight, Violet swats my hand and tells me to get my own damned bacon.

"Why would I do that, when it's so much tastier off your plate?" I reply with a wink. I move to grab a second piece off Violet's plate, but this time, she grabs my wrist and says *no* like my next move could be my last. Which, of course, only makes me laugh. It's a running gag between Violet and me, actually, since our last tour, when Violet and Jackson tagged along. Violet would say something to Jackson and then turn to me and say the exact same thing, in the same tone, implying I've got the maturity of a toddler. Honestly, it never fails to amuse me.

"Go," Violet says, pointing at the door. "Bacon will be your reward when you get back from talking to Amy, and telling her the truth, like a big boy."

"Fine." I grab a piece of bacon off a communal plate in the center of the table and point at a stack of blueberry pancakes. "Leave those for me. I'm hung over and hungry, and I'm sure I'm gonna want to eat my feelings when I get back."

"Be totally honest with her," Violet says. "But *gentle*."

"I'll handle her with kid gloves," I say, before heaving out a long, dejected sigh. "Believe me, making sweet little Amy O'Brien sob when I tell her that kiss was a huge mistake isn't at all how I want to be spending my Sunday morning."

TWELVE

AMY

As Colin's body gyrates on top of me, I clutch his naked, hard ass and unleash ten years' worth of desire in a singular, guttural growl. I turn my head to invite his lips to mine, and the second Colin's tongue enters my mouth, my body releases a rolling orgasm that yanks me out of my dream . . . and back into reality, where, oh my God, I'm having an *actual*, rolling orgasm in real life! I lie still for a long moment in my hotel bed, enjoying the unexpected pleasure, and then sigh happily.

Wow.

That was a first for me—climaxing, in real life, due to a sex dream. It'd be the perfect way to wake up, if it weren't for the horrific hangover making me feel like I might barf.

Yawning, I stretch and groan, letting the amazing memories from last night wash over me. That kiss with Colin! It was supernatural! And what in the dirty-talking perfection was the stuff Colin whispered into my ear afterward? I wish I could remember all of it, but I can't. I remember him whispering about wanting to eat my pussy. I also remember him grabbing my hand and yanking my arm out of my socket and—

Oh, God.

Our mothers.

I remember now.

We turned that corner, and there they were.

Shit.

Did Colin ever text me last night to finish what we started downstairs? Did I pass out before receiving his text? I reach for my phone, but before I've swiped into my texts, Colin's name pops onto my screen as an incoming call.

"Good morning," I say, my heart racing with excitement.

"Good morning," Coin replies. "I hope I didn't wake you."

"Nope, I'm up."

"Can we talk? I'm standing in the hallway. I'm not sure which room is yours."

My stomach sinks. Colin's tone isn't flirtatious. On the contrary, it's tense and apologetic. *Regretful.* And I know, just this fast, this "talk" he wants to have isn't code for "let's finish what we started last night!" No, Colin genuinely wants to talk. Undoubtedly, about our kiss being a horrible, awful, regrettable mistake.

"Uh, sure. Give me five minutes."

"Take your time."

"I'll let you into my room to sit while you wait for me."

"Great."

I head to the door and open it, and sure enough, Colin is standing in the hallway in sweats and a T-shirt. Oddly, though, he's not facing me. He's facing the room immediately across from mine.

"Hi."

Colin whirls around and palms his forehead. "Well, that explains it." Shaking his head, he points. "708."

I don't know what he's talking about. And I'm too nervous about my impending doom to ask. So, I simply open the door and let him pass inside.

Colin's body language is as tight as his voice was on the phone, confirming my earlier hunch. He's here to tell me last night was a mistake that will never happen again.

"What's up?" I ask, my stomach twisting into knots.

"Why don't you do whatever you need to do first," he says, gesturing to the bathroom. "And then we'll talk."

"Great," I squeak out lamely.

Once inside the bathroom, I close the door, put my phone on the counter, and do the bare minimum of my morning routine. But when I grab my phone again, intending to head back into the room to face my certain slaughter, I'm slammed with a montage of memories that stops me in my tracks.

Ball Peen Hammer. Blue hair and dimples. The Sure Thing!

Oh, God.

Get your hot ass to my room! Eat my pussy and do The Sure Thing to me! Fuck my brains out until we both see God!

No, no, no!

Please, God, no!

Our amazing kiss fulfilled my biggest childhood fantasy about you.

Now it's time for you to fulfill my far more adult fantasies about you.

My pulse quickening, I swipe into my texts with Colin . . . and instantly turn unalive when I see my two, unanswered texts. Panicking, I quickly google, "How to unsend a text," and it's instantly clear from the results I'm totally fucked.

I tilt my head back, willing aliens to beam me up from this hotel bathroom and disappear me forever. But little green men don't come to save me, and I know I can't remain in this bathroom forever. And so, eventually, I take a deep breath, pull up my proverbial big-girl panties, and drag my hung over, embarrassed ass into the next room.

Colin rises from an armchair when I appear. And when I wordlessly take a seat on the edge of the bed, inviting him to crush me with whatever hammer he's got at the ready, Colin resumes his seat and takes a deep, halting breath.

"About last night," he begins. "I was *really* drunk."

It's all I can handle. Colin's remorseful tone, the look of apology on his face, everything about his body langue is screaming his message, loud and clear. *He feels sick about what happened last night.*

"I was shitfaced," I blurt. "Smashed. I barely remember anything that happened."

He looks deeply relieved. "Same." He pauses. "You remember me kissing you?"

Of course, I do, dumbshit. "Yeah, I think I vaguely remember that."

"I shouldn't have done that," he says. "You're like a little sister to me. "

Okay, well, hold on a minute there, sir, I think. I mean, I could understand Colin saying he's not attracted to me, when he's sober. I could understand him saying the alcohol gave him epic beer goggles. Or perhaps made him pity me. But I can't accept the idea that booze made Colin kiss his little sister, and grind his hard-on into her, and say he wanted to eat her pussy, unless he's willing to admit that exact same scenario could happen with one of his *actual* sisters, if he'd consumed the same amount of booze as he did last night.

"You're Logan's little sister," Colin continues. "Which makes you mine, basically."

"Does it, though?" I ask, my eyes narrowed.

Colin pauses, apparently surprised by my snarky tone.

"Well, yeah," he says.

Shoot. I didn't mean to say what I did out loud. I intended to merely *think* it, while standing here agreeing with whatever bullshit Colin said, so we could fast-forward to the part where Colin leaves and we never mention my unfortunate text to him.

But now that I've said what I said, I can't take it back. Indeed, I feel obligated to elaborate on my comment.

I clear my throat. "I get the gist of what you're saying. You're not sexually attracted to me, when sober. You were wearing beer goggles last night."

"No. Amy, *no*."

"But don't insult me by saying I'm like a sister to you, unless you can also look me in the eye and tell me there's some amount of alcohol you could consume that would make you tongue Caitlyn or Chiara, and press your hard dick into her pelvis, and then tell her you want to eat her pussy and do The Sure Thing to her, until she's 'speaking tongues' and 'seeing God.' If you can look at me with a straight face and say that to me, then, fine, I'll believe I'm like a sister to you. I'll also believe you're a sicko, but that would be beside the point I'm trying to make at this time."

Colin looks flabbergasted. *And I'm loving it.* Maybe I shouldn't have said everything I just did, but I'm all out of fucks to give. If Colin came here to reject me, which he plainly did, then at least let him do it with some integrity. I don't care how much we both drank, I know the fireflies I felt during our kiss were *mutual*! Colin might not remember feeling those fireflies today. Or if he does remember them, he might deeply regret them. Either way, I know he felt them, every bit as much as I did, whether they were caused by alcohol or not.

"About my text," I say, deciding to face my humiliating text message, head-on. "I warned you Drunk Amy has no filter."

"Your text was fine. You were reacting to what I'd said to you on the patio. This is my fault. I'm the one who fucked up here. Not you."

What's his fuck-up, though? The kiss? The stuff he said to me afterward?

But before I've mustered the courage to ask for clarity, Colin continues speaking. "The important thing," he says, "is that I don't want you thinking you're not sexy or attractive. You are. You're sexy as hell, Amy. Also, fun and funny and smart."

"Okay, this isn't helpful to me. It's confusing. I get what you're saying, generally. You shouldn't have kissed me. You were drunk. Blah, blah. Let's just move on, pretend everything from the kiss until this moment never happened, and never talk about any of this again. Sound good?"

"It sounds great. Yes. But before we erase last night from our memories, there's something important you need to know. I should have told you this last night, when you were crying on the patio, but I was too drunk to think straight. After you left my mom's house the other night, I called Caleb, like you suggested."

"Oh, wow."

"And it went great. And while we were talking, Caleb told me why nobody hit on you during the tour. Amy, after that game of 'Never Have I Ever,' Caleb tucked you in and then went back out and told everyone you were off-limits."

"What?"

Colin nods. "He considers me like a brother, and you'd told him your connection to me. So, in his mind, he was doing you—and me—a favor by keeping those horny crew guys from bombarding you for the rest of the tour."

"What the hell? But I wanted at least some of those horny crew guys to bombard me! That's half the reason I went on the tour, in the first place—to get to walk on the wild side!" I jerk to standing and begin pacing the small hotel room. "How dare Caleb do that to me! He had me thinking, the whole time, I'm totally unfuckable!"

"I know. I'm so sorry." Colin sighs. "That's not the case. Caleb felt the need to designate you as off-limits precisely because you're so fuckable. That's the real take-away here. That's what you need to understand."

I stare at Colin for a long beat. *Is he* stupid? If I'm so fuckable, then why didn't *he* fuck me last night? But I'm done talking about that. In fact, I never want to talk about it again.

"Thank you for telling me about this," I say stiffly. "I can't begin to tell you what a relief it is to me. I thought there was something wrong with me. I thought nobody found me the slightest bit attractive."

"Never believe that bullshit Nate said to you. He was negging you. You're a stone-cold, perfect ten, Amy O'Brien."

Again, I stare at Colin, willing him to put two and two together—to realize he's giving me mixed signals here to the point of being a total douchebag. If I'm such a perfect ten, if I'm so fuckable and attractive, then Colin would be ripping my clothes off right now and doing everything he said to me last night. Not rejecting me.

"Okay, well, thanks," I say. "Good talk. Are we ready for everything that happened from our kiss until now to be erased from our memory banks?"

"Absolutely." He smiles and sighs. "Whew. I'm so glad you're reacting so calmly. I thought for sure you were gonna cry and I was gonna feel like shit . . ."

I narrow my eyes, yet again, feeling anger rising inside me. What the ever-loving hell? He thought he was going to come here and break my little heart, did he? Even though I know, for a fact, he was every bit as into that kiss as I was! I didn't imagine his moans. I didn't imagine his hard dick pressing feverishly against me! But *I'm* the one who's going to shed a tear that we'll never get to do the things he promised me last night? Ha! Maybe I was planning to reject *him* when I woke up this morning! Did he ever consider that?

I clasp my hands in front of me. "Do you still feel comfortable having me work for you on the movie?"

"Of course," Colin says. "I'm excited about that. I think having a friendly face with me that week will be a fantastic thing for me. It'll be a win-win."

"And am I still invited to be your plus-one to Laila's birthday party?"

"Of course. Nothing's changed, Ames. We were drunk. Drunk people do stupid shit. You said yourself Drunk Amy has a track record of doing and saying highly regrettable things. Well, unfortunately, so does Drunk Colin."

Dick.

I suck in my cheeks for a long moment, feeling the urge to punch his handsome face. That kiss wasn't "highly regrettable," and I'm insulted he'd say that. But, again, I decide to let it slide for now, to save face over my unfortunate texts.

"Gotcha," I finally say.

"So, we're good?" Colin asks, his eyebrows raised.

"Yep. We're great. Same as before the kiss. Friends. Honorary siblings. Nothing more. *Poof.*"

Colin exhales like I've taken the weight of the world off his shoulders. "Awesome." He shifts his weight. "So, are you hungry? Violet ordered enough breakfast to feed an army. It's already been delivered to the room."

"Let me throw on some clothes."

"Take your time."

I rummage into my overnight bag, grab some clothes, and head into the bathroom. And when I emerge a few minutes later, I've got full clarity. Colin doesn't want to be anything but friends with me, despite the fireflies we both felt during that kiss? Fine. That's his choice. But he'd better be good and ready to live with the consequences of his choice.

"Whew! I'm starving," I say, striding across the hotel room. I grab my purse and keycard and follow him when he walks to the door and opens it for me. "Thanks." Smiling sweetly, I pause in the doorway. "Thanks so much for telling me what Caleb did to me during the tour," I say. "I can't tell you what a confidence boost it's giving me to know the truth about that."

"Good. You should be confident. You're amazing."

"And so are you, my friend. Look, I promise I won't mention our kiss again, once that door closes. But I feel the need to thank you for kissing me last night."

He looks confused.

"I fully accept the fact that you didn't feel sparks when we kissed. But I sure did. Which means you were absolutely right: I'm *not* defective. I've absolutely got all my working parts. In fact, I'm now convinced I'm an intensely sexual person, who's ready, willing, and able to have an extremely active and fulfilling sex life with the right guy—someone who wants me as much I want him."

Colin's nostrils flare, but he says nothing.

"I hope that doesn't freak you out to hear, since I'm like a sister to you," I add, and somehow keep myself from snickering as I do. "But that kiss was so incredible for me, I had a sex dream about you this morning and woke up having a real-life orgasm."

"Uh . . ."

"That's a first for me! Awesome, right? Ha! I guess that means, whether you like it or not, you're the first man to give me an orgasm. Whoops. Don't worry, *brother*, I'll take that naughty little secret to the grave." I wink and then pivot like I'm going to leave the doorframe, but quickly return to his shocked face. "Oh! Also, thank you for telling me about The Sure Thing. Thanks to you, I watched Ball Peen Hammer's video about it on repeat and now I'm super pumped to find someone to try it out on me. Someone who gives me fireflies when he kisses me. I know that *someone* won't be you, of course. I fully accept that. But now that I know about that video, I can show it to whichever lucky guy I decide to have sex with next." I cross my fingers. "Hopefully, the technique works the way Ball Peen Hammer says it does—because, damn, that sounds fun. Can't wait to try it out!"

With that, I ditch the doorway and sashay down the hallway, swinging my hips as I go. I have no idea which room is Dax and Violet's, so I don't know where I'm going. But I don't need to know. Surely, after Colin picks his jaw up from the floor, he'll catch up to me and lead me to our destination. In the meantime, though, I wouldn't have missed provoking the look on Colin's face a second ago, for all the money in the world.

THIRTEEN

COLIN

I do a quick lap of my living room, making sure everything is neat and tidy for Amy's imminent arrival. I'm not anxious about seeing Amy again, only excited. Thankfully, after that awkward brunch on Sunday with the gang, everything went back to normal between Amy and me. In fact, every time Amy and I chatted on the phone in the evenings this week to talk about our respective days—Amy's been working in the mail room at her father's law firm this week, while I've been doing costume fittings and rehearsals in anticipation of next week's shooting schedule—the vibe between us has been every bit as comfortable and easy as it was in Seattle before I screwed everything up with that kiss.

No, the thing making me nervous about Amy's imminent arrival is the simple fact that she's an O'Brien. Growing up on Cedar Street, the O'Brien house was the biggest and fanciest on our block, while mine was by far the smallest and most modest. While Amy's house was stylishly decorated and immaculate, mine always felt "lived in" and in need of repairs. And so, knowing what kind of house Amy grew up in, and therefore considers normal, I can't help wanting to knock her socks off with the home I chose for myself, and then had decorated to my taste, when money wasn't an object.

There's a knock at the front door and I barrel to it excitedly, my heart pounding—and the second I behold Amy in my doorframe, my eyes telescope in and out like I'm Donald Duck beholding Daisy Duck in a polka-dotted bikini. Who is this red-haired *femme fatale* standing in my doorway?

"Wow!" I blurt like a fool. "You look amazing, Amy!"

Amy bats her eyelashes, playing the part of Daisy Duck to a T, without even realizing it. "Why, thank you. So do you." She giggles when I don't move. "May I come in . . .?"

"Oh! Yes. Please do." I grab her suitcase, feeling flustered. "Lemme get that for you."

"Thank you. It's got wheels, Colin."

"Oh."

Disregarding the wheels, I carry Amy's bag into my house, still staring at her in disbelief. Her newly red hair makes her green eyes pop almost supernaturally. And speaking of things that look supernatural . . . Good lord, Amy's tits are otherworldly! What magic spell has Amy cast on them to make them defy gravity this way? She couldn't have gotten a boob job this past week, could she? No, she's got to be wearing a push-up bra with extra padding. Or maybe the neckline of her low-cut dress is creating some kind of optical illusion?

"Your house is beautiful," Amy says, gliding into my living room.

"Thanks. Wow. Your hair is fire. You look gorgeous."

"You like it?" Amy touches her glorious mane. "I didn't tell you about my little transformation because I wanted to see your honest reaction."

"My honest reaction is I *love* it. The red brings out the green in your eyes."

"That's what everyone keeps saying! I've never gotten so many compliments in my life—even from strangers!"

My stomach clenches. What strangers? People at her father's law firm, where she's been working this week . . . or dudes in bars?

Oh, God, no.

Did Amy go home with some random dude this week and show him Keane's video about The Sure Thing? The odds are low, considering Amy worked long hours every day and then chatted for hours on the phone with me every evening afterward. But even if the odds are low, the mere thought of anyone laying a pinky on Amy is driving me fucking crazy.

"I know it's silly," Amy says. "But what you told me about Caleb warning everyone off me during the tour boosted my confidence like crazy. And then, getting so many compliments this week boosted it even more. Thank you again for telling me about that. It changed everything for me."

That's it. That's what's so different about Amy—her *confidence.* In fact, I'd even call it *swagger.* I'm sure Amy felt beautiful at Logan's wedding last weekend in that pretty purple dress. But it's clear the siren standing before me feels *sexy* as hell. Indeed, the girl's now got sex appeal oozing out her pores.

"So, can I have a tour of the house?" Amy asks with a wave of her hand.

"Of course." I clear my throat. "Follow me."

I lead Amy through my house, and she oohs and aahs and compliments everything. When we arrive in my bedroom, Amy oohs and aahs again. But this time, seeing her standing next to my bed makes me feel the impulse to throw her down onto it and fuck the living hell out of her.

"Such a beautiful bedroom," Amy says, looking around. "I love it, Colin."

"Thanks," I say, turning away from her, so she won't see the erection growing in my pants. "Lemme show you the room I've got for you."

We cross the hall and enter my guest room, and Amy oohs and aahs, yet again. When she notices a bouquet of lilies sitting on the dresser, she squeals.

"Lilies are my favorite!" she says excitedly.

"Yeah, I know. That's why I got them."

She looks shocked. "How did you know I love lilies?"

"I overheard your conversation with Alessandra at the wedding. And I know your mother always had fresh flowers in your kitchen, so I thought having fresh flowers in your room—your favorite kind—would make you feel at home."

I've rendered her speechless. Shit. Were the flowers a misstep? Too much? I was only trying to welcome her. Let her know I'm excited she's here. But I think maybe in my effort to erase the awkwardness I felt during brunch last weekend, I quite possibly over-corrected.

"The flowers cost thirty bucks at the grocery store," I say quickly. "They were on display next to the checkout line, so I grabbed them, last minute. It was nothing."

Amy presses her lips together. "It was very thoughtful of you. Thank you."

I feel my cheeks turning hot. Shit. I don't even know how to act around her anymore. I thought I was being nice getting those flowers for Amy, but now I see it was all wrong for our agreed-upon platonic friendship.

"Uh, I'll get your suitcase, so you can unpack and wash up before we head out."

"How soon are we leaving?"

"An hour or so, if that works? We're going to Dax's to pre-party with the gang before heading to Laila's party."

"Yay. I can't wait to see everyone. Oh! Can you tell me some of the famous people I'll see at Laila's, so I can flip out here, in advance, rather than embarrassing myself at the party?"

"Just be yourself at the party, Ames. Whatever your honest reaction might be, people will love it."

Amy shakes her head. "I walked into walls, repeatedly, during the tour—each and every time someone famous came backstage. Trust me, we don't want a repeat of that tonight."

"Speak for yourself," I joke. But ultimately, I tell Amy the guest list for tonight's party, as far as I know it, concluding with, "And of course, Savage's bandmates will all be there."

Amy's face lights up. "All of them, you think?"

"As far as I know."

"Their drummer?"

My heartrate increases, slightly. "I assume so. Kendrick is Savage's best friend and a good friend of Laila's."

Amy smiles broadly but says nothing, and the hair on the back of my neck stands up. Kendrick Cook is a good-looking guy. A badass drummer. Also, single, as far as I know. He's got game, but he's not a douchebag. In other words, he's perfect for Amy.

Uh oh.

"Kendrick isn't a good bet to hire you," I say quickly. "He's a low maintenance kind of guy, like me, so—"

"Oh, I don't want to meet Kendrick Cook so he'll hire

me," Amy replies. "I just want to meet him because he seems nice in all his interviews."

Excuse me?

In all his interviews?

When did Amy start checking out interviews of Kendrick Cook? This past week, after I threw on the brakes in Seattle, or before then? Has Amy had a longstanding crush on Kendrick, or is he the consolation prize she's set her sights on, now that I'm not an option? Frankly, I'm not sure which scenario I'd prefer. Either one makes my stomach twist and my heartrate increase.

Amy grins at whatever she's seeing on my face. "What can I say? After living next-door to you, and being on tour with Caleb, I guess I've got a soft spot for drummers."

Fuck.

Jealousy throttles me, even though I know I have no right to feel this way. I'm the one who threw on the brakes last weekend. I'm the one who said that kiss couldn't ignite anything between us. And yet, suddenly, I feel determined to keep Kendrick Cook away from Amy tonight, far away, the same way I kept that Luke guy away from her last weekend.

"Is everything okay?" Amy says, tilting her head to the side.

I inhale deeply. Remind myself of the list of reasons why turning Amy down in Seattle was the right thing to do. "Everything's great."

"Good." Again, she smiles. "Well, I guess I'd better jump into the shower so we can head over to Dax and Violet's."

Shower.

My brain shows me Amy's wet, naked tits in the shower. They're pink from the hot water. Glistening and mouth-watering.

"You want a cocktail?" I choke out. "I'm gonna make myself one."

"Great. Surprise me. You can leave it on the dresser for me, if I'm still in the shower when you come back, and I'll enjoy it while getting dressed."

Shower. Enjoy. Naked. Tits.

In a flash, I see myself getting into that shower with Amy. Sinking to my knees, eating her pussy and making her come, while hot water rains down on my head. I imagine myself pulling her from the shower and laying her wet body down on the bed mere inches from where she's standing now, and doing The Sure Thing to her, until she's speaking in tongues.

"Sure thing," I whisper hoarsely. And when Amy arches her perfect eyebrow, I quickly add, "One surprise cocktail and one suitcase, coming up."

Jesus. With my skin on fire and my heart pounding in my chest, I bolt out the room . . .

But not fast enough to miss hearing Amy shout after me, "Thank you so much, Colin! You're such an amazing . . . *friend.*"

FOURTEEN

AMY

When Colin and I enter Dax and Violet's expansive living room, we're greeted by Dax and Fish. When we venture farther into the spacious room, we discover Violet and Alessandra sitting on a couch, engaged in a FaceTime call, while Dax and Violet's tow-headed toddler, Jackson, sits on his beautiful mommy's lap.

When Violet sees Colin and me, she enthusiastically calls to Colin to come join the call. "It's Keane and Maddy!" she says excitedly. "Maddy's two days past due and about to pop!"

Colin heads over to Violet and Alessandra on the couch, while I hang back with Fish and Dax in a corner bar area. But after a moment, Violet calls to me.

"Amy, come meet Dax's brother and his wife! I told them all about the wedding last weekend and they want to meet you!"

"Oh, great."

I begin walking toward Violet, feeling wracked by nerves

and excitement. I can't believe I'm about to come face to face
—albeit on video chat—with Ball Peen Hammer! A guy
who's explained The Sure Thing to me, in explicit detail, at
least five times, and then made me laugh endlessly after I fell
down the "Ball Peen Hammer" rabbit hole this past week by
devouring every single video in his YouTube series, and then
binge-watching both seasons of his slick dramedy on Netflix,
too.

From what I've gathered, Keane and his wife, Maddy—
whom Keane calls "Maddy Behind the Camera" in all his Ball
Peen Hammer videos—rarely add new content to their years-
long web series nowadays. But that didn't keep me from
feeling like I knew the couple, inside and out, by the time I
reached their most recent video.

As much as I loved all the Ball Peen Hammer videos, I
loved watching Keane Morgan even more as an actor in his
scripted show. Perhaps because I'd watched all his silly videos
prior to watching his show, I felt particularly connected to his
character, above all others, even though he's only a side
character.

Fidgeting with excitement, I sit down next to Colin, who's
already laughing easily with Keane and Maddy on Violet's
phone. *And there he is.* Keane Morgan. Blonde these days,
like on his Netflix show, and looking even more handsome on
his couch next to his wife than he does under professional
lighting.

"Guys, this is my friend, Amy," Colin says, as I get settled
next to him. "We grew up together."

"Hi!" I chirp, while waving like a dope.

"Remember my buddy, Logan, who lived next door to
me?" Colin says to Keane. "He came with me to your garage

a bunch of times to watch our rehearsals and smoke weed with us."

"Oh, yeah," Keane says. "Cool guy."

"Amy's his little sister. She might have tagged along with Logan to watch us rehearse, a time or two. Not too many, probably, since that would have meant we couldn't smoke weed."

"Oh, sorry about that," I say. "I had no idea. Whoops. Yeah, I definitely came with Logan a time or two, I think." Actually, I came to Dax's garage to watch Colin's band rehearsing exactly *four* times over the years. But who's counting?

"Oh, *yeah*!" Keane says brightly. "I remember you! Little Orphan Amy!"

Maddy laughs. "Take it as a compliment he's given you a nickname, Amy. Keane never does that with anyone he doesn't like."

Keane laughs. "True. You were hilarious, as I recall. I remember you cracking everyone up."

"Not intentionally, I'm sure," I reply. "And from what Colin said, I think my 'hilarity' might have been mostly because you were stoned."

Keane chuckles. "And she's still got it! Ha! I remember you had a big ol' mop of curly hair back then and you always seemed like you were playing to the crowd in the back row of a huge Broadway theatre." He winks. "Hence, the nickname."

I can't help laughing. "That's the perfect description of me as a kid."

"And look at you now," Keane says. "You've got the red hair to make my nickname a premonition."

"So sorry, Amy," Maddy says, but she's clearly loving her husband's sense of humor.

"No worries," I say. "Considering what a little weirdo I was as a kid, I think I got off easy with that nickname."

"You were a cute little weirdo," Keane says, and warmth spreads into my core. I knew I liked this man, after watching him online for hours and hours. But just this fast, I know I absolutely adore him.

Colin and Fish get up to grab drinks, and Dax engages Keane and Maddy in a conversation about some upcoming trip to Seattle. So, while all that's happening, Violet, scoots closer to me, pulling her son, Jackson, who's still sitting on her lap, along with her.

"I *love* your new do, Amy!" Violet says. "You have the perfect coloring to pull off red hair!"

"I was just about to say the same thing," Alessandra interjects, sitting on my other side.

"Thank you so much. I'm so happy to see you both. I had such a great time with you last weekend."

"So did we." Violet cranes her neck to address the little boy in her lap. "Jackson, this is Auntie Amy. Say hello."

"Hello, Auntie Amy."

Oh, my heart. Without hesitation, I launch into conversation with the kid about his cool light-up shoes. But when the FaceTime call ends and Fish takes a seat—an armchair—Jackson abruptly stops talking to me, slides off his mommy's lap, and beelines over to his Uncle Fish's lap.

"Don't be offended he dropped you like a hot potato the minute Fish's lap became available," Violet says, laughing. "Jackson's been obsessed with his 'Unkie Fish' since day one. When Jackson toured with the Goats as a baby, Fish was the only one who could get him to fall asleep for two solid months."

"Aw, that's so cute."

"I think I'm going to grab a bite in the kitchen," Violet says, standing up. "You ladies want to come, too?"

"Yeah, sounds great," I say, as Alessandra says the same.

And off we go.

In the kitchen, I grab a plate and begin loading it with appetizers, but before I've completed my task, both Violet and Ally lean over the island counter and energetically ask me what's going on with Colin.

"Are you two on a date tonight?" Violet asks, her blue eyes sparkling.

"No, we're just friends," I reply, my tone conveying my disappointment. "I'm his plus-one tonight." When both women frown, I add, "It's okay. Colin's not interested in anything more than that, so . . . Such is life." I smile. "So, hey, ladies . . ." I put down my plate and lean over the island opposite them, my energy matching theirs. "Feel free not to answer this question, if it's too personal, but . . . are either of you familiar with a sexual technique called The Sure Thing? Keane has a 'Ball Peen Hammer' video about it, in which he says the technique gives woman 'honey bunches of O's' in a short period of time."

Violet and Alessandra laugh.

"Oh, Keane," Violet says. "Yes, I'm very familiar with that technique. Ally?"

Alessandra blushes, looking far less comfortable with this topic than Violet, but she nods and says, "I'm very familiar with it, too."

"And it works?"

Both women smile and nod.

"Wow. I'd never even heard of it before Colin mentioned it to me last weekend at the wedding! I googled it and wound up watching Keane's video on it, several times. Does

Keane's technique work as well as he said, or did he exaggerate?"

"I've never seen Keane's video on the topic," Violet says. "Dax told me never to watch it." She laughs. "But if Keane says the technique gives women 'honey bunches of O's' in a short period of time, then, yes, I can confirm it works, as promised."

"Holy crap."

"It's not 'Keane's technique,' by the way. His two older brothers, Colby and Ryan—but mostly Ryan, from what I've been told—came up with the technique years ago and named it, and then told the younger guys how to perform it." She smirks. "Of course, since Keane's the big YouTube star, he gets all the credit for being the Godfather of The Sure Thing. But Dax said the lion's share of credit goes to his brother, Ryan. I'm not surprised by that. Ryan's extremely . . . How shall I put this, without embarrassing myself? *Alpha*?" Violet giggles and leans onto the kitchen island again, a smirk on her gorgeous face. "Why are you asking about this, Amy? Are you hoping Colin will do The Sure Thing to you?"

Hell yes, I think. Instead, what I say is, "No, that's not going to happen. Colin and I had a drunken kiss at the wedding. But after that, we talked about it, and he decided we're only going to be friends. I asked about the technique because, if it's real and works the way Keane said, then I'm planning to find someone, someday soon, to do it to me. Admittedly, I would have preferred that someone to be Colin, but I've accepted that's not in the cards. So now, my Plan B is to find someone nice and cute, someone I like a lot, who could watch Keane's video and make it happen for me."

Violet considers this for a moment. "Hmm. I'd suggest you keep your expectations low, at first, if the guy's never done it before. From what Dax has said, the basics of the technique are always the same, but every woman is different, so there's a bit of trial and error needed with a new partner. I haven't seen Keane's video, like I said, but he's a huge bullshitter, in general, so it wouldn't surprise me if he exaggerated about how easy it is to make it work."

"Oh."

"But don't worry, the technique *does* work, once your man figures it out. It's incredible."

Alessandra nods, still blushing.

"So, yeah, if you find someone you like, and he's willing to watch Keane's video and figure it out with you, then you'll eventually get to experience something that will blow your mind, girlie. You won't believe what your body can do when your partner knows what he's doing."

Again, Alessandra nods. But the poor girl looks like a vine-ripened tomato at this point.

"Thanks for the info," I say, trying to sound calm. When I raise my drink to my lips, my hand is shaking so violently from adrenaline and excitement, I have to quickly put down my cup to keep from spilling. But it's too late. Both women have noticed me wigging out and are now buckled over laughing.

After a bit more talking, Violet, Ally, and I return to the living room—and to my delight, during the ensuing conversation with the full group, I feel every bit as comfortable as I did last weekend at the wedding. Even more so, because Jackson has apparently anointed me his new favorite person.

"Jackson never sits on a new person's lap!" Violet says, after Jackson leaves Fish for me. "Daxy, look!"

Dax marvels with Violet at how quickly their son has

taken to me, with Dax saying, "Usually, if Fish Taco is here, nobody else, including me, exists."

"I hope you know this makes you my arch nemesis," Fish says, wagging his finger at me with mock menace, and everyone in the room chuckles.

The conversation shifts to something new, but I'm too engrossed in conversation with the cutie in my lap to participate. As Jackson talks to me, I run my hand through his soft, blonde hair and steal an occasional sniff of his kiddie shampoo. Suddenly, Jackson surprises me by sliding off my lap, grabbing my hand, and commanding me to come play Legos in another room.

"*Au revoir*," I say to the room, doing the Queen's wave with my free hand. "I'm off to play."

"Auntie Amy isn't your babysitter, honey," Violet says to her son. "When Mrs. Sampson gets here, she'll play Legos with you a little before bedtime." Violet looks at her watch. "Speaking of which, where is Mrs. Sampson? She's never late."

"I'll play with him until she gets here," I offer. For one thing, Jackson hasn't stopped pulling me out of the large room, despite what his mother said. And for another, I'm a sucker for a cute kid who likes me.

"Are you sure, Amy?"

"Absolutely."

By chance, my gaze meets Colin's before I exit the room, and the look on his face as he watches me with Jackson sends warmth oozing into my core. I can't read his expression with confidence. But it sure seems like he's looking at me the same way he did on that patio last week, right before leaning in to kiss me.

When Jackson and I arrive in the playroom, he retrieves a

box of Legos from a shelf, and we get settled onto the floor and begin building. A few minutes later, Violet appears and sits next to her son on the floor.

"Mrs. Sampson isn't coming, Donut," she says. "So, I'm gonna play Legos with you tonight, okay?" She whispers to me, "Her daughter was in a car accident. She's okay, thank God, but Mrs. Sampson doesn't want to leave her tonight." She touches Jackson's blonde head. "I'd certainly stay with my kid, too."

"Thank goodness she's okay. How scary, though."

"I can't imagine."

"Do you have another babysitter you can call?"

Violet shakes her head. "I tried and struck out. But that's okay. Jackson and I will have a fun Mommy and Me Night. Right, Bubba?"

"Why don't I watch him?" I ask. "Go to the party, Violet. I insist."

Violet pulls a face that tells me she's not having it. "You came to LA early, specifically to go to this party with Colin."

"Yeah, I know, but I don't even know Laila. This birthday party was nothing but a networking opportunity for me, a fun thing to do—but I'll still have lots of chances to network next week on Colin's movie set. Laila's your friend. You should be there to celebrate her birthday."

My logic seems to be making headway with Violet, so I pile on. "I love kids. I grew up babysitting everyone on my street. Honestly, I'll have more fun playing Legos with Jackson than trying not to embarrass myself in front of a room full of celebrities, while also trying to pretend I don't feel anything but platonic friendship for my 'date.'"

Violet looks at me sympathetically. I guess I shouldn't

have said that last thing to her, but I'm sure it didn't come as a surprise.

Before Violet's replied to me, Dax enters the playroom with Colin and Fish, saying he's secured someone named Amalia to come babysit. "Amalia said she's on her way."

"Oh, fantastic. Thanks, babe." Violet hops up and kisses her husband. "Amy volunteered herself as tribute to watch Jackson, so I could go to the party, and I'm embarrassed to say I was considering it." She smiles down at me on the floor. "Thank you for offering, Ames."

"I was being sincere. Please, take me up on the offer another time. I'll hopefully be living in LA. I'd love to help you, whenever I can."

Violet smiles broadly at me. "You're such a sweetheart."

"I wouldn't have let you or Amy stay behind," Dax says to his wife. "I'd have stayed home with Action Jackson before letting either of you miss the party. In fact, . . ."

"No, Daxy," Violet says. "You're coming to the party." She looks at me. "He always thinks he'll hate every party, and then he always winds up having a blast."

"Yeah, we couldn't have let Amy stay behind, anyway," Fish says. "Colin needs Amy to show up with him to keep things from being awkward."

My brows knitted together, I look at Colin, not understanding Fish's comment. When Colin's eyes meet mine, the guilty, pissed look on his face tells me Fish just spilled the beans on something Colin fervently wishes he hadn't. When Colin says nothing, I shift my gaze to Fish. The bean spiller.

"What about me coming to the party with Colin would make things less awkward for him?" I demand. And when Fish gapes like a fish on a line in reply—like a Matthew Fishberger on a line—I look around the group for edification.

"What am I missing?" I look at Colin again and gasp with my epiphany. "You dated Laila Fitzgerald?"

"No, no," Colin says, waving at the air. "Laila and I are friends and nothing more. We've never even kissed."

I narrow my eyes. The air in the playroom feels thick. There's obviously something Colin's not telling me, and his friends are maintaining their silence, so that *Colin* will be the one to explain it to me. "Colin, tell me what's going on."

Colin rolls his eyes. "It's nothing. Last month, I saw Laila, by chance, at a few different parties and events, including when I shot my episode of *Sing Your Heart Out.* That day, I wound up telling Laila I'd maybe be interested in starting something with her, if she was interested, and she told me, thanks but no thanks. She said she's not interested in me as more than a friend, regardless, but also that she had a new boyfriend. Savage. Unfortunately, he came into the dressing room where Laila and I were talking and immediately jumped to some conclusions that weren't right. It was a bit heated for a second there, but I explained I didn't know about their relationship and that Laila had just turned me down. And that was it. All good. No biggie."

I stare at Colin for a long beat, mentally carving my initials into his tattooed chest, while simultaneously feeling weirdly rejected and humiliated. Of course, Colin went after Laila Fitzgerald after his breakup with that gorgeous dancer! Of course, he thought a glamorous popstar is the kind of woman he belongs with, given who he's become!

Colin rolls his eyes at whatever he sees on my face. "Amy, don't think twice about this, okay? Laila and I are friends. We're signed to the same label. I was newly single and heartbroken, and I figured, *Why not see if something could happen here?* But I've never even kissed Laila and I'm certainly not sitting around pining for her, if that's what you think."

"Why would I care if you're pining for Laila?" I say. "We're nothing but friends, right? You can pine for whoever you want. It's none of my business."

The group collectively shifts their weight. Some people look at the ground. Others shoot death-glares at Colin. Some simply clear their throats. But every single person looks painfully uncomfortable.

Fish speaks first. "Tonight's the first time our group will be hanging out with Savage and Laila, as a couple, so Colin figured—"

"I know what he figured," I say. "That it'd make things less awkward if he showed up tonight with a date." I gasp, as yet another epiphany strikes. "The 'date' he was seen canoodling with on Instagram last weekend!"

Colin glares at Fish. And that's how I know I've hit the nail on the head. *And that makes me seethe.* How *dare* Colin let me think he was the saint who invited me to Laila's party as a *favor* to me, the saint who posted that photo to make Nate feel like an asshole, when, in reality, Colin was using *me* to smooth over his humiliation at the hands of Laila, the whole time!

In response to me glaring at Colin, and Colin therefore glaring at him, Fish throws up his arms and shouts at Colin, "How was I supposed to know you hadn't told her?"

"Don't you dare be angry with Fish for telling me the truth," I say to Colin. "He didn't blow it by being honest with me. You blew it by *not* being honest."

"I didn't mention it because the main reason I invited you to the party was to help you. So why mention I was also incidentally getting a benefit out of it, too?"

"Because you manipulated me!" I whisper-shout, so as not to scare little Jackson. "Because if I'm truly your friend, then you should have trusted me to want to help you! Frankly, I'm relieved to hear you're getting something out of bringing me tonight, because it means I don't owe you nearly as much as I thought. The fact that you don't know I'm *dying* to be of service to you, to finally do something nice for you, the way you always do nice stuff for me, is what pisses me off the most, Colin. You thought you had to manipulate me to do your bidding, when all you had to do was ask."

Violet, Fish, and Alessandra are all looking at me like, *You tell him, girlie*, while Dax is looking at Colin, like, *Dumbass*. Which means there's not a single facial expression in the group that makes me feel like I'm out of line or overreacting. And so, I persist.

"As a favor to you, I'll play the part of your 'date' tonight, when we arrive at the party. And I'll keep doing it until we're sure Laila and Savage have seen us together. But after that, all bets will be off, my friend. After that, I'm going to mingle like the extremely *single* woman I am. Who knows? I might even meet a nice drummer who has a thing for redheads." As Colin's jaw muscles pulse, I turn to Violet and Alessandra, both of whom look positively delighted. "Would you ladies join me in the kitchen, while we wait for the babysitter? All of a sudden, I feel like doing a couple shots."

FIFTEEN
COLIN

I'm a flaming pyre as I watch Amy chatting across the crowded party with none other than Kendrick Cook, the broad-shouldered, easy-going drummer of Fugitive Summer, the band whose song "Hate Sex High" is currently number one in the world.

I keep telling myself I'm feeling nothing but protectiveness, not jealousy, in this moment—as any good big brother would feel while watching a handsome, muscular, wildly successful musician flirting with his little sister. I keep telling myself I'm watching out for Amy the way I did when we were kids. The way I did when that groomsman, Luke, hit on her at the wedding. But it's a hard sell, given what I know about Kendrick. Despite his looks and success, he's as far from a douchebag as a man can get—which means he's objectively a perfect fit for Amy, if I were trying to set her up with a friend.

Which I'm not.

I think I'm particularly flustered because Fugitive Summer's hit song is pure sex in aural form. That's not merely due to Savage's raunchy lyrics and sexualized vocals, as a casual fan of music might assume. Nope, as a drummer myself, I know a song can't be *that* sexual without having a nasty beat that hits people squarely between their legs. And I also know, as a drummer myself, that a guy can't bang out *that* dirty a beat, unless he's got some damned good rhythm behind closed doors, too.

Fuck!

As promised, Amy entered the party on my arm and let me introduce her to our hosts as my date. She flirted with me a bit whenever Savage and Laila were nearby, all in the name of fulfilling her promise to me. The nano-second the party filled up and got crowded and crazy, and people started mixing and matching and dancing to the blaring playlist, Amy ditched my ass on a bullet train and went off with Violet, not me, to make the rounds.

For the first hour, I managed to remain pretty chill watching Violet introducing Amy around. But when Violet introduced Amy to our good friend, popstar Aloha Carmichael, who then escorted both women over to Kendrick Cook, who'd prior to then been chatting in a corner with his brother, Kai, almost all semblance of chill left my body. Still, even then, I was able to cling to a shred of my chill.

But no more. Not since Violet, Aloha, and Kai drifted away, leaving Kendrick and Amy chatting alone, their faces mere inches apart, their demeanors flirtatious. Yeah, that's when I flipped my motherfucking lid. Inwardly, anyway. I haven't left my spot or moved a muscle, other than breathing, clenching my teeth, and sipping my drink, for the past twenty minutes. But inside, I feel like a volcano on the bitter cusp of eruption.

Kendrick seems so nice in all his interviews, Amy said.

What interviews?

My chest heaving, I yank out my phone and tap Kendrick's name into my browser, eager to see why and how Kendrick comes off as so fucking "nice" in "all" his interviews. Unfortunately, the music is too loud to watch any of the video links that pop up, so I click on the first written interview—one of Kendrick and his big brother, Kai, the bass player of Fugitive Summer. A brief skim of the piece quickly reveals why Amy made her comment about Kendrick. He comes across as a truly awesome guy. Self-deprecating, charming, and funny. *Asshole.*

I click on the next interview, another one with Kendrick and his brother, Kai, and midway down the piece, my jaw nearly clanks onto the floor:

Interviewer: What about you, Kendrick? Who's your celebrity crush?

Kendrick: Hmm. I guess maybe Amy Adams.

Kai: What do you mean you 'guess'? After you saw her in **Enchanted** *as a kid, you wanted to grow up and marry her.* **Enchanted** *was your first foray into porn, dude.*

Kendrick: He's not wrong. The only reason I hesitated is I couldn't decide between Amy Adams and Emma Stone. When I saw Emma in **Superbad,** *it was love—lust—at first sight.*

Interviewer: Ah, you've got a thing for redheads.

Kendrick: Guilty as charged. But not just any redhead. The most irresistible combination to me is red hair, light eyes, a killer smile, and a goofy personality. If ever I find all that in one person, I'll be putty in her hands.

Kai: Dude, don't lie.

Kendrick: I didn't.

Kai: You conveniently left big boobs off the list to make yourself seem more noble than you are. Don't let my little brother fool you into thinking he doesn't notice that kind of thing. Kendrick Cook's a boob man, through and through.

Kendrick: Again, he's not wrong.

Interviewer: What about you, Kai?

Kai: Me? I'm an ass man.

Interviewer: No, who's your celebrity crush?

Kendrick: To be clear, if a woman's got all that other stuff I mentioned, nice boobs are only icing on the cake. I don't want to come off like a total asshole here.

Kai: Too late. Your secret's out. You're secretly a dick.

I look up from my phone, feeling like every molecule in my body is going to physically explode. Amy dyed her hair *specifically* to attract the attention of Kendrick fucking Cook tonight! The realization makes me want to bolt over there and beat the shit out of Kendrick, even though my rational brain knows he's done nothing wrong. Amy's the one who turned herself into his ideal woman. *What the fuck?*

I take a deep breath and tell myself to calm down.

But I'm not calming down. Not at all. In fact, I'm now moving toward Amy, planning to yank her away from Kendrick and call her out on her bullshit . . . and then drag her into a room and fuck the living hell out of her.

No.

Stop, Colin.

Somehow, I force myself to stop walking.

She's Logan's little sister, asshole. She's off-limits. And Kendrick is a great guy. What are you doing, dumbass?

Yeah . . . No.

My internal dialog has done nothing to cool my jets.

Off I go, once again.

Trembling with adrenaline, I reach Kendrick and Amy across the party. At which point, Amy greets me pleasantly, as does Kendrick. Hmm. I don't know what I was planning to say when I got here, but whatever it was, their pleasant greetings of me have made me feel like flying into a maniacal rage, out of nowhere, wouldn't be a good look for me.

"Excuse me, guys," Amy says brightly, before I've figured out what to say. "I need to pee!"

"I'll wait for you right here," Kendrick replies.

"You'd better!" Amy turns and skips away, but not before flashing me a truly murderous look.

"She's so cool," Kendrick says, watching Amy disappear into the crowded party.

"Mm-hmm."

"I like how sweet she is," Kendrick continues. "While still being direct and no-nonsense. It's such an attractive combination."

My breathing turns instantly ragged. "Amy's direct and no-nonsense about *what,* exactly?"

Kendrick pauses, apparently surprised by my question. He twists his mouth, obviously choosing his words carefully. "Just, you know. She was straightforward about what she's looking for, which I found refreshing."

The thumping of my heart is gaining speed. My breathing is shallow. "Amy was 'straightforward' about *what,* exactly?" I'm shouting now.

Kendrick cocks his head. "You're not with her, are you?

Amy said she grew up next-door to you and that you two are like siblings."

I can barely breathe. But I manage to say, "That's right."

Kendrick exhales and takes a sip of his beer. "Amy told me why it looked like she was your date tonight when you first got here. That was cool of her to do that for you, huh?"

"Mm-hmm."

Kendrick chuckles. "Savage is such a nut job sometimes. But, trust me, you don't need to worry about him being pissed at you. He knows he overreacted the other day. He wasn't even pissed at you, I don't think. He was going through some stuff and took it out on you."

"It's all good."

"So, hey, I saw the news about the movie. Congrats, man!"

"Thanks."

"When does filming begin?"

"What, *precisely*, did Amy say to you that was so 'direct' and 'straightforward' and 'refreshing'?"

Kendrick blinks like I've slapped him. "Uh . . . I think that should probably stay between Amy and me—out of respect for her privacy."

Fucking hell. In a huff, I throw back the rest of my drink, hold up my empty to Kendrick like I'm in need of a refill, and take off to find Amy. When I find her, she's talking to a group of women—Aloha, Violet, Alessandra, and Laila—outside one of the bathrooms.

I march to the group of women, my audacity fueled by booze and jealousy, and touch Amy's shoulder. "I need to talk to you. *Right fucking now.*"

Everyone stops talking and looks at me, shocked.

"You'll have to wait," Amy says calmly, ignoring the

smoke coming out my ears. "Aloha is in the middle of telling a story."

"It's okay," Aloha says, looking between Amy and me.

"Yeah, this is urgent," I say, before grabbing Amy's arm and physically dragging her away.

SIXTEEN

AMY

Colin grabs my arm and pulls me down a short hallway and into a nearby bedroom, where he slams the door behind us and practically tosses me into the room like a rag doll.

"What the fuck?" I shout.

Colin's dark eyes are glinting in the moonlight that's streaming through a nearby window. As he approaches me, he looks feral. Primal. *And hot as hell.* "Did you dye your hair to catch Kendrick Cook's eye?" he shouts.

Well, that took a turn. "Yes. Partly."

"Jesus Christ, Amy!"

I put my hands on my hips. "So, let me get this straight: you don't want me, but nobody else can have me? Is that how this works in the world according to Colin Beretta?" He's positively seething. *And I love it.* I scoff. "Not that it's any of your business, but my hairdresser in Seattle has tried for years to convince me to go red. So I figured—"

"Don't bullshit me, Amy."

"I'm not! Yes, I admit when I found out Kendrick has a

thing for redheads, and I figured I'd probably meet him tonight, that gave me the little push I needed to finally do it. But I'd been thinking about going red for a while."

He's fit to be tied. "What 'direct' and 'refreshing' thing did you say to Kendrick out there?"

"That's what Kendrick said? That I'm *refreshing*? How sweet!"

"What'd you say to him?" He's shouting. Losing his mind.

"It's none of your goddamned business."

Colin takes a step forward, his dark eyes burning like hot coals. "You asked him to fuck you, didn't you?"

"What if I did? Kendrick is a handsome, sweet guy who's obviously got zero issues with fucking Logan O'Brien's little sister, unlike you. Our conversation was fun and easy. He smells good and made me laugh. Oh, and he's got the most gorgeous lips and teeth and eyes. So, yes, I told Kendrick about my sexual history and asked him if he'd be willing to be my teacher this week, every night after I get off work with you, no strings attached. And Kendrick said he'd be 'honored and thrilled' to do that with me." My lip twitches as I try not to smirk too wickedly. "Not that any of that is of your concern, *brother.* If Logan were here, I certainly wouldn't tell him any of that. So, I don't see how—"

Colin's lips crash into mine. His tongue finds mine as his muscled arms snake around my waist and pull me to him. And just like that, every atom inside me explodes with relief and excitement and white-hot lust. Out of nowhere, Colin leans back and holds my face, firmly in his palms. "*I'm* gonna be your teacher every night this week—no strings. I want the same deal you offered to Kendrick, Amy."

I nod effusively. "Yes."

"This is gonna be no strings."

"Yes. Whatever you say."

Colin drags me to the nearby bed, throws me down on my back, pulls up my dress, all the way, revealing my bra. In a frenzy of excitement, he pulls my bra off my breasts, and begins devouring me like a beast—like his very life depends on getting my nipples and flesh into his mouth. He's groaning as he kisses, licks, and caresses me. Losing every ounce of his sane mind.

"I guess Kendrick's not the only boob man," I mutter to myself, just as the song blaring in the distant party becomes "Hate Sex High," which provokes a tidal wave of cheers and shrieks in the other room.

"Fuck me to this song," I beg, writhing on the bed. "Do The Sure Thing to me while this song is playing." It's a depraved request, considering Kendrick is the one making those sexy drumbeats on the recording, and I just ditched that gorgeous man—and the arrangement I made with him—to come in here with Colin and make the same arrangement with him, mere moments later. Even so, Colin is the only man I truly wanted. The only man I've *ever* wanted. Surely, Colin knows that.

"I won't do The Sure Thing to you here," Colin mutters, his voice awash in arousal. "And I'm not gonna fuck you here, either. But I'll sure as hell make you come, baby. Easy as pie." He leans down and kisses my mouth, this time stroking my clit from the outside of my cotton panties as he does. As his tongue tangles with mine and Fugitive Summer's sexy song provides our soundtrack, Colin's fingertip swirls and massages that hard bud throbbing inside my panties, sending my arousal up and up and up . . .

.   .   .

I fucked with your body, baby
You fucked with my mind
You said it meant nothing to ya
But you came three times
Girl, you came three times
You came three times
Cuz you're chasing
A hate sex high

La la la la la la la . . . Hate Sex High
La la la la la la la . . . Hate Sex High

As "Hate Sex High" continues turning me on from the other side of that closed door, Colin's fingers continue stroking me on the outside of my soaked panties, inching me closer to having an orgasm with another person than I've ever felt in my life. Why isn't Colin slipping his fingers inside my panties, like I'm aching for him to do?

"Relax," Colin whispers into my ear, his fingers still stroking me through my undies. "This is gonna take thirty minutes or so, so don't worry about the time. Just relax and enjoy it."

Thirty minutes? Holy shit. No wonder Perry never even came close to getting me there! I had no idea it takes that long!

Colin opens my thighs, camps himself between them, and begins kissing and nipping at the sensitive flesh around my panties. And when I begin moaning like crazy with anticipation, he *finally* slides his hand inside the fabric, but without taking my undies off, and dips a couple fingers inside me, making me growl with pleasure.

His fingers slick with my arousal, he begins sliding them from my wetness to my clit and back again, several times, before massaging my clit with his wet fingers in slow, languid circles. And all the while, his tongue in my mouth is mimicking the movement of his fingers. It's outrageously pleasurable and exciting. Like nothing I've felt before, as a matter of fact.

"Oh, God," I blurt, suddenly hurtling toward ecstasy on a rocket.

"That's it, baby," Colin whispers breathlessly in my ear. "You're so fucking sexy in the moonlight. Take a deep breath. Focus on how good this feels. On how good it's gonna feel when I take those panties off and eat your pussy like a starving man."

Out of nowhere, my body seizes sharply, and then everything inside me pauses, like I'm in suspended animation. Then, suddenly, it's pure ecstasy as my body releases the best, most pleasurable and intense orgasm of my life, by a long mile.

"Yes," I choke out, gripping the comforter underneath me. "Colin! Yes!"

Colin slides his fingers inside me as my internal walls ripple and warp. "Good girl. Oh, that's a good one."

I sigh with satisfaction when the ripples fade away.

"Did that feel good, beautiful?" he asks, smiling.

"So good. I thought you said it'd take thirty minutes! But that wasn't even close!"

Colin chuckles. "I lied. I knew it'd take less than five. I just wanted you to relax and not stress. Orgasms are mostly mental for women. It's all about getting you out of your head."

I exhale happily again. "You're amazing. Wow. That felt so good."

"And that was what I can do, leaving your cute pink panties *on*. Just think what I can do for you when I've got you naked and spread-eagle on my bed like a picnic lunch."

I bite my lower lip. "Let's do it. I'm on the pill. Make me your picnic now."

He chuckles. "Patience." But the glint in his eyes tells me he likes my enthusiasm. "When I fuck you for the first time, I want you to be able to let go completely. And that's not guaranteed to happen here, where we can hear the party on the other side of the door." He slides his fingertip underneath my chin and grins. "When I fuck you for the first time, sweetheart, I want to be certain I've got your undivided attention."

A shaky exhale escapes me as I nod my assent.

"Come with me, puppet." He slides my bra back down, and then my dress, and puts out his hand. "We're going to say goodbye to our friends. Then, make sure you've got all the photos you need to impress that agency, just in case. And last but not least, I'm gonna spy on you with a rock-hard boner while you tell Kendrick Cook there's been a change of plans."

[Go to http://www.laurenrowebooks.com/hate-sex-high-music to listen to "Hate Sex High" by Fugitive Summer]

SEVENTEEN
COLIN

I pull into my garage and turn off my car's engine—and when I look at Amy sitting next to me, the expression of unadulterated glee she's wearing makes me chuckle, despite the carnal urges that have been throttling me since we left Laila's party.

Amy unbuckles her seatbelt, clearly intending to exit the car on a bullet train, so I command, "Stay put. I'll come around to grab you."

"*Grab* me?" she echoes excitedly, practically panting with excitement.

Trying not to laugh, I exit the car and bound around the back, planning to scoop my little newbie puppet into my arms and carry her into my house. That's what a proper Fantasy Man would do in this situation, I think. But the second I open Amy's car door and see the forest fire in her green eyes, the bloom in her cheeks, the way her tits are rising and falling, my plan flies out the window, supplanted by primal instinct. Suddenly, I'm too ravenous to do anything but drop to my knees and taste her, right here and now.

I grab Amy's thighs and roughly pivot her body toward me, making her gasp, and then yank up her dress, spread open her legs, and drop to my knees. As Amy's breathing turns shallow and erratic, I slide off her shoes, making way for her undies next. I massage both feet, briefly, while smirking up at her like a lion tracking his prey, and when I can't wait another second, I lean forward, take her pink panties between my teeth, and yank those fuckers down.

When her panties are at her knees, I crook my finger inside them and yank them all the way off, while nipping and teasing Amy's inner thighs with my lips and tongue.

Even before I've come close to her pussy, Amy is already groaning loudly. Whimpering like she's in delicious pain. And that's how I know this girl's a ticking time bomb, about to go off.

Her panties off, I run my palms over her inner thighs, getting my little newbie relaxed and acclimated to my touch.

"Breathe," I whisper, looking up at her. "Relax and breathe. Grab my hair while I'm eating you, if you're feeling it. Dig your nails into my shoulders, if that's what you want to do. You can't hurt me. Scream as loudly as you want, Amy. You can't embarrass yourself. Whatever feels good, whatever turns you on, do it. As long as it's real and honest and not a performance for *me*, that's what I want out of you."

When she nods effusively, I lick my lips, lean in, and get to work. I start off kissing my way up her inner thighs, while gently brushing my fingers over her slit. Back and forth, my fingers go, making her yearn for more as my mouth zeroes in on its landing strip.

As my mouth gets closer and closer to her pussy, and my fingers continue teasing her, Amy begins moaning and gyrating in her seat. She's spreading her legs wider to give me full access to her. Snapping her hips forward and back, nonverbally begging me, in the most primal of ways, to fuck her. And this is all before my tongue has even brushed Amy's bull's-eye.

I dip my finger inside her, to see what I'm working with here, and my body jolts with pleasure to find her already soaking wet for me. I slide my finger in and out, in and out, priming the pump. When her body tells me she's ready for me to ramp things up, I spread her pussy apart with my finger and thumb, all the way, baring her swollen clit to me—a sight that makes my mouth water and my cock jolt.

I'm dying to lean in and assault that hard bud staring at me. But I know Amy's basically never been eaten before. At least, not right. I want to make sure to give her plenty of time to relax into it.

I blow on her clit. Little puffs of air to let her know I'm coming in hot and there's nothing to fear—nothing to recoil from— and when she moans and writhes in response, clearly turned on, I slide the pad of my thumb inside her, getting it nice and lubricated, and then press it down firmly against her clit, while feverishly kissing and licking the flesh surrounding my thumb.

Holy fuck. Amy is already on fire. In response to my gentle assault, she fists my hair, shoves herself into my thumb and mews like a kitten. *A sex kitten.* And that's how I know she's ready. Time to start eating this pussy cat, in earnest.

My thumb still in place, I run my tongue over her slit several times, getting her acclimated to the sensation. I harden my tongue and slip it inside her wet entrance, and then flicker and lick, getting as deep inside her as I can go.

In reply, Amy groans and coos and begins gripping my hair, even harder, letting me know she's aching for it. Dying for it. *Begging for it.*

My cock aching and my heart pounding, I release my thumb and replace it with my hungry lips and tongue and teeth. And the woman goes gloriously ballistic on me. As my mouth continues its hungry assault, I slide two fingers inside her and find her G-spot, which I'm thrilled to discover is swollen and malleable, and stroke her.

The movement of my fingers is languid, at first. Once again, I'm getting her acclimated to my touch—taking the edge off whatever apprehension she might still be holding onto. As my fingers stroke her, my mouth swirls and flicks and eats. Around and around my tongue swirls, while my fingers beckon her orgasm, the pressure and intensity of my strokes becoming increasingly insistent. I'm no longer getting Amy acclimated. No longer leading her gently down the path. I'm dragging her. Commanding her. Ordering her to come for me. *Right fucking now.*

Amy releases a primal growl that reverberates through my garage. She's clearly on the bitter cusp of having an intense orgasm. Her first vaginal one, I'd guess, versus a clitoral one, since she's the only person who's ever gotten her body over the finish line before now. It's just a hunch, but I'm guessing this orgasm is about to blow Amy's mind.

Her groans are downright desperate now, her pussy soaking wet beneath my tongue and fingers. She digs her nails into my shoulders, hard, which unfortunately are covered by a Henley shirt at the moment, so my flesh doesn't get to feel the full extent of the painful pleasure.

Shuddering with arousal at Amy's sounds, I slide a

fingertip to her anus and tap the sensitive flesh there, while continuing my assault inside her with my other hand. I'm letting her body know time's up. *I demand her orgasm now.* And that's all she wrote. The final straw for my little newbie head case. Her body instantly unravels.

As Amy roars with pleasure, her inner muscles clench and unclench against my fingers inside her. She's cursing, growling, and screaming through her orgasm, losing her mind as those waves of pleasure ripple inside her body. *Delicious.*

When Amy comes down from her climax, she's got tears running down her face.

She wipes them and apologizes, and I tell her that's perfectly normal. An involuntary reaction during a moment of pure euphoria.

"You're amazing," she whispers, her body shaking from adrenaline. "A sex god."

I chuckle. "I thought you said you'd be a challenge for me. At least an intermediate ski slope." I touch her chin playfully. "But you're a bunny slope."

She looks thrilled. "Am I really?"

"Oh, yeah. Absolutely. You're a sex kitten, Ames." I smile wickedly. "This week is gonna be fun."

Amy bites her lip. "What's next?"

"I'm gonna fuck you right, for the first time in your life."

I rise to my feet, scoop her into my arms like I was planning to do before, and carry her into my house, pausing only to enter the code on my alarm and toss my phone and keys into a dish. When we reach my bedroom, I lay my beautiful little toy down on my bed, as she coos and purrs, while I begin slowly removing her clothes.

I'm moving like I've got all the time and patience in the

world, even though inwardly I'm a kid on Christmas morning. Thank the lord above I had the foresight to jack off in a bathroom at the party, right before we left, or I'm positive I'd have splooged in my pants during Amy's orgasm in the garage. Everything about that moment was nirvana to me, including knowing Kendrick Cook is probably lying in bed right now, jerking off to Amy Adams or Emma Stone lookalikes on Pornhub, while I'm the guy who got to eat this little newbie's pussy tonight.

When Amy's naked body is splayed out before me, I lean down and bury my face in her perfect tits, the same way I did in that guest room at Laila's party. Only this time, I take my time. I lick and kiss and devour, languorously, while gently stroking her slit. I'm leaving her clit alone for now. Giving her time to regroup, so she'll be ready for the hardware that's going to bang against it with each rocking thrust of my body in short order. The hardware she's got no idea about, at the moment, but will hopefully learn to appreciate when the time comes.

When I'm sated for now by my meal of Amy's tits, I release her hard nipple with a loud pop and straighten up until I'm straddling her on the bed, fully clothed, while she's lying beneath me, naked and panting. With a lick of my lips, I get off the bed and begin peeling my clothes off as she watches me silently with wide, appreciative eyes.

Wearing nothing but my briefs, I crawl beside Amy on the bed, my dick straining behind the fabric, and wordlessly lay her hand on my straining bulge and glide her fingertips to the metal hoop attached to the base of my dick.

Amy gasps in shock at the unexpected sensation. "What . . .?"

"It's a piercing," I explain calmly. "It won't go inside you when I fuck you. It'll never hurt you or cause discomfort. Its only purpose is to stimulate your clit with each thrust, to help you reach orgasm while I'm fucking you."

From the outside of my briefs, she cautiously fingers the small ring of metal attached to my dick, her eyes wide. Clearly, she's not sure what to think about this unexpected loop of metal, just yet.

"It's gonna make you come harder than you did in the garage," I say, smiling. "Only with my cock inside you." My smile turns naughty. "The holy grail."

"Can I see it?"

"I thought you'd never ask."

I peel off my briefs and reveal myself in all my glory, and to my relief, Amy looks like she's peeking straight into heaven . . . albeit through a peephole. She's obviously beyond excited. But, still, not ready to barrel through the wide-open door to the left.

"Is that a Prince Albert?" she asks, tentatively touching my piercing.

"No, that would be *here*." I bring her fingers to my tip, which is now slick with pre-cum. "Like I said, this type of piercing never goes inside you."

Amy grips my length and slides her palm up and down, her chest rising and falling with excitement. "I'm excited. I'm all yours."

I let out a shaky breath. "I'm gonna make you feel incredible, baby."

"I know you will. I trust you."

"Your only job here is to relax and *receive*—I want you to react with complete honesty. No worrying about doing it right. And no trying to put on a show for me. Don't fake a single moan. Do you understand?"

Amy nods, though I doubt she fully grasps what I'm saying to her. No worries, though. She'll understand soon enough.

Quaking with anticipation, I remove Amy's hand from my cock and crawl on top of her. As my tip teases her clit, I kiss her deeply for a long moment. And when our kisses become feral and desperate, when I'm positive she's dying for me to penetrate her, to *pound* her, I place her thighs onto my shoulders, finger my target to ensure she's wide open and ready for me, and push myself inside her, as far as I can go, until I'm balls deep and her body has relaxed and molded to mine.

When I know she's adjusted to my body's invasion of hers and is ready for a good, hard fucking, I raise her arms above her head and begin rocking, slowly, in and out, feeling enraptured by every sublime sensation. Every breath we take. In and out, as our bodies find their rhythm together. As my tip bangs against her farthest reaches. I'm in fucking heaven.

It doesn't take long for Amy to lose herself completely. As I begin fucking her, hard, Amy lets go. She moans loudly. Grips my shoulders and chest. Runs her hands across the planes and grooves of my pecs. My shoulders. My biceps.

Every nerve ending in my body, but especially my cock, feels electrified in this moment by tiny spasms of pleasure. I haven't had sex without a condom since Kiera and I'd forgotten how much better it feels. How much more natural and right. Although I can't imagine this rightness I'm feeling with Amy is solely attributable to the absence of a condom. If I'm being honest with myself—which is something I've tried hard not to do in relation to Amy this past week—I've never felt this level of rightness while fucking anyone in my life, whether there's been a condom between us or not.

I take a deep breath to steady myself, to banish that realization from my head. And when I know I've regained control of myself, at least for now, I pick up the pace of my movements. I begin rocking in a way designed to make that little hoop of metal hit Amy's bull's-eye, at a steady, rhythmic pace, bound and determined to push her to the bitter edge of release on a bullet train.

With a loud moan, Amy grabs my bare ass as I fuck her and digs her nails into me, making me growl at the delicious pain, which, in turn, only makes Amy lose her mind even more. I lean into her ear and tell her she's hot as fuck and feels like heaven. I tell her she feels so good, I'll fantasize about fucking her for the rest of my life. Maybe I shouldn't have said that last thing, come to think of it. That was probably stupid. But oh well, it was true. Regardless, the comment has had its desired effect.

As the words leave my mouth, Amy arches her back and screams my name before coming so hard underneath me, she not only bursts into tears again—she damn-near bursts into flames. Once again, like in my garage, I feel Amy's innermost muscles squeezing and clenching, ferociously. Only this time, I get to feel that sublime sensation—the bliss of her orgasm—against my cock. It feels so good, so fucking heavenly, my eyes roll back into my head as I continue riding her through it.

It's the sensation I fantasize about, often. The one I crave like none other, and I simply can't hang on through it a second longer, try as I might. Amy called me a sex god earlier in my garage. But the truth is I'm only a man—a mortal one with a very mortal cock. And when my cock gets physically milked like this, there's nothing this mortal man can do but release.

My eyes rolling back, I pull out and come all over Amy's incredible, heaving tits—not because I'm worried about her diligence in taking her birth control pills. But because I'm an animal marking my territory. At least, during this week of our arrangement. For the next ten days or so, until my scenes are done and I've found her a permanent gig that meets my specifications, I'm going to pull my little puppet's strings and show her what her body can do—provided, of course, I'm her puppeteer.

I'm not proud of myself for reveling in the fact that Amy will never have sex this good with someone else. She doesn't know it, and I don't plan to tell her, but I'm positive when she leaves my bed she'll be sorely disappointed by the next guy. The simple truth is that someone else could touch her exactly as I've done, kiss her the way I have—hell, another guy could have the same piercing and similarly sized cock—and Amy won't even come close to coming as hard as she's done with me. Why? Because I'm her fantasy, come to life, and I know it. The one she used to spy on while I practiced my drums in my bedroom . . . in a spot I *knew* she could see from her bedroom window.

It's gonna suck for her, after this week. When she finds out I'm the only one who can get her off this way. When I've ruined her for anyone else. A piece of me is genuinely sorry to do that to her, honestly, but an even larger piece of me doesn't care. In fact, that larger piece of me is reveling in it. Knowing I'm going to fulfill this woman's fantasies this entire week, and become her gold standard for getting fucked right, forevermore.

At the thought, I grip Amy's face and devour her mouth, putting an exclamation point on the cum I've left on her tits. And it's clear from her enthusiastic reaction she's experiencing aftershocks of pleasure.

"That was amazing," she whispers with a smile, as her body comes down. "Thank you, thank you."

I slide off her and lie alongside her, incapable of speaking, thanks to the unmistakable wings and lights in my belly. I take a deep breath and push through them. Ignore them. Deny them. "There's no need to thank me," I whisper. "Trust me, the pleasure was all mine."

EIGHTEEN

AMY

I snuggle next to Colin in bed and lay my cheek onto his bare chest, too exhausted to continue exploring his body any longer. Dawn isn't here yet, but it's threatening. For the past three hours, we've been tangled up in Colin's bed, variously talking, messing around, having sex, and talking some more. But it's clear we're both too spent to do anything more than lie here now and chat a bit more before falling asleep.

"I meant to ask you," Colin says softly, his fingertips brushing up and down my bare back. "What happened when you talked to Reed and his fiancée tonight? I saw Violet bring you over to them and I was dying to know if anyone brought up the time you walked in on them during the tour."

"Nope. Nobody said a word about it. Reed didn't even recognize me, I'm pretty sure, unless he's a brilliant actor."

"Oh, he is."

"But Georgina recognized me immediately. I saw it in her eyes. She pretended to be meeting me for the first time, though, so I played along. Violet was there, and I had no desire to embarrass that poor woman again. Plus, I'm still bound by my NDA, and I take that shit seriously."

"Not seriously enough to not tell me everything that happened."

"You don't count. I trust you with my life."

Thankfully, Colin's body language remains relaxed in the wake of my comment. In fact, he pulls me closer to him. Regardless, though, I should probably be more careful about what I admit to him, going forward. If I let my guard down too much with Colin, who knows what stupid thing I'll say that will reveal me to be the creeper weirdo I am?

"So, why didn't you do The Sure Thing on me tonight?" I ask, deciding to change the subject.

"That technique works best when the woman is completely relaxed and confident, and I didn't think you'd be able to get there with me yet, not without me boosting your confidence a bit first about how easily you can come with me."

I press myself against his naked body and sigh contentedly. "You're so good at sex. How are you so damned good? Wait. Don't answer that."

He chuckles. "The answer isn't what you think. I mean, yes, I've been lucky enough to have plenty of practice. Sex is like anything else. Practice makes perfect. But I had a huge head start as a teen, thanks to Dax's older brothers giving the younger guys some helpful tips and tricks. Dax's second-oldest brother, Ryan, has been especially helpful. He's my Master Yoda on anything relating to sex and women to this day. Any question I might have, I still call him first, and he never fails to give me fantastic advice."

"Sounds like I owe Ryan Morgan a big thank you for tonight. He taught you well."

"Yeah, but I'm the one who learned how best to put his tips and tricks into practice over the years. So, it wasn't all him."

I snort. "Thank you both."

He laughs. "I'm just teasing. Like I said before, the pleasure is definitely all mine. Sex with you is so damned fun, Amy—the way you go crazy at my simplest touch turns me on. Something as simple as a kiss with you is like . . . *Jesus.* I've never been with someone who reacts like you do. You are a unicorn. And not because of any welt on your forehead."

My heart is pounding. "Really?"

"Absolutely."

"I'm so relieved. I was scared I'd be boring to you, with all the sexual experience you've had."

"*Boring*? No. It's quite the opposite. I've never had this much fun in my life."

My heart stops beating. My breathing halts. Is he being literal? Does that mean we just had the best sex of *his* life, too? That can't be.

"In bed," Colin quickly adds. "Well, and out of it, too, of course. You're fun all the time. Obviously. So much fun. But I just meant that . . ." He trails off, and I can feel his body tightening up.

"Oh, I totally knew what you meant," I say breezily, even though I have no idea what he meant. I stroke his bare chest gently, luring him back to a relaxed state, and decide to change the topic. "So, tell me about that piercing. It must have hurt like a mofo when you got it."

Colin takes a deep breath, and I feel his muscles next to me turning supple again on his exhale. "It didn't hurt all that much. The woman who pierced me said it's the same level of pain as getting an earlobe pierced."

"Oh, well, I screamed bloody murder and sobbed my eyes out when I got my ears pierced, so . . ."

Colin chuckles. "How old were you?"

"Ten."

"Okay, well, I was twenty-five and drunk off my ass. Plus, Ryan already had the same piercing and told me what to expect. He's the one who'd plied me with tequila and brought me to the place to get it. So, I knew I was in capable hands."

"So, you wanted to be like Ryan, eh?"

He laughs. "Basically, yeah. As usual. I've always idolized that guy. When he initially got his dick pierced, I was maybe . . . fourteen or so? He told the group about it, and I thought he was so damned cool. But then I kind of forgot about it. Until two years ago, when things weren't going well with my ex, I called Ryan for some advice. Kiera's birthday was coming up and I told Ryan I wanted to give her a memorable birthday present. That's when he suggested the piercing. I'd already bought her every other sex toy under the sun, so I figured, 'Why not?' Of course, I now realize there was no birthday gift in the world that could have staved off our inevitable break-up. Things weren't going well because we were a ticking time bomb. But at the time, I gave it the ol' college try."

"Why were you and your ex a ticking time bomb?"

"You really want to hear about this, while you're lying in bed naked with me?"

I pause, so I don't blurt, *Hell yes! I've been dying to know what happened between you and that gorgeous dancer since you deleted her from your Instagram account!*

I clear my throat. "Yeah, I'm curious. I told you about Perry and me, so . . ."

"True." Colin pauses. "Basically, I felt like my ex was

addicted to drama and excitement. It always felt to me like she was testing me, wanting me to jump through hoops to prove my feelings for her. Picking fights so I'd grovel, even when I didn't feel like I'd done anything wrong. Giving me ultimatums. On her side of things, she thought I was uncommunicative and boring as shit. At least, when I'm not on tour. The thing I kept trying to explain to her is that my career is so batshit crazy and unpredictable most of the time and requires me to be 'on' so much of the time, I don't want my most intimate relationships to feel like a rollercoaster ride. I want them to be a safe haven, you know? Rock solid. But safe things were boring as shit to her."

"How long were you with her?"

"Almost five years, on and off. I hung in there much longer than I should have, in retrospect, because I'd met her right before the band took off on our first world tour—as the opener for Red Card Riot, as a matter of fact. I think I liked knowing, for certain, she'd gotten with me before I'd become 'Colin from 22 Goats.' That went a long way with me. Whatever else drove me to the brink of madness with that woman, I always knew she wasn't in it for the money or fame."

Well, I wouldn't be with you for the money or fame, I think. *I couldn't care less about that.* But what I say is, "So, you got a piercing on your dick to keep things from being boring as shit to her?"

He laughs. "Yeah, I suppose so. That wasn't my first foray into trying to spice things up for her. But in the end, the piercing, along with all my other attempts, weren't enough because *I* wasn't enough."

"For *her,*" I say. "You're more than enough, Colin. Just not for *her.*"

He kisses the top of my head. "You're very sweet. Sorry I went into such detail."

"I asked, remember?" My heart is thrumming as I dare to ask the thing I've been dying to know this whole time. "So, do you think you'll get back together with her at some point, or . . .?"

"No. We're done. If she asked me to take her back, I'd say no."

I sigh with relief, even though I know full well I don't have a shot in hell of being with Colin, long-term. It doesn't matter, though. Lying here naked with him, it's still a lovely thing to confirm he's not lying next to me, wishing I could be *her*.

"Enough about my ex," Colin whispers. "Let's not talk about anyone else either of us has ever fucked the rest of this week, okay? This whole week is about you and me. Nobody else even exists."

"Sounds amazing. Although I should warn you it's going to be difficult for me not to fangirl if I get to meet Seth Rockford this week."

Colin chuckles. "Sorry to break it to you, but he's a massive douchebag."

"*What*? Noooo!"

"Yep. Gary Flynn, my director, secretly warned me about Seth. Told me not to believe a word out of his mouth."

"But when everyone asked you about Seth Rockford at the rehearsal dinner, you said he was a 'prince' when you met him! You said he's 'every bit as cool as he seems in all his movies'!"

"You think I'm gonna tell the truth and risk someone posting what I said, only a week before I'm set to shoot my first movie with the guy? I didn't know your brother's groomsmen all that well. And I didn't know Kennedy's bridesmaids at all. I'm not gonna risk fucking up this movie for myself. It's a dream come true."

"I'm so happy for you. And for me. I can't wait to watch you and see, firsthand, how movies are made."

"I meant it when I said I'm excited you're gonna be there with me, Ames. I think your presence on-set will go a long way toward helping me relax in what's surely going to be a stressful situation." Without warning, he turns me onto my side like I'm a rag doll and positions my backside against his front. "Okay. Time to sleep, my little puppet. All this talk about the movie makes me realize I want to do some last-minute prep on my scenes tomorrow, which means I'd better get some sleep."

I make a soft sound of agreement, and Colin pulls me even closer into him.

For several minutes, I revel in the warmth of his embrace. The smoothness of his fancy sheets beneath me. As his breathing slowly becomes rhythmic against my back, I think about my amazing night. The glamour of Laila's party. The famous faces I met, all of whom were so nice to me. That was probably due to the fact that Violet was introducing me around, more than anything. Violet's a big cheese, being the wife of Dax Morgan and the little sister of Reed Rivers. Not to mention, she's close friends with one of the biggest stars in the world, Aloha Carmichael, and runs a popular charity lots of stars scramble to support.

But, still, whether or not everyone's graciousness toward me had anything to do with me, and everything to do with Violet, it still felt incredible having so many famous, high-profile people treat me like I belonged at that party. Like they were sincerely excited to meet me.

And what about the absolute best part of the party? Namely, the tortured look on Colin's face when I started flirting with Kendrick! Ha! I thought the top of Colin's head was going to pop right off! I was genuinely attracted to Kendrick and figured he'd be a fantastic Plan B, if I could swing it. But I can't deny I'm beyond elated my Plan A worked out, instead.

My brain tries to recall the image of Colin's face as he stared at Kendrick and me talking, but my actual memories are beginning to get scrambled up with images from a dreamscape, as my mind begins slipping away. Try as I might to stay awake and continue reveling in every amazing moment of the best night of my life, I simply can't remain conscious.

I feel my breathing slowing down and matching Colin's behind me. I feel my body surrendering to total relaxation and my limbs turning heavy, yet light as a feather. Until, finally, I feel myself drifting away into the most blissful sleep of my life.

NINETEEN

AMY

I *smell bacon.*

I open my eyes and confirm, much to my thrill, I'm lying naked in Colin's bed, rather than in my pajamas in his guest room across the hall. Which means the best night of my life wasn't a dream! It happened! I'm really here!

Giggling to myself, I roll out of bed, throw on a pair of undies and a T-shirt from Colin's drawer, and pad happily into Colin's kitchen, lured by the scents and sounds of breakfast cooking.

And there he is. Colin Beretta. The hunky sex god who rocked my world last night and made all my fantasies come true. Colin is dressed in nothing but gray sweatpants, lean muscles, and ink this morning, while standing at his stovetop, stirring something in a pan. And the sight of him sends a whole new round of fireflies coursing through me.

"Good morning," I say, entering the kitchen.

"Good morning," Colin replies. "I hope you're hungry."

"I'm starving. Last night was a workout." I peek over his

tattooed forearm at the food he's preparing. "That looks yummy. I didn't know you can cook."

"I'm a Beretta." He tells me about the meal he's preparing —a pesto-veggie frittata—and offers to make me a coffee on his fancy machine.

"That's a coffee maker?" I say, as Colin gets to work on my requested drink. "It looks like a robot."

"It's top of the line, from Italy," he says. "A total indulgence on my part. But, hey, I never know what to do with my money. I've got the house of my dreams. Three cars. I've paid off my mom's mortgage and bought her a car. I've also bought both my sisters cars—which is all they'll accept from me. So, why not buy stupid stuff like the world's most ridiculous coffee maker for myself and everyone I love for Christmas?" He hands me my drink and, not surprisingly, it's incredible. Which is what I tell him.

"It's as good as any cappuccino you can get in Italy," he says proudly.

"It sure is."

"You went through there during the tour?"

I nod. "Rome. My time in Italy was way too brief. I'd love to go back one day." I lean my hip against the kitchen counter. "Can I help you?"

"Nope. Just relax."

"I can do that." I take a sip of my cappuccino and let my mind wander.

"What are you thinking?" he asks after a moment.

"Huh?"

"You're scowling."

"I am?"

"Like this." He pulls a face.

"Oh. I didn't realize that."

"What were you thinking?"

"Nothing much."

Colin stops what he's doing and stares me down. "Okay, let's set some ground rules for this week. You're gonna have to speak your mind around me, Amy. If you're worried about saying or doing the wrong thing all the time, that's going to get in the way of me being able to deliver everything you've asked for this week. Sex doesn't happen in a vacuum. It's best when two people are super comfortable with each other, across the board. Not just in bed. It's best when there's trust."

"I trust you."

"Okay, great. I trust you, too. So, tell me what you were thinking about when you scowled."

My heartrate increases. "Just that . . . if you're serious about not knowing what to do with all your money, you could give a nice chunk of it to charity every year."

"I already do that."

I sigh with relief. "I'm so glad to hear that. What charities and causes do you donate to the most?"

"Well, you know Violet runs a cancer charity, right? For kids with cancer and their families?"

I nod. "She told me about it at the wedding. It sounds incredible. She's my hero."

"Yeah, she's passionate about it. So, of course, I give Violet's organization a big, fat check every year. Plus, Reed throws a few charity galas at his house each year and all three of us Goats always go to those events and wind up donating a small fortune. Plus, we perform at several charity concerts every year. Sometimes, we'll donate 'lunch with a Goat' or whatever to an auction. That kind of thing usually raises a pretty penny."

"Oh, wow. All that sounds amazing. I'm so glad you guys

do all that stuff. I believe those who have the most in life have a duty to give back—to look out for those in need."

"I believe that, too." But he looks unsure. He returns to the food in the pan, looking deep in thought. Eventually, he says, "Dax and Fish do more of that stuff than I do, to be honest. I'm happy to give, when asked. But I'm not leading the charge on that stuff."

"No?"

Colin shifts his weight. "You know what? I'm gonna take this conversation as a sign I should be doing more. I'll call my manager after breakfast and tell him to send me a list of some good charities I should consider helping, if I can."

"Oh. I wasn't trying to guilt you into—"

"I know you weren't."

"It sounds like you do a lot."

"Not really, considering what's sitting in my bank account. I've been feeling like I'm not doing enough with my money and platform for a while now. This conversation is only confirming something I was already feeling, deep down." He flashes me a crooked smile that reminds me of the ones he used to flash me when we were neighbors. "Thanks for speaking your mind. I want you to keep doing that with me, okay? No matter what."

I feel myself blush. "Okay. I'd ask the same of you."

"You got it."

We share a shy smile, before Colin returns to the stove and stirs the contents of his pan again.

He asks, "Would you do me a favor and run lines with me, as I finish making breakfast?" He motions to the nearby kitchen table and sure enough, there's a script sitting on it, its pages tagged with a host of colorful sticky notes.

"You got it, boss." I sit down at the table, put down my

coffee mug, and grab the script. "Oh, wow. You've got *six* scenes! I didn't realize that."

"Only three where I speak, though."

"This is so exciting!" I flip to one of the sticky notes and peruse the page. It's riddled with highlights and scrawled notes in the margins, all of which I find fascinating. "So, you're Private Sherman?"

"Yeah. I'm the 'dumb jock' who gets blown to bits in an accident during basic training."

"Oh, no. Poor Private Sherman."

"His memory lives on."

"Which scene do you want to work on first?"

"Let's do the poker party. My easiest one. Green sticky note."

I open to the designated page and skim the dialog. As Colin said, the scene depicts a poker party among Colin's character and the other soldiers in his unit. It's a light-hearted scene, it seems to me. One that's meant to establish each character's essential personality, with Colin's character coming off as a bit of a cocky fuck.

"Just so you know, I'm not gonna *act* right now," Colin warns. "I'm gonna speak my lines in a neutral way, so I don't get locked into specific inflections and speech patterns before we shoot the scene for real in front of cameras."

"Okay."

"That's what my acting coach told me to do, so I retain spontaneity for the real thing."

"Awesome."

"I don't want you thinking I'm the world's shittiest actor."

I chuckle. He's so cute. "No judgment. I know you'll smash it when the time comes."

Colin turns around and leans his hard ass against the

kitchen counter next to the stovetop. "The thing is . . . everyone else in the cast has lots of acting experience. Gary—the director—said I'll bring 'fresh energy' to the cast, but I don't know. It's pretty intimidating being the new kid on the block and working with all these seasoned actors."

"Well, they might have more movie acting experience than you. But they don't have more performance experience. They've never performed in front of thousands of screaming fans, all over the world. And it's not like you've never been in front of cameras before. You've modeled and done countless interviews and music videos. Plus, you did that stint on *Sing Your Heart Out*! You were great on that show, by the way. So funny and charming."

Colin's face is unreadable to me. Without replying to my pep talk, he turns off the stove, grabs plates from a cupboard, and begins plating our breakfast.

"What are you thinking?" I ask, when he still hasn't said a word. "You promised we'd speak our minds this week, remember?"

Colin sets my food before me and sits next to me at his round kitchen table. "I'm thinking you're sweet. Also, that's all the same stuff Gary said when he initially offered me the role. What I fear, though, regardless of what Gary said, is that he actually hired me as nothing more than a publicity stunt—because me being in the movie, even in a small role, will bring my band's fans into theaters and reach a whole new demographic that normally doesn't give a shit about Seth Rockford movies."

"Okay, but do the two things have to be mutually exclusive?" I ask. "I'm sure it's true, if you weren't Colin from 22 Goats, the director wouldn't have known you exist, unless on this alternate timeline you'd decided to become an actor in LA. However, just because you've got fans to contribute to the marketing effort doesn't mean you didn't also earn your spot in the cast. I heard the audition story you told at the rehearsal dinner. Nobody cast you without first confirming you'd be perfect for this role. I have to believe someone as brilliant as Gary Flynn wouldn't cast anyone in any movie, if he didn't honestly believe in them. That man is a living legend. Why would he risk screwing up this movie—and his *legacy*—for a PR stunt? No way, Colin."

Colin is blushing. "Thank you for that. That was all great to hear."

"It's all true. So, tell your pesky imposter syndrome to stop talking shit inside your head, or it'll have to answer to *me*. And let's not forget, I'm the woman who handled Caleb Baumgarten's bullshit for nine months. I'm not someone to be trifled with, honey."

Colin bursts out laughing. "Clearly not." He picks up his fork, which makes me do the same, and we begin eating the scrumptious meal he's prepared for us with gusto. As we eat, I compliment Colin on his culinary skills, and he tells me how he made the food. Which then leads to him telling me stories about how his mom and two older sisters always kept him busy in the kitchen as a kid. Until, eventually, we're pushing aside our plates and I'm picking up Colin's script to help him run lines on the poker party scene.

"That was awesome!" I say, after Colin's delivers his last line in the scene.

"Did I get all the words right?" he asks.

"Every single one of them."

"I have to get all of them *exactly* right. No improvisation allowed, unless the director specifically asks for it."

"You delivered every word perfectly like a true professional." I wink. "You want to run the other two scenes now?"

Colin looks far more relaxed now than he did before breakfast—like a whole new man—as he nods and replies, "Let's do it."

We run his two other two scenes with lines, and Colin mostly nails his dialog, only requiring a few corrections.

When we're done with both scenes, I put his script down on the table and praise him.

"Now that I've heard you," I say, "I'm positive Gary Flynn didn't hire you as a PR stunt. He hired you because you're a natural."

Colin's face lights up. "That's the exact word Gary used about me! Same with my acting coach!"

Oh, my heart. He's darling in this moment. So vulnerable and sweet. I lay my hand on his on the table. "I'm so happy for you, Colin. I know you've dreamed of being an actor since you were a kid. I'm so excited to have a front-row seat to you making your childhood dream come true."

Colin looks utterly shocked. "How do you know I've wanted to be an actor since I was a kid? I've never told anyone about that. Not even my family."

"You told Logan when I was in the room, hiding behind the couch."

He laughs. "What?"

I giggle. "You guys were watching a horror movie. My mother said I was too young to watch it with you, so, when she went to bed, I snuck out of my room and hid behind the couch to watch. And that's when I heard you telling Logan that's what you wanted to be when you grew up—an actor in a movie, like the one you were watching."

Colin lets out a sort of half-chuckle of astonishment. "I

don't even remember saying that. It's funny you remember that."

"Who knows why certain memories take hold inside a person's brain," I say casually, even though I know exactly why I've always remembered Colin's comment: because anything that boy has ever said or done in my presence that gave me a window into his soul immediately got filed away in a special drawer inside my brain labeled "Colin."

"This movie really does feel like a childhood dream come true," Colin admits. "I haven't said that to anyone else. I don't want to jinx it or come off like a total dork. Plus, I've been lucky enough to have so many dreams come true with my band, and I don't want to come off like a greedy motherfucker."

"There's no quota on dreams," I say. "As far as I'm concerned, they can be infinite."

His chest heaves. "I like that."

"You're allowed to keep dreaming and reaching for even higher stars, no matter how successful you've already been in life," I say, my eyes locked with his. "In fact, I'd be a bit sad for you, if you didn't."

His nostrils flare. He doesn't look away and neither do I. The air between us at the kitchen table suddenly feels electrified.

"Can I tell you something?" he whispers.

"Of course."

"I'm deathly afraid I'm going to embarrass myself tomorrow. Fail to meet expectations and get fired on the spot."

"That's not going to happen.. Even while running lines, you *became* Private Sherman before my eyes. I know you discount my high opinion of you, because you think *I* think you can do no wrong. But I'm telling you, you're an *objec-*

tively fantastic actor—a true natural—and everyone tomorrow will think so. Not just me. And so will everyone who eventually sees the movie."

Colin bites his lower lip, his cheeks flushing gorgeously. "The truth is, Amy . . . with my band, I've been feeling like the caboose for a while now. So, getting cast in this movie felt like more than a childhood dream coming true. It's a chance for me to spread my wings and prove to myself—and the world—that I can actually *earn* something."

"What? Colin, that's crazy. You have to know you're an insanely talented drummer."

"Yeah, I know that. I'm super confident about that. But I didn't have to audition to get into 22 Goats. It just sort of happened to me. And the truth is my beats aren't all that complicated. Dax and Fish could have found any other talented drummer to play them. There's no shortage of good drummers in the world. Even excellent ones. Anyone could do what I do."

"No. You can't discount the intangibles. The chemistry you three have—the creative input you contribute directly and maybe inspire indirectly the other guys, simply because you're there. I personally don't believe 22 Goats would have taken off like it did without all three of you in the group. All three of you were essential. Magic."

Colin smiles. "I appreciate you saying that. I know Dax and Fish both feel that same way. To be clear, they've never once made me feel like I'm riding their coattails or don't deserve an equal one-third cut of our royalties. Early on, we decided to give writing credit to '22 Goats' for all our songs, no matter who contributed what, and Dax and Fish have never squawked about that over time—even though, as things have progressed, it's become clear Dax and Fish are the real writers in our group. I contribute my drum parts and an occasional lyric or melody idea. But Dax and Fish do the lion's share of the writing. Plus, they now co-produce all our albums together. Fish also sings fucking amazing back-ups, in addition to playing bass and synth and guitar. And, of course, Dax sings main vocals and plays guitar, along with writing and producing . . ." He breathes out a long exhale. "We never talk about it, but the gap has definitely widened between their contributions and mine over the years. With each passing year, the more money that rolls in, the more I feel like I'm not completely earning my share. But see, the thing is I'm not *capable* of doing more for the band. I'm not like Dax and Fish. I don't wake up with random riffs and melodies in my head demanding to be turned into a song." Colin runs his hand through his hair. "That's why this movie is such a big deal to me. Whether I slay this role, or fuck it up, it's gonna be all on *me*. That scares the shit out of me, honestly, but being scared is exactly what attracts me to doing it. The band hasn't scared me in a very long time, if I'm being honest. Like I said, I'm the caboose. I play my drums and have fun and let them take all the risks while I rake in the money, along with them. But with this movie, I'm the one taking all the risks. I'm the one putting my neck out there, with nobody to hide behind, and it feels amazing."

My heart is crashing in my chest at the openness he's showing me. The vulnerability. "Thank you for telling me all that," I say softly. "I know you're going to slay your performance, Colin."

"I've never told anyone else this stuff. Not even Dax and Fish or Ryan."

"I totally get it. I had the same mindset about the tour. I wanted to do something scary and outside my comfort zone, even if I crashed and burned. I didn't want to play it safe anymore. I didn't want to have any regrets."

Colin nods and holds my gaze for a long moment, his dark, soulful gaze sending my heartrate through the roof. He grins after a moment. Bites his lower lip. "What's your dream, Amy O'Brien? Something tells me it's not becoming a celebrity personal assistant—not that there's anything wrong with that."

My breathing turns instantly shallow.

If I were to answer Colin's question with complete honesty, I'd tell him my dream is and has always been to become a mom one day. To have a family. Yes, I want to work hard at something in the foreseeable future and be able to pay my own way in life. I want to feel proud of myself for being able to do that.

But, still, at the end of the day, the thing I dream of the most, which is what he's asked me about, is having a family of my own with someone I love—someone who wholeheartedly loves me back. I know full well society says that's an antiquated, weird dream for a twenty-three-year-old woman. Which means it's not something that should be admitted out loud, especially not to the man you've had a lifelong crush on, who's *finally* relented and made your fantasies come true. All of which leads me to reply dishonestly to Colin in this moment, despite my earlier promise to always speak my mind this week.

"I'm still figuring out my dreams," I say softly.

"That's understandable," Colin replies. "You're still young. It's a big deal you figured out you don't want to go to law school. Figuring out the stuff you *don't* want to do gets you that much closer to what you do."

I try to force air deep into my lungs, but it's not possible.

"I think working for you this week will go a long way toward helping me figure things out. Thank you again."

"It's nothing. My pleasure. As long as we're being honest, I didn't ask you to work for me, only as a favor to you. I'm also getting something out of it. You have a way of making me feel relaxed and calm, like nobody else, Ames. And that's the kind of energy I want to surround myself with this week."

"I'm glad to be able help you. I'd do anything for you. Always. All you have to do is ask."

Colin arches an eyebrow. "Is that so?"

A grin unleashes across my face at his sexual tone. "Absolutely."

"Well, in that case . . ." Colin smiles lasciviously, confirming what I sensed a moment ago: he's suddenly feeling hella horny. His dark eyes blazing, Colin motions to my empty plate. "You want more?"

I shake my head. "It was delicious."

"And so is your pussy." With that, he rises from the kitchen table and grabs our two plates, revealing the unmistakable outline of an erection bulging behind his sweatpants.

"Well, hello, sir," I say playfully, my eyes trained on Colin's hard-on, and he chuckles in reply. Wordlessly, he rinses our dishes in the sink and places them into his gleaming dishwasher. But finally, he turns to face me, and says, "It's time, Amy O'Brien—time for you to experience The Sure Thing."

TWENTY
COLIN

After carrying Amy over my shoulder from my kitchen, I hurl her down onto my bed like a hunter tossing down his haul and she squeals excitedly. Man, she's easy to please. So fucking fun.

"A few ground rules," I say, sliding my fingertip underneath her chin while trying to keep my face stern and commanding. "As I've said before, your job is to do nothing except react, honestly. No faking. No performing. Understand?"

Amy nods enthusiastically, looking like she's gripping an electric fence, and it takes all my restraint not to burst into laughter at her adorable facial expression.

"Good girl," I manage to say calmly, even though this girl is making my spirit soar and my dick pulse. "I don't want to hear a single sound from you that isn't one hundred percent authentic. I need to be able to read your body and cues. That's how I'll know when it's time to do the next thing. You'll mess me up if you're putting on a show for me. Do you understand?"

She nods like a bobblehead and breathes out, "Yes."

My heart is palpitating. As excited as I am to get going, I'm feeling a bit nervous here. How else to explain this first-time-ever speech I've given? Normally, I jump right in, no instructions given. But this is a unique situation. The first time I'll be doing this technique on a woman who not only knows about its existence, in advance, but has also watched Keane's motherfucking video providing step-by-step instructions. That's a huge disadvantage for me, since the element of surprise is a critical ingredient to making the technique work like gangbusters. The Sure Thing works best when the woman you're fingering is wondering, "What the fuck is he doing to me?" Not, "Oh, I thought it'd feel better than that."

Plus, the dirty-talk component of the technique is all fucked up for me now. Besides being hot and always a good idea, a constant flow of whispered words is supposed to keep a woman from thinking too much. It gets her out of her head. Which, in turn, helps her relax enough for my fingers to work their magic on her.

But now, thanks to me drunkenly babbling to Amy about The Sure Thing like an idiot, she not only knows to expect dirty talk during this technique, but she's also most likely going to grade me on my performance the whole time. Maybe she'll think, "Huh. I expected the dirty-talk to be so much hotter than that!" And that right there would be enough of a distraction to keep her from getting into the necessary mindset for the magic to work.

"I'll do everything you say," Amy says, staring up at me from the bed. And she's so damned hot in this moment, so eager, I forget my predicament and lean down to kiss her.

When our tongues meet and begin dancing, Amy's body jolts and jerks like I'm licking her clit. I suddenly realize my worries aren't rational. I can make this work for her, whether she's seen that video or not, as long as I switch things up from the video enough to keep her guessing.

My confidence rebooted, I grip Amy's neck gently and stare into her green eyes. "Go into my bathroom and take a long, hot shower. Use the handheld spout on the massage setting, directly on your clit." Her lips part in surprise. "Pull it off before you come. If you reach orgasm on your own, we'll need to do this another time. Don't worry, if that happens, I'll still eat you and fuck you. But we won't do The Sure Thing today, if you come in the shower. Do you understand?"

Amy bites her lip and nods.

"When you're feeling relaxed and turned on in the shower, get out and dry off, and make sure to pee. Even if you think you don't need to go, *try*. It's important you know for a fact you have an empty bladder when you leave that bathroom. Do you understand?"

She nods.

"Good girl. Go. Take your shower—and take your time. We're not in any rush here."

Amy salutes me, turns, and practically gallops into my bathroom . . . which thankfully gives me time to gather supplies and perfect my game plan.

I grab a couple things from my kitchen. And then a few items from a toy box in my walk-in closet. I grab some white, fluffy towels from a hallway closet and lay them down over my sheets. I close the shades on my bedroom windows and turn on some sensual music to low. And, finally, I strip off my clothes and sit on the edge of my bed, waiting for Amy like a big cat with a hard-on, awaiting his prey.

"Hi," Amy says shyly. And I swear to God, when I look at her, I physically swoon a little bit. She's gorgeous. Her wet hair is combed back, drawing focus to every curve and line of her blushing face. Her nipples are hard and her tits mouthwatering. But the best part? That little smile of anticipation. This girl is ready. Already on the brink of her first orgasm.

"Why the towels?" Amy asks, motioning to bed, but she's no sooner asked the question than she notices the bottle of chocolate sauce on the nightstand. "Oooooh, fun. I don't remember *that* being talked about in Ball Peen Hammer's video!" She squeals. "I'm game, though." She squeals again.

I chuckle softly at her exuberance. Not to mention, at how fucking amazing I am. I didn't lay those towels down to protect my sheets from a little smear of chocolate sauce. I'm not going to douse the girl in the stuff, for fuck's sake, only tease her with it enough to throw her a curve ball and make her feel a bit naughty.

No, I laid those towels over my sheets because, God willing, my little newbie puppet is about to experience her first squirting orgasm before I'm done pulling her strings. Of course, there's nothing to gain by explaining that to her, however, since Keane didn't talk about squirting in that particular video. So, why raise her expectations about what's going to happen to her, even further? No, the best approach is to keep Amy soundly in the dark about that, and let it shock the hell out of her when it happens.

Breathing hard, though I'm trying not to, I grab a bottle of edible massage oil off my nightstand—spiced vanilla scent—and lead Amy to sit on the edge of my bed. When she's seated, I douse my palms with oil and begin massaging her shoulders. "Clear your mind," I whisper, before brushing my lips against her neck. "Think about nothing but my touch, baby. The fact that your clit is pulsing. Think about how wet you are for me."

I kiss my way down her neck, and she moans softly at every touch, making my erection pulse with excitement. I can't believe this live wire worried she's not sexual, when in reality she's the most sensitive and reactive woman I've ever been with.

"Inhale through your nose, sweetheart. Do you smell that?"

"Mmm. Vanilla. I love it."

"It's edible."

"Ooooooooh."

I try not to laugh. Even in the midst of sexual arousal, this girl is like an adorable cartoon character come to life.

"Inhale again," I whisper, after I've gained control of my urge to laugh, and Amy follows instructions while I continue kneading her shoulders. When her muscles feel sufficiently supple under my palms, I guide my little puppet onto her back on top of the towels. "Do you trust me, puppet?" I ask.

"With my life," she whispers back. And the thing about Amy O'Brien is I know she's being literal. This girl would place her very life in my palms without the slightest hesitation, without realizing I'm not even close to worthy.

"Nothing should cause you any pain," I whisper. "But you might feel uncomfortable and anxious, right before you feel fucking amazing. You'll probably feel like you need to pee, right before you have the best orgasm of your life. But you need to trust me when I tell you to relax and push through it and let go. For this to work, you have to trust me and not resist what I'm telling you to do."

When Amy nods, I open the drawer of my nightstand, pull out four soft cuffs, and begin slipping them onto her ankles and wrists. I've never tied anyone up for The Sure Thing before. At least, not ceremoniously, like this. The two things have never gone together in my mind. But I need to pull out all the stops with Amy. Thanks to that video, and me being her lifelong Fantasy Man, she's got the highest expectations regarding what's about to happen to her. And I'm hell-bent on exceeding all of them.

After securing each cuff to its nearest bedpost, I step back and admire my handiwork. Amy is glorious right now. Naked and spread-eagle on the bed. Twitching and panting with anticipation. My cock straining, I grab the vanilla oil and dribble it onto her bare torso, thighs, and pussy, that last spot making her moan. I massage her hips and thighs for a bit, making her yearn for the moment when I'll get to work in earnest.

For a while, I don't touch anywhere near Amy's pussy. I already know I can easily get her off the usual ways. But getting her to come as hard as *this* technique is designed to do —getting her to let go *that* fully for me—will require a much longer than usual build-up.

When Amy begins gyrating and writhing against her straps with enthusiasm, I grab the chocolate sauce off the nightstand. I drizzle it onto her hard nipples and breasts, and then lick it up with fervor while letting the tip of my cock slide up and down her slit.

The effect on Amy is hard to miss. Just this fast, she's going batshit crazy on me. And that's a mighty good thing, since I am, too.

When the chocolate is gone, I stretch open Amy's pussy with my fingers, all the way, baring her swollen clit to me. I blow on her pussy as she moans with excitement at every subtle stimulation. Then I flicker my tongue against her hard, swollen bull's-eye, teasing her some more, before leaning in to . . .

Holy shit.

Amy's having an orgasm already! I wasn't expecting that.

As Amy groans and writhes through her pleasure, I slide my fingers inside her, straight to her G-spot, and stroke that swollen patch as her body ripples and clenches around my fingers, in an effort to keep that orgasm going for her as long as possible. Clearly, it's nothing but a simple clitoral orgasm, based on what I've done to her thus far and what I'm feeling inside her. A run-of-the-mill O that's an insult to the intense kinds I'm going to be unleashing from deep inside her soon. But, hey, she seems to be enjoying this little appetizer, thoroughly, so good for her.

Not giving Amy's body a chance to regroup from her little orgasm, I begin stroking her G-spot with firm, confident strokes—and it's easy to ascertain the effect on her. That her pleasure is quickly skyrocketing with each precise stroke.

Breathing hard, I lean in and give Amy a deep, passionate kiss that tightens my balls, and she replies by gasping into my mouth in a way that tells me something big has just happened inside her. A sharp tightening, I presume. Whatever it was, it's clearly shoved her right to the very brink of ecstasy.

My heart crashing, I press my lips to her ear, still stroking her G-spot methodically. *This is it.* The moment I need to push her into the abyss with a steady stream of dirty talk.

"You're hot as fuck, baby," I whisper, my dick throbbing and seeping with wetness. "You've got delicious, perfect tits. The tastiest pussy I've ever eaten. You feel so fucking good when I fuck you—tight and warm and perfect—it's like your body was made for mine."

"Oh, God, *yes*," Amy chokes out, thrashing against her four bindings.

"Come for me," I whisper. It's something I never say,

simply because it's demoralizing for both parties if it doesn't work. But this time, I have zero doubts. She's on the bitter cusp of realizing. The ragged edge. All she's waiting for is my command. "Come now, baby," I grit out. "Do it. Relax. This pussy is mine and I'm telling it to give me what I want."

With a guttural growl, Amy releases forcefully, which sends my own pleasure spiraling, along with hers.

"Fuck me," she whispers as her body comes down. "Colin, I want you inside me."

"I haven't even done The Sure Thing to you yet," I say, smiling.

"*What?*" Amy shouts. Not surprisingly. I figured she'd lose her mind to find that out.

"Those orgasms were appetizers," I say. "I'm laying the foundation to get your body ready to be turned inside out."

Amy's eyes saucer. "*Oh my fucking God.*"

I laugh heartily at her expression. "Relax now, sweetheart," I say. "Let me take care of everything. You're about to feel something you didn't even know was possible—something a session with a vibrator can't even come close to achieving for you."

As Amy releases a string of excited, incredulous sounds, I return to the top drawer of my nightstand and grab the toy I've stowed there—an egg-shaped vibrator about the size of my palm that features a rubber spout that's perfectly designed to encapsulate the hood of a woman's clitoris. Unlike other vibrators I've enjoyed incorporating into my fun, this beauty never touches a woman's most sensitive nerve endings, but instead blows streamlined puffs of air onto its target. Which means, it's perfectly designed to complement my piercing. Thanks to this genius invention, I can stimulate Amy's clit, gently and precisely, as we embark on The Sure Thing together, while not worrying I'm *over*-stimulating it. That's important for a guy like me, with a hoop of metal attached to my dick. Because it means Amy's clit will still be open for business for my piercing by the time I get around to finally fucking her at the end of this magical carpet ride. Which, of course, is the whole point of this for me, besides giving my partner pleasure. Getting to experience the holy grail for myself.

After quite a bit of research, I ordered this vibrator as a Valentine's gift for Kiera, but then never got the chance to give it to her, thanks to her dumping me. And so, my meticulously researched gift sat in my toy box in my closet for months, wrapped in heart-covered paper, taunting me. Reminding me that, no matter what I tried, I was never enough.

But now, I couldn't be more thrilled my ungiven gift was still sitting there in that toy box, still in its packaging, when I went into my closet to formulate my game plan for Amy's wild ride. Indeed, I can't think of another woman I'd rather use this toy on for the first time than the little redheaded puppet tied to my bedposts—a woman who sends rockets of arousal shooting through me in ways I've never felt before.

I show Amy the egg-shaped contraption I'm planning to press against her clit. I explain what it does. How it works. And when she says she's excited for me to use it on her, I gleefully get to work.

I gently place the rubber opening precisely around her swollen clit and turn the thing on at its lowest settings. And as the vibrator begins pelting Amy's most sensitive spot with meticulously directed puffs of air, she instantly starts moaning at the tops of her lungs. So loudly, in fact, the sexy sounds lurching from her seem to be reverberating off the walls of my bedroom.

As I continue holding the Womanizer in place, I lean down and lick Amy's tits voraciously. I suck and bite her nipples. Whisper into her ear. I know I'm cheating a tiny bit by letting this miracle of modern engineering do some of the heavy lifting for me. But there's no margin of error here. Amy thinks I walk on water, and I need to prove her right. No matter what. At least, when it comes to *this*.

When I'm positive Amy's on the bitter edge of a clitoral orgasm, despite the fact that I've kept the vibrator on its lowest setting this whole time—seriously, the thing is barely doing anything at all—I slide my fingers deep inside her, way past her G-spot this time, to her magical A-spot—a place deep, deep inside Amy's body, as deep as my fingers can go, until I find the spot that feels like a seam.

When I find exactly what I'm looking for, I begin stroking that spot, beckoning Amy's orgasm to come out to play, while whispering yet another non-stop stream of dirty-talk into her ear. And, of course, through it all, my little helper—the Womanizer in my palm—remains in place and never stops doing what it's ingeniously designed to do.

It doesn't take long before I feel a sudden, sharp tightness seize my hand—a tell-tale shudder that informs me Amy's deepest core muscles are on the brink of releasing in explosive fashion.

My breathing hard and erratic, my excitement spiraling, I stay the course in every way, without variation. I continue stroking with one hand while keeping that vibrator in place with the other. I continue whispering to Amy that my dick has never been this hard, this wet. That I've never wanted to fuck anyone else the way I want to fuck her. Which is true. I tell her she tastes so good, I almost come every time I eat her. Also, true. I tell her, in every conceivable way, she's the sexiest, hottest, tastiest woman alive. All true. And soon, I feel her body squeeze my hand inside her so sharply, so forcefully, I know it's coiling up in anticipation of releasing like a hurricane.

I keep going, staying the course, expecting that orgasm to release for me, any second now . . . but to my surprise, that tightness doesn't release.

No worries. I'll help her along.

Dizzy with arousal, I slide my fingers to Amy's G-spot, dig my fingertips into that rough, swollen patch until I find a certain corded band buried underneath—the gland that's a tripwire for female ejaculation. When I get my fingers in place, I go for it, milking that gland with authority, without mercy, the same way I'd squeeze the last bit of toothpaste out of an almost-empty tube.

But still, to my shock, nothing happens. Goddammit, she's holding back. Too self-conscious to let go that last little bit and push through and release the pressure building inside her—a sensation I've been told feels exactly like a full bladder.

"This is the moment I told you about," I blurt hoarsely, returning to stroking her G-spot the usual way as I speak. "Baby, trust me. It's time to let go. You feel that pressure inside you?"

"Mm-hmm."

"Feels like you're gonna pee?"

"I am. I think I'm gonna pee! We should stop!"

"No, this is it," I say. "Those are the same muscles that release when you pee, but this time you're gonna come. So hard, you won't believe it. Relax those muscles the same way you do when you pee. Exactly like that. Don't hold back. Release. *Trust me.*"

As she shakes and convulses, I slide my fingers back to her A-spot and get her going hard again. And soon, I feel her ratchetting right back up to where she was before.

When I'm sure she's on the brink again, I slide my fingers back to her G-spot, back to that buried cord, and milk her, hard, yet again, while cooing into her ear.

"Don't fight me on this," I growl into her ear. "I'm telling you to let go and you're gonna fucking do it. Right fucking now."

With a loud roar, Amy digs her nails into my forearm, convulses sharply, and then hurtles into the most glorious, squirting orgasm I've ever seen in my life—one that gives me nearly as much pleasure as it's so obviously giving Amy. As she loses control of herself, completely, she thrashes in her bindings. Screams and then babbles incoherently about how amazing she feels. And then, predictably, starts begging me, desperately, to fuck her.

"It's not time for that yet," I say, my body on fire. "Baby, we're just getting started." With that, I remove the toy, crawl between her spread-eagle legs, and lick up her cum—my trophy—as she unleashes a stream of delicious noises and whimpers.

When I've completed my task, I kiss and lick and worship the rest of her body, careful to leave her pussy alone for a bit to regroup. When she starts making all the right tell-tale sounds again, the ones that tell me her body's ready to go again, I slide my fingers inside her, all the way to her A-spot, and start again, from the very beginning.

There's no need for me to get an assist from the Woman-izer this time around. Now that Amy's learned how to let go completely, how to trust me and her body's signals, I'll need only my fingers and voice from this point forward. In fact, I'm pretty confident I'll be able to get at least two more orgasms out of her with my fingers before fucking her and getting one more. The holy grail.

Twenty minutes later, I've successfully pulled two more massive orgasms out of Amy, exactly like I thought I would—though neither one was a squirter—which means she's now a glorious, moaning animal who can't stop begging me to fuck her. I'd love to keep going, but I'm too turned on. Plus, I have a feeling, if I don't get inside her now, she'll pass out from exhaustion and the holy grail will elude me.

Panting with excitement, I release Amy's soft cuffs, place a pillow underneath her lower back to maximize my angle and ensure maximum friction with her clit, draw her arms above her head, and plunge myself deep inside her like a man possessed.

At the invasion of my body inside hers, Amy growls and squeezes my hands, while I grunt and groan with relief and pleasure. Oh, my fuck, heaven itself couldn't feel more pleasurable than this. She's as wet and warm and perfectly molded to me as I've ever felt. I feel drugged by the sensations of pleasure overtaking me as my body rocks in and out of Amy's feverishly. I feel physically drugged. Like someone has shot physical bliss straight into my bloodstream.

My head spinning, I grind my piercing against Amy's clit with each beastly thrust, and, within minutes, I feel Amy's innermost muscles tighten and clench sharply around my cock, letting me know she's all cued up. I whisper into her ear for a bit, saying everything I know works best on her. And soon, forceful waves of pleasure begin milking my cock, launching me straight into the most eye-roll-inducing, intense orgasm of my life. By far. The pleasure gripping me, slamming into me, is so profound, so merciless, so consuming, in fact, for a moment I feel in serious danger of passing out.

As my body explodes and my vision literally blurs, I collapse, and then lie still on top of Amy for a long moment, trying to catch my breath.

That's when I finally process something I just heard Amy say, in the midst of all that pleasure. Hold up. Did Amy say she *loves* me, in the middle of that euphoric mutual orgasm, or did I imagine that? Because I'm ninety-nine percent sure I heard Amy say the "L" word just now. *Loudly*. Shit.

As the euphoria I've been feeling fades, a slight panic begins taking its place. Did she say she *loves* me? Oh, fuck. I think she did. Which means I've definitely let things get way too intense, too fast here. This is only day two of Amy's weeklong sexual education, for fuck's sake, and I already feel like we're butting up against the outer boundaries of our agreed-upon "no-strings" arrangement. Why'd I tell Amy all that stuff at breakfast? Why'd I open up like that? I've never told anyone that stuff. So, why'd I think it'd be a good idea to tell *her*?

Okay, that settles it. I need to cool my jets. Slow things down. Stop running off at the mouth. From now on, I need to remember our arrangement. *No strings. No promises. No leading her on to think otherwise.* It's one thing to role-play being Amy's fantasy man and another thing to start believing it myself. One of us has to keep a clear head here—remember this isn't a fairytale and I'm not her Prince Charming. And that person is going to be me.

I t seems like Colin has been unusually quiet today, ever since he twisted my body into squirting pretzels after breakfast. He hasn't been rude to me during the past six hours or so. On the contrary, he's been exceedingly polite— the same way he'd treat the receptionist in the lobby at an important job interview. Unfortunately, however, that's not the way a man should treat the woman he's fucked four times in the space of twelve hours.

I'm hoping Colin's weirdly polite demeanor toward me doesn't mean he's feeling anxious about something. But if it does, please, God, let him be feeling anxious about his first day on the set tomorrow, rather than about the unfortunate thing I blurted during my final, mind-blowing orgasm earlier.

I love . . .!

That's what I blurted to Colin during that final, massive O.

And I've been stressing about it, ever since.

Luckily, Colin had an orgasm while I said it, right on the heels of mine, so I think the odds are high he was too distracted to hear a word I might have said. Also, those two little words were buried in a stream of other ones, rambling ones, so that's helpful.

Plus, I was miraculously able to clamp my lips together and stop myself from saying the final word on the tip of my tongue—*you*. In fact, after a beat of weird silence, I managed to take a sharp left turn and add an entirely new ending to the phrase I was thinking. *Your cock*!

That's what I wound up shouting, I think, as Colin came inside me, so that all of it, put together, turned into: "I love your cock!" At least, I think that's what I said. Maybe that's wishful thinking. The more likely scenario is that I'm now dealing with the fall-out of me making a flat-out declaration of love to Colin during the height of pleasure.

Shit.

Either way, whatever did or didn't come out of my mouth in that moment, Colin has been acting weird, ever since. Right after sex, he kissed my cheek, said he was going to work out, shower, and then study his script. "No need to help me run lines," he said, as I lay in bed, freaking out about what I'd said. "I'm going to do some exercises my coach taught me."

"Cool," I replied lamely, my mind racing. "Do whatever you need to do. I'll keep myself busy today." And that's exactly what I've been doing, while inwardly worrying about what I might or might not have said in the throes of ecstasy.

First things first, I organized Colin's digital calendar, with his permission, creating a color-coded system for him to quickly surmise if an event or obligation relates to his personal life, band, budding career as an actor and model, or "other"—that last category including stuff like cross-over promotional appearances, charity events, and parties that might serve as networking opportunities.

After that, again with Colin's permission, I contacted his

manager to see if we could devise some better systems for Colin in terms of the way he's apprised of his various offers and opportunities. Based on something Colin told me last night, while we were tangled up in each other after sex, he sometimes feels overwhelmed and bombarded by the craziness of his life. So, I figured I'd try to streamline a few things for him, if I can.

Following that, I checked on Colin to find out if he was hungry or needed anything, and when I found him sitting in his backyard with his script in hand, I brought him a bite to eat, told him to sit under an awning so he wouldn't show up sunburned on the set tomorrow, and then—again, with Colin's permission—launched into devising an organizational plan for his entire house—for every closet, drawer, and cupboard. And then, with my plan in place, I drove off to an organization superstore across town in Colin's gleaming Ferrari, where I gathered all necessary supplies, using a credit card supplied by Colin.

Side note: I didn't want to drive Colin's Ferrari, and even told him the Range Rover was probably more my speed. But Colin said a "smoking hot woman belongs in a smoking hot car," so I giggled like a fool and relented . . . and then proceeded to drive that damned sports car so slowly and carefully, I got cursed and honked at probably eight times in the space of fifteen minutes, confirming what I'd tried to explain to Colin in his garage: along with my zero chill, I've also got exactly zero "need for speed."

After a quick stop at the grocery store, I drove back to Colin's house, *slowly*, where I unloaded the groceries and organizational supplies and got busy building a shelving unit in Colin's garage. But after an hour of manual labor, I was too exhausted and hungry to keep working, so I went back inside, showered, slipped into some soft clothes, and went in search of Colin to see if he was feeling hungry, too.

When I found the man of the house, he was reclined on his couch, fast asleep, with his dog-eared script on his chest. Admittedly, I stood over him for a long moment like a nut job, admiring his beautiful face in repose. The man is so freaking handsome. But after I snapped out of it, I headed into the kitchen, poured myself a goblet of wine, turned on a Spotify playlist of today's top hits, and started cooking dinner. Which brings me to the present moment.

That wine is in my belly now. The meal is simmering in a skillet. And, thankfully, I'm now feeling much more confident that Colin's weirdness from earlier had nothing to do with me and everything to do with his big day tomorrow.

I turn off the burner to let my sauce thicken, but before I've turned away from the stove to grab some lemons from a bowl on the counter, I feel firm hands on my hips. A soft kiss on the side of my neck. I smell the faint scent of Colin's shampoo.

"That smells amazing," Colin says behind me.

I turn around and slide my arms around his neck, and he rests his palms on my ass in reply.

"Hello," I whisper.

"You've been a busy little bee today," he replies.

"I like keeping busy."

"I never expected you to actually work for me. The PA job is supposed to be a networking opportunity for you."

I shrug. "I'm getting a salary as your assistant. I might as well earn my money."

"But I'm not the one paying you."

"Either way, I'm your paid personal assistant this week. I like working hard. I like being helpful."

"Well, damn, this is a pickle."

I raise an eyebrow. "How so?"

"If you're going to take your job seriously, then that means I'm fucking my personal assistant. And that makes me a douchebag."

I giggle. "I won't tell anyone, if you don't."

"But *I'll* know."

"I'm sure you'll find a way to live with yourself." I snicker. "Are you hungry?"

"Starving. And I guess I could eat food, too." He presses himself into me, and he's hard as a rock.

"There's no way I'm letting this dinner sit a minute longer. It's already over-cooked. Tell that hard-on to take a chill pill for now."

He looks down. "Take a chill pill, dude." When he looks up, he's smiling adorably. "He said he'll do his best. But no promises."

"That's all anyone can do. Do me a favor and set the table. Also, grab us a couple beers from the fridge. I got a variety pack of different craft beers at the store. Thought it'd be fun for us to try them out throughout the week."

"Great idea."

While he gets to work, I plate our food. And a moment later, we're sitting at Colin's round kitchen table, feasting on the over-cooked meal I've prepared. As we eat, the vibe between us is relaxed and easy, the same way it was this morning at breakfast. And I'm beyond relieved about it. Whatever I might have blurted during sex, it's clearly water under the bridge now.

As we're eating, "Hate Sex High" begins playing at random on the "today's top hits" playlist, and I immediately spring to life. "I love this song!" I say, bopping to the sexy beat in my chair.

"Based on its current position on charts around the world, I don't think you're alone in that."

"Do I detect a hint of jealousy?" I ask.

"Not at all. I'm stoked for Fugitive Summer's success. Not only because they're our friends, but a rising tide floats all boats. Any time a River Records artist has a smash hit, that's more money in the coffers for everyone's marketing budgets."

"Wow. I never thought about it that way."

"Music is a business. And hit songs are very, *very* lucrative for a label."

I listen to the song for a moment. "Even if music is a business, it's still art—a form of personal expression."

"Of course."

"And you can plainly tell Savage had something vitally important he wanted to say here."

Colin laughs. "What clued you in? How many times does he say she came *three* times?"

We both laugh at the raunchy lyrics.

"Do you think Laila was pissed at Savage for calling her out by name as the woman chasing a 'hate sex high'?" I ask.

Colin shrugs. "If Laila was ever upset about it, then she'd made peace with it by the time of the party last night. I talked to Dax and Fish today while you were out about some band stuff. And during our conversation, Fish said when this song came on last night—while you and I were messing around in that guest room—everyone started dancing and singing along like crazy, along with the band. Fish said Laila was singing louder and prouder than anyone else, especially on the raunchiest parts."

I run my fingertip down the bottle of beer on the table in front of me. "During today's phone call, did you happen to tell Dax and Fish where we were when this song came on last night?"

Colin cracks a lop-sided smile. "There was no need. I'd already told them about us last night, as we said our goodbyes to everyone."

I smile, taken aback. "I thought we were going to keep this thing we're doing a secret."

"Only from our families, so they don't flip out and assume we're jumping into something more than we are. But I have no problem with our friends knowing what we're doing. Do you?"

There's so much to unpack in what Colin just said, I don't even know where to begin.

He furrows his brow. "You're pissed I told our friends what's going on?"

My heart skips a beat that he's now *twice* referred to *his* friends as *ours*. "No, I'm happy our friends know."

"It didn't occur to me *not* to tell them the truth. I'm sorry if I—"

"No, no, I'm glad you told them." I grab my beer and take a long sip, hoping to camouflage the fact that I'm feeling tongue-tied and confused. We can tell *this* group of people about us, but not *that* one? We can eat meals together and lie in bed naked and tell each other intimate things we don't tell other people . . . we can kiss and have sex and snuggle . . . And basically act like we're in a committed relationship, in front of the whole world . . . *other than with our families?*

After putting down my beer, I take a big bite of food, yet again trying to hide the fact that I'm deeply confused. Well, shit. I can't remain silent forever. I might as well ask Colin at least one of the questions that's been rattling around in my brain since last night.

"So, did you feel like last night was a success for you, in terms of erasing any awkwardness between you and Laila and Savage?"

"Yeah, last night was great. I'm happy for Laila and Savage—anyone could see last night they're a match made in heaven." He presses his lips together, looking apologetic. "I'm sorry I had an ulterior motive when I invited you to the party. You had every right to be pissed at me about that."

"Yes, I know. But I forgive you. Next time, however, ask me for something you want, directly, rather than manipulating me to get it."

Colin smiles wickedly and then bites his lip in a way that feels tantalizingly sexual. "You're hot when you're pissed at me, Red. *Red hot.*"

He's never called me Red before. I must admit, I like it. "I'm not pissed at you. I'm annoyed with you."

"Still hot."

As we're exchanging lustful looks, "Hate Sex High" comes to an end and none other than "Fireflies" by 22 Goats begins.

"Ugh. Skip it," Colin says.

"No. This is my favorite 22 Goats song."

"I've heard it a time or two."

I giggle. "You're gonna have to deal with it. I love this song. I especially loved getting to watch a private performance of it at the wedding. What a dream come true for Logan and Kennedy."

Colin shrugs. "Logan said it was Kennedy's favorite song. We were happy to give them the memory."

I listen as the song heads into its first chorus. "Are you singing backups here?"

"No, I don't sing on our tracks. I leave that to Fish and Dax."

"You sang along to this part at the wedding."

"When we perform live, I'll sing along to choruses, where we might need extra vocals to add volume. But I don't sing during the recording process, when Dax and Fish can easily layer in multiple vocal tracks of themselves."

"But don't you want to sing, sometimes? You have such a beautiful voice."

He looks surprised. "When have you heard me sing? Did I sing in the shower this morning?"

"You had a solo in a Christmas pageant one year. Remember that? You and Logan were shepherds."

Colin looks flabbergasted. "How the hell do you remember that? I was eight or nine, so you had to be four or five."

"Maybe I've seen a video of it? Either way, your voice was beautiful. So rich and expressive—so much better than any of the other kids. And let's not forget I stood next to you at Logan's birthday parties, several times, so I heard you singing 'Happy Birthday,' and sounding better than anyone."

Colin chuckles and picks up his beer. "I enjoy singing. The sensation of it. I do it in the shower, quite a bit. But in front of an audience? No, thanks. I remember feeling like I had crippling anxiety for two weeks leading up to that Christmas pageant, and then felt like I was gonna barf the whole performance. Thanks to that experience, I harbor zero delusions about me taking the mic away from Dax or Fish, at our concerts. I'm perfectly happy banging away on my drums in the back and singing along to choruses."

I know Colin is trying to infuse his story with self-deprecating humor, but his vulnerability is peeking through. He
suffered "crippling anxiety" as a kid? That's an awfully strong
choice of words. An incredibly sexy choice of words, if you
ask me.

I rise from my seat at the table and move to him, like he's
pulling me on a string. Every version of Colin is gorgeous to
me. But Vulnerable Colin lights my fire like nobody else.

When I reach Colin in his chair, I straddle him, slide onto
his lap, and kiss him deeply. Colin returns my kiss with
passion, until we're both gyrating and grinding into each
other. Making out like horny teenagers.

To my surprise, as the song reaches its third chorus, Colin
begins whisper-singing along with the track into my ear, and
then doesn't stop singing along during the quiet, intimate
outro:

Oh, Fireflies
Oh, In your eyes
Oh, Fireflies
Oh, In your eyes

Fireflies
Fireflies
You got me feelin' 'em
With you
And nobody else
You're a flower
A road
A destination

Would give my soul to the devil
My soul to the devil
To feel
Those
Fireflies
In my belly
Again

As the song ends, I rise from Colin's lap and remove every stich of my clothing as he watches me with dark, hungry eyes and does the same. When our clothes are crumpled on the floor, I sink to my knees and take his straining, hard length into my mouth. I lick and suck and worship him, saying everything I can't say in words, without defying the express boundaries of our arrangement: *I'm all yours, to do with as you please. Even if that's breaking my fucking heart.*

I don't want to care this deeply for a man who views me as a non-starter. But so it is. I love him. Always have and always will. He's my kryptonite, and I can't change that, though I wish I could. I'm going to get my heart broken in a few days, when it's time for our "no-strings arrangement" to end. But as I kneel before Colin and worship his cock with my mouth, I decide to exist only in the present and enjoy this romantic, white-hot ride, even though I know Colin will almost certainly break my heart in the end.

[Go to http://www.laurenrowebooks.com/22-goats-fireflies to listen to "Fireflies" by 22 Goats]

TWENTY-TWO

COLIN

I think it's possible I'm not quite as terrible an actor as I thought I'd be. Or, hell, maybe I am, and I got lucky yesterday. I've certainly played poker with my best friends lots of times in real life, so filming a fake poker party didn't feel like much of a stretch. When we shoot today's scene, on the other hand—the one my acting coach calls my "tantrum" scene—I'm sure I'll find out acting isn't quite as easy-peasy as it seemed yesterday.

Thank God, Amy is here with me. Not only because her calming energy and sweet smile have a way of putting me at ease, but because she's unexpectedly found a way to make herself incredibly useful. Not only to me, but to several other actors and higher-ups at the production company, too, including the woman in charge of production assistants. Clever girl.

At present, I'm sitting with Amy in the mess tent. As we've been eating lunch at our small table, she's been running lines with me for this afternoon's big tantrum scene—the one where my character, Private Sherman, has a testosterone-infused freak-out after searching frantically for, and failing to find, his lucky penny.

"Mind if I sit here?" a male voice asks, interrupting Amy midsentence. And when we turn to look, none other than the A-list star of our movie—Seth Rockford—the man whose name gets any project in Hollywood greenlit—is standing at the edge of our table.

"Hey, Seth. Yes, of course." As Seth sits with his plate, I gesture to Amy. "This is Amy O'Brien, my good friend and personal assistant."

Seth nods at Amy. "Hello."

"I'm so excited to meet you, Mr. Rockford! I'm a huge fan!"

"Call me Seth. Thank you." Seth shakes Amy's trembling hand. "Love the hair. I'm a sucker for a pretty redhead."

Oh, no, he didn't.

"*Ooh*," Amy coos, her cheeks blooming to match her hair. "Thank you. I dyed it recently. I'd been wanting to go red for a long time."

"I would have thought it's natural. You've got the perfect coloring for red hair. It brings out the gorgeous green of your eyes."

Gorgeous green?

Pretty redhead?

Oh, fuck no.

Did the man not hear me say Amy is my "good friend"? Doesn't he realize that's code for "I'm sleeping with her"? I already knew Seth is a secret asshole, based on some stories people have whispered to me, but I'm definitely getting a firsthand glimpse of his assholery now. Is he not going to at least *ask* me if I'm fucking my assistant before hitting on her?

Or does he think every young, fawning, obviously star-struck woman is his for the taking?

I clear my throat, loudly, reminding Seth I'm still sitting right here, motherfucker, and ask, "So, Seth, how are you feeling about the shoot thus far?"

Seth wrenches his eyes off Amy and ignores my question. "I need a small favor from you, Colin."

"Oh."

Amy pops up. "I'll let you two talk shop!"

"You don't need to go, sweetheart," Seth says. "This little favor isn't confidential."

Sweetheart?

"No, no," Amy says, turning beet-red. "I'll leave you two *actors* to chat. Margaret asked me to help her with something when I had the chance, anyway. Bye now!" She flashes me a beaming smile that makes my heart skip a beat. And I know, without a doubt, Amy has no idea she was just hit on, in earnest, by the top-paid actor in Hollywood, but instead thinks it's a thrilling thing for *me* that Seth has plopped himself down at our table to ask me for a favor.

"Text me if you need anything, boss!" Amy calls out as she turns to go. "Bye, Mr. Rockford—Seth!" And off she goes, practically tripping over her feet as she skitters away.

"She's cute," Seth says, watching Amy careen away.

"Yeah, I've known her for a long time. She's very special to me." He's still watching Amy running away. I clear my throat. "So, what's this favor, Seth?"

Seth peels his gaze off Amy's departing frame and flashes me his best movie-star smile. "My fifteen-year-old son is a huge 22 Goats fan, and it's his birthday next month."

Here we go. Despite what I'd heard about Seth being an extremely "transactional" kind of person, I was pleasantly surprised at how welcoming he was to me at the table read the week before last. He was so warm and welcoming toward me, in fact, I thought perhaps the gossip I'd heard about him was sour grapes or exaggeration.

But now, in a flash, I know it was all true—that Seth was grooming me last week to pave the way for this request, whatever it's going to be. Surely, a guy with an ego the size of Seth Rockford's won't be satisfied to get the usual VIP treatment—backstage passes and front row seats to a show. No, my gut tells me he's going to ask for something much bigger than that.

"My son just started playing drums," Seth continues. "I was hoping you'd come by my house in the next few weeks, before the production moves to Hawaii, and give him a private lesson."

I cringe. It's an even bigger ask than I was anticipating. Why do rich, powerful people always think they can have anything or anyone they want because of who they are? I've met quite a few people like Seth the last few years, and I'm constantly amazed at how incapable they are of forging genuine friendships—the kind I have with Dax and Fish and all of Dax's siblings. With Logan, too. When Logan asked me for that favor for Amy a year ago, the first-ever favor he'd asked me for, he sounded sick to his stomach. Even after I'd said it was nothing, no problem at all, Logan apologized profusely.

But Seth Rockford? Ha! He expects me to come to his house to give a newbie drummer a private lesson, just because he asked. If the situation were reversed, if I had a son who was a fan of Seth Rockford movies, and my kid was enrolled in freshman drama class at school, would Seth happily come to *my* house and give *my* son acting lessons, as a favor to me?

Of course, he wouldn't! Because it'd be the height of narcissism for me to even *ask* one of the top-paid actors in the world to humble himself that way! But how could I possibly say no to *the* Seth Rockford, who's not only the star of our movie, but also credited as a co-producer?

"Sure thing, Seth," I reply, even though I want to tell him that's not a "small" favor.

"Don't worry, I'll pay you back," Seth says. "I overheard you telling Margaret your little redhead is looking for a permanent PA position after your scenes are in the can. I'll make sure your friend gets hired and assigned to me, personally, once we get to Hawaii." He winks.

Hell to the fucking no. Every fiber of my body is recoiling at the thought of Seth coming anywhere near Amy. But what if my gut is wrong and this mega-movie star is genuinely willing to help Amy get a plumb assignment—and in Hawaii, no less—with zero expectation that sucking his dick would be one of her job duties?

Nope. I can't deny what my gut feeling is telling me. *The man can't be trusted.*

"I wouldn't talk to Margaret about Amy yet," I reply. "Thanks for the offer, but I think she's got a few irons in the fire."

Seth makes a face like my comment is pure lunacy. "Don't be silly. You're doing a favor for me, so I'll do one for you. That's what friends do for each other." Seth smiles broadly, but the skin around his eyes doesn't crinkle. True, that could be because of the copious amounts of Botox in his face. But I'm inclined to think it's because of his good old-fashioned *insincerity.*

Amy appears, out of nowhere. She's breathless. Adorable. Trying to act like this is totally normal for her. But her excitement is wafting off her. "Hi! Sorry to bother you, gentleman. Hello. Sorry. Margaret told me to fetch you two and tell you to go to hair and makeup now, please." She throws up her arms like she's yelling surprise at a birthday party. "They're setting up for this afternoon's exciting scene!"

TWENTY-THREE
COLIN

"Quiet on the set," the assistant director says.

We're in the barracks set, built for us by the movie's design team. Cameras are set up and ready to go. All actors in this scene, including Seth and me and Rob, the actor who plays Private Hawkings, are on our marks. All necessary crew members are now in position, while all unnecessary ones, including Amy, have found an unobtrusive place to observe. We're only waiting on Gary, our director, who's apparently framing his shots in the monitors tent.

While waiting, I decide to use the time to think about Private Sherman's emotions and headspace.

In this scene, after frantically looking for my lucky penny to no avail, I conclude my best friend, Private Hawkings, must have swiped it, since he's the one who razzed me about my superstitions during the poker party. And that conclusion sets me off. Not because of the missing penny, itself. But because I'm scared shitless to die in combat and the penny is my irrational way of coping with that fear. Thinking my best friend took it from me, when he knows I believe it's the one thing standing between me and certain death, feels like a mammoth betrayal to me. So, what do I do? I lose control and rant about the stupid penny.

In preparing for this scene, my coach told me to think about a time when I've felt rejected or betrayed by someone I cared deeply about. So, of course, I thought about Kiera. But even with such a perfect person to think about while practicing the scene, I've never felt in rehearsals like I've reached my fullest potential.

I've been hoping when the time came, when I was in costume and in front of cameras, and I could feed off the other actors' energy, I'd rise to the occasion. Fingers crossed I'm right about that, or the jig will finally be up. If I crash and burn during this scene today, I think it's likely Gary will finally realize he messed up by casting a drummer, instead of an actor, to play Private Sherman.

"Okay, everyone," the assistant director says. "Gary's ready. Ready, Colin?"

I find Amy's adorable face at the back of the crowd and take a deep breath. "Ready."

Gary appears, sporting big-time dad energy, as usual. "Everyone set," he says. "Rolling . . . and . . . *action.*"

And off we go.

As rehearsed, I begin rummaging through the footlocker at the edge of my cot, searching frantically for my lucky penny. When I can't find it, I tell myself to think about Kiera dumping me. But when I straighten up and turn around to deliver my lines . . . it's not Kiera's face I see. *It's Amy's.* Specifically, I'm suddenly imagining Seth gripping Amy's red hair, as he pushes her down and forces her to suck his cock, all in the name of him doing *me* a motherfucking favor.

I lose my shit.

Not about some stupid penny.

For real.

Without conscious thought, my scripted lines pour out of me, like I'm thinking of them on the fly. I'm in a weird, alternate dimension right now. I'm Private Sherman, saying all the right words. Feeling all the right rage toward Private Hawkings, while still being *me.* The guy who'd fucking kill Seth Rockford if he lays a motherfucking pinky on my woman.

Mine.

Mine.

Mine.

She's all mine, motherfucker! Every bit as much as that motherfucking penny!

"Cut!" Gary yells. And everyone on-set applauds and whoops. "Great job, Colin. Excellent."

Trembling, I look at my director to find him smiling. The other actors tell me that was a great take, and I thank them softly. Eventually, my gaze lands on Amy in the far back. And when it does, I know, even from this distance, she's sobbing.

When our gazes mingle, Amy smiles through her tears and blows me an enthusiastic kiss with both hands, and I can't help smiling broadly in reply. Amy's reaction was the one I wanted to see most in this moment—even more than Gary's. Amy's the one I trust to tell me the truth. Not in words. But with that expressive face of hers. The girl can't hide a single emotion, no matter how hard she tries. And thanks to Amy's face, I know I kicked ass. *I know it.* Which means I can finally breathe deeply for the first time today.

"Let's do that again," Gary says calmly. "Just to have some options during editing."

"You got it," I reply. I find Amy's face in the back again and wink, before returning to Gary. "I'm ready whenever you are."

TWENTY-FOUR

"Colin was amazing today," I say. "He's as good as any actor you could possibly name."

Colin throws his head back next to me and laughs uproariously. "Don't lie to them, Ames!"

"I'm not! You were incredible."

Colin and I are at his house, sitting on his couch while catching up with the new Mr. and Mrs. O'Brien on FaceTime. At the beginning of our call, we talked about the wedding and honeymoon, from which Logan and Kennedy returned last night. After that, we talked about Laila's birthday party— although Colin and I didn't mention what we did in Laila's guest room. And now, we're telling the happy couple about the first two days of shooting on Colin's movie.

"I can't wait to watch tomorrow's big scene," I say, clapping my palms together excitedly. "Private Sherman is going to die a bloody, dramatic death!" I turn to Colin next to me on the couch. "Do you know if Gary's sticking to the planned shooting schedule tomorrow?"

"Yeah, he said it's full steam ahead. After we get my death

scene in the can, he said we'll resurrect me and shoot all my earlier non-speaking scenes for the rest of the week."

"What are your non-speaking scenes?" Kennedy asks.

"Group scenes, basically," Colin replies. "I think there's going to be a montage of basic training. You know, stuff where everyone in the unit shines their boots, cleans their guns, and does physical training. I think there's gonna be some 'man-candy' stuff, too. Shower scenes showing our asses or whatever."

Logan laughs. "Sounds like they know how to sell tickets to half their audience."

"Yeah, the half that includes me," Kennedy says, giggling.

"And me!" I add enthusiastically, and instantly regret it. That was okay for me to say, right? It doesn't mean I'm having sex with Colin, if I'm excited to see his bare ass in a shower. Kennedy said the same thing and *she's* not secretly screwing Colin.

Oh, God, I'm terrible at lying and keeping secrets! Colin should have made me sign an NDA. Then I'd know for sure how to keep my big mouth shut.

Logan says to me, "Are you still staying at Colin's house?"

My heartrate spikes. "Yeah, that's most convenient for me, since we're driving to the same place every day."

"Don't worry, I hooked Amy up with my best guest room," Colin quickly adds.

I feel myself blush at the lie. Why are we lying to Logan, again? Especially when all Colin's friends know the truth? I know Logan used to be intensely protective of me when we were much younger. But I can't imagine he'd lose his mind to find out Colin and I are sleeping together. He knows I was with Perry in college for a year, so he can't reasonably think

I'm still a virgin. And even if he did think that, so what? I can have sex with anyone I want and that's none of my big brother's business.

"You guys wouldn't believe the way Amy has organized my entire house in the short time she's been staying here," Colin says, drawing me from my thoughts. "Everything is labeled and organized, top to bottom."

"Oh, I believe it," Kennedy says. "When Amy came to visit us for a weekend, she packed a label maker with her."

"What the fuck, dude?" Colin says. "You didn't pack a label maker to come to my house! I feel cheated."

"Don't," I reply. "I bought one with your credit card."

Everyone laughs.

"Amy's made herself indispensable to me on the set," Colin says, smiling at me. "I didn't even think I'd want a PA this week. I figured I'd introduce Amy around and let her loose to charm the right people. Instead, she's been running around like crazy, doing a million things for me. Making herself useful in ways I couldn't have predicted. While *also* charming all the right people. Honestly, now that she's been on-set with me, I can't imagine doing this gig without her."

"Thank you," I squeak out, as fireflies ravage my belly.

"She's impressed everyone," Colin continues, much to my thrill. "When she went to get me coffee on day one, she got coffee for ten other people. And I'll be damned, on day two, she remembered everyone's orders and brought them their favorites, without being asked. Not only that, while delivering those coffees, she overheard one of the actors saying it was the anniversary of him meeting his wife, so she left a bouquet of flowers and a bottle of champagne in his trailer for him to bring home to his wife after work. He was blown away."

"It was nothing," I say, waving at the air. "There was a

flower stand a few doors down from the coffee place and I sweet-talked the caterer for that bottle of champagne."

"It was the fact that you thought to do it at all, without being asked, that was so impressive," Colin replies. "He was grateful."

"Hopefully, he'll be 'grateful' enough to hire you," Kennedy says, holding up crossed fingers.

"Actually . . ." I say, shifting my position on the couch. "On that note, I've got some big news, everyone. I've been waiting for a break in the conversation to tell you about it." I pause for dramatic effect. "Right before we left the studio today, the woman who manages all the production assistants —this woman named Margaret—offered me a permanent position on the production assistant team after Colin's done shooting his scenes!"

Kennedy and Logan whoop, but Colin seems less enthused.

"It's not a done deal yet," I explain, my stomach twisting into knots. "I told Margaret I'd think about it."

"Why didn't you say yes, right away?" Logan asks.

"In a couple weeks, I'd have to head to Hawaii for three months. I'm tempted, now that I've seen how interesting a movie set can be, but I was hoping to stay in LA for a bit."

"Are you nuts?" Logan says. "LA will be there when you get back!"

Kennedy and I share a look. She knows about my lifelong crush on Colin. Surely, she knows I'd rather stay in LA to be with him, rather than work three thousand miles away, even if the job is on a fancy movie set in Hawaii.

"We'll see," I reply vaguely, before shifting the conversation and asking Logan and Kennedy a question about their honeymoon. We already talked about the topic earlier in the call, but, luckily, they answer my question, and nobody mentions that job offer again.

Eventually, the call winds down and it's time for good-byes. I send smooches to my brother and sister-in-law, while Colin tells them it was great catching up, and we disconnect the call.

"So, you're not gonna take that job, are you?" Colin says.

My heart is beating like a humming bird's. Does that mean he's hoping I won't?

"I haven't decided yet," I reply honestly.

Colin looks agitated. He runs his hand through his dark hair and exhales. "Whatever you decide to do, just don't let Margaret assign you to Seth. I don't want you working for him, personally."

Anger surges inside me. That's what Colin is thinking? Not that he doesn't want me working three thousand miles away for the next three months?

"I didn't ask for your opinion," I snap. "And, frankly, I don't want it."

Colin looks shocked. "Well, that's too fucking bad because I'm giving it to you, anyway." His dark eyes flash. "I don't want you working personally for Seth fucking Rockford, Amy. Absolutely *not*."

My eyebrows lift sharply. "Excuse me?"

"I've got a gut feeling about him. Heard some things. I told you he's got a rep for being a douchebag."

"There are two sides to every story. Seth's been perfectly charming to me."

"He's grooming you."

I scoff. "Grooming me to have *sex* with me? Is that what you're implying?"

"Correct."

I throw my head back and laugh. "That's preposterous! Seth Rockford is a huge movie star. One of the biggest in the world. And I'm a nobody!"

"That's exactly why he thinks he can fuck you, if that's what he wants to do. Because you don't matter, in his eyes."

I'm floored. "I've talked to the man twice in two days! Both times, for like, twenty seconds. Your 'gut feeling' is based on *those* interactions?"

"And his reputation, like I said. Also, I don't like the way he watches you like a lion tracking his prey."

"Oh my God, you're insane. Not to mention, way out of line. If I got offered a job working personally for one of the biggest movie stars on planet Earth, I'd be stupid to turn that down, especially based on nothing but someone else's 'gut feeling.' Even more so when that 'someone else' with the gut feeling is a guy who's too ashamed of me to admit he's fucking me to my brother!"

Colin rolls his eyes. "I'm not ashamed of you. If I were, I wouldn't have told my friends about us."

"But not Logan and Kennedy."

"We both agreed to the terms of this arrangement."

"Did we? My memory is you demanded that condition of me and I took what you were offering."

"Amy, come on. I told you what a pressure cooker this situation would be for me, if our families knew about us. I told you how the weight of their expectations would make things way too intense, too fast."

"You didn't say any of that."

"I did. But if not, let me tell you this little nugget now: my mother has *expressly* informed me she's always wanted Beretta-O'Brien grandbabies!"

My mouth hangs open as my heart lurches with glee.

The tortured look on Colin's face tells me his shocking revelation wasn't meant to enthrall me, as it has. Quite the opposite. But I don't care. His mother has always dreamed of Colin and me getting together? Hot damn, that's an incredible thing to find out! A huge compliment! *Well, momma always knows best,* I think, my eyebrow cocked. But I'm not brave enough—or maybe *stupid* enough—to say it.

"Okay, never mind about that," Colin says, reacting to whatever he's seeing on my face. "That was meant to freak you out, the same way it freaks me out."

"I'm freaked out," I assure him. But even I can hear the lie in my tone. "Whatever," I say quickly. "Let's go back to your 'gut feeling' about Seth. Let's pretend you're right and he'd try to fuck me six ways from Sunday in Hawaii."

"He would."

"Okay, even if you're right about that, which you're *not*, give me one good reason why I shouldn't say *yes* to a no-strings arrangement with *him*, the same way I've said *yes* to one to *you*?" I've bowled him over with that comment. *And I love it.* I forge ahead. "Why wouldn't I jump into a fun little fling with Seth Rockford in paradise? He's a handsome, dashing—"

"*He could be your father!*"

"Yeah, and I've got daddy issues! We're a match made in heaven."

"Amy, for fuck's sake!"

"Seth is divorced, right? And I'm a single girl. So, what would be the harm in having a little fling with a rich, handsome movie star?"

Colin's breathing fire. But the fucker says nothing. Does he know I'm bluffing? Is that why he's able to keep himself from *begging* me not to go? Or does he simply not care enough about me to ask me to stay?

I'm suddenly enraged. Even if Colin *knows* I'm bluffing, so what? Is it too much to ask for him to say he can't stand the thought of Seth, or anyone else, touching me? Doesn't he know I'd throw myself at his feet and declare my undying love for him, if only he'd say that?

Oh.

Wait.

Duh.

Colin *does* realize I'd do that, which is exactly why he's *not* saying any of it.

Shit! This gorgeous, infuriating asshole is dancing through raindrops! Having his cake and eating it, too! He wants all the benefits of my fawning adoration without any of the responsibilities or commitments on his end!

I rise from the couch and pace Colin's living room, wracked by anger. "You don't want me enough to tell Logan and Kennedy about us," I huff out, "but you don't want anyone else to have me, either? Well, screw that! You can't have it both ways. Either what we're doing is no-strings and I'll be single when this week is over—which means you have exactly *zero* say in what or *who* I do after this week—or I'm your girlfriend and you're an asshole for not telling our families about me!"

Colin's chest heaves. "It's not that black and white. We've been doing this for less than a week, Amy! If we tell our families what's been going on, they'll start planning our wedding —and that's not an exaggeration." He shakes his head. "I'm not ready for that. Not even close. *Are you?*"

Of course, I am, you stupid man! Don't you realize I'm the creeper who's loved you my whole fucking life? That I already know for a fact, sadly, that I'll never want anyone else the way I want you? That's what I'm thinking as I stare into Colin's stupid, tortured face. But wild horses couldn't make me say any of it. In fact, I'd sooner die than admit that pathetic truth to him. It's hard enough admitting it to myself.

Using all my strength not to burst into tears, I open my mouth and tell the biggest lie of my life: "Of course, I'm not ready for that. I'm only twenty-three."

Colin's shoulders soften. He exhales from the depths of his soul. "Okay, good. All I'm asking is that you promise me, if you wind up working on the production after I'm done, you won't let them assign you to Seth. It's a simple request."

I scoff. "Request *denied.* I absolutely do *not* promise you that."

"Goddammit, Amy!" Colin runs an exasperated palm over his face. "Okay, promise me this: you'll let me know the second it seems like I'm right and Seth wants you to suck his cock as one of your job duties."

"And what if he does? You'll hop a flight to Hawaii and come beat him up?"

"If that's what it takes to keep you safe, yes," he says, without hesitation.

Oooh, I like that answer. But I keep myself from showing it. "Are you implying he'd be *assaulting* me in that scenario? Because, as mentioned, I'm pretty sure I'd say *yes* if he made a move on me."

Colin narrows his eyes. "In that scenario, Seth would be your *employer*, which would make your yes *legally* unreliable. You might say yes, because you felt like you couldn't say no. Because you thought your job was on the line. Since Harvey Weinstein got exposed, the film industry takes that kind of shit seriously, Amy."

"What the fuck are you talking about? I don't care what the 'film industry' might think in your hypothetical! In mine, I've entered into a consensual fling with Seth—a handsome, charismatic movie star, without feeling an ounce of pressure about my job. In *my* hypothetical, I wouldn't consider consensual sex with a handsome man an unsafe activity, requiring you to hop a flight to 'save' me!" I smirk at the smoke coming out of Colin's ears and decide to twist the knife. "Unless, of course, you're worried about Seth not using a condom with me. Is that the kind of 'unsafe' activity you're worried about? Because if that's the case, if you're asking me to *promise* to make Seth use a condom when he rails me, each and every night in Hawaii, and some mornings and lunch breaks, too, then okay, I promise."

Oh, man. He's losing his mind. Which, of course, was my intended result.

Colin fists his hair, his dark eyes bugging out. "There's no way you're honestly attracted to that blowhard!"

"I am." *I'm not.* "Honestly, I'd be excited about a handsome, rich, older man hitting on me." *Ew.* "Maybe I'll enjoy calling an older man *daddy* while he's railing me, three times a day in Hawaii."

Whoa. I thought I was playing with fire by saying such incendiary stuff to Colin, especially that last thing. But, no, it seems I was detonating a nuclear bomb!

"Not gonna happen, Amy! No fucking way." In one fluid motion, Colin lurches at me, picks me up, flips me over his shoulder, and stomps toward the hallway.

In his bedroom, Colin throws me down on his bed and proceeds to rip off my clothes like they're on fire. When I'm naked before him, breathless and panting, Colin peels off his own clothes, flips me onto my hands and knees, tells me I'm a bad girl, spreads my legs, and begins eating me out from behind while fondling my hanging breasts.

Almost immediately, I'm delirious with pleasure. Moaning. Grunting. Making sounds that don't sound human.

"Who's your daddy now?" Colin mutters behind me, before biting my ass, hard, and slapping my ass cheek. "You make me so fucking hard when you're a bad girl," he mutters, before plunging his full length into me from behind.

I growl with pleasure as he fills me, all the way, while gripping the comforter beneath me to steady me. As my body relaxes and molds to his, Colin begins pounding me, fucking me, *railing* me, mercilessly, in a way he's never done before. He's not teaching me what my body can do this time around —he's showing me what *his* body can do, when I've been a *very* bad girl. *And I'm loving it.*

As he fucks me, Colin begins fingering my clit with one hand while fisting my hair with the other. "You're *mine,*" he grits out. "This pussy is all *mine.*" Still thrusting into me like a beast, Colin pulls my head back by my hair. He kisses and bites my extended neck—that second thing probably leaving a mark—a sexy thought. And when I'm feeling right on the brink of release, Colin gruffly whispers into my ear, "I'll kill him or anyone who touches you, Amy."

I know he's not being literal. Frankly, I don't know what role-play this is. How this rough sex and possessive dirty talk meshes with the way Colin lied to my brother earlier. But fuck it all. I don't care. This is the hottest thing I've experienced in my life and I'm going to enjoy it.

"Come for me," Colin commands. "And say my name when you do."

It takes a few more thrusts and swirls of Colin's magical fingers against my sweet spot, but soon enough, pleasure explodes inside me as warm fluid gushes out of me. I choke out Colin's name, as commanded, as my orgasm shatters me, and a moment later, he releases inside me with a loud groan. My limbs give way as pleasure grips me, making me face-plant onto the mattress, and Colin follows me down.

"Holy shit," Colin murmurs after a moment, his chest cleaved to my back. "Jesus Christ, Amy. *Oh my God.*"

It's not the declaration of undying love I'd kick a puppy to hear from him. And I know dirty sex didn't come close to resolving the issues we argued about before lust turned him into Hurricane Colin and swept me into its path. But I'm so high on euphoria and sexual satisfaction in this moment, I don't even remember what pissed me off.

Like Colin said, it's been less than a week since we started having sex, and Colin isn't the one who's had an eternal crush on *me*. Whatever Colin might be feeling for me beyond broth-erly affection at this point, it's a brand-new thing for him. Whereas for me, this is the fulfillment of a lifelong fantasy. And so, while still feeling high on the outrageously dirty plea-sure Colin just delivered to me, I decide to accept things as they are, for now, rather than thinking about how I wish they'd be.

TWENTY-FIVE

COLIN

"They're ready for you, Colin," Amy says, peeking her cute little red head into my trailer.

"Thanks, babe." Fuck. I didn't mean to call her that. Fuck, fuck, fuck. I inhale deeply, place my script on a table, and follow Amy toward the set. If she noticed my endearment, she's pretending she didn't. Which works for me, considering I'm about to shoot the toughest of my three speaking scenes—my dramatic death—and I can't let myself lose focus right now.

We're shooting on the "firing range" set this time, where poor Private Sherman will die after his former best friend, Private Hawkings, makes a tragic mistake. As it turns out, my best friend did, indeed, swipe my lucky penny. Not out of malice, but to help me get past my stupid superstitions. Oops.

I won't find out what Private Hawkings did before dying in his arms. But the audience will, when Private Hawkings tearfully admits what he did later on, in a dramatic scene with Seth's character—and then, for the rest of the movie, tries desperately to atone for his sin.

"This scene is part of your gray matter, at this point," Amy whispers as we walk toward the firing range set. "There's nothing more you could have done to prepare. *You're ready.*"

As usual, she's read me like a book and knows exactly what to say to reassure me. "Thanks," I choke out, my voice tight. "Yeah, I've got this."

Amy brushes her arm against mine as we continue walking. And I'm grateful. Surely, she knows I'd love to hold her hand and squeeze it right now. But what professional actor would do that with his PA as he heads to set to shoot his biggest scene? I'm not a kid being dropped off at nursery school, and Amy's not my mommy. Under the circumstances, she's chosen the perfect way to touch me.

Shit.

I'm nervous.

Thankfully, Gary told me not to stress about the stage directions in this scene. Particularly, the part of the script that says "Private Sherman sheds a tear" as he delivers his last line to Private Hawking. Gary said tears aren't necessary to convey intense emotion. And that's a mighty good thing, because I don't think I've shed a single tear since my parents' divorce when I was a kid.

"You ready?" Gary, our director, says, as Amy and I reach the set.

"Ready."

"We'll film your close-ups first, Colin."

"Sounds great."

Rob, the actor playing Private Hawkings, appears and we exchange brief words before Gary begins explaining what he wants from us. He explains the explosives and special effects that will be used later, when our stunt doubles perform this scene after we're done. And, finally, Gary asks if we have any questions.

"Not me," Rob says.

I look to the spot where Amy said she'd stand and find her face. Instantly, calmness washes over me. "No questions from me," I say, returning to Gary's face. "I'm good to go."

We practice the blocking a few times, choreographing how and where I'll fall when I'm hit in the chest by friendly fire. Gary explains we'll redo portions of the scene again, from a wider angle later this afternoon, at which point the frame will clearly show my bloodied, ragged torso. But for now, Gary says, we'll do the scene in close-up to capture my face.

"Got it," I say, my stomach flip-flopping.

Rob and I get our guns from the prop master, take our marks, and wait. And then wait some more. And when Gary eventually calls "action," off we go, performing our choreographed moves, as rehearsed.

Thankfully, I don't mess anything up. At the exact right spot, Gary calls out "explosion!" for now—his voice to be replaced by an actual explosion, later—and I react accordingly, jerking back and clutching my chest, before falling to the ground, exactly as rehearsed.

Gary says everything was great, but let's do it again. So, we do. Four more times, until Gary confirms he got everything needed from that particular angle. Moving on. It's time for me to say my lines, in close-up, while dying on the ground.

Cameras are quickly set—two handhelds, plus one hovering above me. Gary says we'll capture Rob's face in close-up next, but for now, this run-through is all about Private Sherman's emotions as he says his dying words.

"Stand by!" the assistant director yells, and I try to get my mind right as I wait. I try to imagine what it'd feel like to know, for a fact, I was dying. To know my life force was rapidly draining out of my body and I had mere seconds left to live. I think about knowing I'll never see my family and friends again. I think about the things I'll miss out on because I'm dying so young. No wife. No kids. No more *Amy.*

What?

Amy.

Amy.

Amy.

She's my dying thought.

My *only* dying thought.

I'll never get to have a future with Amy.

What the fuck? I'm supposed to be thinking about my parents' divorce right now! That's what my acting coach told me to do, after we talked about various emotional triggers in my life. But out of nowhere, as I look into Rob's blue eyes, I see Amy's green ones. *I'm going to lose my chance with her, forever.*

"Action!" Gary says, prompting Private Hawkings to frantically shout his line.

Tears prick my eyes as my best friend holds me and I choke out my last words on this earth. I tell Private Hawkings to find the girl I love back home and tell her I love her. Tears flood my eyes. "Tell her to get married and have babies and live a long and happy life," I manage to say, struggling to get the words out, as tears roll down my cheeks. "Tell her not . . . to live the rest of her life . . . in love . . . with a dead guy."

TWENTY-SIX

AMY

"What an adorable house!"

As Colin parks his Range Rover in front of it, I'm looking at a small, ivy-covered home in North Hollywood that's enclosed by a rose-covered white picket fence—a house owned by none other than Keane "Ball Peen Hammer" Morgan and his wife, Maddy. We're visiting the couple on our way home from Colin's third day of shooting, after being invited to come meet the newest member of the Morgan clan: little Billie Morgan.

As it turned out, Maddy went into labor the night of Laila's birthday party, mere hours after we hung up from that FaceTime call at Dax and Violet's. And now that the exhausted new parents have made it home from the hospital with their bundle of joy, they've invited Keane's little brother, Dax, and his two best friends to come by.

When Keane and Maddy's front door opens, we're greeted not by Keane or Maddy, but by a strikingly handsome hottie with ocean-blue eyes and charisma for days. A man who looks like an older, tattooed amalgam of Keane and

Dax Morgan, albeit with slightly darker hair than both of them.

"What are you doing here, Ryan?" Colin blurts, confirming my suspicion. Colin wraps the hottie—Ryan Morgan, I presume—in an enthusiastic hug and the two men laugh and pat each other's backs.

"I'm in LA for business—getting stuff lined up for another bar location," the man replies enthusiastically. "I figured I'd come meet my baby niece while I'm in town. Someone's gotta sit Keane down and explain the daddy gig to him, or that poor little girl's gonna grow up thinking he's nothing but a Jungle Gym."

Colin guffaws. "There's no better man to explain the job. It's so great to see you, Rum Cake. You look great."

"You too, Colinoscopy. Congrats on the movie. I've been meaning to call you."

"No worries. We're both busy. Yeah, it's been a blast." He motions to me, as I stand next to the men fidgeting excitedly. "Speaking of the movie, this is my good friend, Amy O'Brien. She used to live next-door to me, growing up. She's been on the set with me this week, keeping me from having a nervous breakdown. Ames, this is the coolest guy you'll ever meet, Ryan Morgan. Captain Morgan. Rum Cake. My Master Yoda. I told you about him."

"Yes, I remember. It's nice to meet you, Ryan." My brain is racing with a thousand thoughts, all at once, including the following ones: *He's gorgeous. Oh my God, he's the one who figured out The Sure Thing! Holy shit, his dick is pierced!*

"You, too, Amy," Ryan says, shaking my hand. "Thanks for taking care of our boy."

"It's been fun."

Wait.

Hold up.

My racing thoughts skid to a stop, as my brain rewinds and fixates on the words Colin used to introduce me to this scrumptious man.

Good friend.

Used to live next-door.

Keeping me from having a nervous breakdown.

It's all true. Nothing false there. And some of it is complimentary. So, why does all of it, put together, feel like a punch to my gut? Didn't Colin say he only felt the need to hide what he's been doing with me from our *families*? So, why did he call me something as platonic as "good friend" while introducing me to one of his best friends?

Although come to think of it, what *should* Colin have called me? I'm not his girlfriend, after all. Should he have been honest and introduced me as his fuck buddy or friend with benefits? As accurate as those labels would have been, they would have been mortifying to me.

My heart stops.

The truth is mortifying to me.

Shit. That's never a good sign.

We follow Ryan into the house, my mind still teeming with thoughts, but the minute I see the adorable scene unfolding in the next room, I instantly forget my own worries and feel swept away by the purest form of wholesome joy. In Keane and Maddy's family room, little Jackson Morgan is sitting on a couch, his legs so short the bottoms of his sneakers are visible. On his lap, he's holding his new cousin, Baby Billie, and cooing adorably at her, while his proud parents snap a thousand photos.

New mommy, Maddy, is splayed out in an armchair, looking exhausted but amused at Jackson's exuberance, while new daddy, Keane, is perched next to his nephew, making sure his daughter's tiny head and neck remain properly supported by Jackson's arm and some well-placed pillows.

When Keane sees Colin entering the room behind Ryan, he pops up and greets him warmly, before surprising me with a warm hug, too. "Welcome, Little Orphan Amy," Keane says. "Come see what I made!"

Maddy giggles from her armchair. "You did nothing special—only what you would have done, anyway."

Keane chuckles. "It never fails to annoy her when I say that. Ha!"

I meet Maddy and greet Dax and Violet and Jackson, and then take a seat next to the little cutie who's still cooing at his baby cousin on the couch. When the photo shoot ends, Keane scoops up his tiny daughter and proudly shows her off to Colin and me. We remark on her eyes and lips and ears, and Keane coos at his baby in ways that make my heart go pitter-pat.

Soon, however, "show and tell" is over, and Keane hands Billie to his wife, who drapes a blanket over her shoulder and feeds her newborn underneath it.

"Did you see me, Uncle Colin?" Jackson says. "I got to hold Billie!"

"Yeah, I saw. You did a great job, little dude."

"I'm big now."

"You're huge."

Without missing a beat, like it's the most natural thing in the world, Jackson crawls onto my lap and makes himself at home. "Did you see me?"

"I did. You were so good with Billie. She loves you."

"I love her. The most."

Everyone laughs and praises Jackson for uttering what I'm quickly learning is one of this group's favorite turns of phrase.

"It's a Morgan thing," Colin confirms to me, as everyone chuckles around me. "The Morgan kids grew up competing to be their mother's favorite—in number one spot, they called it. The one she loves the most. Over the years, they started saying it all the time to each other." Colin turns to Jackson. "Who do you love the most, Action Jackson?"

"Billie Goat."

Everyone laughs wholeheartedly.

"And Mommy and Daddy," Jackson quickly adds. He looks around. "Where's Uncle Fish?"

"He's coming, Bubba," Violet assures him.

"What about me?" Colin asks. "I'm right here. And I'm way cooler than Fish."

Jackson shakes his head and Colin clutches his heart like Jackson's thrown a dagger into it. And once again, I find myself marveling at how loose and relaxed Colin seems around these people, his very best friends, compared to how brooding and guarded he can be around people he doesn't know nearly as well.

Conversation ensues. Maddy and Keane tell the group the story of Billie's birth, and not surprisingly, considering who our storytellers are, their tale makes everyone laugh. Midway through the story, the doorbell rings and Ryan pops up to answer it. When Ryan reappears, he's got Fish and Alessandra in tow.

As Fish and Alessandra enter the room, Maddy removes the blanket from her shoulder to reveal a sleeping Billie in her arms. Of course, Fish and Ally fawn over Billie for a few minutes, the same way Colin and I did earlier. Another round of photos is taken, and the sleeping baby is passed around the room. After Fish passes Billie to his beloved girlfriend, rendering his lap newly open for business, Jackson quickly seizes his opportunity and beelines straight from my lap to his Uncle Fish's.

"You do realize this makes you my mortal enemy," I say to Fish, as Jackson climbs aboard, and the mock scowl Fish flashes me tells me he remembers his similar comment to me from the other night.

"Are Zander and Aloha coming over?" Dax asks, as his wife is handed Billie. And because I've watched every single Ball Peen Hammer video in existence, I know he's referring to Keane's longtime best friend, Zander Shaw, who appeared in several early episodes, as well as Zander's popstar wife, Aloha Carmichael, both of whom I met at Laila's birthday party.

"No, Z and Aloha had to leave for London today for some big award Aloha is getting, so they met Billie in the hospital."

"You want to hold her?" Violet asks Colin, since he's the only one who hasn't held the baby yet.

"Absolutely," Colin says, surprising me with his enthusiasm. "Gimme that baby!"

Violet slides the baby into Colin's tattooed, muscled arms, and the minute he smiles down at her, both my ovaries explode like mini nuclear bombs. This isn't a run-of-the-mill swoon I'm feeling right now. This is a Code Red Cat Five Hurricane overtaking me.

"Hey there, Billie Goat," Colin coos at the sleeping angel in his arms, before leaning down and smelling her fuzzy hair. He says something about how good she smells . . . *I think?* And everyone agrees and starts talking about the scent of a newborn baby being the best one in the world. *I think?*

Honestly, I can't be certain what the fuck anyone is saying

around me, because the second I saw Colin holding that baby, smiling at that baby, cooing at that baby, my brain melted, right along with my ovaries.

"When Zach was born, I'd sit and smell him for hours, like a total wack job," Ryan says, laughing.

"Yeah, I did the same with Jackson," Dax says.

I clear my throat. "How many kids do you have, Ryan?"

"Two for now," Ryan says. "Zachary and Claire. Hopefully, we'll have another one on the way soon. We've been working on it, diligently." He grins.

Lord have mercy.

No wonder Ryan Morgan is Colin's Master Yoda! The man is sheer perfection. Insanely gorgeous. Clearly, comfortable in his skin. Charming and confident, while somehow *not* coming across as cocky. *And he wants more babies*? I feel like I need the crash cart.

Ryan addresses Keane. "Have you finished shooting the third season yet, Peenie?"

Keane nods. "We wrapped a couple weeks ago."

"Lucky timing," Ryan replies.

"Yeah, it was perfect. This way, Mad Dog and I can both stay home with Billie for three months. After that, Maddy's got a couple cool projects lined up in New York, so Billie and I will travel with her for that stuff. And when we get back, it'll be perfect timing for me to start shooting the fourth season."

"I didn't know you'd already gotten picked up for another season," Ryan says. "Congrats, Peenie!"

Keane laughs. "We got picked up for *three* more seasons. Guaranteed."

"What?" Ryan gets up and hugs his younger brother, effusively, while the room congratulates him. Once seated again,

Ryan bats his brother's thigh. "So, are we gonna see more of your character in future seasons? I'm sick of having to fast-forward through all those other storylines to get to yours."

Violet adds, "I second that. I hope the producers have noticed what a fan favorite you are, Keaney. It's all over the internet. People want to see more of you."

Maddy snorts. "Do you hear that, honey? People want to see *more* of you."

"Well, 'people' are gonna be in luck, then!" Keane booms, and the pair chuckles. Keane continues, "Actually, they're gonna see a whole lot more of me throughout the third season, culminating in me doing the Full Monty in episode six!"

The room explodes with questions, prompting Keane to confirm, "Yep. You can see every inch of The Talented Mr. Ripley. The camera lingers on him in *excellent* lighting."

Ryan seems annoyed with his younger brother. But Keane only laughs and transforms into Ball Peen Hammer before my eyes. "Yee-boy!" he bellows. "Money, fame, power! It'll all be mine, thanks to that lingering shot of my peen!"

"He's not wrong," Maddy says. "It's a great career move. Plus, I think it's great Keane's challenging societal norms regarding male versus female nudity. People get so uptight about male nudity— somehow, that's shocking and rated X— and yet, everywhere we look, we see female bodies on display, used to sell every product under the sun. If you ask me, Keane is doing a great thing normalizing male nudity."

"I'm doing God's work," Keane says reverently. "One lingering dong-shot at a time."

"Keane, the internet is *forever*," Ryan says. "People are gonna get crafty and press pause at the exact right second, and then screen shots of your dong will be everywhere."

"Nobody's gonna need to 'get crafty,' son," Keane replies

proudly. "A person could have the most delayed reflexes in the world and still get a perfect *head* shot of The Talented Mr. Ripley." Keane snickers. "See what I did there? I've been a dad for less than a week, and my dad jokes are already on point."

"Exactly how long is this *lingering* shot in 'excellent lighting,' Peenie?" Dax interjects.

Fish adds, "Count it off for us."

"Why don't I show you, instead?" Keane says, standing.

"No!" Violet blurts, averting her eyes.

Keane bursts out laughing. "Not like *that*. I have a rough cut of the episode on my laptop. Due to the, *ahem*, sensitive nature of the scene, I got final approval of the edit."

As Violet sighs with relief, Ryan pops up, clearly intending to follow his brother into the other room to watch the scene. "Come on, Peenie Weenie!" Ryan booms. "Show me your lingering dong!"

"Kewl," Keane says. "All joking aside, I'd appreciate you telling me honestly if you think the porridge is too hot, too cold, or just right."

"Oh, I'll tell you, honestly," Ryan says. He looks at the group. "Don't leave me hanging here, guys, along with Peen's peen. Someone else has to come with me to see this porridge."

"I'd appreciate as much honest feedback as I can get," Keane says, sounding surprisingly earnest.

Dax and Colin exchange a look I'd caption, *Fuck my life.* But they both stand, reluctantly, to join the effort. And once that happens, Fish sighs and guides Jackson off his lap, clearly intending to follow suit.

"Thanks, lads!" Keane says. "Ladies? Any of you want to check out my porridge, too?"

"I've already seen your porridge, many times," Maddy deadpans, before pointing to the sleeping baby in her arms.

"Yeah, I think I'm good," Violet says. "I'd rather not think about your porridge while sitting across from you at Thanksgiving every year."

Ally shakes her head, looking like a deer in headlights, so I do the same, not that anyone is looking at me, the new girl.

"Suit yourselves, ladies," Keane says. "But trust me, you're missing out!"

With that, Keane and his band of brothers and best friends march out of the room to take a nice, long *lingering* gander at Ball Peen Hammer's penis. Apparently, in notably *excellent* lighting.

TWENTY-SEVEN

AMY

With the men out of the room, Violet asks Maddy if she's as comfortable with Keane showing his ding-dong to the world as it seemed earlier. And Maddy confirms, yes, she's one hundred percent comfortable with it—that, in fact, she thinks it's not only hilarious and fun for her exhibitionist husband to bare it all to the world, but, also, she says, she believes it will be a show-stopping, buzzworthy moment in the show, which will, in turn, create a social media frenzy, that, in turn, will wind up being a fantastic career move for Keane, like she suggested earlier.

"I suppose, if I didn't trust my husband completely, I might freak out about the attention he's going to attract," Maddy concedes. "But I know Keane belongs to me, completely." She smiles down at her baby, who's fast asleep in her arms. "And now, to Billie, too. I never doubt Keane, when it comes to loyalty. He's rock solid. And let's not forget, he was a stripper when I met him. I know how much he loves baring it all. So, let my man have his fun at work, as long as he's all mine, in real life."

Violet and Maddy talk about the parallels for her, in terms of Dax being a worldwide sex symbol—although a reluctant one, in Dax's case. But I'm pulled away from eavesdropping on their fascinating conversation by a little blonde nugget tugging on my shirt. It's Jackson, holding up a wooden puzzle he's apparently pulled out of his mommy's tote bag.

"Will you play with me?" he asks.

"I'd love to, Jackson."

I slide off the couch and sit on the floor next to him, and we begin figuring out the simple puzzle together. But after a few minutes, someone says my name, drawing my attention. When I look up, it's Maddy who's addressed me.

"Colin's an actor now," Maddy says. "Would you be upset if he showed his crown jewels in a movie?"

"Oh, I don't think I'm entitled to have an opinion on that, since we're not a couple."

Maddy looks surprised. "You and Colin aren't dating?"

I shake my head, feeling embarrassed. "No. I mean, yes, sort of, in the sense that we're not merely platonic friends. But it's casual. No labels or strings." *Except for the fact that I love him.* "We grew up together," I add quickly, reacting to the three stares I've provoked. "And Colin thinks there'd be too much pressure from our families if we jumped into a relationship, out in the open, so . . ." I trail off, realizing I sound like a pathetic doormat.

The truth is mortifying to me. There's no way around it. I've been letting Colin feed me tiny little breadcrumbs this whole time, whenever *he* chooses, when what I want—and deserve—is the entire goddamned loaf!

Violet looks sympathetic. "Colin's engineered a little

'friends with benefits' arrangement while you're staying at his house this week, has he?"

I nod, acknowledging the pitiful truth, not only to her, but to myself.

Violet's blue eyes flash with anger. "Colin wants to have sex with you, and play house with you, and bring you to parties and to my house to hang out, until we're all head over heels in love with you . . . all while telling you it's only casual?"

"In fairness, we both agreed."

"But that's not what you want?" Violet says. "You agreed because you figured some of Colin was better than nothing?"

I swallow hard and nod.

"But now you feel like his side chick. His guilty pleasure. You feel like he cares more about your brother's feelings than yours."

This time, she's issuing statements, not questions. And I can't stop nodding like a bobblehead. "Get out of my head, Violet Morgan," I whisper, trying to deflect my embarrassment with humor. But Violet's not smiling at my remark, so I clasp my hands and press my lips together, feeling bare and vulnerable under her blue gaze.

Alessandra shifts in her seat. "For what it's worth, I can tell Colin really likes you. Every time I've seen him with you, it's obvious he's totally smitten with you."

My heart leaps with hope at Alessandra's pronouncement . . . until I see the look of skepticism and fury Violet and Maddy are exchanging.

"You two don't agree," I say.

Violet returns to me and smiles sympathetically. "Of course, we agree Colin is smitten with you. That boy is happier around you than he's ever been. That's what makes what he's doing so infuriating."

My breathing catches at Violet's implication: *Colin is happier around me than he was with his gorgeous dancer?*

"How can Colin be *this* clueless?" Maddy asks.

"I don't know," Violet says. "I know that boy's not the most self-aware tool in the box, but how can he ask Amy to accept something casual and hidden, when it's so obvious she's the best thing that's ever happened to him?"

I clutch my heart, too overwhelmed and excited at Violet's statement to react in words.

Violet leans back in her seat and addresses me. "Answer me this, Amy. What kind of relationship would you want with Colin, if you could wave a magic wand and have anything at all?"

"Anything?" I shrug. "I'd want what you have with Dax." I look at Maddy and Alessandra. "What all of you have. Eventually. For now, I'd be thrilled to be his girlfriend, out in the open. And if that went well, then, yeah, I'd want what you all have. A commitment. A promise of forever." My eyes drift to Jackson next to me. Then to Billie in Maddy's arms. "A family."

When my chin begins trembling, Violet moves from her chair to the floor, right next to me, and hugs me. And the minute she wraps her arms around me, I can't hold back my tears.

"Does Colin know how you feel?" Violet asks, stroking my hair.

"Yes and no," I say through a sniffle. "I'm sure he knows I've always had a crush on him. We've never talked about it, but I can't imagine I've hidden it well. Plus, I basically admitted my lifelong crush in a drunken text I sent to him the night of the wedding. But there's no way he could understand the way my childhood crush has now morphed into a very adult love that's as deep as any ocean."

"Oh, honey," Violet coos. "You poor thing! You can't keep doing something 'casual' with a man you *love*. It's impossible."

"That's what I'm figuring out," I admit. "It was fine, at first. *Fun*. But not anymore. I'm turning myself into pretzels telling myself I'm fine with casual when I'm not. I should have put my foot down last night, when Colin lied about us to my brother and sister-in-law during a FaceTime call. I was so hurt and pissed when we ended that call, but then our argument turned into this hurricane of lust, and I temporarily forgot everything he'd done to hurt my feelings." I blush. "Colin's *really* good at sex. It's hard for me to remember my own name when we get going."

Maddy laughs. "Good sex will do that to you."

"And then, Colin was awe-inspiring on the set today," I continue, "so I was too blown away by him to remember how I've been feeling. But now that I'm talking about it with you ladies, I'm realizing I can't keep lying to myself. Good sex is only a temporary fix. My hurt feelings aren't going to disappear. They're only going to grow, if I keep pretending I'm fine being his guilty pleasure."

When tears prick my eyes again, Violet hugs me. So, I cry on her shoulder for a moment, while the other women whisper words of encouragement. When Violet and I disengage, Jackson crawls into my lap and hugs me.

"Thank you," I say to my little friend.

"It's okay," Jackson says, patting my arm. "I love you."

"I love you, too."

"That's so sweet of you, Donut," Violet says. "We should

always help the people we love when they're sad. And we should always be honest about our feelings when we love someone."

I look at Violet and feel a tidal wave of love for her. She's a stunning woman. Dark hair in a bob. Big blue eyes. Chiseled cheeks. But I've come to realize she's even more beautiful on the inside.

"I'd give anything to hear Colin say to me what Jackson just did," I admit.

"Maybe he will," Alessandra says hopefully. "If you say it first?"

I shake my head. "If that's how Colin is feeling, he wouldn't have lied to my brother last night. I know he cares about me. I know he's having fun with me. But casual is all he's willing to give me."

"And that's not enough for you," Violet says.

"No. Not anymore. Not nearly enough."

Violet nods. "What I'm about to say might sound harsh, but I'm only saying it because I've been in your *exact* shoes with Daxy and done precisely what I'm about to suggest to you."

I look at her expectantly, already certain I'll do whatever this gorgeous woman instructs, if it'd give me the slightest chance of winding up with Colin the way she's wound up with Dax.

Violet levels me with fierce, blue eyes. "You need to come clean with Colin about your feelings, without holding back, as soon as possible, and let the chips fall where they may."

Shoot. I suspected she was going to say that.

Violet continues, "You should give Colin a fair chance to respond, of course. But if that stupid man doesn't *fully* reciprocate your feelings in a way that honestly feels like *enough* to you, if he stops short of giving you what you know, down deep, your heart *needs* to be happy, then you should end your 'arrangement' on the spot and leave Colin's house."

I nod, but I'm trembling.

"Colin's not the best at processing his feelings quickly," Violet says. "Even when it comes to stuff with the band, he's always the one who needs more time than the other guys to think about different opportunities and offers. And from what I've seen, he's even slower to process in his personal life. It's not you, Amy. Colin is a tough nut to crack. So, my suggestion is you should tell him what you're feeling, give him the chance to respond, and if he's not giving you what you need, then leave and give him time to process his emotions—while discovering *exactly* what it feels like to lose you for good."

"I agree with everything Violet's said," Maddy chimes in. "I've been in your shoes, too—with Keane." She looks down at Billie in her arms. "And I'm positive I wouldn't be here now, if I hadn't drawn a line in the sand with that man."

I look down at the top of Jackson's head and discover he's fallen asleep in my arms, with his little cheek pressed against my breast, and full clarity slams into me. As much as I'm dreaming of a future with Colin, I need to be willing to let him go, for real this time, if he's certain he can't imagine a future with me. I love Colin. But he's not the only man in the world. And if he's not willing to love me, out in the open, the way I deserve, to shout about his love for me from the rooftops, to proudly tell our families about us and introduce me to *everyone* we meet as his girlfriend, then I need to find someone who will.

"I'm going to follow your advice, to a T," I say. "I'll do it tonight."

Maddy smiles at me kindly. "If things don't go the way

you're hoping and Colin starts sending you texts and voice-mails over the next few days, I'd suggest you ghost him for a little bit."

"Yep," Violet says.

"You're both here in LA," Maddy adds. "If he has something important to say to you, let him say it to you, in person."

Violet touches my arm. "If you wind up leaving Colin's place tonight, come stay with me. We've got an empty guest house for you."

"Thank you. It's so sweet of you to offer. But if things don't go well with Colin tonight, I won't want to stay where he'll likely come around. I'll want to give myself some time to lick my wounds, without seeing him for a week or so."

"Do you have somewhere else you can go?"

I nod. "A couple friends have said I can crash at their places, anytime."

We talk a bit more about Colin and my strategy, until Violet shifts the topic.

"There's something I've been wanting to ask you," Violet says to me. "I hope this isn't a weird time to bring this up . . . I know I'm not what you've had in mind during your job search, but would you consider working for *me*?" When my lips part in surprise, Violet elaborates. She says I'd be working for her, personally, not for Dax—at her house. She says she's been wanting a full-time assistant/right-hand woman for some time now but hasn't pulled the trigger yet because she's been skittish about hiring a stranger to enter her family's home and life. "But I trust you completely, Amy," she says. "And I know you'd be perfect for the job I have in mind."

"What would the job be, exactly?" I ask.

"You'd help me with my cancer charity some, but mostly,

you'd help me launch my dream of designing wedding dresses. You'd also probably help get me organized, in general, and lend a hand with Jackson, as needed." She looks at her son, asleep in my arms. "I can't believe how quickly he took to you." She looks at me hopefully, her blue eyes sparkling. "So, that's my pitch. What do think?"

I don't hesitate. "I think *yes*. I accept your job offer."

Violet laughs. "I'd understand if you need to think about it, now that things might be up in the air with Colin."

I shake my head. "No matter what happens with Colin tonight, we'll always be friends. He's not a factor in my decision-making about this. My answer is yes."

"But we haven't even talked about salary yet!" Violet proposes a figure that's almost five times what I made during the RCR tour—a number that makes me feel like tipping over in shock. But, somehow, I manage to nod and calmly reply, "That sounds great. My answer is still yes!"

Violet whoops, and so do I.

"When would you like me to start?" I ask.

"How does a week from Monday sound? Keane and Maddy are taking Billie to Seattle tomorrow to spend a week with the Morgans, and Daxy and I are going to join in. It's my mother-in-law's birthday on Sunday, so we're throwing her a surprise dinner party and getting everyone together under one roof as her gift. She's going to flip out."

"That's so sweet. Yeah, a week from Monday is perfect. Do me a favor, though: don't tell Colin about my new job before then, not until I've shown up for my first day of work. Once I've told him my feelings tonight, I want his reaction to be based on nothing but his honest feelings. I don't want Colin deciding to be with me, simply because he realizes he's going to be seeing me all the time, anyway, and I'm the path of least resistance."

"So smart," Violet says. "Okay, I won't say a word. And neither will Daxy."

"Thank you."

"My lips are sealed, too," Alessandra says. "I won't tell Fish about the job, so he doesn't feel like he's keeping something from Colin. Poor Matthew is the worst at keeping secrets. I'll spare him the torture."

I inhale deeply. "Thank you, guys. Wow, I feel like such a huge weight has been lifted off me. I didn't realize how much this 'arrangement' with Colin has been twisting me into knots until we started talking."

"The truth shall set you free," Violet says.

"And it can also hurt," I say, exhaling. "Here's hoping I don't get hurt *too* badly tonight."

A commotion draws our attention—the men re-entering the room, all of them laughing and razzing Keane.

Maddy smiles at the jocular group. "Well, what'd you boys think of Peenie's peenie?"

"Babe, I keep telling you. Don't call it a 'peenie.' That makes it sound small."

"Sorry, honey. What'd you boys think of Peenie's porridge? Do you think he should ask for a shorter edit on the shot, or let them keep it, as is?"

"I'd say that depends," Ryan says. "Does Peenie Weenie want his audience to be able to count the veins in his porridge?"

"Oh, absolutely," Keane replies.

"Okay, then," Ryan says, settling onto the couch. "Then in that case, I'd say the porridge is 'just right.'"

TWENTY-EIGHT

COLIN

"Everything okay over there?" I ask.

Amy and I are driving home after visiting Keane and Maddy, and ever since we got into the car, Amy's been unusually quiet. She's typically chatty in the car. But not this time.

At my question, Amy turns from her passenger-side window, and I know the minute I see her tightly drawn features, she's been having deep thoughts over there.

"Everything's fine," she says.

But it's all I get.

"What have you been thinking about?" I prompt, even though my clenched stomach is telling me to leave it alone.

"Billie," she replies. "I was thinking about how happy Keane and Maddy seem to have her."

"Yeah, exhausted, too."

"They're 'happily exhausted.'"

Uh oh. I don't think I'm going to like where this is headed.

"You were adorable with the baby," Amy adds. "I felt like

I was watching that story your mom told us the other night—
the one where you held me after my parents brought me home
from the hospital."

Oh, fuck. I'm positive I'm not going to like where this is
headed.

"Did you see the sassy look Billie gave Maddy at feeding
time?" Amy continues. "You can tell she's going to be a spitfire like Keane."

"Keane's not a spitfire. He's a flamethrower."

Amy laughs and my shoulders soften. Maybe this conversation isn't headed where I think, after all?

"Do you think you might want kids one day?" Amy asks.

And . . . my shoulders tighten again. "Sure. One day," I
reply. I already know Amy's answer to the same question. As
a little girl, she was always playing with dolls whenever I
came over to play video games with Logan. But, still, out of
politeness, I ask her, "Do *you* want kids one day?"

"Oh, definitely."

It's not a surprise.

Wordlessly, I steer my car off the main highway and make
all appropriate turns to make our way to my canyon-side
street.

"How many kids do you imagine yourself having?" she
asks, breaking the silence.

Fuck. "Two or three, maybe." *Fuck.* "You?"

"I don't want to pick a number and jinx myself," she says.
"For all I know, I could have fertility problems or meet the
love of my life much later than I hoped. Or never."

Oh, Jesus Christ. The poor woman is wearing her heart on
her sleeve. When she said the words "love of my life," she
looked at me with such palpable longing, I could feel it all the
way down in my soul. "Yeah, life can be unpredictable."

"But I suppose if I could wave a magic wand and get *exactly* what I wanted," she says, "I'd have four or five kids."

My eyebrows ride up to my hairline. That's a couple more kids than I thought she'd say. Don't people who grow up with two kids in their family usually imagine themselves repeating the cycle? I shift my hands on my steering wheel and mull that over.

"That's a scary thought to you?" she says, apparently reading my body language.

"No, I wouldn't say scary. There are five kids in the Morgan family—four boys and a girl—and they're the coolest family I know."

"The three Morgan brothers I saw in action tonight seem super close."

"The whole family is like that. All five of them and their parents."

"The Morgan parents are still married?"

"Yeah. Happily, it seems."

Amy's green eyes blaze. "That's what I'd want. A big, close-knit family like the Morgans, where everyone always gets along and loves being together."

"When did I say they 'always' get along? Because believe me, it's shocking to me Ryan didn't off Keane at some point. Or Kat, the lone sister, didn't off Ryan or Keane."

Amy giggles. "I would have preferred having a love/hate relationship with Logan. He was too old to play with me, or even argue with me, growing up. He just sort of ignored me, like I was an inescapable nuisance." She pauses. "What do you think is the Morgan parents' secret to staying together? I've never seen a happy marriage, up close."

"Neither have I. My mom is happily married now, but she married my stepdad after I'd already moved out."

"So, what do you think is the secret to the Morgan parents' success?"

I pause to think about it. "I guess . . . they genuinely like each other? That sounds basic, but it's kind of astonishing. They make each other laugh a lot. And it's clear they don't sweat the small stuff. Plus, at the end of the day, they're both one thousand percent committed to their family."

Amy lets out a shaky breath. "That's what I want one day. A family like that."

We've reached my house now—and, clearly, the truth about what Amy was actually thinking about earlier when I asked her. My breathing shallow, I turn into my driveway, pull my car into the garage, and press the button to close the garage door behind us. And, finally, when Amy still hasn't spoken, I gather the courage to look at her.

Yep.

It's exactly as I feared. She's feeling deeply moved. Indeed, there are tears pricking her eyes. Which means my hunch was correct: this conversation has been a prelude to Amy asking me about the future. Specifically, if I can imagine myself giving her the kind of future she just described.

But how can I possibly know that already? As of now, I know I've got love in my heart for this woman—this beautiful, gentle soul who brings something out of me, like nobody else—and I have for a very long time. But I *also* know Amy only thinks she's in love with me, because, for reasons I've never fully understood, I've always felt inspired to don a red cape around her. And now, I'm reaping what I've sown. This girl worships me like a hero, because that's exactly what I've trained her to do—even though I know, down deep, I'm not capable of delivering that illusion forever. Who could?

"You look like a trapped animal," Amy says.

"I feel like one," I admit.

"Why?"

"Because I know you've got expectations I'm not going to be able to fulfill, long-term."

Amy looks deflated. "When I told you what I dream about for my future, I didn't mean right now. I meant 'one day.' All I'm asking for now is honesty."

"About what?"

"Your feelings for me. Do you think you *could* be the man in my dream one day in the distant future? Do you at least feel yourself falling for me enough to take the risk of telling our families about us now?"

I press my lips together. *Shit.*

"Because if you're sure, sitting here now, you could *never* want our families to know about us, then we should end this arrangement now." When I stare at her, speechless, she takes a deep breath and says, "The truth is I already know I'm in love with you, Colin. Madly in love. And now that I'm sure of that, every second I pretend *not* to be, every second I pretend doing something casual with you is enough for me, it's beginning to feel more painful than fun. It's beginning to feel like rejection."

My heart squeezes at the forlorn look on Amy's beautiful face. "We've only been doing this for less than a week," I manage to whisper.

Amy's eyes flash. "*You've* been doing this for less than a week. My heart has belonged to you for a lot longer than that."

My heart is racing. "Amy, please. This is too much, too fast."

Amy scoffs. "Do you think I want to feel that way about you, Colin? Of course, I don't! I know I'm a creeper for loving the same boy my whole life! Who does that? I'm gross. *Blechh*! *Ew*! But I can't help what I feel! I'm Jacob the Were-wolf when he sees Baby Renesmee!"

"*What?*"

"Never mind. The point is that I know I'm a werewolf freak-a-doodle, but I can't help it. The bottom line is I need more—and *deserve* more—than a no-strings fuck buddy arrangement you don't tell my brother about."

"You're not my fuck buddy. Don't insult me."

"Yes, I am! You lied to Logan and Kennedy about us! If fucking me and hiding it from the people we're closest to doesn't make me a fuck buddy, then I don't know what would."

"You know why we're not telling our families about us! You said you agreed!"

"I've changed my mind."

I exhale in frustration. "I tell you, constantly, how much I care about you, Amy! Maybe not with words, but with the things I do for you."

Unexpected anger explodes across her face. "You explic-itly told me you were doing those nice things for me because I'm Logan's sister! You said if the situation were reversed, Logan would do the same for you! So, forgive me, if I don't interpret your favors to my *brother* as evidence of how much you care about me. Don't get me wrong, I'm grateful for what you've done for me. But in the context of this conversation, in the context of me expressing the brutal truth about my feel-ings for you, I call bullshit!"

With that, Amy darts out of my car and marches into my house. So, of course, I follow her, feeling like my heart is palpitating at an irregular clip in my chest.

"Amy!" I call after her.

She whirls around to face me in the middle of my living room, her green eyes on fire.

"You want to hear *my* 'brutal truth'?" I ask, my pulse pounding loudly in my ears.

"That's all I want."

I take a step forward, my chest heaving. "You only *think* you're in love with me, when in reality, you're 'in love' with a fantasy—a perfect version of me that doesn't even exist!"

Amy snorts. "You think *I* think you're *perfect*?"

"Yes. Absolutely."

"Ha! News flash, babe, I lived next-door to you for fourteen years! And during that time, I saw *plenty* of times when you were anything but perfect. I saw you being impatient or downright rude to your mother and sisters! I saw you being moody and entitled at times, too. I saw more than one girlfriend leaving your house in tears because you'd lost your temper—which I could hear you doing, by the way—and you didn't say sorry when you should have!"

My jaw hangs open. *Well, this took a turn.*

"How dare you accuse me of only being in love with a 'fantasy version' of you, when that's the only version of yourself you've ever been willing to show me!" Amy takes a step toward me, breathing hard. "Answer a question for me—something I've been wondering for years." Her nostrils flare. "You *knew* I used to spy on you from my bedroom window every night while you practiced your drums, didn't you? You knew I was there, watching you!"

Holy shit.

"Answer me!" she shrieks. "And tell me the fucking truth!"

I can't deny it, so I nod slowly.

"You knew it!" she screams. "Ha! You knew I was there,

all along—watching you, slobbering over you, fantasizing about you—and you fucking *loved* it. I bet it stroked your ego like crazy to feel like a rockstar with a fangirling audience every night! It made you feel like you were king of the world to know there was a dopey tweener next door idolizing you!" She shakes her head, her lip curling. "You performed for me because it made *you* feel good to have me worship you, and now you have the audacity to tell me I can't possibly love you because you were too successful at manipulating me?" She scoffs and takes another step forward. "Well, let me enlighten you about something, Colin." She leans forward. "*I'm not an idiot.* Maybe I was back then, but not anymore. Looking back now, I know *exactly* what you were doing and why—and that what you were doing was actually kind of douchey. Definitely *not* the actions of a *perfect* man."

I open and close my mouth, too shocked to speak.

"And what about when I moved away?" she says. "You think *I* thought you were perfect then, when you didn't even think to keep in touch with me? When it didn't even cross your mind to check in on me, after my parents got divorced, and Logan went to college, and I had to go to a new house and new school and make all new friends? You knew how shy I was around new people and that I used to talk to you when I didn't feel like I had anyone else who gave a shit! But I guess out of sight, out of mind. I moved away and ceased to exist, as far as Mr. Budding Rockstar was concerned?"

My breathing is shallow. Holy shit. *She's right.* I was a total prick.

"I'm sorry," I eke out. "My band was starting to get lots of gigs by that point and—"

"Yes, I know. And I also know you were far more important to me, than I was to you. To you, I was nothing but

Logan's kid sister. But, still, it hurt. So, don't you dare tell me I'm standing here thinking you're perfect! That's truly laughable!"

"You were much more to me than Logan's kid sister," I concede. "You're right. We were friends, and I was a self-absorbed little shit to drop you like a hot potato."

Amy processes that. "Thank you. I accept your apology. To be fair, I was fourteen and you were eighteen and in a band. Frankly, it would have been weird for you to stay in touch with me. I'm just telling you, whether it was rational or not, I felt abandoned by you—and therefore knew you weren't even close to perfect. But if I stupidly thought you were perfect then, I certainly would have figured out the truth at Logan's wedding."

"*What*? I was Prince Charming at that wedding!"

"You stood me up after our amazing kiss!"

"Oh." I grimace. "Yeah, I was drunk."

"That's no excuse! You knew that kiss gave me fireflies! *You knew that,* and you got off on that, the same way you got off on me spying at you playing drums through my bedroom window. So, you whispered all those amazing things into my ear, to keep those fireflies swirling in my belly, to keep your ego stroked, and then you left me sitting in my hotel room, waiting for a text that never came. I sat there like an idiot, waiting for you to show up and do everything you'd promised me, Colin. What kind of asshole leaves a girl hanging like that?"

"I tried to come to you, but you'd texted me the wrong room number!"

"*What*?"

I nod effusively. "When I got your text, I beelined out of Daxy's room so fast, I practically tripped over my feet. But then some old lady answered the door and screamed at me for waking her up."

Amy palms her forehead. "Oh my God." She gasps. "Did you drop a bottle of booze in the hallway?"

"Yeah! When that old lady chewed me out!"

Amy rolls her eyes. "It doesn't matter, in the end, though, considering your decision the next morning to 'let me down easy.'" She snorts. "Trust me, if I didn't know you were *imperfect* before then, I would have figured it out."

I exhale. "I thought I was doing the right thing."

"Yeah, and I thought you were being too big a coward to do what you truly wanted to do."

"It's not being a coward to say, 'Hey, let's not get both our families all riled up before we know, for sure, if—"

"But that's not what you said!" she shrieks. "You said I was '*off-limits*' to you. Because, apparently, you care more about my brother's imaginary feelings than your own. But, okay, fine. Let's pretend I thought you were perfect when I showed up on your doorstep in LA." She snorts again. "Trust me, I didn't. But let's say I did. Well, guess what? I would have figured out pretty damned skippy you're a deeply flawed motherfucker."

"What the fuck? I rolled out the red carpet for you! I got your favorite flowers for your dresser!"

"And that was very sweet of you. Thank you. But this is a conversation about how you're not perfect, and, unfortunately, thoughtful flowers don't erase the fact that it turns out you can be a moody, broody, closed-off, self-absorbed, manipulative motherfucker who gets off on having a little puppy following him around and fawning over his every smile. A puppy who takes whatever little breadcrumbs he deigns to drop on the floor for her to gobble up, knowing full well she's dying to be fed the entire freaking loaf."

Heat floods my cheeks. Shit. Amy's not taking any prisoners. I'm being decimated here.

"Oh, did I hit a nerve?" Amy challenges. "Are you ready to stop hearing the brutal truth yet?"

"Not if you've got more of it to tell me."

"Oh, I do."

"Then give it to me, Red. All of it."

"Gladly." She paces back and forth in my living room, gearing up. "I don't love the fact that you've got three cars, and that stupid behemoth of a coffee maker that has no business being in a home where only one human bachelor resides. That thing is built for restaurants!"

"That's what makes it so fucking cool!"

"I wouldn't give a crap what you spend your money on, if you spent a little more of it on making the world a better place. *But you don't.* You were sweet to take care of your mom and give your sisters cars. And I'm thrilled you support the charities you do. But you've clearly got more money than you know what to do with, and also an amazing platform and some time on your hands, and the fact that it doesn't even occur to you to do something really meaningful with all that tells me you're more selfish and materialistic than my ideal man would be."

I smirk. "Guilty as charged."

"Also, it drives me bonkers the way you shove things into drawers and closets, without the slightest bit of organization. You're cool with things *looking* neat and perfect, on the outside, when, underneath, they're a hot mess!" She levels me with two pools of green fire. "In my opinion, that's a metaphor. You look amazing and perfect, on the outside.

You've worked hard to make it so—and kudos to you for that. But underneath that perfect body and ink, let's face it, babe, you're a hot fuckin' mess!"

I press my lips together. Yet again, she's not wrong.

"That would *also* be fine with me, since, as I've mentioned, I'm a creeper werewolf and not even close to perfect myself. As we both know, a freaking cereal commercial can easily make me sob. Also, I get frazzled easily and can't keep a poker face to save my life. But see, I know all that about myself, whereas you don't even realize what a hot mess you are—how guarded and closed-off you can be from your true emotions, whatever they may be." She puts her hands on her hips. "Do you even know why you love acting so much?"

I cross my arms over my chest, matching her position. "Enlighten me."

"It's the only time you give yourself permission to express your honest emotions, without holding back, and without feeling embarrassed about them. Acting forces you to dig deep inside yourself, in a way you don't normally allow yourself to do."

Goosebumps. They're suddenly erupting all over my arms and neck, raising every hair on my body. Holy shit. She's amazing.

"I don't know what turned you into this paragon of bottled-up masculinity," she says, "but it's insanely frustrating for anyone who loves you! Which I do." She exhales. "I could go on and on, but there's no point, when the bottom line is that I'm willing to look past your many, *many* flaws and accept them—and *you*—*the real you*—exactly as you are. Without trying to change you, other than organizing your fucking closets. Because that's what love is, you stupid fucking dumbass. It's accepting the bad with the good and loving all of it, because you know one doesn't come without the other."

My breathing hitches. This woman is melting my brain and causing my heart to race.

Her anger softens. She takes a deep breath. "Okay, I've told you *most* of the reasons you infuriate me. Now let me tell you some of the reasons you make me adore you." Amy smiles shyly. "You've got a heart of a gold, Colin Beretta, and so much more love to give than you even realize. One smile from you melts me, all the way down in my soul. Oh, man, you just do it for me. You're passionate and talented. So talented, I'm in awe of you. You're funny and thoughtful. Generous and kind. A good listener. You're loyal. You'd throw yourself in front of a moving train for the people you love the most. And despite what I said about you being self-absorbed at times, you're also shockingly humble and down to earth, considering how talented and gorgeous you are and everything you've accomplished." The tenderness on her face flashes to anger again on a dime. "*That's* why I constantly swoon for you, motherfucker! Not because I think you're anywhere close to *perfect*!"

I'm short of breath. Oh my God. This was the best ass-whooping I've ever received in my life. And I thought my mother was an assassin? Holy fuck. Amy's more beautiful to me now than ever.

"What?" Amy says. "Spit it out. Whatever it is, I can take it."

I blow out my cheeks, not sure how to accurately express the cocktail of emotions flooding me. I'm feeling over-whelming love for this woman in this electrifying moment. Not to mention, white-hot *lust*. But also, anger. So much fucking anger, that she's demanding I dance like a monkey for her. Most importantly, however, I can't wrap my head around the love I'm feeling being the real deal, the kind that would make sense to tell our families about this quickly. I don't want to fuck up and speak those words, prematurely, or wrongly, considering what's at stake here.

"What are you thinking?" Amy demands.

"I'm thinking a lot."

"Like what?"

"Mostly, I'm thinking I'm crazy about you and don't want what we've been doing to end. But I'm also thinking you've been staying with me for less than a week and I'm not ready to say the words you want to hear, on command. It feels like an ultimatum to me. A test. And I fucking hate that kind of shit."

Amy nods. "That's fair. Unfortunately, the kind of shit I hate is feeling like I'm your dirty little secret."

"That's not fair."

"I think it is. Sorry if it seems like an ultimatum to you, but I need you to call my brother and tell him we're dating. It's as simple as that. I don't need the magic words from you, as long as you feel like you're falling for me and could ultimately imagine yourself saying them. On the other hand, if you want me to stay here and keep doing what I've been doing because I'm fantastic at organizing your closets, making you dinner, and sucking your cock, then hire a housekeeper and find yourself a groupie and let me go."

I exhale in frustration. "That's unfair. You know I care deeply about you."

Amy pauses briefly before ultimately shaking her head. "That's not enough for me. I want someone who wants to shout from the rooftops about me. Someone who'd write a love song about me, if he could. I want someone to swoon over me, the way I swoon over him. And if you're not even sure enough about your feelings for me to call my brother and tell him we're dating, then you're clearly not going to be that someone. Which means it's time for me to move on."

She stares at me, giving me a chance to respond, and when I press my lips together, too overwhelmed—not to mention too pissed—to speak, she marches out of the living room in a huff.

I follow her down the hallway and into the guest bedroom, where she grabs her empty suitcase from the closet and begins packing. And that's it for me. The sight of her packing—the reality that she's following through with leaving me—sends me into a panic. Fight or flight kicks in for me . . . and in this case, I choose *fight*.

I'm not proud of myself for it, but I start screaming at her. I command her to stay. I tell her she's overreacting. Not giving me enough time. Being melodramatic and overly sensitive. I order her to stop and listen to me, and when she does, her chin trembling, I'm tongue-tied and lame. I feel so much love for this woman! But it's love I refuse to name right now, because it's too much, too soon and I refuse to be commanded to react the way she wants.

Amy's bag is packed and zipped now. Her nostrils flaring, she pulls her suitcase off the bed, grabs her phone, and begins tapping angrily on it.

"What are you doing?"

"Ordering an Uber. It'll be here in four minutes." She looks up from her phone. "Anything else you want to scream at me, you'd better do it now—although I should warn you, everything you've screamed at me for the past five minutes has only made me more certain I'm doing the right thing."

Without waiting for me, she drags her suitcase toward the bedroom door, and I follow her.

"I'm sorry I yelled," I say. "I shouldn't have done that. I'll work on that. But this feels like a huge overreaction to me. You haven't even landed a job yet! We agreed you'd stay long enough for me to help you land the perfect job!"

"I already did. I've been offered my dream job and accepted it."

"What? *No*! There's no way I'm letting you work for Seth Rockford!"

She doesn't reply. She keeps marching furiously away from me, dragging her suitcase along with her—and when her bag wobbles on its wheels, I lurch forward and grab the damned thing myself and carry it to my front door, even though I have zero intention of letting her leave.

At my front door, I stop and whirl around. "Don't go," I plead. "And please don't work for Seth."

Amy's face looks the same way it did when she ran away to "Genovia" as a kid. For a second, I'm certain she's going to throw herself into my arms. But no. After a moment, she pulls herself together, squares her shoulders, and says, "This isn't goodbye. We'll always be friends. I simply don't want to be your fuck buddy anymore. If you decide you want more with me, out in the open, if you want me to be your girlfriend and shout about me from the rooftops, then let me know, and I promise I'll give you a shot . . . *if* I'm not already dating someone else by then." She gazes out my front door. "My Uber's here. Will you bring my bag to the car, please?"

My breathing catches. "Where are you going?"

"To my friend's, until it's time to start my new job." She gestures to her bag, sternly, so I reluctantly carry it down the front walkway to the waiting car.

At the curb, I put Amy's bag into the trunk, while she slips into the car's backseat. Without looking at me, she closes her door, looks forward, and says something to the driver.

As the car pulls away, I know in my bones I've fucked up. I know I love her. But how can I trust these feelings after less than a goddamned week? It'd be pure selfishness to take a leap of faith that big, when I'm not sure the foundation we're both standing on is rock solid.

I watch the car driving down my street, praying Amy will miraculously tell the driver to stop and turn around. But no. Ten seconds after pulling away from the curb, Amy's Uber turns the corner and disappears for good.

Fuck.

For several minutes, I pace the sidewalk in front of my house, losing my mind. I don't want to go back into my house, if Amy's not there. I don't want to sleep in my bed, if Amy's not lying next to me. I don't want to cook in my kitchen, if I'm not cooking for two. And I sure as hell don't want to go to the studio tomorrow without Amy being there to make it all better and more fun.

Oh, God.

What have I done?

I love her.

I know I do.

I feel it in my soul. Way down deep.

So, why couldn't I say it to her?

Because I'm not fucking crazy, that's why.

I pull out my phone and press the button to call Amy, and then grunt in frustration when it goes straight to voicemail. At the beep, I leave a rambling message that paraphrases every-thing I already said to her in the house but get cut off midway through by a computerized voice asking if I want to re-record my message or send it, as is.

"Fuck!" I shout, before pressing the option to re-record.

Beep.

This time, I keep it short. "It's me. What you're asking is unreasonable at this point. That doesn't mean what we have has to *end,* for fuck's sake. Let's take things slow. How is that an unreasonable request? Jesus!" I sigh. "Call me, Amy. *Please*. Bye."

TWENTY-NINE

COLIN

I check my phone. But once again, there's nothing from Amy. No return call. No text. No voicemail. Obviously, she's been ghosting me. *And it fucking sucks.*

It's Sunday night, four days since Amy left me. But it feels like four hundred. At the moment, I'm sitting on my couch, eating a cold burrito and drowning in misery and regret. My dream job has been over for two days now. But rather than celebrating the accomplishment with Amy, I've been sitting here for two days, alone and miserable.

Ryan.

All of a sudden, my honorary big brother's name pops into my head like a thunderbolt. Why haven't I called him? Ryan always knows what to do to fix everything, especially when it comes to women! The Morgans literally call him their family's *fixer*!

My heartrate increasing, I grab my phone and place the call, and, thankfully, my Master Yoda picks up immediately.

"Colinoscopy!" Ryan booms. "How the hell are ya?"

"Hey, Rum Cake. I'm shitty. How are you?"

"That's too bad. I'm great. It's Momma Lou's birthday, so the whole fam is here at the house, throwing her a surprise birthday dinner."

"I didn't know it was your mom's birthday. Wish her a good one from me. I'll talk to you later."

"No, no. Now's a good time. I'm sitting here with some of the fam, watching the game while we wait for the dinner bell. Can I put you on FaceTime and let everyone say hi to you, or are you feeling the kind of 'shitty' that requires a private conversation?"

"Meh, go ahead and put me on FaceTime. I'll take all the help I can get at this point."

We press the right buttons and two seconds later I'm staring at Ryan and his three brothers—Colby, Keane, and Dax—plus, their brother-in-law, Josh, who's become a brother to us all since he married Kat several years ago. Maddy's there, too, passed out against Keane's broad shoulder. Plus, there's a whole gaggle of kids in the room. In fact, every single man on my screen is holding a baby or a kid. Most amusingly, Colby's second youngest, Mia, is sitting on her Uncle Dax's lap, facing him while playing with his long blonde hair, which at present is littered with an array of bows and sparkly clips.

"Colin says he's doing 'shitty,' guys," Ryan informs the group, after basic greetings are administered. "What's going on, brother?"

I tell everyone the gist of my shitty situation and admit I'm intensely second-guessing my reaction to Amy's comments the other night.

"I got defensive," I admit. "I was pissed she was demanding I tell her brother about us, before I was ready. But now that I've had a chance to think about it, I can see how me *not* telling Logan made Amy feel like I was hiding her."

"Well, you were hiding her, to be fair," Ryan says.

"But not from you guys! Not from anyone but our families."

Ryan flashes me a look I know all too well—a look that tells me I'm a dumbshit. And just this fast, I know I fucked up. Royally.

"I wasn't ready to tell her brother!" I shout. "Is that a crime?"

"No," Ryan concedes calmly. "But it certainly gave your girl the answer she was looking for, eh? Good for her for walking out. That's a confident woman. The best kind."

I roll my eyes. "Ryan, come on. How could I tell Amy's brother and our families about us after *this* short a time?"

"What do you mean?"

I explain the timeline, as I see it.

"But you've known this girl your whole life, right?" he asks. And when I nod, he adds, "Okay, so you already knew all the most important stuff, going in. You knew she wasn't a bunny boiler. That's huge. You knew she's exactly who she appears to be. Also, huge."

"But we knew each other as kids. It's been less than three weeks since I've known her as an adult."

"Yeah, but people don't change all that much. You knew ninety percent of her by the time you slept with her. You've just been getting to know the other ten percent since then."

I'm speechless. I hadn't thought about it like that.

"I mean, I'm not trying to push you into anything," Ryan says. "You're the one who knows if you click with her or not."

"It's not about whether I 'click' with her," I say. "We've

always had a crazy connection. Honestly, I feel like I know her, inside and out. The problem is that she doesn't really know *me*. She thinks she does. Whew! You should have heard the way she chewed my ass the other night. But the thing she doesn't realize is how weirdly nice and generous I always feel compelled to be around her. For instance, the other day, I heard her say, *once,* that lilies are her favorite flower. *Once.* And not even to me. So, what'd I immediately run out and do? Buy her some fucking lilies! Who does that?"

Colby, the eldest Morgan brother, laughs. "A man in love does that, dumbass."

Josh, Kat's husband, chimes in. "I'm not trying to push you into anything, either, Colin. But I feel like I should mention the right woman will bring out the best in *you.* If a woman doesn't do that, she's not The One."

"Amen," Ryan says, and Colby quickly agrees.

Dax pipes in. "You haven't noticed how Violet makes *me* a better man?"

"Mad Dog has certainly done that for me," Keane says.

"To put it mildly," Colby mutters, and everyone on the call, except for me, chuckles.

I suppose I'd join in the chuckling, if only a cavalcade of memories from my relationship with Kiera weren't slamming into me right now—a rapid-fire montage of all the times Kiera and I fought over the stupidest shit and brought out the absolute worst in each other.

Being around Amy feels like the polar opposite of the shit show that was my relationship with Kiera. Being with Amy feels calm and happy. Natural and *right.* But, still, my rational brain simply won't stop clinging to the timeline here.

"It hasn't even been three weeks since Amy and I saw each other for the first time in almost a decade," I say. "Could anyone trust the kind of intense feelings I'm having for Amy, this fast?"

"Could *anyone*?" Ryan asks. "Absolutely. Can you? Only you can answer that, brother."

Colby adds, "Rum Cake's right. Only *you* can know if your feelings are the real deal. That said, I'm a believer in 'When you know, you know.'"

"When did you know?" I ask.

"Oh, I knew Lydia was The One the second I saw her. Everyone thought I was crazy, but I *knew*."

My eyebrows shoot up. That's shocking to me—it's totally unlike our careful, methodical Colby to jump in, head-first, like that. "Wow, man. That's intense."

"It was," Colby agrees. "*But I knew*. So, I went with it, and never looked back." He looks down at the sleeping baby in his arms. "And it turns out, it was the best thing I ever did."

I'm blown away. Colby isn't the kind of guy to leap before looking. "What about everyone else? How long did it take you to know your wife was The One?"

The guys reply to my question with answers ranging from "after one conversation" to "about a month." All of which is shocking to me. Even Kat's husband, Josh, who says he fought his true feelings for "way too long," seems to think it's entirely possible for me to have reliable, real feelings for Amy this quickly.

But before I've figured out how to reply to the latest round of information, the Morgan family's lone daughter, Kat, appears on-screen. She hands a baby to her husband, Josh, who hands her an older one in return. And when Kat realizes I'm on FaceTime, she pops over next to Ryan to greet me.

"Hey there, Colinoscopy! Wish you were here!"

"Hey, Kitty Kat. Nobody invited me."

"Oh, I'm sorry! Violet said you and Fish have a work thing in LA tomorrow."

"Yeah, we do. It's all good. Fish and I have to appear in the finale of *Sing Your Heart Out* tomorrow. Tell your mom happy birthday from me."

"I will. So, what's going on? Why the big pow-wow?"

Mia on her Uncle Dax's lap interjects, "Uncle Colin's girl-friend broke up with him because he wouldn't say 'I love you' when she said it to him. And now he thinks he messed up and should have said it. So, he's asking everyone how long it took them to say it and everyone is calling him a big dumb-dumb."

Everyone bursts out laughing, including me.

"I couldn't have explained it better myself, Mia," I concede.

The guys give Kat a bit more information, and to my surprise, Dax's diabolical sister looks deeply sympathetic. "Violet's been telling us this same story in the kitchen, actually. And we've all reached the same conclusion: You're a big dumb-dumb."

"Lovely," I mutter. "Amy won't return my texts and calls, but she's called Violet and told her everything."

"That's what women *do*," Kat says with a dismissive wave of her hand. "We cry on our besties' shoulders when our hearts get broken."

My heart squeezes. "In my defense, this is a tricky situation, Kat. Way trickier than Violet probably explained to you. My mom told me the other day she's been dreaming of Beretta-O'Brien grandbabies. So, I think it was wise and considerate of me not to jump the gun and subject Amy to—"

"Screw your mother!" Kat says. "And screw Amy's brother, too. From what I've heard, your girl didn't demand you to put a ring on it! She just doesn't want to feel like your hidden, guilty pleasure! And I can't say I blame her. People don't hide the ones they love. They shout about them from every mountaintop! So, if you're not willing to proudly call that woman your girlfriend to *everyone* you know, not just to the group that's most *comfortable* for you, then I think she did the right thing. Good for her."

"Who's this?" a female voice sings out, before I've decided how to reply to Kat's disemboweling of me. A second later, the birthday girl herself—Louise Morgan—appears at Kat's side, looking like an older, cookie cutter version of her gorgeous daughter.

Louise looks beautiful tonight, as always. Not to mention, a little tipsy. She's wearing a glittering birthday crown atop her blonde bob, while holding a wine goblet in one hand and a bundled baby in her other arm—a baby who's obviously Ryan's, based on his reaction to the bundle.

"Helloooo, Colin!" Louise sings out gaily when she sees my smiling face. "How are you?"

"I'm good. Getting some advice from the Morgan Mafia. Happy birthday."

"Thank you so much." She giggles. "The kids surprised me with a full house as my birthday present!"

"So, I see."

"I wish you, Matthew, and Zander could be here, too. Our family isn't complete without *all* my kiddos."

"I'm sorry to miss it. Fish and I have a work obligation in LA tomorrow. And I think Zander is in London with Aloha for some big event."

"Oh, I didn't mean to imply I'm upset with any of you for not being here. I know you're all busy. Just saying I love you, that's all."

"I love you, too, Louise."

Bam.

I love you.

The minute those words glide out of my mouth, so fucking easily, I realize I *also* love Amy. Of course, I do. In a different way, obviously. But also, weirdly, in a surprisingly similar way, too.

All of a sudden, I realize Louise Morgan is Amy's walking Pinterest board. She's Amy thirty years from now. And even more importantly, Louise is the person who's trained me, for half my life, to love someone who, on the one hand, feels like family to me—she's been a second mother to me—while also inspiring lust in me, during my formative years.

I haven't felt anything close to lust for Louise Morgan recently. As an adult. But back in the day? Hell yeah. And so did all the Morgan boys' friends. In fact, growing up, Louise Morgan was the ultimate MILF for a whole lot of randy teenagers, a fact I know to be true because we all talked about it, endlessly. Fish, especially, had a *massive* crush on this woman, during his teenage years. And yet, we all still loved her like a mother figure, at the same time, and still do to this day.

So, if that's the case, then why can't I love Amy, in a similar way? In some sense, like a brother would, only in that I want to take care of her and protect her and fix all her problems . . . But also in a decidedly *un*-brotherly way, too. In the sense that I want to rip her fucking clothes off, every goddamned time I see her?

It's a startling revelation to me. A new way of looking at things that makes everything click into place for me.

I love Amy.

I've always loved Amy.

And I always *will* love Amy.

And nobody else.

And I *also* want to fuck the living hell out of her!

Oh my God.

What more could a man possibly want, if not all that?

Amy's words from the other day suddenly slam into me: "If you want me to be your actual girlfriend and shout from the rooftops about me, then let me know, and I promise I'll give you a shot . . . *if I'm not already dating someone else by then.*"

Oh, no.

I've been such a fool!

"Gotta run, guys!" I blurt, interrupting something Kat is saying to me. "Happy birthday, Momma Lou! Sorry, Kat! I gotta go!"

"Wait!" Kat shouts. "I have more to say to you about this Amy situation."

"There's no need!" I shout. "I just figured everything out. I've got to hang up now, so I can call her and tell her I've been a fool and I love her to the moon and back again!"

"Oooh, how exciting!" Louise says.

But Kat is breathing fire. "*No!*" she shouts. "No! Don't do that!"

I'm hyperventilating with excitement and anticipation. But Kat's tone was too authoritative to ignore. "What do you mean no? Kat, I have to go!"

"Colin, you absolutely cannot hang up and *call* this poor woman to say you love her for the first time!" Kat says. "That ship has sailed. The price of admission has gone way up now."

"What are you talking about?" I ask, genuinely confused.

"She's saying you gotta grand gesture the fuck outta her, brah!" Keane shouts from the back.

"Language, Keaney," Mrs. Morgan says, pointing at little Mia on Dax's lap.

"I've heard Uncle Keaney say worse than that before," Mia mutters, as Ryan is saying, "Keane's right, dude." Ryan grimaces. "*Ach.* I hate saying that, in any context. But Kat and Keane are both right—words won't be enough anymore. I mean, you also need to say the words. And don't scrimp on them. But at this point, you're gonna need to ride in on your white horse before saying all the right words."

"Sweep her off her feet, Colinoscopy!" Keane calls out.

"You need to do something that takes her breath away!" Kat agrees enthusiastically. "Something that shows her how much you've been listening to her. Something designed specifically for *her.*"

"Shit," I mutter. "I mean, shoot. Sorry, Louise."

"I've heard it all before," Mia mutters.

I run my hand through my hair. "Okay, I hear what you're saying. Any suggestions?"

"We don't know the girl like you do," Kat says. "What would make her feel like you've moved mountains to—"

"I've got it!" I blurt. "I know what to do!" I'm shaking from adrenaline. I leap up from my couch and pace around my living room, feeling electrified. "I've gotta go, guys! Thank you, Morgan Mafia! I love you the most!"

"Give us a hint!" Kat shouts.

"No time for that. Gotta go. I'll fill you in later."

"Go balls to the walls, Colinoscopyyyyy!" Keane yells.

"Roger!"

'Rabbit," the entire group responds, even Mia on Dax's

lap. Because that's what any Morgan worth their salt always says after hearing the word "roger," in any context.

I end the call with the Morgans and immediately place one to my brother in arms, my piscatorial best friend: Matthew Fishberger.

"Fish Tacoooo," I say enthusiastically, after he picks up the call. "I need you and your guitar and your big ol' song-writing brain, *pronto*."

"Huh?"

"I need you to help me write a love song."

"Wait, *you* want to write a love song?" Fish asks. I don't blame him for being shocked. It's the first time I've made this kind of request, in the history of our friendship.

"Yep. I'm going to write the most perfect, heartfelt love song in the history of the world for Amy—and we both know I'm gonna need a *lot* of help to pull that off."

"Am *I* gonna be the one to sing this love song to Amy, or—"

"No, *I'm* gonna sing it to her, dumbass! Obviously. She's *my* girlfriend!"

"Whoa."

"Chop chop, Matthew! Get your ass over here. We don't have a lot of time."

"How long do we have?"

"We have to write it tonight, so I can sing it to her tomorrow. We'll swing by the movie studio tomorrow before we head over to the *Sing Your Heart Out* taping."

"I'm confused. I thought you were done shooting all your scenes for the movie."

"I am. But Amy's been ghosting me, and I have no idea where she's been staying, so I'm gonna surprise her at work tomorrow. I'm pretty sure she's gonna start work on the movie set tomorrow, now that I'm no longer there. So, we're gonna show up and I'm gonna sweep her off her feet! Ka-bam!"

"Why has Amy been ghosting you?"

"Because I'm an idiot. I'll tell you about it in person. Are you coming here or am I going there? Time's a-ticking."

"You'd better come here. I just smoked a huge bowl."

I chuckle. "Okay, I'm on my way. Stay awake for me."

"You'd better pack an overnight bag. Depending how long it takes us to pound out this 'perfect' love song, you might want to crash here tonight, so we can drive to the studio and the taping together tomorrow."

"Good thinking. I'll be there in twenty, Fish Head. Thanks."

"Make it forty and grab me a pizza on your way. Ally's having dinner at her mom's tonight. I'm hungry."

"There's no time, Fish Head."

"You want to exploit my songwriting skillz, then you need to feed me, Seymour."

"*Fine*. One pizza coming up. Stay awake for me."

"Make it two pizzas." He snorts. "I smoked *a lot* of weed."

Where does this lanky man put all the food he eats? "Fine," I say, exasperated. "*Two* pizzas. Just don't pass out on me before I get there."

"Roger."

"Rabbit. See you soon."

THIRTY

COLIN

"**P**ut a fire under your lanky ass, Matthew!" I shout at Fish, as he sloooowwwwly grabs his guitar case out of his car's backseat.

"You're a madman," Fish replies calmly, straightening up with his guitar case in hand. "We've got plenty of time."

"No, we don't!" I shout in reply, beckoning furiously for Fish to hurry the fuck up. "We're short on time, as a matter of fact, thanks to the surf sesh you *insisted* on having after breakfast!"

Fish rolls his eyes as he languidly closes his car door and presses a button to lock up. "You need to take a very large chill pill, my dude. It's all gonna work out fine."

We're in the VIP parking lot of the studio where I worked last week. Shooting on my scenes is over, but production has resumed today for everyone else, after taking the weekend off. Luckily, when I texted the production manager, Margaret, and told her I'd left something behind on-set last week—and could I swing by with my bandmate, Fish, to retrieve it?—she said no problem, she'd put our names on the list.

And now, here we are. Poised and ready to sweep Amy off her feet with the world's most honest and intimate love song, written especially for her and performed by *me* in front of every crew and cast member we worked with last week! How's that for grand gesturing the fuck outta Amy O'Brien?

When Fish is finally ready to go, I begin sprinting toward the security check-in area. When we get there, the guard recognizes me from last week—but, unfortunately, he also recognizes Fish. Which means he suddenly realizes, oh my God, he was chatting with the drummer of 22 Goats all last week and didn't even realize it! He asks for a selfie with both of us and then goes on and on about his love of 22 Goats. Which would be okay, I suppose, if Fish didn't elongate the conversation by talking about music with the guy for half my life.

When I can't take it anymore, I blurt, "Sorry, man. We'd love to stay and chat, but we're running late."

"Oh, no worries!" the guard calls to our backs. "Great talking to you!"

"That was rude, dude," Fish says as we jog toward the main production area.

"My life's happiness hangs in the balance, Fish. He'll live."

We make it inside the bustling heart of the production area and stop to look around, both of us breathing hard.

"Do you see her?" Fish asks.

"No. I'll ask Margaret, the woman in charge of production assistants. Come on."

I take off running, figuring Fish will follow. And, God bless him, he does. But before I've located the woman I'm looking for, I spot our famed director, Gary Flynn, chatting with a small group that includes his longtime personal assistant. *Perfect.* Gary's assistant is the eyes and ears of this place! She'll know exactly where Margaret is—and maybe even Amy.

But as we approach the small group, I overhear something that stops me dead in my tracks. "Where the hell is Seth?" Gary, our director, is saying.

His assistant replies, "He said he'd be 'running lines' with his new PA in his trailer and we shouldn't bother him 'for at least an hour.'"

"Are you fucking kidding me?" Gary shouts, taking the words right out of my mouth.

My heart stampeding, I pull a one-eighty—a sudden maneuver that sends Fish crashing into my chest—and then, as Fish stumbles back and tells me I'm a lunatic, I grab his lanky arm and physically drag him toward Seth's extra-large, extra-luxurious trailer on the perimeter of the large studio lot.

When we arrive at our destination, Seth's trailer door is locked. Gritting my teeth, I yank on the handle, furiously, trying to gain entry in any way possible, even if it means breaking the latch or pulling the entire door off its hinges.

"Dude!" Fish yells, as my movements become more frantic. "Calm down, Colin!"

But I'm not listening. In fact, I'm a man possessed. "Open up, Seth!" I shout, variously banging and yanking on the door. "It's Colin Beretta! Open up!"

"You might want to tamp down the crazy, just a tad, my brother," Fish warns. "There's security all over this lot."

But, again, I'm not listening. The past five days of being ghosted by Amy, while reliving our heated conversation in my head on a loop, have pushed me to the brink of lunacy. How could I have let Amy go without telling her what's so clear to me now? *I love you, too.* Why was that simple truth so hard for me to say at the time? I swear, if I'm too late and Amy's inside this trailer, getting railed by Seth Rockford—and she actually wants that fucker over me—I'll never forgive myself.

Out of nowhere, the door swings open and a shirtless Seth appears before me, his dark eyes bugging out. "What the fuck is wrong with you?" he bellows. "Is there a fire?"

Without answering Seth's question, I push past him, hollering Amy's name. And when I find the living area in the trailer empty, I march straight into the tiny bedroom like a bull in a China shop.

When I barge into the bedroom, I find a naked brunette clambering to cover herself with a sheet, and quickly turn away, my cheeks blazing.

"What the hell is wrong with you?" Seth yells behind my back in the doorframe, as the poor woman shrieks and scrambles.

My eyes still averted, I call out to the woman, "You're Seth's new PA?"

"Get out!" she screams.

"Do you want to be here?"

"Of course! Get out!"

"Sorry." I turn around, drag Seth by his arm into the living space, and yell, "Where's Amy?"

"*Who?*" Seth looks genuinely confused, which pisses me off even more.

Flooded with adrenaline, I shove Seth's back into a nearby wall and pin him there with a forearm against his bobbing Adam's apple. "Amy. My *girlfriend*. The redhead you're planning to fuck in Hawaii!"

Seth looks stupefied. Not to mention terrified. I know he's a good actor. Sort of. On occasion. But my gut tells me he's not faking this reaction.

"I haven't seen that redhead since she was with you!" he gasps out.

I lessen the pressure against Seth's Adam's apple, feeling confused and off-kilter. "She's been assigned to you."

"Not to my knowledge. Ask Margaret about her assignment. Why would I know anything about a fucking PA's assignment?"

"Because you said you'd get Amy assigned to you as a favor to me!" I boom. "Although we both know you were planning to do that for nobody but yourself."

Seth scoffs. "Amy's a mousy little thing. I was never gonna—"

I slam Seth against the wall again, this time even harder than before, and his eyes nearly pop out of his head in shock. "Keep my girlfriend's name out of your fucking mouth, or I'll kill you."

Seth grips my forearms. "Get your hands off me!"

"Colin!" Fish yells behind me. I feel his hands gripping my shoulder. "Colin, stop!"

Seth pushes on my chest while Fish pulls me back, so I relent and take a step back. I'm trembling with rage, but in control enough to back off. That is, until Seth points at me and shouts something that instantly hurtles me into an uncontrolled rage.

"You just committed career suicide!" Seth seethes. "Over a mousy little PA I'd never stoop to fuck, anyway!"

Without commanding my body to do it, I haul back and punch Seth's famous face, crashing my fist into his nose with a loud crack that sends blood instantly gushing from his noggin like a geyser.

Howling in pain, Seth covers his face, as Fish leaps forward and grabs ahold of my cocked arm with surprising force. A high-pitched shriek unleashes behind me—the brunette from the bedroom is apparently standing in the doorway, and when I turn toward the noise, I see her wrapped in a sheet, screaming bloody murder.

Fuck.

My body quaking with adrenaline, I sprint out the trailer, prompting Fish to follow on my heels. For at least a full minute, the two of us Goats flee the scene of my crime, heading vaguely in the direction of the main production area. But when I realize Fish is cackling hysterically behind me as he runs—laughing so hard, in fact, the gap between us is beginning to lengthen considerably—I stop running to let him catch up.

Finally, when Fish comes to a stop next to me, he bends over, rests his palms on his thighs, and laughs his ass off for an eternal moment. "That was epic!" Fish shouts. "Awesome!"

"It's not funny," I gasp out. "Seth's a powerful guy, Fish. He could demand my part gets recast. He could press charges."

"Bah. Fuck it, shit happens." It's the catchphrase Fish coined in middle school that turned his lifelong nickname into an acronym. He continues, "Did you see the look on Seth's face when he realized you'd punched him? Bwaahaa! That was amazing!"

I run a palm over my face. "I don't know what came over me. He dissed Amy and I totally lost it. It's like I had an out of body experience."

"Hey, you said you wanted to grand gesture the fuck outta Amy, right? Well, mission accomplished! You couldn't have grand gestured her better than *that*."

I rub my forehead. "I'm fucked, Fish."

He puts his palm on my shoulder. "I have a feeling everything's gonna be just fine. But if not, so what? There'll be other movies—whereas, this was your one and only chance to beat the shit out of Seth Rockford to defend your woman's honor." Fish hoots with glee, which makes me laugh, too, even though I know I shouldn't.

"Unfortunately, I'm gonna look like a loose cannon psychopath to Amy when I tell her this story," I say, "since I can't tell her what Seth said about her. He basically called her unfuckable, Fish—and that's one of Amy's biggest insecurities. But if I don't tell her about that, then why did I beat the shit out of Seth Rockford? Because he looked at her the wrong way a couple times last week? Making her think I'm a nut case isn't quite the grand gesture I was going for here."

"Tell Amy the opposite," Fish says. "Tell her Seth was talking shit about how much he wants to fuck her, so you snapped."

"Oooh, I like that version." I twist my mouth. "I'll have to tell Amy something about what happened, after the cops show up at my house and arrest me for assaulting Seth Rockford."

Fish snorts. "That's not gonna happen. But if did, it'd be worth it."

I shake my head and exhale loudly. "Fuck. I guess I should tell my director what happened, so Seth doesn't find him first and spin things to make himself sound like some kind of hero. Come on."

Fish and I begin wandering around, looking for Gary, and eventually find him in the tent with the monitors, surrounded by a bunch of people, including the woman I was looking for earlier—Margaret, who's in charge of production.

"Hey, Gary," I say, coming to a stand next to him. "Sorry to interrupt."

"Colin!" Gary says warmly, turning to greet me. "Great to see you!"

"You might not feel that way after I tell you what I've done." I take a deep breath and tell Gary the story of what happened in Seth's trailer, although I don't mention the PA in Seth's bed to protect her privacy.

"I totally overreacted," I admit. "Seth wasn't physically threatening me. He made a crack about my girlfriend, Amy— my PA last week—not being attractive enough to have sex with, and I lost it. He was a douchebag, but that was no excuse for me to physically attack him."

Gary looks distressed. "Shit, Colin."

"I know. I'm sorry."

"Seth's a producer on the movie."

"I know." I hang my head. "I know you went out on a limb to cast me. I'm sorry I've let you down."

Gary exhales. "Seth's gonna demand we reshoot all your scenes with another actor. He might even file a police report. He's a vindictive motherfucker."

"That's why I wanted you to hear it from me first. I fucked up, but I don't want him making shit up and piling on."

"Excuse me," Fish says politely, holding up his index finger. "Sorry to interrupt. I'm Matthew Fishberger, Colin's bandmate. I was there when Colin clocked Seth, and I believe Colin has left out a critical detail. Namely, the fact that there was a naked PA in Seth's bed when we burst in there."

"Fish, no."

Fish waves me off. "Are head-honcho producers supposed to have sex with their PAs? Especially a new one, who wouldn't be nearly as comfortable telling her boss to fuck off when he hits on her? I thought that's a big no-no."

"Fish, let's not drag that poor woman into this."

"But wouldn't she have to give a statement as an eyewitness, if Seth tried to press charges against Colin or get him
kicked off the movie?" Fish asks. "That's the only reason I've
brought her up—because I have a feeling, when Seth realizes
that, he'll probably want to let bygones be bygones."

My mouth clanks open. Holy shit! He's a genius!

Gary looks at Margaret, his eyebrows lifted, before
returning to Fish. "You're exactly right, Matthew. *Yes*, any
eyewitness to what happened would most definitely need to
give an official statement, *if* Seth were to report what
happened with Colin." He looks at Margaret again. "But given
the circumstances, I can't fathom Seth would want to do that."

"I'll handle it," Margaret says tightly, before taking a few
steps away, with her phone already pressed to her ear.

Gary returns to Fish and me. "Don't worry about a thing,
Colin. I'm positive Seth won't say a word about what
happened. In fact, what I think happened is Seth accidentally
smashed his face while choreographing a fight sequence with
our stunt coordinator."

"How very masculine of him," Fish mutters. "That's so
alpha."

Gary looks at me sternly. "You got lucky this time, Colin.
If that PA hadn't been there, you'd be fucked, and I wouldn't
be able to help you."

I exhale an ocean of relief. "I'm sorry I lost my temper."

"You should be." He claps a palm on my shoulder and
leans forward to whisper. "But don't be *too* sorry." He snickers. "I'll deny it if you repeat this, but you did what half of
Hollywood has been wanting to do to Seth for years." He
smirks. "Including *me*."

Fish hoots with glee, but I'm too relieved to join him.

"It's gonna be fine, Colin. But don't you dare fuck up like

this on our next movie together. This is a lucky, one-time free pass."

"I'm gonna do another movie with you?" I ask.

Gary smiles. "Of course. I always like working with my favorite actors, again and again. Surely, you know this about me."

I feel myself blushing. "Yeah, I've noticed that. I'd *love* to work with you again, Gary. Any time."

"Good. I've already got something in mind for you. It's shooting next year."

My heart feels like it's bursting. "Whenever you call me, I'll come running. Working with you has been a dream come true."

Someone calls to Gary and he tells them he'll be right there.

"I'll let you go," I say. "I know you're slammed. Thanks for everything. Again, sorry."

"I'll call you after I get back from Hawaii," Gary says. "Let's never speak of the incident in Seth's trailer again."

"What incident?"

"Good boy." With that, Gary walks away and returns to his monitors, while I stand aside with Fish and wait for Margaret, who's standing nearby, to end her phone call. Finally, when she does, I beeline to her with Fish in tow.

"Sorry to bother you," I say to Margaret. "Can you tell me where Amy's been assigned?"

Margaret looks confused. "Amy doesn't work here. She left the production when you did." When I look at Margaret blankly, she adds, "I offered Amy a permanent position, but she said she'd decided to take another job—her 'dream job,' she called it."

I'm stupefied. "Did Amy identify this 'dream job'?"

"No." Margaret tilts her head. "I'm surprised she didn't tell you about it."

I grimace. "We had an argument. You're *sure* Amy doesn't work here, in any capacity?"

"I'd know if she did."

Fish nudges my arm. "We gotta go, or we'll be late for the taping."

"Taping?" Margaret asks.

"We're contractually obligated to appear in the finale of *Sing Your Heart Out,*" Fish explains.

"Fun," Margaret says. "Colin, when you see Amy, tell her if her dream job doesn't pan out, I'll snap her up in a heartbeat."

"I'll tell her, if I ever find her."

Fish and I say goodbye to Margaret and begin jogging back to Fish's car in the parking lot.

"Where the hell is Amy working?" I grumble as we reach Fish's car. "What could her 'dream job' possibly be, if not working on a big-budget Hollywood movie in Hawaii for three months?"

Fish unlocks his car and we both slip inside.

"And why didn't Amy tell me about her new job?" I demand, feeling deflated. "Where has she been staying? Why is she ghosting me? Fish, I'm losing it."

Fish looks sympathetic but says nothing. When he starts his car, I sigh, pull out my phone, and call Reed Rivers' right-hand man—a guy named Owen who always knows what's what at River Records.

"Hi, Colin."

"Hey, O," I reply. "I'm short on time. Remember Amy O'Brien—my buddy's sister who got assigned to Caleb during the RCR tour?"

"Yeah."

"Do you know if she recently signed on for another tour?"

"I'd have to check."

"Could you do that now?"

"Hang on." A few minutes later Owen returns. "Her name isn't listed on any current or upcoming crew roster."

"Fuck." I pause. "Can you give me the number for that Nate guy who works sound?"

"Hang on." There's a short pause, and then, "I just texted you Nate's contact info."

"Got it. Thanks, O. You're the best."

I hang up with Owen and send a text to Nate:

Me: Hey, Nate. This is Colin Beretta. I have an important question. Here's a selfie to prove it's me.

I snap a selfie and send it. I don't have time for Nate to wonder if someone is pranking him, and I've learned from past experience a selfie is the quickest route to side-stepping that entire conversation. Luckily, Nate replies instantly:

Nate: Hey, Colin! Great to hear from you! What's up?

Me: Remember Amy O'Brien, C-Bomb's PA during RCR's tour?

Nate: Yeah.

Me: Who from the tour would have invited her to crash at their place in LA?

Nate: Lots of people. Everyone loved Amy.

Me: Top pick?

Nate: Maybe our tour manager, Melanie? She was especially fond of Amy.

Me: What's Melanie's number?

Nate texts me the number and I immediately call it. But the woman doesn't answer, so I leave a voicemail, just as Fish is parking his car in the VIP parking area for *Sing Your Heart Out*. Before I exit Fish's car, however, I tap out another text to Nate. Something I wish I could say to the fucker in person— preferably, while pressing my forearm into his bobbing Adam's apple. But such is life. It's filled with disappointments.

Me: BTW, I heard you called Amy "a six, at best" during the RCR tour. Just so you know, she's my girlfriend now. And that woman is a stone-cold, perfect TEN, motherfucker.

THIRTY-ONE

COLIN

"Five minutes!" the production manager of *Sing Your Heart Out* calls out. And all of us in the greenroom, a group that includes Fish, me, and a British popstar named Phoebe, acknowledge her announcement.

The fourth "guest mentor" of this season's singing competition, Kendrick Cook, isn't here in this greenroom with us because he's currently onstage playing drums behind Savage and Laila's duet. But the minute I get the chance, I'm going to ask Kendrick if he knows Amy's whereabouts—and God help me, if it turns out she went straight from my bed to his, I'll never forgive myself.

My phone in my pocket rings with an incoming call from Melanie—the tour manager I called earlier—and I gasp and quickly answer.

"Melanie! Thanks for calling me back."

"You said it was urgent."

"Yeah, it is. I'm calling about Amy O'Brien—C-Bomb's PA on his last tour?"

"She's a cutie."

"I thought maybe she's been staying at your place the last several days?"

"No, I'm on Watch Party's tour now. I haven't talked to Amy since the RCR tour ended. Is she okay?"

"She's fine. I need to talk to her about something personal. Who do you think from the RCR tour might have offered Amy a place to crash in LA this past week?"

"Hmm. Could be anyone. Everyone loves Amy."

"I know the feeling," I mutter, just as the production manager for *Sing Your Heart Out* appears and says it's time for our group to follow her.

"I gotta go," I say to Melanie on the phone. "Do me a favor and send me the crew sheet from the RCR tour."

"I don't have it handy, but I can get it."

"Thanks. I owe you one."

We say goodbye and hang up, and I follow the group out of the greenroom. As we walk, I get Fish up to speed, concluding with, "As soon as Melanie sends me that crew list, I'm gonna call every name on it, until I find Amy."

"That could be a lot of calls," Fish says. "I'll help you."

"Thanks, Fish Head. That's why I love you the most."

We reach our destination—the left wing of the stage—and wait for our cue to walk onstage and celebrate this season's winner. For now, however, the host of the singing competition is onstage, drawing out the suspense.

As the host does her thing, I notice Kendrick Cook standing in the opposite wing and feel sick to my stomach at the sight of him. He's a fit, handsome dude with a beaming smile and a heart of gold. How could I have been so stupid *not* to lock Amy down the other night, and risk pushing her straight into the arms of someone like Kendrick Cook?

"Addison Swain!" the host of the singing show bellows

onstage and the studio audience loses their shit at the "big reveal" of the winner's name. Streamers sprout from the ceiling as music begins blaring, and a moment later, Laila Fitzgerald barrels onstage to congratulate the young winner. Finally, a production assistant cues the three of us—Fish, the British popstar, and me—and we head onstage to join the celebration, exactly as we're contractually required to do.

In the midst of the dance party, I spot Kendrick whooping it up with Savage across the expansive soundstage, so I grab Fish's arm and pull him over there for moral support.

When we reach Savage and Kendrick, we all high-five each other for the cameras, and then make a show of having a great ol' time as the blaring music continues, until the director yells, "We're clear!"

"Catch you later," Savage mumbles, before beelining across the stage toward his girlfriend, Laila.

"Well, *that* winner wasn't a surprise to me," Kendrick says amiably.

But I don't have time to talk about the show. "Have you seen Amy since Laila's party?" I ask. And when Kendrick looks at me blankly, I add, "The redhead who was 'direct' and 'refreshing.'"

"Ooh." Kendrick flashes a snarky look. "No, I haven't seen her since she left the party with *you*." He cocks an eyebrow. "Uh oh. Does this mean you weren't able to teach her what she was dying to learn?"

"No, I taught her everything she wanted to learn and more." Annoyed, I turn to leave but stop when Kendrick calls out to my back, "She's at Caleb's."

I whirl around. "Caleb's? Are you sure?"

Kendrick nods. "I was talking to him on FaceTime the other day about a drum sequence I was working on. And who did I see in the background, organizing the shelves in Caleb's home studio, but the redhead from Laila's party. I was like, 'Oh, fuck, C-Bomb, no. Please tell me that's not *Colin's* redhead.' And Caleb goes, 'Yeah, it's her. Do me a favor and tell Colin you saw her here. Right away. Please.' I wasn't planning to touch that with a ten-foot pole. I didn't want to be the guy responsible for sparking yet *another* beef between RCR and 22 Goats. But now that you're asking me about her, directly, I'm not gonna lie to your face." He raises his palms and grimaces. "Don't shoot the messenger! This is between C-Bomb and you."

I roll my eyes. "C-Bomb isn't fucking her, KC. He's *harboring* her."

Kendrick furrows his brow. "Huh?"

I run my palm down my face. "Amy and I had an argument. Caleb's obviously been helping her ghost me."

"Are you sure? That doesn't sound like C-Bomb."

"I'm sure. Thanks for telling me. Sorry I was a dick the other night. I was fighting my attraction to her. I'm sure Amy genuinely liked you."

"No worries. I figured out the situation pretty quickly. I hope everything works out for you two."

"Thanks. Me, too." I grip Kendrick's palm, sideways, confirming there are no hard feelings, and Fish does the same. And then, Fish and I race out of the studio and into the cool night air.

The second I get settled into Fish's car, yet again, I place a call to Caleb.

"What took you so long?" Caleb says in greeting.

"Is Amy still there?"

"She is. At the moment, she's organizing my bedroom closet. Yesterday, it was my kitchen cupboards and home office. Before that, my garage, home gym, and home studio. And for three days before all that, she didn't stop crying on my fucking shoulder. *Please*, Colin, get your ass over here, tell the girl you love her, and give me my life back!"

I laugh. "I'm on my way. I should tell you: you're on speaker phone and Fish is in the car."

"Hola, Fish Tacoooo!"

"Hey, C-Bomb. Long time, no talk."

"Way too long."

Fish looks at me, shocked, before replying, "I agree. Do you think you might be willing to say the same thing to Dax?"

"I've been talking to Amy about doing that very thing, as a matter of fact—whenever she's taken a break from crying or 'helping me,' that is. Amy's helped me look at several things from a new perspective. Don't let her green doe-eyes fool ya. She's a sniper."

"She is," I agree. "She kicked the shit out of me the other day."

"Oh, trust me, I know. I've heard all about it. How'd you finally figure out Amy is here?"

"Kendrick."

He chuckles. "Thank God. Amy made me swear I wouldn't call you and tell you she's here. But she never said I couldn't tell Kendrick to tell you. Ha! What's your ETA?"

"Fifteen minutes," Fish supplies.

"Don't tell Amy I'm coming," I interject.

"Of course not," Caleb replies. "I wouldn't miss the look on Amy's face when you show up here for anything."

"So, she's working for you now?" I ask, even though I know it's a foregone conclusion.

"No," Caleb says, surprisingly. "I promised Amy I

wouldn't tell you about her new job, if you called, though. So, you'll have to ask her about that yourself."

"I will. Right after I sweep her off her feet."

"Please, don't fuck this up, man," Caleb pleads. "There's nothing left for the woman to organize here, and I'm not wired to be anyone's shoulder to cry on for this fucking long."

I chuckle. "Don't worry, brother. I'm riding in on my white horse as we speak. As a good friend of mine called it, I'm gonna grand gesture the fuck outta her."

THIRTY-TWO

AMY

As I'm reaching for a pair of shoes on a high shelf in Caleb's walk-in closet, I hear a voice behind me, saying my name. *Was that Colin?* My heart in my mouth, I whirl around and discover, yes, it was! He's standing in the doorway of Caleb's closet with Fish and Caleb a few feet behind him—and he looks gorgeous!

"Colin," I gasp out.

He looks tentative. "You didn't answer any of my texts or calls."

My heart is a jackhammer in my chest. "I figured you'd find me, if you had something important to say to me." I nod at Fish in greeting, and suddenly realize he's holding a guitar at the ready. My jaw falls open. "Fish is here to sing 'Fireflies' to me?"

Colin grins. "No, sweetheart. I'm going to sing to you—but not 'Fireflies.' A song I wrote for you, the love of my life, with an assist from Fish." As my jaw clanks open, Colin takes my hand and leads me out of Caleb's closet and into the bedroom, where he deposits me on the edge of Caleb's bed, while Caleb takes a chair and Fish stands to Colin's side with his guitar.

I'm a deer in headlights. Colin wrote a song for me? And he's here to sing to me? *And he called me the love of his life*?

"I only supplied the guitar chords," Fish says, tuning his guitar. "Colin wrote the melody and every word. This one's all him, Amy—straight from his heart."

Well, that's it. Even before Colin's started singing, I'm already on the verge of throwing myself into his arms and telling him I love him. That I've been miserable without him. The embarrassing truth is that, ever since I left Colin's house the other night, I've cried an ocean of tears and been wracked with regret. I was too hasty! Expected too much!

In fact, only moments ago, while organizing Caleb's closet, I resolved to go to Colin's house tomorrow morning, first thing, and tell him we'll work it out. Find a middle ground. Take our time! And now, Colin is here to sing a love song he wrote for *me*—the woman he just called "the love of his life"? *Swoon*!

"This is called 'Swoon,'" Colin whispers, a shy grin on his face.

Goosebumps. They're erupting across every square inch of my skin!

Colin chuckles at whatever he's seeing on my face, before nodding at Fish, taking a deep breath, and launching into his song:

First time I saw you I loved you the most
Don't remember that day, I trust what I'm told

How could you doubt the effect of your smile?
It parts the clouds

Saw you again, like no time had passed
Except for the curves under that purple dress

You wished for a love song, your wish my command
I'm singing to you now

You make me swoon
Baby, you just do it for me
Swoon
In my soul down deep

Love you to the moon
And right back again
Baby, you're perfection to me
A stone-cold, perfect ten
Swoon to the moon and back again

If you're a creeper, then call me one too
My pulse through the roof any time I'm near you

Don't ever doubt the effect that you have

You drive me wild
Those green eyes and that smile

You make me swoon
Baby, you just do it for me
Swoon
In my soul down deep

Love you to the moon
And right back again
Baby, you're perfection to me
A stone-cold, perfect ten
Swoon to the moon and back again

I'll love you till I'm old and gray
Love you from beyond the grave
Love you forever and a day
Love you more than words could ever say

You make me swoon
Baby, you just do it for me
You make me swoon
In my soul down deep

Love you to the moon
And right back again
Baby, you're perfection to me
A stone-cold, perfect ten

Swoon to the moon and back again

By the time Colin finishes his stunning song, tears are streaking down my cheeks, my heart is a stampede of wild horses in my chest, and, of course, I'm swooning. Riding a wave of love and excitement, gratitude and relief, I pop up from the edge of Caleb's bed and fling myself into Colin's waiting arms.

"I love it!" I shout. "I love you so much!"

Colin takes my tear-streaked face in his palms. "Every word is the truth. I love you to the moon and back again. I'll love you forever and a day." With that, Colin crushes his lips to mine.

Fish and Caleb cheer like they're watching a smooch on a kiss-cam at a basketball game, which prompts Colin and me to laugh into each other's lips and fall into a tight, fervent embrace.

"Live with me," Colin says into my hair. "Be mine forever and I promise I'll never stop shouting from every rooftop about my love for you, as long as I live."

I pull back from our hug to wipe my cheek and discover Fish and Caleb have left the room.

"You don't have to promise me forever," I say. "We can take it slow. I just need to know you're not—"

"I don't need or want to take it slow, Amy. You're The One. I'm done dating. I'm done looking. I'm committed to you—to building a life with you and only you. Forever."

I'm shaking. Reeling. "Are you sure?"

"I'm sure. I've always loved you—my whole life. If I had another hundred lives to live, I'd love you, and only you, in all of them."

I fling myself at him again, too overwhelmed with joy to speak.

Colin's hard chest heaves against mine. "Come work for me, Ames. I don't want you working for someone else who—"

"I'm working for Violet!" I shout excitedly, and then giggle at the look of complete shock on Colin's face. "I'm starting on Monday after Dax and Violet get back from Seattle!"

"Violet?"

I quickly tell him the gist and he's every bit as thrilled as I am.

"That really does sound like your dream job!" Colin says.

"And guess what else?" I say, jumping up and down like toddler. "Violet told me yesterday she wants me to travel with her, whenever she and Jackson join Dax on tour, so she can keep working while she's on the road!" I squeal. "That means I'm gonna get *paid* to travel with *you*!"

Colin guffaws with me. "Well, I would have been happy to pay you to do that."

I giggle. "I'd much rather have Violet as my employer and you as my boyfriend. But thank you."

Colin's dark eyes are sparkling. "That big family you dream about having one day? I want that, too. I want all of it, Amy, anything you dream about, I want it—as long as it's with you."

My breathing hitches. "That's not even close to what I was demanding of you the other day. I only needed to know you could imagine—"

"I know that. I understand now what you were saying to me. To be clear, I don't want to get started on *all* of that stuff, immediately. I'd like to have some time alone with you, before we jump into the next step. But I want you to know I'm one hundred percent all-in. None of what you said scares me. It only makes me excited about our future."

Well, that's all my poor little heart can take. Up until this moment, I've managed to pretty-cry this whole time, the way beautiful actresses do in period flicks—with gentle, poetic tears tracking slowly down my cheeks. But now, all bets are off and I'm a weeping, sobbing, snotty mess—letting loose with an ugly-cry that's almost certainly contorting my face in the most embarrassing of ways.

"Aw, Ames," Colin whispers, pulling me into his hard chest.

As I sob against him, Colin rubs my back and kisses my hair. He coos at me softly and says he loves me. Until, finally, I calm down enough to speak.

"This is even better than any fantasy. It's perfect."

"Even though *I'm* not perfect?"

"Correct."

Colin chuckles. "What clued you in? Damn." He winks playfully. "You ready to call your brother now, Red?"

I suck in a sharp inhale. "Yes!"

Colin pulls out his phone, and a moment later, Logan's smiling face appears on his screen.

"Hey, guys," Logan says. He frowns. "What's wrong, Amy?"

"Those are tears of joy," Colin reports calmly.

"Shocker," Logan deadpans.

"Is your wife nearby?" Colin asks. "I'd like to tell you both what's caused Amy's happy tears."

"She's right here." He yells over his shoulder. "Baaabe!"

There's a beat. And then Kennedy appears. "Hey, guys." Kennedy frowns. "What's wrong, Amy?"

"They're 'tears of joy,'" Logan reports.

"Oh, good."

All appropriate greetings are administered, before Colin gets down to brass tacks.

"So, guys," Colin says, "the reason I called is to inform you that I'm head over heels in love with Amy O'Brien and she feels the same way about me."

Kennedy whoops and Logan says something I can't make out above her celebration.

"Loving Amy is the easiest thing I've ever done," Colin says through the din. "And I want you—and the whole world —to know it. She's gonna be living with me, permanently. Forever. She's The One. I'm done looking, and she is, too." He looks at me. "Right?"

"Right."

He exhales with relief.

I roll my eyes. "You knew that, Colin." I smile at my brother and Kennedy. "Are you guys surprised?"

Logan and Kennedy look at each other and snicker, before Logan answers "nope" and Kennedy replies, "Not at all."

"We saw you two at the rehearsal dinner," Logan says. "And then at the wedding reception. We're not blind."

"Oh my God, Logan," Kennedy says to her husband. "I had to point it out to you!"

"Yeah, but once you did, I wasn't blind anymore."

Kennedy giggles.

"You're not pissed at me?" Colin asks my brother. "Not that it would matter. I love Amy, no matter what anyone thinks. But I'd prefer not to piss you off."

"Why would I be pissed?" Logan asks. "You're like a

brother to me. This is best-case scenario, as far as I'm concerned."

"Me being like a brother to you is exactly why I thought you'd be pissed," Colin admits.

Logan looks genuinely dumbfounded.

"Well, I'll be damned," Colin says, as I swat his broad shoulder.

"Are you gonna call both sets of parents next?" Logan says. "Because I should warn you, my mother is gonna lose her shit. She's always wanted you and Amy to get together."

"What?" I shout. "When did Mom say that?"

"Every time Colin was a better big brother to you than me. Which happened a lot." Logan smiles tenderly at me. "I'm thrilled for you, Amy. Always follow your heart. Take whatever path calls to you and run with it. Fuck the O'Brien way."

I clutch my heart and nod, tears re-emerging in my eyes. He doesn't need to explain that last comment any further. I know precisely what he means. "Thank you, Logan. I love you so much. You, too, Kennedy."

"We love you, too," Logan replies. "So, when did you two get together—the night of the rehearsal dinner, or did you exercise superhuman restraint and wait till the night of the wedding?"

I motion to Colin to answer my brother's question, exceedingly curious to hear his answer.

Colin purses his beautiful lips, contemplating. "Hmm. Well, our connection started the night of the rehearsal. There was an instant attraction between us that only grew exponentially the more we talked. But we kissed for the first time at the wedding reception, so I'd say that's when our *romance* began. After that kiss, it was game over. There were sparks.

Fireworks. Fireflies. It was everything the best love songs are written about."

I hold my breath, wondering if he's planning to tell Logan and Kennedy about the love song he wrote for me, given what a natural segue his last comment would be for that part of the story. But, no, Colin's next comment makes clear the beautiful song he wrote is a special, *intimate* gift from him to me.

"Now, if the question is how long I've *loved* Amy, then that's a different answer," Colin continues, after shooting me a shy smile that makes my heart skip a beat. "Call me a creeper, guys, but I've loved Amy my whole life—from literally the moment I first saw her."

Kennedy gasps and clutches her heart, thoroughly swept away by Colin's romantic words, and our foursome talks a bit longer about Colin's comment and our great news in general. Eventually, however, Colin wraps up the call.

"Gotta go, guys," he says. "There's something I want to do, before Amy and I call our parents." We hang up the call, and Colin grins mischievously at me. "Let's go find Fish and Caleb. I'd love their help with something."

We find the duo downstairs in Caleb's living room, looking like they're having a jovial conversation.

"Hey, guys," Colin says, as we enter the room. "I wanna make it Instagram official with Amy, and I'd love to have you both in the shot."

I inhale sharply in surprise, not only because Colin is willing to announce our relationship to the whole world—but because he wants to do it in such a shocking way. Since C-Bomb and Dax had their falling out several years ago, the members of Red Card Riot and 22 Goats haven't been photographed together. And now, Colin is planning to post a photo of two members of 22 Goats with Red Card Riot's iconic drummer . . . and lil ol' me?

To my surprise, Caleb leaps up energetically, as does Fish, with both men saying they'd love to help out. Without hesitation, all three men huddle around me, with Colin sliding his arm around my shoulders, and Colin snaps the momentous shot. When he shows it to me, it's after he's already posted it to his Instagram account—and the caption he typed underneath the photo makes me feel physically dizzy:

Two Goats, a Red Card Rioter, and the love of my life who makes me swoon.

"Well, that's not gonna fly under anyone's radar," C-Bomb says dryly. "In about ten seconds flat, that post is gonna break the internet."

"That's the idea," Colin says. He addresses me. "You want my ex to see that post? If so, I'll have to unblock her on Instagram."

I can't help snickering. "Hell yeah. I'm probably a petty bitch, but I want every woman you've ever dated, had sex with, or merely kissed—every groupie who's ever dreamed of sleeping with you, every girl I saw sneaking through your side gate as a teenager, every boy who didn't ask me to a dance in high school, and every girl who made fun of my hair growing up—to see that photo and wish they were me."

All three men guffaw at my surprisingly diabolical response, as I break into peals of gleeful laughter along with them.

"Done," Colin says. He grins broadly. "Now that I've

posted it, I think we'd better call our parents, *pronto*. Otherwise, in a matter of minutes, someone else is going to steal our thunder and tell them the good news first."

[Go here: http://www.laurenrowebooks.com/swoon-song to listen to Colin sing his song "Swoon" to Amy]

THIRTY-THREE
COLIN

When Amy and I reach my moonlit bedroom—or, rather, from this day forward, *our* moonlit bedroom—I stow her suitcase inside the doorway and immediately begin kissing her ravenously while peeling off her clothes. I've had a hard-on since leaving Caleb's house, a primal ache coursing through me like a mania to consummate the lyrics of my song—to express the same sentiments and promises contained in my lyrics, only this time with my body. If Fish hadn't been giving Amy and me a lift home, if I'd been driving, I would have found some dark, secluded place to park, so I could have fucked my woman a full half-hour ago.

When Amy's naked before me, I rip my own clothes off, tossing each article of clothing this way and that as I guide her to the bed. When we're both naked, I lay Amy down onto her back and begin worshipping every inch of her, every soft curve, murmuring words of adoration as I do.

As our mutual excitement soars, Amy begins making delicious sounds of pleasure that send pre-cum seeping from my tip. Breathing hard, I spread her thighs wide and dive head-first into her sweet pussy like a starving man. I flicker my tongue over her hard, swollen clit while sliding my fingers inside her and stroking her, methodically.

It doesn't take long. In record speed, Amy yelps, grips the comforter underneath her, and comes like a freight train against my fingers and tongue.

That first one under my belt, I lie on my back, pull Amy's quivering frame on top of me, grip her hips, and guide her onto my cock. I want to see her face as I make love to her. I want to see her green eyes flash when I tell her I love her while fucking her.

Why did I think romantic love had to be hard and painful to be real? Was it from watching my parents as a kid? Was that idea reinforced after watching my sister, Chiara, go through her painful divorce?

Well, now I see. True love can be easy and natural and right, like it's written in the stars. Like it's always been with Amy.

My whole life, the harder someone's love felt to attain, the more I wanted it. Perhaps, I wanted to prove I wasn't a quitter. Or that I was *worthy*. But now, suddenly, I realize love has always been so fucking hard for me, as far back as my teens, because I was never with the right person. *I wasn't with Amy.*

Our synchronized movements have become furious and passionate. If we keep going like this, we're going to break my bed. Gasping for air, I sit up and devour Amy's hard nipples. When I'm on the bitter brink of release and hanging on by a thread, I grasp Amy's face and look into her eyes. The green eyes that have lured me in and melted me from my earliest memories.

"I love you," I choke out. "I'll always love you. *Forever.*"

Amy chokes out the magic words in reply, before her eyes roll back. With a guttural growl, she digs her fingernails into my shoulders and comes with sublime force. As her innermost muscles send shockwaves of pleasure into my cock, I release along with her—and not only physically. As I come, I release everything that's been holding me back until now. Fear of getting hurt. Fear of not being enough. I resolve to give this woman all of me, forever, the good and the bad, without holding back, in a way I've never done with anyone else. I'm Amy's now. All of me. I'm committed to her and only her—to building a future with this woman, for the rest of my days.

As our heart rates settle down, we hold each other, our foreheads pressed together. I wrap my arms around her and kiss her tenderly, feeling overwhelmed with love and joy and peace.

"I'm so happy," Amy whispers.

"I've never been happier in my life."

"I never even dreamed this big."

The unbridled love I feel for Amy is making me feel like I could leap tall buildings. It's making me feel like there are no rules or boundaries. "You can go off the pill, any time you want," I whisper. And the minute the words leave my mouth, I feel nothing but excited about them.

Amy looks skeptical. "*Any* time I want?"

I nod. "It could be tomorrow or five years from now. No need to say a thing about it to me, in advance. In fact, surprise me. There aren't enough surprises in life. Good ones, anyway."

If I weren't holding Amy in my arms right now, I think it's fifty-fifty she'd flop over and face-plant onto the mattress in shock. I laugh at the way her body is turning to jelly in my arms and lay her down next to me.

"You okay?" I ask, as we lie alongside each other and cuddle.

"You're *sure* about what you said?" Amy asks.

I nod. "Choose your own adventure, Ames. I'm all in, whatever you decide to do."

I can practically hear Amy's heart thumping inside her chest. "If you change your mind, you'll need to tell me. Otherwise, I'm going to rely on this conversation."

"Go for it."

She's blown away.

"Okay, wait. A caveat. I know you're excited about your new job, and in a perfect world, I'd like to do a little traveling with you and the band before we have a baby to consider. So, come to think of it, I'd prefer you wait maybe six months before you pull the goalie."

"Oh, I never would have done it before then. I can't imagine I'd do it in less than a year. I'd want your movie to come out before we have a baby. It's going to be a huge hit, Colin. Probably lifechanging for you, and I want you to be able to enjoy that, fully, without being pulled in too many other directions. I'd also love having some time when it's just you and me."

"Cool. We'll have a year with the goalie in place, and after that, all bets are off. Surprise me."

She bites her lip, looking like she's holding her tongue.

"What?" I ask, and when she looks sheepish, I add, "Whatever you're thinking, spit it out, babe. From now on, we need to agree we'll always speak our minds."

Amy exhales. "I'd need to be wearing your ring before I'd feel comfortable pulling the goalie." She makes an apologetic face. "It's not that I don't believe you when you say you love me forever. It's just that—"

"Dude, I'm gonna put a ring on it." I chuckle as Amy's body relaxes into mine. "Didn't you listen to my lyrics? I'll love you till I'm old and gray. I'll love you from beyond the grave. I'll love you forever and a day. I didn't pick those lyrics because they rhyme. Of course, I'm gonna marry you! You think I wanna be eighty years old with five kids and fifteen grandkids with my *girlfriend*?"

She squeezes me tight. "I love you so much."

"I love you, too." I kiss the top of her head. "Don't worry. You won't have too long to wait. A ring will be on your finger long before you start thinking about pulling the goalie."

"I can't believe this is happening," she whispers, before pinching my nipple *hard*.

"*Ow*. Dude!"

She giggles.

"Aren't you supposed to pinch *yourself* when you can't believe something?" I say, laughing.

"Oh yeah. Sorry." She pinches herself and frowns. "Well, that's not nearly as fun."

I laugh and kiss the top of her head again. "I love you so much."

"I love you, too." She kisses my shoulder. "Baby, you just do it for me."

It's one of the lyrics from my song, of course. So, I sing it back to her.

"Was that performance tonight a one-time thing?" she asks. "Or will you ever sing me that song again?"

"I'll sing it to you every night of your life, if you want," I say.

"I do."

"Then so it shall be, milady. Your wish is my command."

She sighs happily, like a Disney princess. "I love you, Colin."

"I love you, too, baby. *And I always will.*"

THIRTY-FOUR

AMY

Six Months Later

"Hey, ladies," Caleb says, coming to a stop in front of Violet, Alessandra, and me.

We three women are sitting on a bench in a far corner of Reed Rivers' spacious patio, not far from the spot where Reed exchanged marriage vows with his bride, Georgina, a few hours ago. Ever since dinner ended and live music kicked off, Violet, Ally, and I have been dancing pretty much nonstop inside the house. At times, we've shaken our asses with our men. But mostly, we've let loose as a trio.

When we came out here to this bench a few minutes ago, I thought we'd throw back a quick drink and catch our breath before heading back inside to boogie again. Given the history between Caleb and Violet, I never would have thought, not in a million years, that Caleb would approach and say hello to our trio before we'd made it back inside.

I hop up to hug Caleb in greeting. We already hugged and said a quick hello earlier, right before sitting down for the ceremony, but I know it's a big deal for him to come over here, so I want him to feel supported and encouraged.

As Caleb and I pull apart from our embrace, he smiles warmly at me, before tentatively smiling at Violet, who's risen from the bench and is now standing next to me, her breathing shallow.

"Hi, Violet," Caleb says softly. "You look beautiful."

It's a heartbreaking compliment, considering everything Caleb divulged to me when I stayed at his house six months ago. This inked mountain of a man unexpectedly poured his heart out to me during those five days, every bit as much I poured mine out to him, so I know, despite his hard outer shell, Caleb's got a gooey-soft center—one he only shows to people who've earned his complete trust.

"Hello," Violet replies softly. She steps forward like she's going to hug him, but abruptly stops herself, which causes Caleb to wilt. But when Violet sees Caleb's body language, she recalibrates and follows through with her initial instinct, widening her arms and giving him a warm and tender hug.

Alessandra and I exchange a look that says, *Should we leave?*

"We'll let you two catch up in private," I murmur, motioning to Alessandra to follow me.

But Violet disengages from Caleb and says, "Stay. There's nothing Caleb and I need to say to each other in private." She fixes her blue eyes on me, and I know from being around her so much these past six months, she's nonverbally telling me she'll cut a bitch—a bitch named Amy—if I take as much as a single step.

When it's clear I'm staying put, Violet returns her attention to Caleb. "I'm so happy to see all the RCR guys decided to attend the wedding, even though you knew we'd all be here. I know it means the world to my brother that both bands could put their differences aside long enough to help him celebrate his love for Georgie."

"My bandmates have always wanted you to be happy, in whatever form that took," Caleb says. "They thought I was being an asshole—throwing a temper tantrum."

"You were," Violet says.

To my shock, Caleb nods in agreement with Violet's comment, before saying, "My band stayed away to keep from pissing me off—as I'm sure Colin and Fish stayed away to show solidarity with Dax."

"And with *me*," Violet retorts. And it takes all my strength to keep my face neutral in response. I'm rooting for Caleb, of course. I love that man. But I can't deny I'm proud of Violet for sticking to her guns and saying what needs to be said, without holding back.

"And later, with my son, too," Violet adds. "Do you know Dax and I have a son?"

Caleb nods. "I've seen photos. He's beautiful, not surprisingly. Jackson, right?"

"That's right. He's our world."

"I'm happy for you."

Caleb's eyes shift, briefly, to me, and I nod my encouragement. We talked about this six months ago, after all. I told Caleb, in no uncertain terms, he'd never be able to find true love again, never be able to feel true happiness again, frankly, if he didn't wipe the slate clean with Violet and Dax and admit his contributions to the cluster fuck and *forgive*.

Caleb clears his throat. "I'm happy for you both."

Violet looks shocked. "Thank you."

Caleb shifts his weight. "I came over here to tell you that. Also, to say I know it was wrong of me to expect my band to stand in solidarity with me, when I was the one being an asshole. I was immature and selfish. I felt stabbed in the heart, and I thought stabbing Dax in his heart in return would make me feel better. But it didn't." He looks at me again, gets encouragement, and returns to Violet. "Amy told me the expression, 'When you hold a grudge, it's like drinking poison and hoping the other guy dies.' And I realized that's exactly what I'd been doing, for way too long." He swallows hard. "I'm sorry."

Violet is visibly floored. "Thank you. It means the world to me to hear you say all that." She looks at me. "Thank you, Amy." When I press my lips together, wishing I could be invisible, she shifts her gaze back to Caleb. "When Dax saw that famous photo of you, Colin, Fish, and Amy, he was elated. He said he hoped it was a sign you were getting closer to burying the hatchet with him. That's all he's ever wanted, Caleb."

Caleb's Adam's apple bobs. The man is covered in tattoos. Some of them kind of scary. He's a towering figure, literally, and also figuratively, in music and pop culture—one of the most iconic and recognizable drummers in the history of music. But right now, he's a vulnerable, broken man—as sweet and unsure as a schoolboy at recess who's praying not to get picked last for a dodgeball team.

Caleb clears his throat. "Maybe you could find out if Dax is willing to talk now?"

Violet's breathing hitches. "I'll go get him. Don't move." With that, Violet sprints away, leaving Alessandra and me standing alone with Caleb.

"Good for you," I whisper.

Caleb nods but looks down at his shoes.

"Um, Caleb, this is Alessandra Tennison," I say, motioning to Ally.

"Hi," Ally says, waving awkwardly.

"Hey. I love 'Smitten.' Congrats on your success with that."

"Thank you. It's been a dream come true."

Caleb half-smiles in reply, but quickly peers past Ally and me, clearly wondering how Violet is faring with Dax. I look at Ally and make a face that says, *Well, fuck if I know what we should do.* And, thank God, a moment later, we're saved by the proverbial bell, in the form of the wedding coordinator's amplified voice inviting "all the single ladies" to come to the other side of the patio to try to catch Georgina's bridal bouquet.

Of course, Ally and I don't consider ourselves "single ladies," in most contexts. We both know we've found our forever person. On the other hand, though, neither of us is wearing a ring, and this is the perfect chance for both of us to get the hell out of here.

"We should go," I say tentatively to Caleb.

"Absolutely," he says, waving us away. "Go, go!"

I lean in and whisper, "I'm proud of you." And then, off we go, with Caleb calling to my back, "Throw an elbow if needed, O'Brien! Be ruthless!"

Laughing, I throw up my free hand as I gallop away, letting Caleb know I've heard his silly advice.

When we arrive at the designated location for the bouquet toss, Ally and I find a good position among the other assembled single women, and the newly minted Mrs. Rivers—wearing a stunning gown designed by her new sister-in-law, Violet—gets into position with her back facing the group.

"Are you ready, Georgie?" the wedding coordinator prompts, and when the bride whoops to signal her readiness, the woman counts down. A moment later, Georgina tosses her bridal bouquet up and back and it flies through the air in a perfect arc . . . *that's headed straight for me.* Oh my God! Gasping, I reach out for the bouquet as it falls straight into my waiting palms . . . and then watch in slow motion as a pair of hands snatch it away at the very last second.

"Damn!" I shout, as Alessandra standing next to me bursts out laughing.

All the single ladies pose for a group photo with Georgina and her friend who caught the bouquet—a co-worker of Georgina's from *Rock 'n' Roll* magazine, apparently. But when a loud cheer inside the house cuts through the party on the patio, everyone outside, including Ally and me, instantly begins traipsing indoors.

All night long, various "super-groups" have graced a large stage inside the house to perform their take on various classic party songs—everything from "Uptown Funk" to "Love Shack" to "Dancing Queen." By now, we all know what loud cheers from inside the house mean: they're surefire signs yet another random combination of famous musicians has walked onstage and is getting situated to perform another party tune.

As Ally and I walk toward the large house, the famous piano intro from one of my all-time favorite party songs—"I Will Survive"—begins blaring, followed by the instantly recognizable voice of Dean Masterson, the frontman of Red Card Riot, crooning the iconic first lyrics.

Shrieking excitedly, I grab Alessandra's arm. "We have to find Fish and Colin to dance to this one! It's my favorite!"

Alessandra agrees, and, together, we turn and survey the patio.

"There!" Alessandra yells, pointing. Quickly, we traipse over to where she's spotted Fish, who's currently chatting with Savage and Laila.

"Come dance with us, Matthew!" Ally yells to her boyfriend. And not only Fish, but Savage and Laila, as well, immediately begin following us toward the house.

"Have you seen Colin?" I yell to Fish, over the loud music as we walk.

"He's onstage!" Fish yells back. "That's him playing drums!"

"What?" I shriek. "Why didn't Colin tell me he was going to play this song tonight—*and with Dean Masterson*!"

"It just happened, spontaneously," Fish says, laughing. "I can't believe it myself. I was just about to come find you two, when you found me."

We pass that same bench from earlier, at a distance, and see Dax and Caleb sitting together, their body language relaxed and amiable. Clearly, whatever they're saying to each other over there, it's going well.

Fish looks elated as he takes in the sight of Dax and Caleb together and says, "Miracles never cease."

"That's thanks to Amy," Alessandra reports. "She's the one who talked some sense into Caleb."

"I barely said anything," I murmur.

"Well, whatever you said, you performed a miracle," Fish says. "Thank you."

When we make it inside the house, we find Violet already on the dance floor, whooping it up with her brother and new sister-in law, as well as Dax's older sister, Kat, and her husband Josh, while Dean Masterson sings his heart out onstage, backed by an assortment of random musicians, none of them from his own band. Of course, my eyes immediately lock onto my hunky boyfriend behind the drum kit. And my heart swells to find him looking like he's having the time of his life.

I begin dancing like a maniac with my friends and singing along to the lyrics, feeling electrified by the energy and excitement in the room. I'm pretty sure every person at this wedding, besides Dax and Caleb, is now crammed onto the dance floor, all of us lured by the dulcet sounds of Dean Masterson belting out this iconic banger.

One of Reed's best friends—the adorable guy who offici-ated the wedding ceremony—begins performing a silly break dance routine in the center of the dance floor that makes everyone cheer and laugh and sends the already sky-high energy in the room through the roof.

Out the corner of my eye, I notice Dax joining Violet on the dance floor. And when I look around the large space, I discover Caleb leaning against a wall in the way back, watching the band and smiling from ear to ear.

My heart soaring at the sight of Caleb's obvious joy, my eyes return to my boyfriend onstage. And this time, he's looking at me. I blow Colin a two-handed, enthusiastic kiss, letting him know I love him and he's gonna get lucky tonight —as always—and Colin laughs and winks at me in reply, without missing a beat in the song.

Unfortunately, all good things must come to an end, even this amazing rendition of "I Will Survive." As Colin pounds out the final beat of the song, the crowd, including me, goes apeshit, and starts demanding another one. I'm too sweaty and thirsty to keep going, however, so I lean into Fish and Ally to be heard above the din and shout, "I'm going outside to get a drink!"

Fish grabs my arm, keeping me in place. "Hang on," he

says, his tone a whole lot more insistent than I'm used to hearing from him.

A second later, Colin's amplified voice says, "Don't go anywhere, Ames. There's something I need to ask you."

Gasping, I turn to look at the stage, and, sure enough, Colin is standing front and center, holding a microphone and looking straight at me.

When my gaze meets his, Colin grins and says, "Mr. and Mrs. Rivers graciously gave me permission to ask you this question tonight, in front of all their guests. Thank you for that, Reed and Georgie." The happy couple whoops from the center of the dance floor, as I stand frozen in place, feeling like my heart is physically lodged inside my throat like a meatball. *Is this it?*

"Amy," Colin says. "My love."

"Holy fuck," I murmur. I clutch Fish's arm to hold myself steady, just in case Colin's next words confirm my hunch.

Colin's Adam's apple bobs. He clears his throat. "Amy, our love story started a lifetime ago, but our *romance* started six months ago at a *wedding*—so I figured a wedding would be the perfect place to start the next chapter of our story. Our *engagement*."

Everyone around me cheers and claps, while I clutch Fish and whimper.

Visibly shaking, Colin kneels at the edge of the stage and holds up a small box, its tiny contents sparkling like crazy under the stage lights. "Amy O'Brien," Colin chokes out, his voice quavering. "You make me swoon from down deep in my soul. I love you to the moon and back again. And I always will. Amy, will you marry me?"

"Yes!" I shout over the heads on the dance floor, and the crowd around me explodes with cheers.

Hooting gleefully, Colin rises, shoves his mic into a stand and then yells into it, "Make way! I'm gonna land *there*." He points at a spot in front of him that's currently covered by humans and barely waits for the crowd to part before leaping off the stage like the rock star he is. Once on the ground, Colin bounds toward me like a puppy in a field of tall poppies, and when my new fiancé reaches me, he slides the glittering ring onto my shaking finger and kisses me passionately, eliciting even more cheers and applause from our audience.

Colin and I kiss and embrace, laugh and exchange words of excitement and adoration. But when my all-time favorite 22 Goats song, "Fireflies," begins blaring from the stage, we break apart and turn to look, both of us curious to see who's playing drums on the song.

It's Caleb.

He's sitting behind the drumkit, banging out the famous groove to "Fireflies," behind Dax and Fish, while Ruby of Fugitive Summer plays keys.

Oh my God.

It's a truly astonishing moment. And not surprisingly, everyone at the party collectively loses their shit. People always go crazy for this song, regardless, but this time, we all know we're witnessing history. Frankly, it would have been a showstopper for Caleb to join Dax on *any* song tonight. But it's *especially* mind-blowing to witness Caleb joining Dax on *this* particular song—the smash-hit love song Dax wrote for his beloved wife, the former Violet Rhodes. Surely, Caleb knows the history of this song, that Dax wrote it about Violet Rhodes, given those final lyrics of the song: *You're a flower, a road, a destination.*

I truly can't believe what I'm seeing. Hearing. *Feeling.*

This song, this moment, is an incredible gift. And not only to Colin and me, as a celebration of our engagement. It's also a gift to Reed and Georgina on their wedding day. For that matter, it's a gift to every guest at this wedding, too, who'll always have an amazing story to tell.

But, mostly, based on what Caleb and I talked about all those months ago at his house, I know this performance is Caleb's highly personal gift from him to Violet Rhodes Morgan. His first and only love. It's his way of letting Violet go, once and for all. He's letting her know he's finally man enough to wish her happiness, in whatever form that takes. *And I couldn't be prouder of him for it.*

Tears pricking my eyes, I throw myself into my new fiancé's arms and sway with him for the duration of the song, until, during the last bit of lyrics, Colin leans in and whisper-sings them into my ear.

"I'm so glad you said yes," Colin whispers, as the song reaches its final note.

"Did you have any doubt?"

"No," he admits, laughing. "But, still, I'm relieved."

I hold up my hand and gaze at my sparkling rock. "It's gorgeous. Thank you."

"You can pick something else, if you'd like."

"No, it's perfect." I smile. "Unlike *you.*"

Colin laughs. It's become our little inside joke these past six months—the fact that Colin isn't a perfect man, but he's perfect for *me.*

"I love you so much," I say simply.

"I love you, too," Colin replies. "And I always will."

EPILOGUE

COLIN

One year later

Shit.

I was so excited to surprise Amy with a strings arrangement of "Swoon" for her walk down the aisle. But now that the moment is upon me, now that Amy is set to appear at the top of that aisle any second now, I'm suddenly worried I've messed up.

Will Amy love the fact that I told the string quartet to disregard her selection for her walk down the aisle and, instead, play my requested arrangement? Or will she be not quite as thrilled with my surprise as I've been assuming, up until this moment?

I shift my weight nervously, take a deep breath, and exhale.

It's become a fun *thing* in our relationship to surprise each other. Amy's told me countless times, in other contexts, she *loves* surprises. But it's suddenly occurring to me that maybe it's a bridge too far for me to surprise her, in front of all these people, with her makeup done so carefully and a photographer at the ready to capture every smile and tear.

Well, it's too late now.

All the bridesmaids are in place. Jackson, our ring bearer, has finished his walk. Even our tiny flower girl, Billie, has made her way down the aisle in her mother's arms. Granted, she was dead-ass asleep. But her dress was cute.

We're standing on a clifftop in Kuai for our wedding, which honestly blows my mind. When I attended Kat Morgan's weeklong destination wedding in Hawaii years ago, I remember thinking, "If I ever find someone I want to marry, and if our band hits it big enough that I've got some money to burn, I'd want to get married just like this." And now, here we are. What a mindfuck. Sure, I imagined it. But I never believed it would happen. And I certainly never thought, not in a million years, the hypothetical bride in that scenario would be Amy O'Brien!

Speaking of which, the strings quartet just started playing their kickass arrangement of "Swoon," which means my bride should be appearing at the top of that aisle, any second now, probably looking flabbergasted by my surprise.

Our officiant for the wedding—Ryan Morgan, who got all necessary paperwork completed to be able to do this for us today—instructs the assembled audience to stand, which they do. All eyes turn to the top of the aisle as "Swoon" swirls through the golden air . . . But Amy doesn't appear.

There's a wall of flowers behind our seated guests, so it's possible Amy is standing mere inches from that opening, pulling herself together. Knowing her, that's exactly what's happening. I'm sure she's identified the song's distinctive melody and now needs a second to gather herself, so she won't sob while walking down the aisle.

Just as I'm starting to worry a bit, Amy finally appears at the top of the aisle on her father's arm, looking more beautiful in Violet's creation for her than I've ever seen her. She's an angel. Ethereal. Glorious. Glowing. Perfect.

Luckily, Amy isn't crying too hard on her father's arm. And even better, it's immediately clear, thanks to her beaming smile, whatever tears she's been shedding are borne of pure joy.

As she floats down the aisle, her eyes latch onto mine, and I feel the smile she beams me all the way down in my soul.

Amy mouths, "Thank you." Clearly referencing the song. And in reply, I mouth "I love you" and "You look beautiful."

Finally, I'm taking my bride's hand from her father's. Leading her to our assigned spot. Whispering to her that she's gorgeous and I love her.

"Thank you for the song," she whispers back. "It's incredible."

"You always say you love surprises." I wipe a tear from Amy's cheek. "I love you."

"I love you, too."

We settle into our spots and Ryan launches into our extremely short ceremony. As short as it is, though, it's still a blur to me, until Ryan says it's time for our vows.

At Ryan's prompting, I turn to Amy, take her hands in mine, and gaze into her gorgeous emerald eyes. "Amy, I promise to love you till I'm old and gray. From beyond the grave. Forever and a day. Amy, I love you more than words could ever say. But let me try to say it, anyway."

Everyone watching us chuckles.

"I promise to always be faithful to you. I promise to

always protect and love you. To listen to you and make you feel safe enough to always speak your mind with me." My chest heaves. "I promise, Amy, I'll always swoon for you, and only you, forever."

Amy bites her lip, like she's trying her damnedest not to weep.

"Amy?" Ryan prompts.

"I need a minute," Amy squeaks out, making everyone, including me, laugh. But soon enough, she takes a few breaths, gathers herself, squeezes my hands, and says, "Colin, I promise to always be the creeper who's totally obsessed with you." Everyone laughs uproariously, even though they have no idea how truly hilarious Amy's comment is. She continues, "I promise to be the best wife and friend to you as I can possibly be, always, and the best mother to all our future babies, should we be so lucky." We share a secret smile, acknowledging the little bean growing inside her—the beautiful surprise Amy told me about only two weeks ago. "I promise to always love you," Amy continues, "not because you're perfect, but because you're perfect for *me*. And I also promise to swoon for you, always and forever. That won't be hard to do. I've been doing it my whole life."

Our smiles huge and our chests heaving with excitement, we quickly exchange rings and share our first kiss, even before Ryan has remembered to shout, "Kiss your bride, Colinoscopy!"

As I kiss my gorgeous bride, I feel euphoric. I've hit the jackpot in this lifetime, in every conceivable way. I've got the perfect wife for me. A baby on the way—our first of many, if we're lucky. Our band is doing better than ever. Our friends are a found family. And my little side career as an actor has taken off like gangbusters, ever since my first movie came out and my performance drew nothing but praise. I'm the luckiest man on earth and I know it. And I'll never take any of it for granted, as long as I live.

"Ladies and gentlemen, I present to you," Ryan booms. "Mr. and Mrs. Colin and Amy Beretta!"

Laughing and whooping, I take my wife's hand in mine, and we float down the aisle together . . . and straight into what we both know, without a doubt, will be our happily ever after.

The End

To hear a full-band version of the song "Swoon" the Goats created together in the studio after Colin got back from his honeymoon with Amy, along with a swoony video you will NOT want to miss, go here: http://www.laurenrowebooks. com/river-records

While you're there, check out music videos for all the songs featured in *Swoon*, plus read tons of extras from the sprawling world of River Records.

If you enjoyed Colin and Amy's group of friends, you'll be happy to learn that most couples featured in *Swoon* already have their own books. Unfortunately, C-Bomb and Kendrick don't yet have their own stories, but they're on Lauren's long list of possible future heroes and she assures you she adores them, too. Sign up for Lauren's newsletter *here:* http://eepurl. com/ba_ODX, so you won't miss any upcoming announcements or releases.

To read about **Fish** and **Alessandra's** friends-to-lovers romance, check out *Smitten,* an interconnected standalone.

To read **Dax** and **Violet's** sexy, angst-filled story, with lots of cameos from Dax's siblings and parents, and to learn what caused the rift between Dax and C-Bomb, pick up *ROCK-STAR.* Note that Dax's book is numbered five in The Morgan Brothers series, but all the Morgans' stories are interconnected standalones that can be read in any order.

Reed Rivers and **Georgina Ricci's** fiery, steamy, suspenseful story is a trilogy that begins with *Bad Liar,* while **Savage** and **Laila** duke it out in an enemies-to-lovers duet that begins with *Falling Out Of Hate With You* and includes tons of original songs.

If you want to find out about the three oldest Morgan brothers, read about **Colby** in *Hero,* **Ryan** in *Captain,* and **Keane** in *Ball Peen Hammer.* All books are interconnected standalones. Ryan's and Colby's books overlap in time, so either one is a great place to start the Morgans. In English, *Hero* is numbered first, while in Germany and Italy, the publishers released *Captain* first. Similarly, *Ball Peen Hammer* is numbered third in the series, simply because numbers were required at one point, but that book was actually released first. However you jump into Lauren's interconnected "Rowe-verse," rest assured you can jump around, in any order, and enjoy the stories completely, without feeling like you're doing it wrong. Readers from all over the world have read Lauren's books in countless ways and orders and thoroughly enjoyed them!

MUSIC CREDITS

The song "Swoon" was co-written by Lauren Rowe and her talented cousin, Matthew Embree. Credits for all other songs featured in *Swoon,* including "Smitten," "Fireflies," and "Hate Sex High," all of which were written or co-written by Lauren Rowe, are listed on Lauren's website, with music videos for all songs, along with spoiler-free extras.

AUTHOR'S NOTE

Thank you for reading *Swoon*! If you're a new reader to me, you've now met several couples who've already found their happily ever afters in my world. I firmly believe those glimpses into other couples' love stories aren't spoilers because all my books (other than *Countdown to Killing Kurtis,* which is emphatically *not* a romance) are clearly labeled as romances, which means, by definition, the main couple in the story will *always* get at least a "happy for now," but usually a "happily ever after," in the end. The fun of any romance is always finding out *how* the main couple reaches their happy ending, against all odds, not the fact that they *do*. Thank you again for reading. Please, find me on social media. I'd love to hear from you!

Thank you to Sophie Broughton, Melissa Saneholtz, Sarah Kirk, Selina Washington, Lizette Baez, Madonna Blackburn, and Geissa Cecilia. Thank you for the amazing cover to Letitia Hasser of RBA Designs.

BOOKS BY LAUREN ROWE

Standalone Novels

Smitten

When aspiring singer-songwriter, Alessandra, meets Fish, the funny, adorable bass player of 22 Goats, sparks fly between the awkward pair. Fish tells Alessandra he's a "Goat called Fish who's hung like a bull. But not really. I'm actually really average." And Alessandra tells Fish, "There's nothing like a girl's first love." Alessandra thinks she's talking about a song when she makes her comment to Fish—the first song she'd ever heard by 22 Goats, in fact. As she'll later find out, though, her "first love" was

actually Fish. The Goat called Fish who, after that night, vowed to do anything to win her heart.

SMITTEN is a **true standalone** romance.

Swoon

When Colin Beretta, the drummer of 22 Goats, is a groomsman at the wedding of his childhood best friend, Logan, he discovers Logan's kid sister, Amy, is all grown up. Colin tries to resist his attraction to Amy, but after a drunken kiss at the wedding reception, that's easier said than done.

Swoon is a **true standalone** romance.

Hate Love Duet

An addicting enemies to lovers romance with humor, heat, angst, and banter. Music artists Savage of Fugitive Summer and Laila Fitzgerald are stuck together on tour. And convinced they can't stand each other. What they don't know is that they're absolutely made for each other, whether they realize it or not. The books of this duet are to be read in order:

Falling Out Of Hate With You

Falling Into Love With You

The Reed Rivers Trilogy

Reed Rivers has met his match in the most unlikely of women— aspiring journalist and spitfire, Georgina Ricci. She's much younger than the women Reed normally pursues, but he can't resist her fiery personality and drop-dead gorgeous looks. But in this game of cat and mouse, who's chasing whom? With each passing day of this wild ride, Reed's not so sure. The books of this trilogy are to be read in order:

Bad Liar

Beautiful Liar

Beloved Liar

The Club Trilogy

Romantic. Scorching hot. Suspenseful. Witty. The Club is your new addiction—a sexy and suspenseful thriller about two wealthy brothers and the sassy women who bring them to their knees . . . all while the foursome bands together to protect one of their own. *The Club Trilogy* is to be read in order, as follows:

The Club: Obsession

The Club: Reclamation

The Club: Redemption

The Club: Culmination

The fourth book for Jonas and Sarah is a full-length epilogue with incredible heart-stopping twists and turns and feels. Read *The Club: Culmination (A Full-Length Epilogue Novel)* after finishing *The Club Trilogy* or, if you prefer, after reading *The Josh and Kat Trilogy*.

The Josh and Kat Trilogy

It's a war of wills between stubborn and sexy Josh Faraday and Kat Morgan. A fight to the bed. Arrogant, wealthy playboy Josh is used to getting what he wants. *And what he wants is Kat Morgan.* The books are to be read in order:

Infatuation

Revelation

Consummation

The Morgan Brothers

Read these **standalones** in any order about the brothers of Kat Morgan. Chronological reading order is below, but they are all complete stories. Note: you do *not* need to read any other books or series before jumping straight into reading about the Morgan boys.

Hero

The story of heroic firefighter, **Colby Morgan**. When catastrophe strikes Colby Morgan, will physical therapist Lydia save him . . . or will he save her?

Captain

The insta-love-to-enemies-to-lovers story of tattooed sex god, **Ryan Morgan**, and the woman he'd move heaven and earth to claim.

Ball Peen Hammer

A steamy, hilarious, friends-to-lovers romantic comedy about cocky-as-hell male stripper, **Keane Morgan,** and the sassy, smart young woman who brings him to his knees during a road trip.

Mister Bodyguard

The Morgans' beloved honorary brother, **Zander Shaw**, meets his match in the feisty pop star he's assigned to protect on tour.

ROCKSTAR

When the youngest Morgan brother, **Dax Morgan,** meets a mysterious woman who rocks his world, he must decide if pursuing her is worth risking it all. Be sure to check out four of Dax's original songs from *ROCKSTAR*, written and produced by Lauren, along with full music videos for the songs, on her website (www. laurenrowebooks.com) under the tab MUSIC FROM ROCKSTAR.

Misadventures

Lauren's *Misadventures* titles are page-turning, steamy, swoony standalones, to be read in any order.

- *Misadventures on the Night Shift* –A hotel night shift clerk encounters her teenage fantasy: rock star Lucas Ford. And combustion ensues.

- *Misadventures of a College Girl*—A spunky, virginal theater major meets a cocky football player at her first college party . . . and absolutely nothing goes according to plan for either of them.

- *Misadventures on the Rebound*—A spunky woman on the rebound meets a hot, mysterious stranger in a bar on her way to her five-year high school reunion in Las Vegas and what follows is a misadventure neither of them ever imagined.

Standalone Psychological Thriller/Dark Comedy

Countdown to Killing Kurtis

A young woman with big dreams and skeletons in her closet decides her porno-king husband must die in exactly a year. This is *not* a traditional romance, but it *will* most definitely keep you turning the pages and saying "WTF?"

Short Stories

The Secret Note

Looking for a quickie? Try this scorching-hot short story from Lauren Rowe in ebook FOR FREE or in audiobook: He's a hot Aussie. I'm a girl who isn't shy about getting what she wants. The problem? Ben is my little brother's best friend. An exchange student who's heading back Down Under any day now. But I can't help myself. He's too hot to resist.

All books by Lauren Rowe are available in ebook, paperback, and audiobook formats.

AUTHOR BIOGRAPHY

Lauren Rowe is the USA Today and international #1 best-selling author of newly released Reed Rivers Trilogy, as well as The Club Trilogy, The Josh & Kat Trilogy, The Morgan Brothers Series, Countdown to Killing Kurtis, and select standalone Misadventures.

Lauren's books are full of feels, humor, heat, and heart. Besides writing novels, Lauren is the singer in a party/wedding band in her hometown of San Diego, an audio book narrator, and award-winning songwriter. She is thrilled to connect with readers all over the world.
To find out about Lauren's upcoming releases and giveaways, sign up for Lauren's emails here: http://eepurl.com/ba_ODX

Lauren loves to hear from readers! Send Lauren an email from her website, say hi on Twitter, Instagram, or Facebook.

Find out more and check out lots of free bonus material at www.LaurenRoweBooks.com.